Where No Man Has Gone Before

From Mary Shelley onwards, ~~~~~~~~~~~~~~~~~~~~~~~~~~ played a central role in the shaping and resh~~~~~~~~~~~~~ fiction, irrespective of its undeniably patriarchal ~~~~~~~~~ *Where No Man Has Gone Before* traces the history of the genre from *Frankenstein* to the present day, focusing on the work of women whose writing has been central to its development this century.

The contributors – writers, readers, and critics of science fiction – examine the work of well-known writers such as Doris Lessing and Ursula Le Guin, as well as others whose work has still to receive the critical attention it deserves. These writers have not only subverted the SF form and its conventions for their own ends, but have also contributed a specifically female voice to a seemingly male genre.

As well as essays on fiction, the collection includes work on the sf film and its implications for women, and also addresses the issue of how the publishing industry has responded to the recent influx of women authors. Perhaps, above all, what this collection demonstrates is that science fiction remains as particularly well-suited to the exploration of woman as 'alien' or 'other' in our culture today, as it was with the publication of *Frankenstein* in 1818.

The anthology will appeal to a variety of readers, including those interested in women's issues in general, as well as to students of modern literary studies, critical theory, film and media studies and, of course, to readers of science fiction.

Lucie Armitt lectures in the Arts Education Department of the University of Warwick, and in the Humanities Department of Bolton Institute of Higher Education.

For
Jean and Eric Armitt

Where No Man Has Gone Before

Women and science fiction

Edited by Lucie Armitt

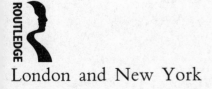

Routledge

London and New York

First published 1991
by Routledge
11 New Fetter Lane, London EC4P 4EE

Simultaneously published in the USA and Canada
by Routledge
a division of Routledge, Chapman and Hall, Inc.
29 West 35th Street, New York, NY 10001

Typeset in 10/12pt Bembo by
Input Typesetting, London
Printed in Great Britain by
T J Press (Padstow) Ltd, Padstow, Cornwall

British Library Cataloguing in Publication Data
'Where no man has gone before': women and science
fiction.
1. Science fiction in English – Critical studies
I. Armitt, Lucie
823.087609

Library of Congress Cataloging in Publication Data
'Where no man has gone before': women and science fiction/ edited
by Lucie Armitt.
p. cm.
Includes bibliographical references.
1. Science fiction, English——Women authors——History and
criticism.
2. Science fiction, American——Women authors——History and
criticism.
3. Women and literature——Great Britain. 4. Women and
literature——United States. I. Armitt, Lucie.
PR830.S35W48 1991
823'.08762099287——dc20   90–8200

ISBN 0–415–04447–2
     0–415–04448–0

Contents

Introduction

I

In this country during the last decade, an increasing amount of interest has been generated around the subject of science fiction writing in general, and that by women in particular. In part the latter has accompanied the very welcome explosion of interest in women's writing of all kinds, which has taken place over the last ten or fifteen years; and in this context one must begin by acknowledging that the relatively recent growth of critical attention paid to women's science fiction is in no small part due to the efforts of certain sections of the publishing industry (perhaps most notably the Women's Press, whose *sf* series has played, and continues to play, a very significant part in this development). But whatever the reasons underlying this growth of interest, the result is that attitudes towards the writing, the reception and the publication of science fiction are also changing – hopefully for the better. For too long science fiction has been relegated lock, stock and barrel to the murky depths of that rather intangible, but often indiscriminately used term 'pulp fiction'. Finally, science fiction is taking the first steps towards overcoming the stigma which it has attracted in the eyes of the literary establishment, and not only has it become an item well and truly on the agenda at conferences, writers workshops and book fairs, but also in higher education establishments, where texts are increasingly included on the more progressive undergraduate syllabuses.

This phenomenon, however, merely highlights an issue which seems to have dogged science fiction throughout its history: the extent to which science fiction and the so-called literary establishment, as represented by the 'academic' or the 'institution' should, or indeed can, interact with each other. Counteracting what I consider to be the very welcome growth of academic interest in SF is a highly defensive 'old school' of science fiction writers and enthusiasts who have largely resented such attention from these quarters. In 1963, Robert Conquest scathingly voiced his irritation at those academics who dare to encompass science fiction within the scope of their concerns:

> We all know how rare it is not to pass judgement on things we know practically nothing about . . . ignorance prevails among literary persons [and] . . . literary training produces, not a natural good taste but simply certain conditioned responses, adequate only in familiar fields.[1]

More recently, if rather less didactically, John Griffiths also recognised that:

> Coming back to science fiction after a decade. . . . The first thing I noticed was that. . . . Into the sometimes irritatingly cosy world of enthusiastic reader and writer of sf . . . had intruded all the exasperating waspishness of the professional academic infighter.[2]

It would, however, be naively over-optimistic, if not quite simply untrue, if I were to suggest that the resistance to this situation is entirely mono-directional. There is still a great deal of prejudice to overcome amongst that 'large educated public which knows its literature, and knows nothing of science fiction'.[3] However, I do believe that the emergence of women's SF as a force to be reckoned with has played a large role in broadening out the readership of SF beyond the specialist clique to the more general reader interested in women's writing and issues, and indeed in contemporary literature *per se*. One of the aims of this collection is to perpetuate and accelerate this process, to whet the appetite of those who as yet remain unconvinced of the significance of science fiction as a literary genre, as well as to provide the initiated with additional food for thought.

Unfortunately, irrespective of its superficially futurist stance, mainstream male-oriented science fiction has traditionally been a genre obsessed with nostalgia and conservativism. On reading certain critical commentaries of the genre published during the 1960s and 1970s one soon becomes profoundly aware of the peculiarly defensive hostility aimed at any would-be progressive (a relative term in this context) who might wish to challenge the authority of the old guard. Such works abound with references to 'the golden age' of SF, which seems to be generally agreed upon as having occurred somewhere between the 1930s and the late 1950s, although there is some disagreement with regard to the start of this era. Significantly, no such disagreement exists over its conclusion, as this is almost unanimously attributed to the dawning of what is generally referred to, often pejoratively, as the 'new age' of SF. The latter is interesting as far as this anthology is concerned, because it is from this point onwards that certain newly published writers of science fiction began to fully recognise its potential for socio-political criticism and/or textual and stylistic experimentation, and notably many of these writers were women.

II

It seems that ever-increasing numbers of women are, for one reason or another, choosing to employ the conventions of the genre (or indeed subvert these conventions) for their own purposes. On occasions women who have achieved recognition through writing science fiction – such as Joanna Russ and Ursula Le Guin – have moved on to publish fiction and criticism outside of the genre. More commonly, however, writers bring to it their considerable abilities as writers known for other forms, most notably perhaps Doris Lessing, Margaret Atwood, Angela Carter and Marge Piercy, whose *Woman On The Edge Of Time* will surely remain one of the landmarks of the genre for decades to come. The wealth of talent which abounds in the writing of these and many other authors is enough to quell the fears of the most reactionary of literary critics, and indeed has begun to do so. The attitude of the entrenched patriarchal core of the SF rearguard is not, however, so hospitable. The peculiarly defensive attitude already noted earlier is frequently employed, not only as a deterrent against the would-be 'literary' critic of science fiction, but also against any large-scale assimilation of the genre by women writers. Once again, Robert Conquest provides us with a prime example of the sort of thinly disguised attitude typical of such criticism:

> For a long time [science fiction] was regarded as an outre form of 'mass-culture'. It was associated with the sensationalism of its lowest type (as absurd an attitude, really, as to condemn

novels about love – e.g. *Anna Karenina* [NB of male authorship] – on account of the sentimental women's serial).[4]

Nevertheless, with regard to women's overall contribution to science fiction there are two main arguments as to the origins of the form, in part depending upon whether one comes to the genre from the scientific angle or (more commonly in critical circles) the literary angle. The former locates its origins in the short fiction of the early-twentieth-century science journals, whilst the latter most frequently traces its conception back to Mary Shelley's *Frankenstein*, first published in 1818. Again, it is interesting to note how begrudging certain critics have been in their acknowledgements of the latter as the progenitrix of a genre which Pamela Sargent considers to have become the American male's 'neighbourhood clubhouse'.[5] Darko Suvin, for instance, refers to Shelley's novel as a 'revealingly flawed hybrid of horror tale and philosophical SF';[6] while John Griffiths argues that a positive renewal occurred within the genre after the Second World War, science fiction 'having escaped at last from the unpromising side track into which this fiction had long been diverted by the man-made bug-eyed monsters sired, or rather damned, by Mary Shelley'.[7]

Finally, Kingsley Amis deals Shelley a strangely back-handed compliment in his comments on the gothic novel as a genre apart from science fiction (and, by implication, clearly inferior to it). In Amis' opinion, the sole exception to this rule '*can hardly help* [my italics] being *Frankenstein*'.[8] For our purposes, there is added significance in the argument which locates the roots of the science fiction genre within the gothic tradition. Seemingly endless debates abound over and around the related modes of the gothic, the fantastic and the supernatural, and their relationship to each other and to science fiction. What they indisputably all share, however, is their general exclusion from what is still frequently considered to be the 'canon' of Great Literature:

> Of the four degrees of relationship of truth to life into which works of fiction may be graded, the impossible, the improbable, the possible and the probable, the novel proper claimed from the beginning to have eliminated from its field the first two. . . . The third was at first held by many to be legitimate, but the greater novelists maintained that they were writing within the limits only of the fourth.[9]

Of course the gothic tradition (particularly during its nineteenth-century heyday) has been dominated by women writers. These two points are clearly not unrelated. One cannot help but consider that throughout the history of literature and publication those forms which have conventionally been 'open' to women are those generally judged to be 'popular' (that is, non-prestigious or 'low-brow'): the romance, the detective story, and of course writing for children. At first sight science fiction, marginalised in itself, may appear inapplicable to this rule, and certainly one could not by any stretch of the imagination consider it a genre dominated by women, even today. However, despite what seems at first glance to be an absence of female involvement, it is quite clear that, from Shelley onwards, women have been central throughout the genre's history: and as a whole have thus had a formative influence on the genre, its parameters, and its preoccupations.

The first section of this anthology focuses on just a handful of the individual authors who have made a formidable contribution to the genre throughout the twentieth century, exploring both the extent to which these writers have subverted the form and its conventions for their own ends, and how they have contributed a specifically female voice to this seemingly patriarchal genre. Liz Russell incorporates continental philosophy, feminist theory and theology into her critical approach to the work of Burdekin and Haldane, in a piece which emphasises the significance of their visionary dystopias to our past, present and future. Sarah Gamble, in her analysis of the works of C. L. Moore, demonstrates that, although outwardly conforming to the masculinist conventions of pulp science fiction, a closer reading of these texts exposes both their deeply subversive potential, and a serious attempt on Moore's part to address the social constructs of masculinity and femininity through her depiction of relationships between the sexes. It is interesting that both Ursula Le Guin *and* Doris Lessing, two writers of indisputable talent, should similarly share a pre-occupation in their fiction with exploring the territory which lies between the twin poles of outer space and the 'inner lands' of the psyche. In both cases, of course, their fiction has always derived from a profound political consciousness, and the two essays which examine their respective contributions to the genre demonstrate very clearly the intrinsic links between these concerns and their employment of the science fiction framework. Susan Bassnett, whose approach to Le Guin's work emphasises its resistance to classification and categorisation, argues that critical approaches on the grounds of gender alone cannot be sufficient in dealing with a writer whose work functions simultaneously as an expression of, and commentary on, the changing face of North American politics; and as an exploration of alternative fantasy worlds. Moira Monteith's approach to Doris Lessing similarly plots a progressive development in her work, tracing the movement away from the earlier realist narratives through to her *Canopus* series. Thus science fiction becomes the latest of a series of phases in which Lessing seems to have been searching for the optimum form for her narrative voice, and one which has enabled a multi-viewpoint structure unattainable through realism, but essential to Lessing's fictive (and political) concerns.

Part II comprises five essays discussing various key issues applicable to women as they emerge in contemporary science fiction. In the first of these Jenny Newman bridges the gap between the early nineteenth and late twentieth century, in returning to the origins of this female tradition in order to offer a reappraisal of contemporary women's science fiction through comparing Mary Shelley's *Frankenstein* (1818) with Maureen Duffy's *Gor Saga* (1981). In so doing, she provides an interesting perspective on the issues of femininity and (pro)creativity, and the identification of the woman as 'monster' in a society which increasingly privileges the use and abuse of so-called 'advances' in the fields of technology in general, and genetic engineering in particular.

For self-evident reasons, women from Shelley onwards have found a particular significance in exploring the figure of the alien or artificial life form from the perspective of the perceived 'Other'. Lisa Tuttle's essay extends the parameters of this approach by examining the relationship between women and animals from this perspective of otherness and difference. Based on recently published works, her discussion of these texts demonstrates a change in attitude on the part of women writers over the last two or three years, producing an interesting new slant on previous arguments around this and related themes. Elsewhere Susan Sontag has commented that:

> The dark secret behind human nature used to be the upsurge of the animal – as in *King Kong*. The threat to man, his availability to dehumanization, lay in his own animality. Now the

danger is understood as residing in man's ability to be turned into a machine.[10]

Increasingly women writers and critics of science fiction are offering new and alternative readings of stock themes and preoccupations. Basing her argument on an analysis of two SF films, *Short Circuit* and *Tron*, Susan Thomas discusses the pseudo-sexual nature of the relationship between the adolescent male and his intelligent machine, and analyses in particular the significance of the female character as the mediator or interloper within this relationship. Taking a Freudian perspective she demonstrates that, far from fearing the dehumanising quality of the machine, the adolescent male looks to it to provide a gratification which he fears in his personal relationships with women.

One of the primary concerns of the science fiction writer is to challenge received notions of reality as it currently exists, and two of the most significant foundations upon which reality is based are time and language (forming the means whereby reality is compartmentalised into comprehensible units). Time as a theme has always been a focus for the science fiction writer, with time travel and disrupted chronologies being a central preoccupation throughout the history of the form. Language, however, has received remarkably little attention. In my own essay I discuss Lessing's *The Marriages Between Zones Three, Four and Five* and Elgin's *Native Tongue* in an attempt to illustrate the significance of language and its structures to the structures of power, stressing the importance of women writers deconstructing not only the language of discourse but also the language of narrative, if existing power relations are to be challenged and subverted.

The final essay in this section provides us with a detailed analysis of the Hollywood star system as employed and upheld by the science fiction film industry. Erica Sheen argues that the underlying ideology of this system functions to privilege the 'naturalisation' of masculinity, in contrast to which femininity becomes deviance or tokenism. From this perspective science fiction, rather than challenging the system through its potential for a radical reassessment of norms, merely functions to reinforce the masculinist code within which it has been so successful.

The final section of the anthology illustrates several problems inherent within SF as 'genre fiction' as they affect readers and writers of the form. Discussing the subject of writing for a specific readership, Gwyneth Jones offers a particularly interesting approach to the issue of writing science fiction for the younger reader. Focusing on Alexei Panshin's *Rite of Passage* and Madeleine L'Engle's *A Wrinkle in Time*, as well as providing a personal perspective on the writing of her recent novel *The Hidden Ones*, she differentiates between 'feminist' and 'feminised' science fiction, and in doing so tackles the difficulties of creating positive characters with whom younger women may identify, and the ideological pitfalls into which the writer of teenage fiction can so easily fall.

Sarah Lefanu and Nickianne Moody both address, in their different ways, the blurring of boundary lines between science fiction and other related popular forms. Sarah Lefanu's piece takes up a theme which has been central to the genre for some time, and which has arisen over the relationship between hard and soft science fiction (a debate in many ways heightened by the increasing involvement of women with the genre). In particular she examines the common ground shared by SF and horror fiction from this perspective. Following on from this, Nickianne Moody's approach moves towards the opposite end of the spectrum, by analysing the recent upsurge of interest in contemporary reworkings of the Arthurian romance legends, and publishers' inclusion of these within their science fiction lists. Her approach to these texts, which often combine the seemingly incompatible elements of a medieval setting with a futurist or, on occasions, extra-terrestrial narrative, examines this 'subgenre' of science fiction from the perspective both of gender and of genre. What are the attractions of these heroic/masculinist legends for the woman reader/writer and how do such reworkings relate to that major popular 'women's' form, the romance?

Science fiction, like any other form of genre fiction, is particularly susceptible to the (often idiosyncratic) marketing strategies of the 'popular' paperback publishing industry. At times this can result in a very obvious tension between the book as a saleable commodity and the creativity of the writing contained therein. Some of the American presses, in particular, seem to favour the disconcertingly gaudy and lurid covers generally associated with 'bodice-rippers' or horror comics, despite the fact that the works themselves are frequently extremely accomplished and sensitive pieces of fiction. This is no trivial observation because it serves to illustrate the power of the publisher with regard to a book's reception by its potential readership. Brian Stableford has commented that 'The label "Science Fiction" does not simply tell a would-be reader something about what a book contains. It also tells him [sic] something about *how it should be read*'[11] – and also, perhaps, by whom. Josephine Saxton provides us with an internal perspective on this phenomenon, as a writer who considers herself to have been the victim of rigid marketing strategies and editorial policies. Despite her anecdotal and, at times, very witty approach to the subject, she illustrates all too clearly the problems of the science fiction 'publishing ghetto' for new authors, and the joint frustrations of being able to reach only a limited readership, and thus of having one's work prejudged (negatively of course) as a result.

III

One of the criticisms frequently launched against science fiction, in common with other fantasy forms, is that of escapism – something which is apparently deemed a lesser preoccupation than those of the realist modes. Undoubtedly all SF novels require some degree of removal from the everyday, as Rosemary Jackson has commented: 'A fantastic text tells of an indomitable desire, a longing for that which does not yet exist, or has not been allowed to exist.'[12] This, of course, necessitates an imaginative leap away from the stark present to the unknown and unfamiliar. However, there is a distinction to be made between this imaginative leap and the aforementioned charge of escapism, and one which becomes apparent on reading this collection as a whole. Women are not located at the centre of contemporary culture and society, but are almost entirely defined from the aforementioned negative perspective of 'otherness' or 'difference'. As such, the need to *escape from* a society with regard to which they already hold an ex-centric position is clearly an irrelevant one. More appropriate perhaps is the need to *escape into* – that is, to depict – an alternative reality within which centrality is possible.

In addition to this, however, good science fiction (whether based on a technological or a socio-political foundation) places great emphasis upon the intrinsic *link* between perceived reality and the depiction of futurist or alien societies. Thus whatever the approach, and whatever the gender, the depiction of an alternative reality is only the first step of an essential reassessment process on the part of both author and reader; making strange what we commonly perceive to be around us, primarily in order that we might focus upon existing reality afresh, and as outsiders. This is a necessary process if we are to challenge what are commonly taken for granted as 'absolutes' or 'givens'.

So authorial preoccupations can be seen to change in accordance with the contemporary socio-political climate, as the current preoccupation with the dystopian vision makes apparent. At a time when the death of the Ayatollah Khomeini has been seen to consolidate rather than undermine the atrocities committed in the name of Muslim fundamentalism in Iran, and last summer's European Community elections demonstrated, once again, an alarming swing to the extreme right wing in West Germany, women are profoundly aware of the fragility of human rights in general, and those of women in particular. In this context the science fiction novel provides a forum for fictionalising frightening possibilities, as well as utopian dreams.

IV

As writers, readers and critics are becoming increasingly aware, the type of writing incorporated under the label 'science fiction' is becoming increasingly diffuse and, as a genre, perhaps even unwieldy. The arbitrary nature of the categorising process becomes clearer when one considers that certain 'science fiction' novels could equally be read as romance (Anne McCaffrey's *Killashandra*), historical fiction (Octavia Butler's brilliant novel *Kindred*) or indeed, as Nickianne Moody notes, murder/mystery (Phyllis Ann Karr's *The Idylls Of The Queen*). Whereas the name, originally deriving from Hugo Gernsback's term 'scientifiction' (coined in 1926)[13] was once a fairly unproblematic referent to a specific type of fictional writing, 'subgenres' now proliferate, with terms such as 'space opera', 'sword and sorcery' and 'technofiction' supplying the perceived need for greater precision. The complex and rather slippery nature of the genre means that limits (however arbitrary) have to be imposed for the purposes of any study. One approach to this is to define the boundaries within which one wants to work, and then to select material within those boundaries for inclusion. Definitions proliferate throughout science fiction criticism, and the would-be collector will have no trouble in finding multiple (often contradictory) examples. But to define something before one starts is immediately to constrain it, to imprison it within a label in relation to which all innovation becomes deviation. My aim in producing this book was to demonstrate the diversity, scope and originality of some of the work currently being undertaken by women in Britain and Europe within the realms of science fiction, and to this end the volume has set its own limits.

There are particular problems facing any science fiction critic working outside the United States. There the genre has, of course, been developed and encouraged as an academic discipline for many years, and for this reason materials (both primary and secondary) which are readily available in that country are often still very difficult to obtain elsewhere. This is just one of the reasons why I hope this collection will help to open up discussions on the subject of women and science fiction in the UK. In 1988, the publication of Sarah Lefanu's book, *In The Chinks of the World Machine*,[14] paved the way for further exploration with her much needed overview of the genre. This volume moves on from that point to focus in greater depth upon specific authors, themes and phenomena. As such it is not, and was never intended to be, a definitive, all-encompassing collection.

C. S. Lewis made an important critical distinction when he warned that 'Criticism of kinds [or genre criticism as it is now called], as distinct from criticism of works . . . is, I think, the most subjective and least reliable type of criticism.'[15] In one sense, *Where No Man Has Gone Before* is a collection of individual pieces, by individual women, on individual works, authors and themes. Subjectivity is therefore its framework. However, the advantage of the edited collection over the individual study lies in the many differences in approach and attitude voiced by the contributors which cohere in the whole. As such I would hazard to claim, in reply to Lewis' warning, that what begins here as 'criticism of individual works' takes on significance in its entirety as one of the more valid examples of 'criticism of kinds'.

ACKNOWLEDGEMENTS

I particularly wish to acknowledge the following, all of whom have been indispensible to the completion of this book: Judith Armitt and Rob Sibley, Mair Evans and David Hughes, Michael and Marjorie Cavanagh, all of whose practical help and support have been crucial at different stages of the writing, researching and editing process; the 'Network' organisation, without which this book would not exist today (and in particular Shirley Foster and Patsy Stoneman for putting me in touch with Sarah Gamble and Elizabeth Russell respectively); Lisa Tuttle who, when all other possible British sources dried up, sent me her own copy of Suzette Elgin's *A First Dictionary and Grammar of Láadan*; and Susan Bassnett whose initial and continued support, advice and encouragement have been an immeasurable contribution to the book's progress and completion.

NOTES

1 Robert Conquest, 'Science fiction and literature', in Mark Rose (ed.), *Science Fiction: A Collection of Critical Essays*, Englewood Cliffs, Prentice-Hall, 1976, 43. Originally published in *Critical Quarterly* 5 (1963): 355–67.
2 John Griffiths, *Three Tomorrows: American, British, and Soviet Science Fiction*, London, Macmillan, 1980, 2.
3 Conquest, op. cit., 43.
4 ibid., 32.
5 Pamela Sargent, Introduction to *Women of Wonder: Science Fiction Stories by Women about Women*, Harmondsworth, Penguin, 1978, 29.
6 Darko Suvin, *Metamorphoses of Science Fiction*, New Haven, Yale University Press, 1977, 127.
7 Griffiths, op. cit., 52.
8 Kingsley Amis, *New Maps of Hell: A Survey of Science Fiction*, London, Gollancz, 1961, 32.
9 A. A. Mendilow, *Time and the Novel*, London, Humanities Press, 1972, 40.
10 Susan Sontag, 'The imagination of disaster', in Rose op. cit., 128. Originally published in Susan Sontag, *Against Interpretation*, New York, Farrar Strauss & Giroux, 1966.
11 Rosemary Jackson, *Fantasy: The Literature of Subversion*, London, Methuen, 1981.
12 From an essay on the mass marketing implications of science fiction in *Foundation* 11. (Here quoted from Griffiths, op. cit., 5.)
13 As quoted by Eric S. Rabkin in 'Genre criticism: science fiction and the fantastic', in Rose, op. cit., 89–101, and selected from chapter 4 of Eric S. Rabkin, *The Fantastic in Literature*, Princeton, NJ, Princeton University Press, 1976.
14 Sarah Lefanu, *In The Chinks of the World Machine: Feminism and Science Fiction*, London, Women's Press, 1988.
15 C. S. Lewis, *Of This and Other Worlds*, ed. Walter Hooper, London, Collins, 1982, 81.

Part I

Writing Through the Century: Individual Authors

Chapter 1

The loss of the feminine principle in Charlotte Haldane's *Man's World* and Katherine Burdekin's *Swastika Night*

Elizabeth Russell

The title of this anthology, *Where No Man Has Gone Before*, in no way describes the dystopian societies depicted by Charlotte Haldane and Katherine Burdekin, for their fictional worlds are men's worlds, ruled by men for men. The women in these worlds have been reduced to their biological function and it is this alone that gives them a social identity. In both novels the women are minor characters and comply with the dominant ideology. They are depicted by silence rather than sound and only exist in so far as they internalise male desire and imagine themselves as men imagine them to be. The women of Haldane's world have been elevated to a pure and intensely 'feminine' level; those of Burdekin's world have been devalued into 'unwomen'. At opposite poles, neither the former nor the latter have the possibility of asserting themselves, of becoming fully developed human beings. In this essay, I shall attempt to decipher their silence in order to make clear the political message that both Haldane and Burdekin – by adopting the voice of Cassandra – try to put over.

Charlotte Haldane's *Man's World*, first published in 1926, depicts a futuristic scientific socialist state which covers North America, Australasia and Europe. Her husband, the geneticist J. B. S. Haldane, had written an essay, *Daedalus: or Science and the Future*, only three years before, in which he suggests that the responsibilities of the future should be left in the hands of a scientific elite. Haldane's essay was answered with scepticism in 1924 by Bertrand Russell's *Icarus or the Future of Science*. Both essays constitute different views of the possibility of science to promote human happiness. For Russell, Daedalus represents the rational scientist whose prime aim is to aid humanity, which he does by taking a middle road, whereas his son, Icarus, represents the irresponsible scientist who does not heed the warnings of others and refuses to be guided. Rash and imprudent, Icarus becomes over-confident of his own abilities and allows his passions to take precedence over his reason. The middle road, the road indicated by Daedalus, represents the perfect balance between head and heart, or – as Nietzsche put it – between the Apollonian and Dionysian.

In the early twentieth century there appeared a great number of scientific utopias which pointed out that the perfect society of the future would be one inhabited by rational thinkers who, like Daedalus, would take the middle road and be aware of the consequences of each act. Daedalus and science was the road civilisation had to follow if it was to avoid self-destruction. The scientific dystopia, on the other hand, was the civilisation of Icarus, the irresponsible scientist who does not take into account the consequences which his scientific experiments may have upon humanity. The conflict between head and heart, reason and emotion, have long been the focus of many a philosophical discussion. Christa Wolf, in her essay *Conditions of a Narrative*, refers to the warning issued by Leonardo da Vinci which runs: 'Knowledge which has not passed through the senses can produce none but destructive truth' and follows his line of thought by adding:

> There could truly be a new renaissance of consciousness if this insight were to bear fruit again, after the long dangerous experiment with abstract rationality, which resulted in thinking that everything is a means to an end. What speaks against this possibility? The fact that the senses of many people – through no 'fault' of their own – have dried up, and that they are justifiably afraid to reactivate them.[1]

Charlotte Haldane's *Man's World* is a discussion of the conflict of head/heart, of rational and abstract thinking/emotion and feeling. It is also the conflict between science and religion. In this, *Man's World* offers little that is original from the other scientific utopias or dystopias of its time[2] but, read from a feminist perspective, it is clear that *Man's World* is essentially an analysis of gender distinctions and a warning of what the effect on society would be 'if the human race could determine in advance the sex of its children'.[3] As the title of her novel suggests, the future for women in a man's world is grim. Women have little or no say in matters of state. Science has solved almost all the problems afflicting humanity but it has not yet been able to control or manipulate instinct. The female population of the scientific state is kept down to a minimum. All girls entering adolescence choose to become either 'vocational mothers' or – if they show no mothering instinct – they are sterilised by the state and doomed to be neuters. Living in a male supremacist society, the women in *Man's World* enjoy the privileges which their status as mothers or neuters allows them, as long as they stay within the limits prescribed to them by the state. The existence of both mothers and neuters, however, is at risk when it is revealed that plans are already under way which, if successful, would reduce the population of mothers (and possibly neuters) down to one woman, who would be solely responsible for the continuation of the race, like 'a sort of human termite queen' (*MW*: 77).

All members of the scientific state are classified according to a rigid hierarchy. The women are mothers or neuters (entertainers, artists, writers or administrators). The men are grouped according to their abilities. The Brain of the state is constituted by the scientists; the Patrol comprises its administrative and executive officers and the Body of the state comprises the 'masses'. There is no room for those who cannot conform to the ruling norms as is the case of the two individualists, Christopher and Morgana, who must be sacrificed (they commit suicide).

In an analysis of the gender distinctions inherent in *Man's World* I shall take Hélène Cixous' table of binary oppositions as a starting point and then discuss C. S. Jung's process of individuation and its application to the novel.[4]

Cixous[5] offers the following table of binary oppositions in her analysis of phallocentrism and shows how women have been allotted the category of 'not man', of absence of word, law and meaning in a hierarchy in which man *is* and woman *is not*:-

Activity	/	Passivity
Sun	/	Moon
Culture	/	Nature
Day	/	Night
Father	/	Mother
Head	/	Heart
Intelligible	/	Sensitive
Logos	/	Pathos

The norms on the left are, according to patriarchal tradition, to be listed under male = positive = master whereas those on the right would bear the reading female = negative = mastered. In order for the one side to acquire meaning it necessarily has to destroy the other. Thus, as activity equals victory in patriarchal thought, it follows that the male is the winner and the female the loser.

Both the mothers (to an exaggerated degree) and the neuters (to a lesser degree) 'fit' the norms described as 'feminine' in Cixous' patriarchal binary table; likewise, the male members of the scientific state fit the description the table presents as 'masculine'. Not only does this equation of femininity leave no space for the development of woman's self or a change in the *status quo*, it also denies men the possibility of achieving wholeness by withholding from them the feminine principle.

The only person who receives any characterisation in the novel is Christopher. Christopher is a seeker of a religion, an individualist in a society of stereotyped people, in search of his self. He is also an artist. He is a musician who takes his inspiration from nature: he learns from the song of the bird, the moaning of the wind, the humming of insects and the murmuring of the stream. As an artist he is tolerated by the scientific state, but Christopher has a defect: he is emotional rather than rational, he possesses a 'mystical understanding of the ways of women' (*MW*: 105) is described as having 'a streak of femininity' (*MW*: 104) and as being 'intermediate sexually' (*MW*: 322) and 'submasculine' (*MW*: 322). People in the scientific state insist that he has not grown up yet and that he needs special assistance to 'think like a man' (*MW*: 265). Christopher cannot and will not think like a man. Furthermore, he seldom thinks, as he himself stresses: he feels.

Applied to the Jungian theory of individuation, which is the quest for self, Christopher's journey seems doomed right from the beginning. Jung believed that a fully developed individual personality must transcend gender; it must not be endowed by either excessive masculinity or excessive femininity. It is true, as Annis Pratt points out,[6] that Jung's definition of 'masculine' and 'feminine' are rigid and almost stereotypical, but it is also true that the same gender stereotyping is present in *Man's World* and I believe that this is what classifies Haldane's novel as a dystopia.[7] To achieve wholeness, each person has to come to terms with, and incorporate, characteristics of the opposite sex into her or his personality. This means that a man would have to listen to what Jung calls the 'inner voices' of his 'anima' which is feminine and a woman would listen to the 'inner voices' of her 'animus' which is masculine. The feminine anima or soul is represented by the moon and is erotic and mysterious, sentimental and irrational. The masculine animus is represented by the creativity of the sun and by the logical and spiritual. To become whole, the individual has to become reconciled with those aspects of his or her personality which have not been taken into account. No one can become whole by repressing the 'inner voices' in the unconscious.

In the individuation process a man might become 'possessed' by the anima and this will cause him to behave in a manner stereotypically expected of women, such as openly expressing emotions like moodiness, sulking, lamenting and tearfulness, whereas a woman who is possessed by her animus will become shrill and opinionated. (The blatant sexism in Jung's theory has recently been discussed in depth by Demaris S. Wehr.)[8] At the beginning of his individuation process, Christopher suffers from neurosis: from a split between his conscious and his unconscious. He cannot relate to the other people in the scientific state, people whom he sees as '100 per cent man and 100 per cent woman' (*MW*: 298), and this, together with the fact that there is no free will, causes the neurosis. By free will he means, not the right to choose between good and evil since both concepts have been dispensed with in this futuristic society, but the right to choose one's own destiny, the right to self-government which is true anarchism. At the same time, he has not been able to enter a dialogue with the 'inner voices' of his unconscious; he is not aware that the basic reason for this split is that the 'problem' is not only an external one (incompatibility with the community and the state) but also one which is internal; and to solve this he has to assimilate his homosexual soul.

One outcome of this neurosis is that Christopher projects onto his much loved sister, Nicolette, what are actually his own characteristics. He imagines she is like him, is a rebel at heart, shares his desire for the mystical and transcends her gender. It is only when Nicolette falls in love with the 100 per cent manly geneticist, and becomes pregnant by him, that she shakes off her homosexuality and slips into the hierarchy as a 100 per cent mother. This ironically helps Christopher is his quest for self. By projecting less onto his sister he enlarges his own personality. He accepts the 'inner voices' of his anima which encourage him to be more emotional, more feminine. But as his individuation process reaches its completion it becomes clear that Christopher's alien-ation from the society he was born into offers no way out except death. With this knowledge, he climbs into his small plane, the Makara[9] (which is always referred to as 'she') and flies higher and higher into the sky in a suicidal flight which seems more like another beginning than an end. Christopher as a 'whole' person would be characterised as follows:

Activity !   — —
!   Moon
!   Nature
!   Night
!   Emotions
!   Sensitive
!   Pathos

A 'feminine' mind within a masculine body has no possibility of survival in a society which insists on polarising gender differences. As Christopher sails higher up into the clouds he ponders:

That word sex (words were like stepping-stones in the pools of thought to-night) – that had to be thrown overboard too, before Christopher could soar freely towards his destination. It was another feeble monosyllable, a euphemism, masking emotions which had been institutionalized by man. You might turn away from it, withdraw, deny, deny, deny – it was useless, down there. Neutrality was not negation. On that ground you were either one of the army of propagatives, or an enemy whom they would ultimately extirpate. Moses and Luther between them had seen to that. Their modern successors did not preach; practice was more efficient. It was not the homosexual body they dreaded, but the homosexual soul; the soul in which the seeds of 'love' were doomed to infertility, the soul that was sufficient unto itself.

(*MW*: 307)

Christopher's femininity is the result of his mother, Antonia, having been disobedient during her pregnancy. She had already borne five sons for the scientists but then, although she knew she was carrying her sixth son, she consciously desired a daughter.

Thus, instead of obeying the scientific state by concentrating on the masculinity of her son, she spent her nine months' pregnancy in 'dreamy reverie' and 'romantic solitude'. When Christopher is born, the near-symbiotic relationship he has with his mother makes his entry into the symbolic order (the law of the father) difficult. Instead of treating him as 'other', Antonia perceives Christopher as an extension of herself and he, in turn, cannot – and does not – repress the female parts of himself.[10] Christopher's individuation process thereby becomes a reversal of that which Sheila Ruth describes:

> Flight from woman is flight from feeling, from experiencing, from the affective; it is flight into distance. It is mind-body split, priority of cognition over feeling, fear of ambiguity (loss of control), preference for deduction over induction, faith in systems rather than responses, pre-occupation with logic to the detriment of aesthetics, and so on.[11]

Although the plot centres on Christopher, the other deviants from the dominant ideology are all women, and personal initiative and the rebellious spirit are all represented by the feminine principle. Antonia is the deviant mother; Morgana, the deviant neuter. Morgana – whose name indicates that she is doomed to die[12] – has been sterilised by the state, desires a child, rebels, and is denounced as 'hysterical' and 'unbalanced': 'She would have to be silenced. She was a nuisance. . . . Women like that were useless' (*MW*: 318).

The polarisation of male/female is more pronounced in *Swastika Night* than in *Man's World*. The mothers in Haldane's dystopia are kept in gilded cages whereas those in Burdekin's dystopia are kept in real cages, their heads shaved and their male babies taken away from them once they have been weaned, so they will not be corrupted by femaleness. First published in 1937, this was one of the many anti-fascist dystopias which appeared in Britain in the late 1930s and early 1940s,[13] but it is different from the others in that Burdekin offers a powerful feminist critique of Nazism by relating power politics to gender politics, and, like Haldane, adopts the voice of Cassandra in warning 'that the pliancy of woman is the tragedy of the human race' (*SN*: 109).

In *Swastika Night*, the Nazis are competing with the Japanese for world power. Europe has been dominated by Nazi rule for 700 years and its strength lies in the Nazi male who believes in 'pride, in courage, in violence, in brutality, in bloodshed, in ruthlessness, and all other soldierly and heroic virtues' (*SN*: 6).

Totalitarianism offers two possibilities to ensure the continuance of the human race. It can either make motherhood especially attractive or it can make it obligatory. The real Hitler began by making it attractive, although his ultimate plans suggest that he considered compulsory motherhood and prostitution.[14] Haldane chose the first option for her dystopia, Burdekin chose the second. Whether mothers are in gilded cages or behind iron bars, the result is the same: their loss of freedom is absolute when their sole reason for existence is reduced to breeding.

The women in *Swastika Night* have been reduced to empty vessels, to 'unwomen'. They possess nothing: no name, no voice, no language they can call their own. They do not possess a soul. Their absolute subjection to man had been relatively easy as it had all begun with rape. The sentences for rape had become lighter and lighter until the rejection right of women was taken away from them. Love then gave way to lust. The women were further punished if they stood up straight 'like a man' or if they wore any garment which enhanced their features. Once they realised what the men wanted them to be, they did their utmost to live up to the new image. By accepting men's idea of their inferiority they not only lost their identity but also contributed to the male supremacist society: 'The human values of this world are masculine. There are no feminine values because there are no women' (*SN*: 108).

Man is active, woman is passive. Man is the giver, woman is the receiver. Daphne Patai has pointed out the similarity of ideas between Von Wied in *Swastika Night* and the Viennese ideologue, Otto Weininger, whose pre-fascist and misogynist work, *Sex and Character*, was published in 1903.[15] *Swastika Night* is, indeed, a critique of fascism but its treatment of gender distinctions also recalls much of the misogyny to be found in the works of Schopenhauer and Nietzsche. It is well known that the Nazis adopted and misinterpreted Nietzschean thought, especially those aspects of it which alluded to the 'super race'.

Some of the most virulent misogynist writing in the nineteenth and early twentieth centuries came from Germany. Schopenhauer, a misanthrope and misogynist, loathed feminine sensuality. He greatly influenced Nietzsche, who assigned women to what he termed the 'slave morality' and denied them an existence unless they could produce an *Übermensch* (Superman). For Nietzsche, women were dark and evil and wished to be 'taken' completely by men. In *The Gay Science*, he writes: 'The woman gives herself, the man adds to himself by taking her.' The Christians in *Swastika Night* consider women to be 'nothing but birds' nests' (*SN*: 183); the Nazis in the dystopia consider women to be the vessels which will carry the warrior foetus. Nietzsche's famous maxim 'Men should be trained for war and women for the recreation of the warrior' received a new interpretation by Mary Daly, who aptly sums up the situation of women in *Swastika Night*: 'Indeed, the War State requires women for the re-creation of its warriors.'[16]

When Katherine Burdekin wrote *Swastika Night* she could not have guessed how horrifyingly accurate her vision of the Nazi régime was to be. The Jewish population in her dystopia has been annihilated and the Christians are tolerated as a sub-race but are termed 'untouchables'. Nietzsche had blamed Judaeo-Christian morality for what he saw to be the degradation and decadence of humanity in the nineteenth century. As Jean Grimshaw points out, he felt contempt for the Christian concept of 'otherworldiness, its emphasis on the spiritual, on self-abnegation, altruism, duty, pity, meekness, humility and poverty'.[17] Mary Daly believes that Nietzsche attributed this type of morality to women and to the feminine principle.[18]

According to Nietzsche there are two types of morality: the master morality and the slave morality. To achieve the former the individual has to act out of a desire of self-affirmation and of self-aggrandisement (this is what Nietzsche terms 'the will to power') and by doing so, the individual will become a superman. The superman (representative of the master morality), must take care not to be corrupted by the 'humanitarianism' of those who acquire the slave morality since:

> they undermine the will to power, they are the levelling of mountain and valley exalted to a moral principle; they make small, cowardly, smug. . . . The man who has become free . . . spurns the contemptible sort of well being dreamed of by shopkeepers, Christians, cows, women, Englishmen and other democrats.[19]

Nietzsche's options, either the master morality or the slave morality, find expression in *Swastika Night*[20] although they have been adapted to fascism:

Master morality	*Slave morality*
Nazi Men	Women
Self-aggrandisement through violence and brutal strength over others	Self-abasement through violence to their selves
Fear of women and female sexuality which they express through contempt	Self-loathing which is the reflection of male desire
Activity	Passivity
Sun	Moon
LIFE	DEATH

The real German Nazis adopted the right-pointed swastika (the sun swastika) as their symbol 卐 which they thought was pure Aryan because it had been used as the cross of the Germanic god of thunder, Thor. There is, however, also a left-pointed moon swastika 卍 which represented the Hindu godess, Kali Maya, the goddess of creation, preservation and destruction. In *Swastika Night*, the sun swastika represents the loss of the feminine principle, the male supremacy over female, militarism over peace and hate over love.

According to the ancient Hindu myth, the world was to come to an end when human beings had become 'violent and sinful, failing to perceive deity in the feminine principle'.[21] After a period of darkness and nothingness, the goddess would re-create the universe and give birth to a new race.

The women have been reduced to 'nothingness' in Burdekin's dystopia. They are described as 'female things', 'female animals' or 'hags'. They have neither a will nor a soul. The fascist empires of the Nazis and the Japanese are also approaching their end, for there is a shortage of baby girls and the percentage of female births is declining rapidly. Thus, the scorpion has given itself a mortal sting. The men in the empires have failed to foresee the consequence of absolute female submission which is, ironically, that it will result in the destruction of male supremacy.

After a period of darkness and nothingness, Kali-Maya will re-create a new race. . . .

In both the dystopias described here male victory over female seems to be evident. In *Man's World* there is no space for the feminine principle to develop freely. Emotion, sensitivity and pathos are crushed unless they are channelled into reproduction of female babies only. In *Swastika Night* the feminine principle has been totally destroyed and the victory of the male over the female seems to be absolute.

There is, however, one main difference between the two dystopias. The vocational mothers in the scientific state are aware of their biological power over men, the power to create life, and do not foresee that this can ever be jeopardised. The ectogeneticist visits the vocational mothers and sums up his concept of their power. Note the binary opposition here between you = women and we = men:

> Let us look back a little. First you had birth control, then you had sex control. The two enabled you to impose your will on us in collective bargaining. Both met, in the beginning with opposition from those of you who would not realise the advantages they brought you. But when you did, you knew an era was beginning for you such as motherhood had never known since dim antiquity.
>
> (*MW*: 75–6)

The time has come, the ectogeneticist continues, to let science (= male-controlled) run its course, and although women's power lies in their biology, this will no longer be the case in the future. If the present is a man's world, the future will be even more so.

The situation in *Swastika Night* is radically different. The women are not aware they possess any power at all. They do not realise the existence of the moon swastika. In a sermon which Von Hess delivers to the women, he unwittingly discloses the secret which threatens to wreck and destroy Hitlerdom. Instead of commanding them to bear strong sons, as was the custom, he tells them to bear daughters. The women cannot believe their ears and hastily convince themselves that Von Hess has made a mistake. Yet:

> If they knew that the Knights, and even der Fuhrer, wanted girl-children to be born in large quantities; that every fresh statistical paper with its terribly disproportionate male births caused groanings and anxieties and endless secret conferences – if the women once realised all this, what could stop them developing a small thin thread of self respect? If a woman could rejoice publicly in the birth of a girl, Hitlerdom would start to crumble.
>
> (*SN*: 14)

Hitlerdom would start to crumble if women developed self-respect, which in turn would come about by giving birth to and rejoicing in female children. On the other hand, Hitlerdom will crumble anyway, without women's self-respect, due to the total absence of female births. Furthermore, women will eventually cease to exist in a world totally populated by males, and this would lead the world into destruction.

Reading *Swastika Night* today with the hindsight of Nazism and the Holocaust is a chilling experience. Read together with Claudia Koonz's *Mothers in the Fatherland*, which is a historical account of how women complied with, or struggled against, National Socialism, *Swastika Night* shows how accurate Burdekin's nightmarish vision was. Koonz suggests that the Nazi creed was easier for women to follow than men, because it stated: 'You are nothing. Your *Volk* is everything' and such a message no doubt harmonises more with women's upbringing than with men's. Koonz continues: 'In the service of this selfless crusade, Hitler's followers discovered their selfhood. Hundreds of thousands of "nobodies" began to feel like "somebodies".'[22]

Koonz's work is an honest analysis of the fascination that fascism held for many women. Klaus Theweleit, in his thought-provoking *Male Fantasies*, insists that fascism is directly connected with hatred and fear of women and with female sexuality. According to Klaus Theweleit: 'What fascism promised men was the reintegration of their hostile components under tolerable conditions, dominance of the hostile "female" elements within themselves.'[23] Moreover, fascism is not a monster that rears its ugly head only now and again, it is always present in our daily relationships with each other.

Charlotte Haldane and Katherine Burdekin both depicted dystopian societies of the far future in which women and life are worthless. The horrifying experiments carried out on the brain in *Man's World* and the glorification of violence in *Swastika Night* are, however, not only crimes of the past, nor of the future, but of our present. This is Cassandra's voice.

> What is past is not dead; it is not even past. We cut ourselves off from it; we prefer to be strangers.[24]

NOTES

The following editions were used for this essay: Charlotte Haldane, *Man's World*, New York, Doran, 1927; Katherine Burdekin, *Swastika Night*, London, Lawrence & Wishart, 1985.

  References to *Man's World* are followed by the abbreviation *MW* and the page number, those to *Swastika Night* by *SN* and the page number.

 1 Christa Wolf, *Condition of a Narrative in: Cassandra*, London, Virago, 1984, 268.

 2 See Patrick Parrinder, *Science Fiction*, London, Methuen, 1980, 76–82 for examples. Parrinder mentions J. B. S. Haldane's essay, *Daedalus*, but refrains from mentioning *Man's World*. Richard Gerber, on the other hand, grants *Man's World* a few lines in his work, *Utopian Fantasy*, New York, McGraw-Hill, 1973, 60.

 3 This quote is taken from Charlotte Haldane's autobiography, *Truth Will Out*, London, Weidenfeld & Nicolson, 1949, 15.

 4 Although Haldane was well acquainted with the work of 'Freud and his successors' (*Truth Will Out*, 34) it is not clear when she read his work and whether she included the work of Jung.

 5 Hélène Cixous' table of binary oppositions is to be found in *La Jeune Née*, written in collaboration with Catherine Clément and first published in 1975. Cixous' theories on femininity and masculinity are further discussed in Toril Moi's *Sexual/Textual Politics*, London, Methuen, 1985, 104–5.

 6 Annis Pratt, *Archetypal Patterns in Women's Fiction*, Brighton, Harvester, 1982, 7.

 7 In *Women's Utopias in British and American Fiction*, London, Routledge, 1988, the author, Nan Bowman Albinski, is correct in stating that *Man's World* can be read either as a utopia (= good society) or as a dystopia (= bad society). She settles for the first option on the evidence of critics' reviews and quotes taken from Charlotte Haldane's work, *Motherhood and its Enemies* (1927). I would insist that it is to be read as a dystopia. In her autobiography, *Truth Will Out*, Charlotte Haldane described herself as being a feminist and a suffragette at the age of 16 (*Truth Will Out*, 304). She also discovers that her mind 'was not in the least scientific, either in discipline or in outlook' (31) and that she had an 'emotional need for a religion, or a substitute for one' (31). These remarks plus the fact that her novel is titled *Man's World* surely would make it a dystopia.

 8 Demaris S. Wehr, *Jung and Feminism, Liberating Archetypes*, London, Routledge, 1988. This essay owes much to Wehr's work.

 9 In Hindu religious myth, Makara was the name of the water monster, which was the steed of Varuna, son of the Hindu sun goddess, Aditi. It is significant that Varuna sometimes appeared as a female and sometimes as an androgyne.

10 According to Nancy Chodorow, because the father does not usually take part in the primary care of children, boys find it more difficult than girls to begin the process of separation and individuation. A girl will identify with her mother, who will perceive her as 'same', as an

extension of herself. A boy will identify with the absent father and will be perceived by his mother as 'other'. See Nancy Chodorow, *Reproduction of Mothering, Psychoanalysis and the Sociology of Gender*, Berkeley, University of California Press, 1978, Ch. 5.

11 Sheila Ruth, *Methodocracy, Misogyny and Bad Faith: The Response of Philosophy*, quoted in Jean Grimshaw, *Feminist Philosophers*, Brighton, Wheatsheaf, 1986, 54.

12 Morgana chooses her name in memory of the biologist Morgan but Morgana was also the name of the Celtic goddess of death.

13 See Andy Croft's article, which lists and discusses anti-fascist novels of that period: *Worlds Without End Foisted Upon the Future – Some Antecedents of 'Nineteen Eighty-Four'*, in Christopher Norris (ed.), *Inside the Myth*, London, Lawrence & Wishart, 1984, 183–216.

14 See Marilyn French, *Beyond Power, Women, Men and Morals*, London, Cape, 1985, 231.

15 See Daphne Patai's excellent critical introduction to *Swastika Night*.

16 Nietzsche's maxim comes from his work *Thus Spoke Zarathustra* and is quoted and contested by Mary Daly in *Gyn/Ecology*, London, Women's Press, 1984, 356.

17 Grimshaw, op. cit., 153.

18 Grimshaw discusses this view by Daly. See ibid., 155–8.

19 This quote comes from Nietzsche's *Twilight of the Idols* and is cited in Grimshaw, op. cit., 154.

20 It must be stressed that Nietzsche would never have approved of the Nazis representing the master morality, nor would he have given his consent to his philosophy being 'used' to promote fascism – as it was by Alfred Rosenberg and Adolf Hitler. Nietzsche's superman was an individualist who used control over self not over others.

21 See Barbara G. Walker (ed.), *The Woman's Encyclopedia of Myths and Secrets*, New York, Harper & Row, 1983, 248.

22 Claudia Koonz, *Mothers in the Fatherland*, London, Methuen, 1987, 79.

23 Klaus Theweleit, *Male Fantasies*, Cambridge, Polity Press, 1987, 434.

24 This quote is from Christa Wolf's *Model Childhood* and is cited by Claudia Koonz in *Mothers in the Fatherland*, vii.

Chapter 2

'Shambleau . . . and others'[1]: the role of the female in the fiction of C. L. Moore

Sarah Gamble

In her essay, 'C. L. Moore and the conventions of women's science fiction', Susan Gubar remarks that C. L. Moore 'is a writer who deserves readers'.[2] The fact that the material for this chapter[3] was compiled mainly by means of lucky encounters in second-hand bookshops is ample evidence of the fact that, however deserving she may be, the work of C. L. Moore is woefully lacking an audience at present.

This may well have a lot to do with Moore's particular cultural and artistic situation as a female writer of science fiction in America in the 1930s. She is associated with the rise of so-called 'pulp' science fiction, a term defined by Peter Nicholls as a form of popular narrative which

> emphasized action, romance, heroism, success, exotic milieux, fantastic adventures often with a sprinkling of love interest, and almost invariably a cheerful ending. . . . It is associated primarily with stories written, usually rapidly, for the least intellectual segment of the sf market: packed with adventure, and with little emphasis on character, which is usually stereotyped, or on ideas, which are frugally and constantly recycled.[4]

It has to be said that much of Moore's work corresponds to this definition: along with her male counterparts, she wrote story after story in quick succession for the cheap mass-produced periodicals known as 'pulp' magazines (so-called because of the poor-quality paper on which they were printed – the word quickly came to be used as a description of the fiction within the magazines themselves). It was through such publications as *Weird Tales*, which published her first short story 'Shambleau' in 1933 and in which many of her subsequent short stories appeared, that Moore made her name.

However, Moore's position as a female writer of science fiction is undoubtedly ambiguous in such a context. The literary phenomenon in which she participated – namely, 'pulp' sf – certainly promoted the popularity of the genre; but it also established it as one almost exclusively dominated by men, where male writers wrote about male heroes for a male audience. Based as it was around technological themes, a topic in which women were assumed to have little interest and certainly no knowledge, science fiction almost automatically assumed their exclusion, both as authors and as characters. As Peter Nicholls comments: 'one of the most shameful facets of genre sf is the stereotyped and patronizing roles which are usually though not invariably assigned to women'.[5] It is significant that the few women who did venture to explore the new genre, like Moore, often used names that were sexually ambiguous (Leigh Brackett or U. K. Le Guin, for example), or adopted male pseudonyms (the most famous example of which is probably James Tiptree Jr, who kept her identity as a female author a secret for many years). Such evasions and deceptions stemming from a fear of male acceptance at either the editorial or the marketing stages in a book's publication also indicate, consciously or not, female authors' own ambivalence about their peculiar position as *female* authors of science fiction. While women such as Moore were pioneers, daring to colonise a traditionally male artistic space, their literature often betrays an unsettling uncertainty about what exactly their role in this genre is to be – an insecurity which tends to be particularly noticeable in such authors' treatment of their female characters, which often dramatises their own doubts and fears.

The American critics Sandra Gilbert and Susan Gubar have identified the female participation, from the 1930s, in such marginal literary genres as science fiction, as women's way of both confronting and evading the politics of sexual conflict by translating it 'into the more openly theatrical terms of species and racial struggle', thus enabling them to feel free 'to express their fantasies about the inexorability of sexual battle as well as their fears of female defeat'.[6] As I have seen from my own experience, many modern readers of Moore's work tend automatically to assume its male authorship. Although it may betray our own lingering chauvinist assumption that science fiction authors are 'normally' male, I think that such a judgement is justified by the content of her work, which dramatised the very 'fears of female defeat' commented on by Gilbert and Gubar. And yet it seems sadly ironic that Moore, one of the earliest – and certainly one of the most successful – American women writers of science fiction, who began her literary career at a time when the male domination of the genre was almost total, is still so disregarded in a supposedly more enlightened age.

I am sure that this refusal to acknowledge Moore's importance to the history of the development of women's science fiction has its basis in the fact that, on the surface at least, her stories seem to conform absolutely to the masculinist conventions of 1930s science fiction. Her most successful character, for example, around whom a great many of her short stories are centred, is Northwest Smith – the kind of lean, laconic, exaggeratedly macho figure seemingly specifically designed to appeal to the adolescent male imagination. On the other hand, another character who is the inspiration for a series of stories is Jirel of Joiry – one of the first sword-and-sorcery heroines in modern fantastic literature, and a remarkably successful creation in the male-oriented world of 1930s science fiction. Any feminist critique of Moore's work, however, must necessarily reconcile these two figures; if we praise her creation of Jirel, for example, we must also attempt to justify the seemingly inherent sexism in the stories involving Northwest Smith.

An examination of Moore's stories as a whole uncovers a consistently recurring subtext, through which Moore examines the whole nature of sexuality and gender differentiation in ways that contain very radical implications. Furthermore, this gender-based conflict is most explicitly expressed through the stories which are most open to accusations of sexism – those involving Northwest Smith.

C. L. Moore's presentation of gender: love and sex

The stories based around her two principal characters, Jirel and Smith, are not startlingly original in structure, following the same repetitive, almost archetypal, pattern – hero encounters and fights an adversary and, after numerous setbacks, wins. Yet this very repetitiveness serves an important purpose by deflecting the interest of the reader away from such extraneous details such as plot and characterisation – which remain unvaried from story to story – and focuses it instead on the pattern of imagery Moore sets up within the body of her work as a whole. The sexual implications inherent in Moore's literature hold the key to an understanding of her presentation of the female principle.

It is interesting to note, though, that the pattern of sexual imagery which forms the basis of most of Moore's stories often specifically *excludes* the heroes themselves. Neither Jirel nor Smith are ever convincingly presented as sexual beings – what sexual and emotional history they do possess is conveniently peripheral to the main thrust of the narrative, and really only exists to establish their credibility as characters. 'Song in a Minor Key' (1957), for example, reveals that Northwest Smith has experienced an intense love affair in his youth. By setting this episode safely in the past, however, Moore shows a vulnerable and sensitive side to Smith's character, while at the same time ensuring that he is distanced from any kind of inconvenient emotional entanglement that might complicate the narrative.

Jirel's personal life is surrounded by a similar sort of ambiguity, even though it forms the content of two stories – 'Black God's Kiss' (1934) and 'Black God's Shadow' (1935). These deal with her love for Guillaume, a rival baron who attempts to conquer her lands. 'Black God's Kiss' ends with his death at Jirel's hands; 'Black God's Shadow' begins with her realisation of her love for him. Conveniently, though, this realisation has come too late – Guillaume is reduced to an impotent wraith who can never be brought back to life. This episode, therefore, fulfils the same function for Jirel as Smith's vague nostalgia for a lost love. It establishes that she does have a sensitive side to her nature (and, maybe just as important in Jirel's case, confirms her heterosexual orientation, which might otherwise be in doubt), while in no way impeding the progress of subsequent narratives in which both her social and emotional autonomy must remain unquestioned.

Smith and Jirel's unintrusive emotional experiences can therefore be seen to immunise them symbolically against the threat of annihilation which the sexual principle continually poses. Sexuality, in Moore's work, is inevitably inherently destructive, and often life-threatening, and her stories are dominated by vampiristic female characters, of which the most well-known is probably the eponymous heroine of 'Shambleau' (1933), a story already comprehensively discussed by Sandra M. Gilbert and Susan Gubar.[7] Smith saves an alien woman from the mob that is threatening to kill her, and takes her home with him. Meek and subdued during the day, at night she reveals her true nature. Under the turban that covers Shambleau's head is revealed 'a nest of blind, restless red worms . . . like naked entrails endowed with an unnatural aliveness, terrible beyond words' (p. 19),[8] and she then proceeds to drain Smith of his life-force in a horrible travesty of the sexual act:

> And in her living cloak she swayed to him, the murmur swelling seductive and caressing in his innermost brain – promising, compelling, sweeter than sweet. His flesh crawled to the horror of her, but it was a perverted revulsion that clasped what it loathed. His arms slid round her under the sliding cloak, wet, wet and warm and hideously alive – and the sweet velvet body was clinging to his, her arms about his neck – and with a whisper and a rush the unspeakable horror closed about them both. (p. 21)

This kind of vampiristic scene is repeated over and over again in the Northwest Smith stories, where he is continually placed in a situation in which he is completely at the mercy of a rapacious alien female sexuality. In 'Julhi' (1935), for example, he encounters a woman whose mouth is 'a beautifully arched orifice, the red lip that rimmed it compellingly crimson, but fixed and moveless in an unhinged jaw. Behind the bowed opening he could see the red, fluted tissue of flesh within' (p. 207).[9] The sexual connotations of this 'orifice', with its similarity to the female vulva, are obvious, for this is the means by which she marks Smith out as her victim:

> He went sick with the shock of what he saw. For Julhi clung to him, relaxed in avid coils. Her eyes were closed, and her mouth was fastened tightly against the flesh of his left breast, just over the heart. The plume above her head quivered from base to tip with long, voluptuous shudders, and all the shades of crimson and scarlet and bloody rose that any spectrum ever held went blowing through it. (p. 228)

In 'The Tree of Life' (1936), he is abducted by an alien god, who, although described in the masculine gender and taking a definitely phallic form, shares the greedy sexuality of Smith's other protagonists: 'The Tree's branches snatched him from its priestess' hands. The fire-colored blossoms burnt his flesh as they closed round him, the hot branches gripping like the touch of ravenous fingers. The whole Tree was hot and throbbing with a dreadful travesty of fleshly life as it whipped him aloft into the hovering bulk of incarnate horror above' (p. 104).[10] All these figures share similar characteristics which emphasise their aggressive sexual hunger – they are 'wet and warm', 'voluptuous', 'hot and throbbing'; they cling, slide, suck and snatch, in what virtually amounts to an act of rape (in the case of 'The Tree of Life', *homosexual* rape – doubly horrifying for such a determined heterosexual as Smith!). Another characteristic which they all hold in common is that they are all associated with the colour red – Shambleau is a sinister travesty of a redhead, Julhi's plume turns shades of 'crimson and scarlet and bloody rose', and Thag, the Tree of Life, has 'fire-colored blossoms'. In other words, they are all scarlet women – both fearsome and fascinating: disgusting, yet compelling.

That sexuality – specifically female sexuality – is consistently associated with threatening images reveals much about the characters' own internalised attitudes towards the subject – to say nothing of Moore's. For the great danger posed by creatures such as Shambleau is that they threaten, in a most basic way, the heroes' autonomous being, annihilating them through their own erotic responses. A recurring detail in the Northwest Smith stories, for example, is how easily he is ensnared by rapacious alien women – because they appeal to his own latent, but strong, sexuality. He does not even attempt to escape Shambleau's embrace because he cannot resist the 'blazing darkness that was oblivion to all else but rapture' (p. 22) that he finds within it. He allows himself to become entangled in the phallic branches of the Tree of Life because he is hypnotised by its 'siren call' (p. 100), and enthralled by the 'flagrant mesmerism' (p. 213) in Julhi's voice. In many ways, therefore, characters such as Smith and Jirel are fighting against externalised representations of their own sexuality, which is precisely what makes such a being so difficult to resist.

Romantic love, as opposed to sex, is another matter, and one that Moore treats entirely seriously in these stories. As has already been mentioned, both Smith and Jirel have experienced love affairs which are portrayed in a very different way from their semi-erotic encounters with voracious alien beings. However, both romances end in either death or separation, and this seems to be typical of Moore's treatment of the subject in her fiction as a whole. In the collection of C. L. Moore's stories compiled for this chapter, there is not a single example of an uncomplicated, happy love affair, for love and death, just as much as sex and erotic annihilation, are irrecoverably linked throughout her fiction. In 'Greater Than Gods' (1939), a man who is in love with two women is faced with a vision of two equally undesirable futures stemming from his commitment to either one or the other. In the end he rejects both, and turns instead to a woman whom he does not love:

> Marta's violet gaze looked out into the room through crystal. Across the desk Sallie's lovely, careless smile glowed changelessly. They had been gateways to the future – but the gates were closed. . . .
> And Bill turned to the gray-eyed woman in the doorway with a long, deep, shaken sigh. (p. 197)[11]

'The Bright Illusion' (1934) is another romance with a twist in its tail, in which a man meets an alien woman in human shape. Although the situation is one similar to that faced many times by Northwest Smith, it turns out very differently. Instead of becoming locked in an erotic battle for sexual control, these two characters fall genuinely in love. However, succumbing to the fatalism that pervades Moore's unhappy romances, they decide that 'there can be no such union for us anywhere in life' (p. 98),[12] and choose to die together rather than to live apart. Moore's message is clear – unrestrained sexuality annihilates the self, while true love can never be fulfilled.

Moore's vision of the future: the battle between the sexes

But *why* does Moore, in all her stories, exhibit such extreme pessimism concerning relations between the sexes? I think that the reason lies in her gynocentric attitudes, which perceive men and women as fundamentally different beings. The science fiction genre, of course, is a literary form which is eminently suitable for the expression of this viewpoint, for, in these stories, the unbridgeable differences between the male and female protagonists are strongly foregrounded by making them literally different species. Thus, gender-based differences of psychology and culture are dramatised and extended by Moore into a more overt physiological and evolutionary context.

Androgyny, with its emphasis on the importance of shared characteristics, has no place in Moore's portrayal of sexuality. This is amply illustrated by the character of Jirel of Joiry. In spite of the fact that Jirel plays a man's role in her society, Moore goes to great lengths to prove the existence of a 'real' woman beneath the armour that renders her sexuality ambiguous:

> The face above her mail might not have been fair in a woman's head-dress, but in the steel setting of her armour it had a biting, sword-edge beauty as keen as the flash of blades. ('Black God's Kiss', p. 101)[13]
>
> She was a creature of the wildest paradox, this warrior lady of Joiry, hot as a red coal, chill as steel, satiny of body and iron of soul. The set of her chin was firm, but her mouth betrayed a tenderness she would have died before admitting. ('Jirel Meets Magic', p. 47)[14]

Lester del Ray is correct (if rather condescending) when, in an introduction to a collection of Moore's short stories, he describes Jirel as 'intensely feminine',[15] because I feel sure that this is precisely the impression Moore is striving for in the Jirel stories. And yet there is another side to the character of Jirel, acknowledged by Moore herself, and that is the similarity she bears to Shambleau: 'If you have read past Shambleau to Jirel, you will probably have noticed what a close relationship the two women bear to one another.'[16] Jirel, with her red hair and blazing yellow eyes, is yet another of the monstrous regiment of scarlet women that parade through Moore's fiction – attractive, feminine, but deadly.

In this sense, Moore both conforms to and subverts a social system identified by the French theorist Hélène Cixous as 'patriarchal binary thought', which splits up human characteristics and concepts into male/female oppositions, and then ascribes a value to them. This can be seen very clearly in Moore's work, in which women tend to be associated with the subconscious, intuition, mysticism, and the realm of night and dream: whereas male characters are intellectual, rational, scientific, and more at home in the world of daylight and of action. Cixous herself sees this duality as ultimately negative, pervading western thought to the extent where the female is permanently rendered powerless and silent. As Toril Moi explains:

> Cixous . . . locate[s] *death* at work in this kind of thought. For one of the terms to acquire meaning, she claims, it must destroy the other. The 'couple' cannot be left intact: it becomes a general battlefield where the struggle for signifying supremacy is forever re-enacted. In the end, victory is equated with activity and defeat with passivity; under patriarchy, the male is always the victor.[17]

Moore, however, preserves these gynocentric dichotomies, but manipulates them into creating a subtext in which female attributes are given new value, thus endowing her female characters with a voice and an active role within the narrative. On the surface, male/female characteristics complement each other – but the deep structure of the text tells a different story, for Moore is in fact continually promoting the female ethic at the expense of the male; hence the recurring images of threatening females in her fiction. One only has to look at the Northwest Smith stories to see this in practice: Smith, deliberately portrayed as the ultimate macho hero, is continually being plunged into situations with which he really cannot cope, and which call into question the real value of his 'male' talents – strength, rationality, an ease with language, and so on. Moore habitually sets up a tension between two worlds – the 'real' one to which Smith belongs, and in which he can control situations and events, and another, symbolic one, which lies outside the realm of normal time and space. Outside the boundaries of his world, Smith is ironically forced to take the role traditionally assigned to the female within the text – victimised, powerless and sexually threatened. This alternative narrative thus neatly reverses traditional value judgements, transferring power from the male attributes to the female. The boundaries between the two narrative spaces are clearly marked – time and time again, in an ironic reversal of the birth process, Smith makes a symbolic descent from a male to a female world. In doing so, he leaves the surface structure of the text behind and enters into a deeper subtext in which lurks the spectre of the frustrated female imagination.

The story 'The Tree of Life' is a case in point, and is a good example of these preoccupations echoed throughout the Northwest Smith stories. Hiding from patrolling police in the ruins of a Martian temple, Smith encounters a girl who telepathically pleads with him for help. Although his chivalrous instincts are aroused by the girl's seeming helplessness, Smith nevertheless perceives a dichotomy between 'the incongruity of speech and power' that the girl's mind conveys:

> Her milky, unseeing eyes held a magnetic power that carried her thought to him without the need of a common speech. And they were the eyes of a powerful mind, the outlets from which a stream of fierce energy poured into his brain. Yet the words they conveyed were the words of a terrified and helpless girl. (p. 80)

Unable, as always, to resist a female in distress, Smith unwittingly leads her to the entrance to another world in which her latent power can be released. Within the shadow cast by the tracery of a metal grille on which the tree of life is represented, Smith experiences a disorienting moment of transition: 'outside the boundaries everything executed a queer little sidewise dip and slipped in the most extraordinary manner' (pp. 82–3), and when he comes to himself again it is to find the roles played by the girl and himself completely reversed: she is now revealed as the priestess of Thag, the Tree of Life, for whom Smith is intended as a sacrificial victim, and he now is the helpless one. 'She was not blind now, nor frightened. She stretched out her hand to him confidently. "It is my turn now to lead you," she smiled' (p. 83).

This episode, which leads into Smith's quasi-erotic encounter with the Tree of Life and eventual escape back into his own world, sets up many of the dichotomies that exist between Smith's 'male' world and the 'female' one into which he has stumbled by accident. At the same time, it explores the nature of female creativity, exposing by means of a series of ironic reversals the role of the female within the conventional literary text. In this sense, the girl functions as a paradigm for the female artist, frustrated and voiceless within the space of a patriarchal narrative, but newly empowered once free of its restrictions.

This preoccupation is demonstrated most clearly through Moore's exploration of the issue of language, always an important theme within her narratives. She uses the metaphor of alienation to expose women's relation to patriarchal speech – and maybe also to dramatise the struggle for feminist articulation within her own consciousness. As the critic Carolyn Burke has commented: 'When a woman writes or speaks herself into existence, she is forced to speak in something like a foreign tongue.'[18] In the 'real' world, Thag's priestess is blind and powerless, and, significantly, she does not share 'a common speech' (p. 80) with Smith – instead she has to close the linguistic gap between them by means of telepathy. Even after the switch of worlds, her words remain 'gibberish' (p. 83) to him.

Not all of Moore's alien women share this attribute, but have to stumble along in human speech as best they can in order to communicate with him at all. Smith, for example, believes Julhi to be 'irrevocably dumb', convinced that her mouth 'in its immovable hinged jaw, could never utter human speech' (p. 208). Her speech – for she can communicate with Smith – is more like music than words, and he comes to realise that her voice is in fact 'primarily not for communication, but for hypnosis' (p. 222), and that her real language is 'a speech of colors' (p. 223). Shambleau, too, is forced to speak to Smith in a language that is not her own: 'I – not talk you – speech', she haltingly explains, and later: 'Your speech – hard for me'. In response to Smith's joking request 'What's yours? I might know it – try me', she replies 'Some day I – speak to you in – my own language' (p. 7). The nature of that language is revealed at night when she takes him in her embrace and whispers 'very softly, very passionately, "I shall – speak to you now – in my own tongue – oh, beloved!"' (p. 22). Smith's encounters thus fictionally dramatise what many feminists believe to be the linguistic situation of women under patriarchy: 'In speech with a man a woman is at a disadvantage – because they speak different languages. She may understand his. Hers he will never speak or understand.'[19]

Although they are forced, therefore, to speak a foreign language in order to communicate with Smith, all these alien women, diverse though they may be, share a common native language which, as Shambleau illustrates, is completely non-linguistic. Normal language can be described in Saussurean terms as a rather clumsy system of a signifier attempting to reflect accurately that which it signifies, whereas these women communicate through a system that rejects words in favour of direct representation. Shambleau's language, like Julhi's, is one of action without any need for speech; and the telepathic ability exhibited by Thag's priestess similarly closes the gap between signifier and signified in order to communicate her thoughts and emotions directly. Although Smith is described by Moore as 'a linguist of repute' ('Shambleau', p. 15), at ease with many different languages and dialects (thus exposing the real patriarchal nature of language), he is completely unable to comprehend the tongue of these alienated females, enacted within a symbolic world in which objects and thoughts can be immediately apprehended without any need to resort to the inevitably inadequate medium of speech. Again, the story 'The Tree of Life' is a good illustration of this point– the doorway to the other world lies within the shadow of an iron grille, on which is represented the image of a tree of life. To pass through that shadow, as Smith finds out, is to discover the reality that lies behind the one-dimensional figure as it exists in his world – Thag, the *actual* Tree of Life itself. The world of the feminine principle, then, is one in which images and symbols are unnecessary, because the reality to which they point can be immediately apprehended.

As well as exploring the difficulties of communication between the sexes, within her stories Moore symbolically hints at the possible discovery of a kind of *écriture féminine*. This is mainly expressed through the recurring motif of some type of random configuration – most commonly a pattern or design, although sometimes music or (as in the case of Julhi) colour. Whatever form it takes, it is a system of non-linguistic representation which holds no meaning at all for Smith, but which is understood well enough by the alien women he encounters. The pattern is often linked to Smith's descent to the other world in which all his patriarchal values are reversed. In 'The Tree of Life', when Thag's priestess runs into the shadow of the grille, Smith sees a hidden significance revealed in the pattern that

> ran over her like a garment, curving to the curve of her body in the way all shadows do. But as she stood there striped and laced with the darkness of it, there came a queer shifting in the lines of black tracery, a subtle, inexplicable movement to one side. And with that motion, she vanished. (p. 82)

The mysterious tracery of the pattern thus functions in a metaphorical sense, opening the way into the female creative space, in the same way that, in the words of Hélène Cixous, *écriture féminine*, 'the language of 1,000 tongues which knows neither enclosure or death' enables the female artist 'to pass . . . into

infinity'.[20] This parallel between the pattern and female creativity
is even more obvious in Moore's story 'Scarlet Dream' (1934).
As in 'The Tree of Life' a pattern is the means by which Smith
enters a world clearly aligned with the female principle – this
time a pattern woven into a piece of cloth, which, when he
studies it, gives him the impression of hidden power, opening
the normal world to 'undreamed-of vastnesses where living scarlet
in wild, unruly patterns shivered through the void' (p. 112).[21]
The piece of cloth is in fact a shawl, and its bright scarlet colour,
as well as its association with an item of exclusively female
apparel, is reminiscent of the dangerous female sexuality of Shambleau and Julhi. The power of the pattern is such that it becomes,
in Smith's dreams, 'one mighty Word in a nameless writing,
whose meaning he shuddered on the verge of understanding, and
woke in icy terror just before the significance of it broke upon
his brain' (pp. 112–13).

Eventually, of course, the twisting design leads him to the
other world that is awaiting him below the surface of the text.
And again it is clearly associated with the female space. In this
realm of literal representation, a symbolic colour (scarlet) actually
becomes that which it symbolises in all of Moore's stories –
blood, described by the critic Susan Gubar as 'one of the primary
and most resonant metaphors provided by the female body'.
Blood has always been closely associated with women through
the biological processes of menstruation and childbirth, and it is
also commonly associated in feminist criticism with female art,
symbolising 'woman's use of her own body in forms of artistic
expression', and echoing the plight of 'the woman artist who
experiences herself as killed into art . . . bleeding into print'.[22] In
'Scarlet Dream' the metaphor is surrounded by a strange, yet
meaningful, ambiguity – the inhabitants of this world drink blood
for their food, yet they also shed it as random victims of a
nameless 'Thing'. Blood is thus simultaneously associated with
life and death, in the same way as it can create both the space
and the means for female creativity, while at the same time
marking out women as circumscribed 'others' in a male society.

On this side of reality, however, the Word, already experienced
by Smith as a subversive symbol susceptible to a feminist linguistic interpretation, adopts a reversed meaning, coming to represent
the constrictions of patriarchal language. It is now, therefore, a
means by which the female reality can be destroyed. Smith

reaches this world by an *intuitive* following of the paths of the pattern, but he can only leave it by placing it within a linguistic system of signification – by *speaking*, an act which transforms the Word (and the world) from literal image to part of the symbolic structure which is language, and thus metaphorically subordinating female art to masculine forms of representation. As the woman who is both his lover and his guide in the other world tells him:

> 'It is death to pronounce the Word. Literally. . . . In the temple there is one room where the Word is graven in scarlet on the wall, and its power is so great that the echoes ring for ever round and round that room. If one stands before the graven symbol and lets the force of it beat upon his brain he will hear, and know – and shriek the awful syllables aloud – and so die. It is a word from some tongue so alien to all our being that the spoken sound of it, echoing in the throat of a living man, is disrupting enough to rip the very fibers of the human body apart. . . . And because the sound is so disruptive it somehow blasts open for an instant the door between your world and mine.' (p. 123)

Once that Word is uttered, Smith is immediately catapulted back to his own space and time – but it is at the expense of the other, which is destroyed. These varieties of other worlds visited by Smith can therefore be seen to exist independently of language, representing a kind of pre-Oedipal state in which female creativity can live outside the subjection of a socialised, patriarchal order. They are worlds in which Smith, as the representative of an almost exclusively male society, full of 'space-ships cleaving the sky with flame' and 'sudden brawls in saloons' ('Scarlet Dream', p. 129), is the *true* alien.

Where, then, does this leave Jirel, whose narratives bear such a close resemblance to Smith's? Although she, too, descends into an alternative world, her position in the text cannot be identical to his, simply because of the difference in sex of the main character. In fact, Jirel does sometimes function in a similar way – in 'Jirel Meets Magic' (1935), for example, she ventures into a strange, enchanted land where she takes on, in a very straightforward way, the role of hero – even down to battling against the 'feminine vengeance' (p. 64) of a malignant sorceress. But while in that narrative she is certainly little more than a female

Northwest Smith her role is more ambiguous in other stories. 'The Black God's Kiss', in spite of a superficial similarity, deviates in several very significant ways from the stereotypical Northwest Smith narrative. Jirel, conquered and imprisoned by Guillaume, deliberately makes the descent to another dimension of reality in a search for the means of revenge – and finds it. Unlike Smith, she does not stumble into this world by accident – she already knows of its existence and how to reach it. (It can almost, in fact, be considered part of her territories, since the gateway is situated within her castle.) Jirel's control over her circumstances continues throughout the story. Jirel does not fight against the female principle in this world, for it is ironically only herself she encounters there – a symbolic extension of her own burning desire for vengeance against the man who has invaded her territories and casually dispossessed her. As she explains to her malicious double: 'I seek a weapon . . . against a man I so hate that upon earth there is none terrible enough for my need' (p. 116). Guided by her other self, she finds the 'semi-human . . . sexless and strange' statue of the black god of the title; a symbolic projection of her own desire to 'unsex' herself, thus freeing herself from any emotional, feminine attachments to Guillaume which might tempt her to accept his male dominance. Instead of fighting against the implied eroticism of the figure, therefore, she accepts it, taking the kiss it seems to offer her. Something 'unthinkably alien and dreadful' enters her soul 'through the union of . . . warm-blooded woman with image of alien stone' (p. 122) – a new and deadly ability to disrupt the patriarchal order. Jirel takes the burden of the black god's kiss back into the rational world, and kills Guillaume in a parody of the classic fairytale motif – a kiss, traditionally a revitalising gesture that can wake sleeping prin-cesses and turn frogs into princes, becomes here an instrument of female vengeance, and another reminder of the fathomless dangers of women's sexuality.

The resemblance between Jirel and Shambleau, another alien-ated, dispossessed female, is nowhere more obvious than in this narrative. While Smith is forever alien and out of his depth outside of his ordered reality, Jirel's adventures in other dimensions put her in touch with different facets of her self. Strange and threaten-ing though these worlds might seem to her, she is at home in them in a way Smith can never be because she accepts that the eroticism she encounters there is her own. Shambleau and her sisters could never be alien adversaries to Jirel, therefore, because she *is* Shambleau – yet another aspect of the vengeful female principle which, while threatening male sexuality, demonstrates a wholly justifiable will to survive in the face of male persecution. Such women are prepared to risk their own lives in the battle to prevent themselves being marginalised, and classified as alien and 'other'.

If these worlds are symbolic extensions of herself, it is not surprising that Jirel is always able to find her way out of them. However, so does Smith, beleaguered though he inevitably is. Every narrative always ends with a return, a re-ascent from the murky, twilight realms of the female psyche into the daylit world of male rationality. A combination of stubbornness, luck and a reliance on sheer physical force always secures Smith's escape. Just as the utterance of a single Word destroys the world of 'Scarlet Dream', so the language of force and of masculine dominance is always sufficient to break out of the thrall of any number of predatory female aliens. Shambleau is shot by Smith's friend, Yarol, and Smith is thus freed from her erotic spell. Smith himself shoots Thag, and immediately finds himself back among the Martian ruins.

Does this mean, then, that Smith has won – and, further, that Moore sees the victory of the male principle over the female as inevitable, even desirable? Although this is certainly a problematic issue, I think that at least a partial answer can be found in the repetitive nature of these narratives. To read any number of them, especially in quick succession, is to gain the impression that, far from winning, Smith has gained only a temporary reprieve. Turn the page, and the whole process – the impulse to aid a seemingly helpless, pretty woman, the descent, the battle with an alien female in a twilit, dreamlike world – begins all over again. And this, too, points to another female attribute; that of plurality. Smith is only a single man, and against him are ranged an infinite number of Shambleau-like beings – alien women with a different world, all waiting to pounce on him. In this sense, all the characters, Smith included, are archetypal figures in an eternal battle, in which the male force (singular) is continually beset by an abstract erotic female principle manifested in a variety of different forms (plural). Although Smith may win individual battles, the war continues.

In a story entitled 'Fruit of Knowledge' (1940), Moore fancifully rewrites the Biblical creation myth, giving men and women entirely different origins, thus implying that the battle between the sexes is inevitable, incessant, and virtually pre-ordained. She recalls an alternative version of the story in which Lilith, 'the Queen of Air and Darkness' (p. 200),[23] not Eve, is the first woman. She is the female principle to God's male, 'her part . . . as necessary as God's in the scheme of creation, for light cannot exist without dark, nor good without evil' (p. 207). The ideological views behind this equation of the female with darkness, evil and negativity would be extremely dubious were it not that Moore is so obviously on Lilith's side. Adam is naive and childlike, and she falls in love with his perfection. When God creates Eve, he merely appropriates Lilith's form – Eve thus becomes Lilith's rival, yet, in a strange way, also her sister.

> Lilith knew it was her very flesh God had taken to mould this pale girl from Adam's rib, using the same pattern which Adam had designed for Lilith. Eve wore it now, and in that shape knew, without learning them, all the subtle tricks that Lilith's age-old wisdom had evolved during the brief while she dwelt in the body. (p. 215)

The creation of Eve, then, has as much to do with Lilith as with God, and in this version of the story Eve's eating of the apple is a conscious act of revenge against Lilith, removing Adam from her influence. Adam is thus reduced to an uncomprehending pawn, being squabbled over by two women – but by the end of the story the sphere of the conflict has widened to include him as well. Rebellious Lilith, always fighting against God's patriarchal authority, vows revenge on both the man and the woman. The children born of the union between her and Adam will 'haunt . . . [Eve's] to their graves. . . . Mine are the disinherited – let them take vengeance!' (p. 234). Part of the pattern of that revenge is Cain, ordained by Lilith 'to set murder loose among Adam's sons' (p. 235).

The three principal characters in 'The Fruit of Knowledge' also highlight the fact that the conflict between male and female is more than just a duel. Adam, Eve and Lilith form an eternal triangle composed of one man and two women – a pattern repeated in other stories. Smith, for example, is often lured into another world by one woman (usually passive, pretty and helpless, like Eve), only to fall victim to a second, who bears an obvious similarity to Lilith. Looked at from a feminist critical perspective, it becomes obvious that these two women are in fact different facets of the same one, echoing women's experience in a masculine society – an experience described by Lorna Irving as 'alienation from the self'. Instead of having a unified psyche, they are forced to become schizophrenic, creating a socialised self to show to the world, while burying angry 'unfeminine' impulses deep within their psyches – impulses which, according to Irving, surface within their art: 'Women's writing . . . seems frequently dominated by the imaginary, by mirrors in which the self is reflected back as other.'[24]

In this respect women share a dual matriarchal legacy – that of Eve, created by a patriarchal God as a helper and companion to man; and that of Lilith, the eternal rebel. In a metaphorical sense, it is the daughters of Lilith, disinherited and repressed symbols of justified female anger, that stalk through C. L. Moore's fiction, exposing the essential weaknesses within the patriarchal principle. This forms the absolute basis of Moore's pessimism concerning the sexes – men and women are fundamentally alien to one another, possessed of completely different attributes and talents. Creatures like Lilith, Shambleau and Julhi are monsters only from a patriarchal perspective – in their refusal to be named and confined within a patriarchal cultural and narrative structure they function as potent symbols of female alienation. Although certain individuals may have a belief in the ability of love to cancel out the differences between the sexes, in Moore's fiction as a whole any kind of reconciliation, however, well-intentioned, would seem highly unlikely.

It is at this point, however, that a fundamental problem in Moore's work has to be faced. While creating, if not consciously, a text which is extremely susceptible to a feminist interpretation, she is either unable or unwilling to confront its ultimate implications. When decoded, her narratives are potentially extremely subversive – the kind of subversion which, as Lorna Irving says, 'effects a fictional break-down of reified male perspectives and often reveals a story that dramatizes the authority of female characters'.[25] However, the endings of these narratives reveal reservations in the mind of the author, who never permits her ideas to reach their natural radical conclusions. This is illustrated in a story which is potentially one of her most extreme, 'No Woman Born' (1944),[26] in which Deidre, a singer disfigured in a fire, is given a new metal body by scientists. As Susan Gubar has already noted,[27] this story contains many conscious references to *Frankenstein*: just as Shelley's monster escaped from the control of its creator, so Deidre demonstrates that her new body has given her powers far beyond those of the men who seek to confine and control her. As Gubar comments, this demonstrates 'Moore's suspicion that the woman who has been placed below man as sub-human might very well turn out to be above him, super-human'.[28] As Deidre's confidence in her abilities grows, the story thus becomes a rather satisfying female power fantasy:

> 'Do you still think of me as delicate?' she demanded. 'Do you know I carried you here at arm's length half-way across the room? Do you realize you weigh *nothing* to me? I could' – she glanced around the room and gestured with sudden, rather appalling violence – 'tear this building down,' she said quietly. 'I could tear my way through these walls, I think; I've found no limit yet to the strength I can put forth if I try.' (p. 284)

However, even here, Moore makes her customary, if rather belated, attempt at an evasion of the issues her narrative raises. Deidre is not, in the end, an adequate symbol of empowered womanhood, for Moore, while emphasising her strength, also emphasises her unnaturalness: 'I think I was an accident. A sort of mutation halfway between flesh and metal, something accidental and . . . unnatural, turning off on a wrong course of evolution that never reaches a dead end' (p. 286). In other words, the powerful woman is a freak, a sport of nature or (as in Deidre's case) technology.

In the end, therefore, Moore seems to retreat from the subversive potential within her narratives, taking refuge in an ultimate plea for balance – always curbing the destructive side of the female psyche at the end of each narrative, even though it is unleashed again in the following story. Stories like 'Scarlet Dream' and 'Greater Than Gods' are extremely critical of all-female societies, putting forward the view that female sensuality can lead to passivity and stagnation. In 'Greater Than Gods' Bill Cory has a vision of the world as a matriarchy – seeing the belief that 'peace and ease and plenty would dominate civilisation, leisure for cultivation of the arts, humankind coming into its own at last, after so many ages of pain and blood and heartbreak' (p. 170) declining into 'a decadent, indolent civilisation going down the last decline into oblivion' (p. 172). An all-male society is just as bad – a remorseless, violent 'machine' (p. 184). Moore's protagonist chooses to face an uncertain future in an attempt to find a balance between two extremes, but, in the context of her fiction as a whole, such a balance seems extremely uncertain. With her deadly kiss, Jirel of Joiry kills the man she loves – a clear example of the vengeful female principle at its most destructive. Yet what else could she do to defend her possessions and her autonomy? This is the agonising dilemma that lies at the heart of Moore's fiction, unsolved and seemingly unsolvable.

The pull towards rebellion countered by an equally strong restraining force in favour of the *status quo* is the irresolvable dichotomy which makes any attempt at analysing the metaphor of the gender conflict in Moore's fiction ultimately inconclusive. Her metaphors of female alienation are potentially powerful and farreaching, but not even a science-fiction writer can envisage a future in which these dilemmas can be satisfactorily resolved.

NOTES

1 This title is (unfortunately) not original – it is taken from C. L. Moore's own essay 'Footnote to *Shambleau* . . . and Others', reprinted in Lester del Rey (ed.), *The Best of C. L. Moore*, New York, 1975, 365.
2 Susan Gubar, 'C. L. Moore and the conventions of women's science fiction', *Science Fiction Studies* 7 (1980), 17.
3 I wish to emphasise that my collection of material for this chapter is far from complete, due to the difficulties I have had in obtaining anything at all by C. L. Moore.
4 Peter Nicholls (ed.), *The Encyclopaedia of Science Fiction*, London, 1981, 485.
5 ibid., 661.
6 Sandra M. Gilbert and Susan Gubar, *No Man's Land: The Place of the Woman Writer in the Twentieth Century*, New Haven, Yale University Press, 1988, 101–2.
7 Gubar op. cit., deals extensively with 'Shambleau'. She returns to that discussion with Sandra M. Gilbert in *No Man's Land*.
8 C. L. Moore, 'Shambleau', *The Best of C. L. Moore*. All quotations from this story in the text are from this edition.
9 C. L. Moore, 'Julhi', *Northwest Smith*, New York, 1981. All quotations from this story in the text are from this edition.
10 C. L. Moore, 'The Tree of Life', ibid. All quotations from this story in the text are from this edition.
11 C. L. Moore, 'Greater Than Gods', *The Best of C. L. Moore*. All quotations from this story in the text are from this edition.

12 C. L. Moore, 'The Bright Illusion', ibid. All quotations from this story in the text are from this edition.

13 C. L. Moore, 'Black God's Kiss', ibid. All quotations from this story in the text are from this edition.

14 C. L. Moore, 'Jirel Meets Magic', in Pamela Sargent (ed.), *More Women of Wonder*, Harmondsworth, Penguin, 1976. All quotations from this story in the text are from this edition.

15 Lester del Rey, 'Forty years of C. L. Moore', *The Best of C. L. Moore*, xi.

16 C. L. Moore, 'Footnote to Shambleau . . . and Others', *The Best of C. L. Moore*, 367.

17 Toril Moi, *Sexual/Textual Politics: Feminist Literary Theory*, London, Methuen, 1985, 105.

18 Carolyn Burke, 'Report from Paris'. Here quoted from Elaine Showalter's essay 'Feminist criticism in the wilderness', in Elizabeth Adel (ed.), *Writing and Sexual Difference*, Chicago, University of Chicago Press, 1982, 20–1.

19 Dorothy Richardson, *Oberland*. Here quoted from Gilbert and Gubar, op. cit., 248.

20 Hélène Cixous, 'The Laugh of the Medusa'. Here quoted from Moi, op. cit., 113.

21 C. L. Moore, 'Scarlet Dream', *Northwest Smith*. All quotations from this story in the text are from this edition.

22 Susan Gubar, '"The Blank Page" and female creativity', in Adel, op. cit., 78–9.

23 C. L. Moore, 'The Fruit of Knowledge', *The Best of C. L. Moore*. All quotations from this story in the text are from this edition.

24 Lorna Irving, *Sub/Version*, Toronto, 1986, 4.

25 ibid., 5–6.

26 C. L. Moore, 'No Woman Born', *The Best of C. L. Moore*. All quotations from this story in the text are from this edition.

27 See Susan Gubar, 'C. L. Moore and the conventions of women's science fiction', in which she compares both Shambleau and Deidre with Frankenstein's monster. She puts forward the view that 'it is the earlier stories that most successfully develop Mary Shelley's identification with the monstrous alien and her concern over the coercive effects of technology on the lives/bodies of women' (p. 17).

28 ibid., 21.

Chapter 3

Remaking the Old World: Ursula Le Guin and the American tradition

Susan Bassnett

In a much-quoted passage from her essay, 'A citizen of Mondath', Ursula Le Guin notes that there is 'little real criticism' for a science fiction writer, and that despite enthusiastic responses from fans serious comment on the quality of a writer's work is hard to find. She makes this point in a general polemic on the particular problems facing a writer of science fiction who wants to write well and yet has no clear measure of how her work is judged in aesthetic terms. Although written in the early 1970s, Le Guin's remarks are still valid; science fiction remains a marginalised literary activity, outside the mainstream, and although critical appraisals have increased in the postmodernist climate of the 1980s, there is still not very much criticism around that a writer might constructively use.

Although an extremely popular and successful writer for adults and for children, whose work has won a number of major literary awards, Ursula Le Guin has not always been treated very kindly by those critics who have actually considered her work. Colin Manlove, for example, who is hardly left of centre, describes her as essentially conservative. In an essay discussing the trilogy of novels *A Wizard of Earthsea*, *The Tombs of Atuan* and *The Farthest Shore* (1968–72), he argues that Le Guin's 'reverence for the past' is essentially conservative and that the workings of magic in the trilogy also express 'the conservative nature of the fantasy'. The novels, like 'most fantasies',

> seek to conserve those things in which they take delight: indeed it is one of their weaknesses that they are tempted not to admit loss. Their frequent looking to the past is conservative in itself: and the order to which they look and seek to re-create is usually

a medieval and a hierarchic one, founded on the continuance of the status quo.[1]

Three years previously, at the Palermo conference on science fiction in 1980, John Fekete accused Le Guin of creating an inadequate utopian vision in *The Dispossessed*, while Nadia Khouri argued that the contradictions in Le Guin's writing 'become aesthetic defects'.[2] In 1988 Sarah Lefanu also complained about contradictions in Le Guin, this time with specific reference to her portrayal of gender roles:

> There is a simple anomaly, or contradiction, at the heart of Le Guin's work. It features very few women; these are restricted either by biology . . . (*Planet of Exile*) or by stereotype . . . (*The Dispossessed*). This is not unusual in science fiction; what is odd is that despite it, Ursula Le Guin should have such a feminist following.[3]

What these and other critical opinions reveal is that it is not easy to assess Ursula Le Guin's work, nor can it be neatly categorised, either in terms of ideology or in terms of genre. In the conclusion to 'A citizen of Mondath' Le Guin appears to be revelling in the fact that her writing defies classification, stating with a rhetorical flourish that 'Outer Space, and the Inner Lands, are still, and always will be, my country'.[4]

In making a distinction between Outer Space and the Inner Lands, Le Guin also deals fairly dismissively with the vexed question of describing a work as science fiction or fantasy. She says simply:

> Along in 1967–68 I finally got my pure fantasy vein separated off from my science fiction vein, by writing *A Wizard of Earthsea* and then *Left Hand of Darkness*, and the separation marked a very large advance in both skill and content. Since then I have gone on writing, as it were, with both the left and the right hands; and it has been a matter of keeping on pushing out towards the limits – my own and those of the medium.[5]

The claim Le Guin is making here is anything but conservative; as a writer, she argues, she has found two modes that both work for her, one described metaphorically as a journey outwards into space, the other as an inner journey, but both seeking to enter new unexplored areas within her own psyche and within her chosen medium. In short, she presents herself in this essay as a radical writer with a social conscience and a sense of artistic integrity, and what this self-definition reveals can, I believe, help to explain the anomalies and contradictions that have perplexed some of her most articulate readers.

All writers are a product of a particular culture at a particular moment in time; the values they bring to their writing, the conventions they espouse, the critical statements they seek to make have a context. Ursula Le Guin is a North American writer, born in California in 1929 into a middle-class home (her father was an anthropologist, her mother a writer), educated at Radcliffe and Columbia, and mother of three children, whose first science fiction novel, *Rocannan's World*, appeared in 1966. Her life spans the period during which the United States has developed into a major world power, the first nation to develop and use the nuclear bomb, while her writing career coincides with the period of United States colonial expansion – into Vietnam, into Central America, into space, and out to the moon.

In 1982 Le Guin gave a talk on science fiction and nuclear war, noting that the post-Holocaust story 'seems to be enjoying a revival'. She attributes this to the world mood of which the Reagan presidency is a symptom[6] and notes that the greater part of this writing seems to come from the North American and British writers. Eastern European writers, despite their well-developed tradition of science fiction, tend not to write about the Third World War, nor do writers from Latin America. Le Guin notes this fact in passing, and does not attempt any explanation of why the southern half of the American continent should have kept away from the post-Holocaust story.

The strength of the North American novel and the Latin American novel in the later decades of the twentieth century needs no rehearsing here. But it is interesting to note the different ways in which the novel has developed in the two Americas. The Latin American novel is essentially concerned with its own history, and the much-used term 'magical realism' is an attempt to describe the blending of fantasy, history and contemporary reality that is so skilfully developed by a wide range of writers. Magical realism may well have its origins in the early travellers' tales, in the exotic accounts of the New World written by the *conquistadores*, in the surviving oral myths of native Indian peoples. For Latin America has, in marked contrast to North America, eschewed the idea of the melting pot. Difference, not sameness, has been a goal and an ideal, unlike the sentiments expressed in verse on the Statue of Liberty which assume that in seeking the embrace of Mother America all differences can be erased. This ideal of forging the New Citizen in the melting pot has a moral and religious dimension also, a legacy of the Puritan tradition of the founding fathers and daughters of the revolution (not, one notes, of wives!).

After the bombing of Japan, after the Cold War years of the 1950s, the purge of leftwing intellectuals and artists, the execution of the Rosenbergs, all of which seriously eroded the ideal of the New Citizen, came the massive campaigns of the 1960s that changed the face of the United States forever. The civil rights movement raised the question of the meaning of Americanness at its most basic level and served as a reminder to everyone that the New Citizen had achieved his wealth and maintained his dignity on the backs of slaves and the underprivileged descendants of slaves. Moreover, following Black civil rights demonstrations, other groups began to organise – Mexican Americans, the much despised Chicanos and American Indians, now known proudly as Native Americans, the original occupiers of the land. The emergence into the public eye of these groups had a great many repercussions, chief among which has been a rediscovery of a neglected history. By the early 1970s North Americans were becoming aware of an archaeological heritage, of the presence of languages other than English (the millions of Spanish speakers had previously been completely marginalised). Suddenly, the fake gothic buildings of the midwest built in emulation of a European past were perceived as far less significant than the ancient Indian settlements in the south-west. In her long poem 'Places Names' (1981) Ursula Le Guin writes about that vanished heritage:

> The people whom the White invaders dispossessed had been
> living here for several hundred years; they called the
> ones who build these mounds the Old Ones. Walk in the
> silence of the vast sacred enclosure among the green
> mounds built above the bones and ashes of the illustrious
> dead
> laid between levels of mica, sheets of mica
> transparent and glittering as eyes, as souls.
> . . . .

So back to the New World, the thin, sick skin we laid
on this land,
the white skin.[7]

Reviewing John Bierhorst's *The Mythology of North America* in
1985, Le Guin sings the praises of Native American culture as a
model for the present:

> The oral literature of the American Indians, transcribed and
> translated, is a treasurehouse for all American readers and
> writers – the only literature entirely rooted in this ground, the
> only words that, like corn and sequoias, begin *here*.[8]

Le Guin's interest in Native American mythology can be seen as
a developing line through her novels, culminating in her most
recent work, *Always Coming Home*. In her early works she relies,
like Tolkien and so many European alternative world writers, on
Norse and Celtic mythology, but then gradually shifts continents,
thereby developing a greater sense of her own rootedness in
America, which also has its political dimension.

In her preface to *The Word for World is Forest*, published in
1972, Le Guin describes her mood at the time of writing, four
years earlier at the height of the Vietnam war in 1968:

> I wrote *The Little Green Men* (retitled) in the winter of 1968
> during a year's stay in London. All through the sixties, in
> my home city in the States, I had been helping organize and
> participating in nonviolent demonstrations, first against atomic
> bomb testing, then against the pursuance of the war in Viet
> Nam.
>   . . . 1968 was a bitter year for those who opposed the war.
> The lies and hypocrisy redoubled; so did the killing. Moreover,
> it was becoming clear that the ethic which approved the defoli-
> ation of forests and grainlands and the murder of noncomba-
> tants in the name of 'peace' was only a corollary of the ethic
> which permits the despoliation of natural resources for private
> profit . . . and the murder of the creatures of the Earth in the
> name of 'man'. The victory of the ethic of exploitation in all
> societies, seemed as inevitable as it was disastrous.[9]

In the same piece, Le Guin admits that in writing *The Word for
World is Forest* she had given in to a great temptation to science
fiction writers and 'succumbed to the lure of the pulpit'. She

noted this tendency in the genre elsewhere, commenting however that generally the preaching was from the opposite ideological position ('most SF has been incredibly regressive and unimaginative') and the galactic empires were derived from the British Empire of the 1880s.[10] Her concern in *The Word for World is Forest* was primarily with what she perceived as the neglected question in SF – the cultural and racial Other – and she returns to this theme again and again in her later works. The creatures that are so brutally treated by the *yumens*, the military invaders from Earth, are gentle peaceloving beings. Their forest is systematically destroyed, they are raped, butchered and treated as slaves. Worst of the exploiters is the *yumen* Captain Davidson, but significantly when the *creechies* resist and win the struggle, they refuse to kill Davidson and send him instead to a desolate, uninhabited island, where he will either learn to dream or sink deeper into his homicidal madness. The novel is a barely disguised parable of the Vietnam war, and one of the most horrific sections is clearly based on the Mai Lai massacre. The narrative voice intensifies the effect, since it is largely written from Davidson's viewpoint, as the following passage demonstrates:

> Hard up as the men were, they didn't leave even one of the females alive to rape. They had agreed with Davidson beforehand that it was too damn near perversity.... These things might be built like human women but they weren't human, and it was better to get your kicks from killing them and stay clean.[11]

Despite the atrocities perpetrated by the *yumens*, the novel ends on a note of hopefulness, with the killing over and reparation beginning to be made as the *creechies* take back their own planet.

The ending of *The Word for World is Forest* touches on a theme that is central to the other novel written in 1967–8, *The Wizard of Earthsea* – the theme of the darkness within the self. Le Guin's own distinction between her left and right hands, between fantasy and SF can be clearly seen in these two novels. In the one, what is placed centrally is the effect on a society of the power of darkness whilst, in the other, what is examined is one man's struggle to overcome that darkness. Ged, the would-be mage, overreaches himself and looses an evil power into the world. The entry of the shadow is described in language that figuratively reminds us of rape: 'Then the sallow oval between Ged's arms grew bright. It widened and spread, a rent in the darkness of the earth and night, a ripping open of the fabric of the world.'[12] Ged can only be redeemed by acknowledging the shadow as part of himself, by speaking its name which is also his own name. In the second novel of the trilogy, *The Tombs of Atuan*, Tenar is redeemed with the help of Ged, now a mature man, and she also comes out of the darkness and learns to speak her own name.

The three novels that make up the Earthsea sequence draw on archetypal images; Le Guin sets up a series of dichotomies – light and darkness, the open sea and the closed tomb, the mage and the priestess, life and death, and she also uses the device of the quest or journey as a frame in each book. She has been criticised for the marginal role of women overall, but clearly the question of sex roles is not her main consideration here. By returning to cultural archetypes, Le Guin inevitably uncovers the patriarchal structuring of the society that produced them, and her principal concern is to look at the way in which the individual of whatever sex faces the darkness and desolation within; failure to face it can result in the creation of a Captain Davidson or a Kossil, the evil priestess who tries to destroy Tenar and teaches her how to kill.

In 1987 Le Guin revised her essay of 1976, 'Is gender necessary?'. The original essay is an account of her own involvement with feminism and her attempt in *The Left Hand of Darkness* to create a society in which sexuality is constructed completely differently and where androgyny is the norm. People exist in a state of non-gender until they come into 'kemmer' when they develop sexually for a brief period randomly either as males or females, and consequently the absence of sexuality is 'a continuous social factor' for most of the time. Le Guin's essay is effectively an attempt to justify herself against some of the criticisms of her alternative sexuality, principle among which was the claim that when not in 'kemmer' her characters are all men and not menwomen. She expresses her support for feminism ('I didn't see how you could be a thinking woman and not be a feminist') but stands firmly against the idea of inventing a new non-genderised pronoun and defends her decision to call all Gethenians 'he'.[13]

But in the 1987 version, she has changed her position on the question of pronouns, pointing out that she had indeed invented a new pronoun for the 1985 screenplay of the novel. She also recognises that she had 'quite unnecessarily locked the Gethenians into heterosexuality':

I now see it thus: Men were inclined to be satisfied with the book, which allowed them a safe trip into androgyny and back, from a conventionally male viewpoint. But many women wanted it to go further, to dare more, to explore androgyny from a woman's point of view as well as a man's. In fact, it does so, in that it was written by a woman. But this is admitted directly only in the chapter 'The Question of Sex', the only voice of a woman in the book. I think women were justified in asking more courage of me and a more rigorous thinking-through of implications.[14]

At the start of both versions of the essay, Le Guin refers to the gathering momentum of the women's movement in the mid-1960s after 'a fifty year halt'. In her introduction to *Planet of Exile* she refers to the 'thirty-year paralysis' of feminism[15] and what both these quotations show is that she perceives feminism as having a tradition and a history, in which she herself has a place. Ursula Le Guin can therefore be placed very firmly in the tradition of United States Liberal feminism that stretches right back into the nineteenth century, and which was from its very beginnings always linked to some specific cause. In the 1987 version of 'Is gender necessary?' Le Guin says: 'At the very inception of the whole book, I was interested in writing a novel about people in a society that had never had a war. That came first. The androgyny came second. (Cause and effect? Effect and cause?).'[16]

The links between nineteenth century liberal feminism in the United States and political campaigns constructed around specific issues such as the abolition of slavery or universal suffrage have been well-documented, as have the links between that liberal feminist line and visions of utopias, of which Charlotte Perkins Gilman's *Herland* (1915) is one of the best known examples. In her edition of feminist documents, Alice Rossi defines the nineteenth-century feminists in terms of two groups – the Enlightenment feminists who she describes as sophisticated, intellectual, urban writers, and the moral-crusader feminists who she sees as native-born Americans from the rural or small-town middle classes.[17] Ursula Le Guin, as a twentieth-century writer, derives her brand of feminism from both lines and the campaigns upon which she focused her energies were concerned with civil rights and anti-militarism for, as I have argued elsewhere, the feminism of the 1960s in the United States was very definitely a resurgence of a social force that had its origins more than a century earlier and continued to be goal-directed.[18] The difference was, of course, that feminism in the 1960s splintered into different factions, with the liberal feminists often viewed as reactionary and elitist and with a whole new dimension being added by Black feminists who questioned the white, middle-class bias of the liberal tradition. It is therefore not to be wondered at that Le Guin could, on the one hand, describe herself as a feminist and believe in that definition wholeheartedly, whilst on the other she could be attacked by other, more radical feminists for the contradictions that many perceived in her writing.

An important strand of the 1960s feminism in the United States was the spiritual dimension. The spiritual has always occupied an important position in the United States' cultural tradition, doubtless a legacy of the early Puritan colonies. Writers such as Mary Daly have posited a feminist metaphysics, and the spiritual has manifested itself in a variety of ways, from campaigns for the ordination of women in organised religions to alternative cultural groupings that celebrate matriarchy and the healing powers of women. Many of these alternative groups set up in the late 1960s and early 1970s drew upon Native American folklore and medicine, and Le Guin appears to be comfortable with this tendency. In a talk given in 1986 called 'Woman/Wilderness' she describes the voice of women in lyrical terms:

> The women are speaking. Those who were identified as having nothing to say, as sweet silence or monkey-chatterers, those who were identified with Nature, which listens, as against Man, who speaks – those people are speaking. They speak for themselves and for the other people, the animals, the trees, the rivers, the rocks. And what they say is: We are sacred.[19]

In a paper given in several different versions and finally published under the title of 'The Fisherwoman's Daughter', Le Guin appears to be thinking through her feelings about feminism, patriarchy and spirituality. The essay is full of quotations from a wide variety of other women writers, and its awkward rather shapeless feel reflects the way in which Le Guin seems to be struggling to articulate complex thoughts. In a central passage she argues for the reclaiming of the idea of woman as mother and writer both, rejecting the 'books versus babies' doctrine in both its patriarchal and its feminist dimension:

White writing, Cixous calls it, writing in milk, in mother's milk. I like that image, because even among feminists, the woman writer has been more often considered in her sexuality as a lover than in her sexuality as pregnant–bearing–nursing–childcaring. Mother still tends to get disappeared. And in losing the artist-mother we lose where there's a lot to gain. . . . My book *Always Coming Home* was a rash attempt to imagine a world where the Hero and the Warrior are a stage adolescents go through on their way to becoming responsible human beings, where the parent–child relationship is not forever viewed through the child's eyes but includes the reality of the mother's experience.[20]

Through her novels, Ursula Le Guin develops her own brand of feminist philosophy, moving from the moral-crusading sentiments of the late 1960s to the more reflective views of the late 1980s, and that shift reflects a wider process of change going on in American society around her. She began by seeing feminism as common sense, as a mode of perception that had a tradition behind it and consequently did not need to be foregrounded. Only later, as the revised version of 'Is gender necessary?' indicates, did she come to question some of her earlier assumptions and to acknowledge that the new feminism both derived from, but also broke with, the earlier version.

Her principle concern in the 1960s was therefore not feminism but the anti-war movement, and the earlier novels reflect that position. *The Word for World is Forest*, though written with passion and commitment, is a dated piece in many respects; stylistically it is still very much in the tradition of tersely written popular SF novels, and its ideology derives from the strong anti-war feelings of so many American leftist intellectuals. Likewise, her most recent novel, *Always Coming Home*, is a work of its time, a vast novel that creates another world not simply by a few invented terms and descriptions of alien beings, but by painstakingly constructing a new society.

The war in Vietnam ended in bitter disillusionment. The United States had suffered a blow to its international prestige, and feelings at home ran high. Through the 1970s and into the 1980s that sense of disillusionment manifested itself in a steady move to the right, in the rise of religious fundamentalism as opposed to spirituality, in a new sense of harshness as notions of a caring society were increasingly dismissed as utopian and costly.

Alternative cultures, now more marginalised than ever, retreated out from the decaying cities. The Equal Rights Amendment (ERA) upon which feminist groups had pinned their hopes was defeated. The scandal of Watergate came and went, and Richard Nixon was elevated to the status of elder statesman in the years of Ronald Reagan's triumphal residency in the White House. Perhaps most significantly of all, the ideology of peace and universal harmony that had been a genuine belief of a great many people from all classes in the late 1960s now came to be perceived as illusory. The more cynical generation of the 1980s showed at best mild amusement, at worst contempt for the people dismissively described as the flower children of twenty years earlier. Ursula Le Guin has noted the way in which fantasy writers have catered for that sense of cynicism and disillusionment. In her essay 'Facing it' (1982) she notes that:

> much current fantasy and science fiction (is) in full retreat from real human needs. Where a Tolkien prophetically faced the central fact of our time, our capacity to destroy ourselves, the present spate of so-called heroic fantasy, in which Good defeats Evil by killing it with a sword or staff or something phallic, seems to have nothing in mind beyond instant gratification, the avoidance of discomfort, in a fake-medievel past where technology is replaced by magic and wishful thinking works. But the science-fiction books about endless wars in space, where technology is magic and the killing proceeds without moral or psychological justification of any kind, probably are written from the same unadmitted despair. The future has become uninhabitable.[21]

She explains this sense of hopelessness as deriving from 'an inability to face the present' and to take responsibility for living in the present in what she terms 'this sacred world'.

Throughout Ursula Le Guin's writing the question of the moral responsibility of the individual is of central importance. Time and again her novels revolve around this issue, regardless of whether they are written in the left-hand or right-hand mode. *The Left Hand of Darkness* is, at bottom, a novel about the love that develops between two individuals and about the way in which each of them confronts their responsibility to the other, to themselves and to the larger communities from which they come. The question of gender difference is, I believe, less important in this novel (even though it has attracted the most attention) than the question of what commitment – to a cause, to a nation, to a person, to one's self – actually means in real terms. Seen in this light, *The Left Hand of Darkness* can be placed in context, and its affinities both with the Earthsea trilogy and *The Word for World is Forest* become clearer.

Le Guin has discussed on many occasions the way in which she views developments in fantasy and in science fiction, the place of these genres in literature as a whole, the response of readers, the hostility and uneasiness they can arouse. The term 'utopia', however, causes her more difficulty and in an important essay entitled 'A non-euclidean view of California' she wrestles with that term and tries in the process to discuss what a genuine utopia might mean for her. She has this to say about the tradition of utopian writing in the west:

> My intent is not reactionary, nor even conservative, but simply subversive. It seems that the utopian imagination is trapped, like capitalism and industrialism and the human population, in a one-way future consisting only of growth.[22]

Utopia, she goes on to argue, has been 'euclidean, European and masculine'. But she is perplexed as to what a non-euclidean, non-European, non-masculine utopia might be. It might, she suggests, possibly be only imaginable by women, though would surely not only be inhabited by women. Using the terminology of yin and yang, she contrasts two versions of utopia:

> from Plato on, utopia has been the big yang motorcycle trip. Bright, dry, clear, strong, firm, active, aggressive, lineal, progressive, creative, expanding, advancing, and hot. . . . What would a yin utopia be? It would be dark, wet, obscure, weak, yielding, passive, participatory, circular, cyclical, nurturant, retreating, contracting, and cold.[23]

The conclusion that she comes to in this essay leads her to the title of her collected essays, *Dancing at the Edge of the World*. Rejecting the two alternatives proposed to utopian writers, either to expose the brutality of the present world or to write escapist, consolatory fiction about an alternative, she states simply that she has no idea what utopia might be. The image she uses is a metaphysical one, that of descending into the abyss, the darkness, and ultimately emerging into the unknown; a form of spiritual death and resurrection:

> I have no idea who we will be or what it may be like on the other side, though I believe there are people there. They have always lived there. It's home. There are songs they sing there; one of the songs is called 'Dancing at the edge of the world.'[24]

Always Coming Home is one version of that other side. It is a huge, carefully crafted novel that is set in an imaginary California of the future, but a future that could also be viewed simultaneously as a past and a present. The title is symbolic; Le Guin herself has come home, from the far galaxies and the Inner Lands, and set her novel in the place where she has her own roots. Her utopia, therefore, is not a European one, nor is it a masculine one, for the Condor people, representatives of a militaristic order live in a dystopic society, where violence, war and social hierarchies create a superclass and a mass of oppressed peoples. It is also a non-euclidean utopia, for in shaping it Le Guin has gone back into North American Indian culture, returning to the Native Americans for an idealised vision of a society where a genuine sense of community exists.

The book is divided into a number of sections. The story line is carried by Stone Telling, the woman who is daughter of a Valley mother and a Condor father and whose journey out of the Valley and ultimately back to it provides the reader with a vision of both the utopian and the dystopian communities. The greatest part of the book is an encyclopaedic account of Valley life, virtually an anthropological study. We read about how they lived: their food, their medical practices, their writing, their pottery, their codexes, their sacred texts, their mythology, their poetry and song, their language, their games and dances, dying and burial practices. There are illustrations of their art, their alphabet, a glossary of their language, drawings of their animals, plants and houses, tracings of their maps, charts of their lodges, societies and arts. Stone Telling's story moves in a linear path, but the construction of the whole society builds up gradually, so that the reader can take the book up and leave off reading it wherever they choose. Translator's notes and authorial comments add to the construction of a sense of authenticity: the map of the town of Sinshan, for example, has a caption saying that it was 'drawn by the Editor with the help of Thorn of Sinshan'.

In 'A non-euclidean view of California', Le Guin points out that her 1974 novel, *The Dispossessed*, contained utopian elements, of which the major one 'is a variety of pacificist anarchism, which is about as yin as a political ideology can get'.[25] *Always Coming Home* takes that pacifist anarchism much further, and contrasts the way of life in the Valley with the 'civilised' life of the militaristic, capitalist Condor culture. Stone Telling admits that she does not understand the meaning of the terms 'barbaric' and 'civilised', and in the section entitled 'Time and the city' the anthropologist I-speaker runs into problems with the same terms:

'They came across a land bridge,' I say doggedly, 'from the other continent –'
'From the west,' Gather says, nodding. But is he talking about the same poeple I'm talking about?
The ones that were met by Coyote? . . .
. . . It is very hard for me to keep in mind that 'people' in this language includes animals, plants, dreams, rocks, etc.
'What human people lived here before your people?'
'Just our people – like you –' . . .
. . . It's hopeless. He doesn't perceive time as a direction, let alone a progress, but as a landscape in which one may go any number of directions or nowhere. He spatialises time; it is not an arrow, nor a river, but a house, the house he lives in. One may go from room to room, and come back; to go outside, all you have to do is open the door.[26]

Le Guin's model for the new culture derives from ancient Indian cultures, and so the imaginary past creates the imaginary future. The reader can share Stone Telling's shock at the cruelty of the Condor world and recognise its affinities to our own world, but the power of the Valley draws her and us back into its embrace, and the value-judgemental terminology of civilisation and barbarism shift their meaning.

In this, too, Le Guin reveals herself to be writing out of a tradition; the clash between civilisation and barbarism has been a central theme for American (North and South) novelists since the eighteenth century. James Fenimore Cooper's Leatherstocking novels, showing the gradual progression of the white settlers into Indian lands and the ambiguities of that 'civilisation' process, are an early example of a form that has continued right up to the present day. *Always Coming Home* is a very American novel in this respect and once again the question of gender is subordinated to the question of pacificism.

Through *Always Coming Home* there is another strand – a series of short sections either about, or narrated by, someone named Pandora. In a section entitled 'Pandora worrying about what she is doing: she addresses the reader with agitation' Pandora is directly equated with the figure from Greek mythology whose curiosity led her to open a box containing all the evil in the world. Pandora here claims to have known what she was doing:

> I knew what would come out of it! I know all about the Greeks bearing gifts! I know about war and plague and famine and holocaust, indeed I do. Am I not a daughter of the people who enslaved and extirpated the peoples of three continents? Am I not a sister of Adolf Hitler and Anne Frank? Am I not a citizen of the State that fought the first nuclear war? Have I not eaten, drunk, and breathed poison all my life, like the maggot that lives and breeds in shit?[27]

Despite this, Pandora claims that at the bottom of the box there may be Hope, and that even if it is empty, there will be room and time – 'time to look forward, surely; time to look back; and room, room enough to look around.'

In the twenty years that separate *Rocannan's World* from *Always Coming Home*, Ursula Le Guin's writing has changed a great deal stylistically. It has matured and developed and she has moved towards a more lyrical mode that owes a great deal to the oral tradition of Native American song and story-telling. The society in which she lives has changed a great deal too, and the anger felt by many Americans in the 1960s has been transformed in all kinds of ways. The growth of the right, the drug crisis, the sense of cynical helplessness felt by many has been countered by a rediscovery of the past, a past that does not owe anything to Europe but rather owes everything to the very peoples once the target of white genocidal policies. The monstrous Captain David-son in one of his manifestations may have succumbed to madness out in the wasteland of exile, but in another manifestation he did indeed learn how to dream.

What has not changed is Ursula Le Guin's profound antagonism to violence and her belief in social equality. Her commitment to feminism likewise remains constant, though by her own admis-sion she has deepened and extended her understanding of what feminism means. For her, feminism must have its political context – in her Bryn Mawr Commencement Address of 1986, for example, she attacks Margaret Thatcher as being the role model for women who want to be female men, and when we recall the enthusiasm for Margaret Thatcher shown by many US feminists at the time of her first election victory in 1979, Le Guin's hostility is a clear sign of where she stands ideologically.

Always Coming Home is, therefore, a work that both breaks new ground and grows out of North American soil. Le Guin shows herself to be part of a literary and cultural tradition and shows also that she has changed the direction of her search for models, looking closer to home than ever before. The alternative world that she has created in such detail is an image of the lost golden age, the pre-conquest world of North America as it might have been. And in creating that tantalising vision of the almost-possible, she raises hopes in her readers of the almost-probable. The last text of *Always Coming Home* is a song 'From the Library at Wakwaha' that serves as a summary of Le Guin's attempt at a utopia:

> I have a different way, I have a different will,
> I have a different word to say,
> I am coming back by the road around the side,
> by the outside way, from the other direction.

NOTES

1 Colin Manlove, *The Impulse of Fantasy Literature*, London, Macmillan, 1983, 31.
2 John Fekete, 'Vettori di cambiamento: razionalità, cultura e società amministrata' and Nadia Khouri, 'Potere, impotenza, utopia: la fantascienza di Ursula K. Le Guin, Michel Jeury e Marge Piercy', both in Luigi Russo (ed.), *La fantascienza e la critica*, Milan, Feltrinelli, 1980.
3 Sarah Lefanu, *In the Chinks of the World Machine*, London, Women's Press, 1988, 132.
4 Le Guin, 'A citizen of Mondath', in *The Language of the Night*, New York, Perigee Books, 1979, 30.
5 ibid., 29–30.
6 Le Guin, 'Facing it', in *Dancing at the Edge of the World*, London, Gollancz, 1989, 102.
7 Le Guin, 'Places, names', in ibid., 64.
8 Le Guin, review of John Bierhorst, *The Mythology of North America*, in ibid., 287.

9 Le Guin, introduction to *The Word for World is Forest*, in *The Language of the Night*, 151.

10 ibid., 151.

11 Le Guin, *The Word for World is Forest*, New York, Berkeley Books, 1972, 86.

12 Le Guin, *The Wizard of Earthsea*, Harmondsworth, Penguin, 1979, 63.

13 Le Guin, 'Is gender necessary?', in *The Language of the Night*, 140.

14 Le Guin, 'Is gender necessary?', redux. in *Dancing at the Edge of the World*, 16.

15 Le Guin, introduction to *Planet of Exile*, in *The Language of the Night*, 140.

16 Le Guin, 'Is gender necessary?', redux. in *Dancing at the Edge of the World*, 11.

17 Alice Rossi, *The Feminist Papers*, New York, Bantam, 1973.

18 Susan Bassnett, *Feminist Experiences: The Women's Movement in Four Cultures*, London, Allen & Unwin, 1986.

19 Le Guin, 'Woman/Wilderness', in *Dancing at the Edge of the World*, 162.

20 Le Guin, 'The fisherwoman's daughter', in ibid., 228.

21 Le Guin, 'Facing it', in ibid., 103.

22 Le Guin, 'A non-euclidean view of California as a cold place to be', in ibid., 85.

23 ibid., 90.

24 ibid., 98–9.

25 ibid., 93.

26 Le Guin, *Always Coming Home*, London, Grafton Books, 1988, 171.

27 ibid., 147–8.

Chapter 4

Doris Lessing and the politics of violence

Moira Monteith

> The question is unavoidable: if we are not on the side of those whom society wastes in order to reproduce itself, where are we?
>
> (Julia Kristeva)[1]

Doris Lessing is a prolific writer who has continued to develop and explore new areas in her fiction. Apart from the central axes of class, gender and race which plot her writing, age is another factor that affects the position from which she starts her work. Unlike the others, age is a variable, and perhaps that is why it is so seldom considered significant in any writer except in relation to subject matter. She herself has labelled it 'the degenerative disease'[2] but there seems no evidence for any deleterious effect on her writing.

Therefore I would like to suggest a developmental or longitudinal[3] approach to her work. However I shall make only a limited use of the extensive interview material available. Often such material is inconclusive or contradictory. For example, Lessing said in 1982:

> 'Well, I don't hold those views now. . . . I don't remember the emotion that made me write that. . . . You see I wouldn't say that at all now because I don't know what good and evil is. But the way I think now is that if writers write truthfully, write really truthfully (it is very hard you know to be truthful, actually) you will find that you are expressing other people.'[4]

The last statement is common to many authors. It presumably indicates a desire not to invalidate the life experience of people they know and observe, and also a desire to be accepted as a reporter or even a mouthpiece. The disclaiming comments in the quotation indicate the very nebulous relationship such answers have with actual texts.

In this essay I intend to focus on one of the major shifts in her writing – the move to science fiction, or space fiction as she prefers to call it. I concentrate on two science fiction novels, *Shikasta* and *The Sirian Experiments*, relating them to the body of her writing and examining the apparent move from realistic presentation. I am particularly concerned with the incidence of violence in her work, a subject area which I suggest is seldom considered in any general way by women writers. She exploits the potential of the science fiction genre to consider violence both globally and historically, but in ways very different from war novels, usually authored by men.

It seems evident that Lessing has always looked for a communal rather than an individual purpose in her writing, and 'expressing other people' is one aspect of this. She inevitably became conscious of the singularity of her viewpoint growing up as a white immigrant in a predominantly black British colony. The imposition of foreign (and patriarchal) ownership was implicit in the eponymous renaming of the land Rhodesia after Cecil Rhodes. She renames it Zambesia in her novels, africanising it to some extent. She became an adherent of the Communist Party and intellectually this gave her a world view, an explanation as to how the world is governed in the way it is, and posited particular views concerning what would happen in the future. But as a communist she was then alienated from the settler society. She had at one and the same time a global outlook and an exceedingly narrow vantage point, positioned by her class, race and gender. She was part of a minority within a minority within a ruling minority. She never completely gets rid of the language of colonialism and alienation, the part that cannot speak for the whole, and so there is always a tension between that language and the desire for SOWF[5] or substance-of-we-feeling. She seems to desire to return to a pre-symbolic state where there is no differentiation between oneself and the other. She repeats frequently that individualism is bad and the good of the whole is what is most desirable. Early experience and ideology are combined in such an injunction. Her separation from the mother coupled with her growing awareness of the divisive nature of patriarchy and colonialism later become rationalised through communist and Sufi doctrines.

But communism has proved to be another of 'the last and greatest of all human dreams'.[6] This implied comparison with Fitzgerald's view of American capitalism fits with Lessing's later view of politics. In *Shikasta*, *The Sirian Experiments* and *Briefing for a Descent into Hell*[7] (Earth) she makes clear her belief that there is no substantial difference between one set of party activists and another, nor between one political dogma and another. It seems likely though that the shattering of such a vision must have been an important factor in preventing her from contemplating a utopian novel, a particular subgenre of science fiction.

With her move to London she became a 'free' woman in the anonymity of the city but writes ironically in *The Golden Notebook* of the lack of freedom for 'free women'. Presumably it was her own experience and perception which led her to portray female characters in such a way that women readers have judged them as ultimately depressing and narrow. Her desire for a community of purpose prevented her from espousing any cause which she deemed partial, for example the women's movement, which she describes as

'very useful because it's broken up set attitudes and allowed a lot of women to feel they've got some support in a very lonely situation. But – it's no use saying what a pity, but it is a pity that they tried to follow men in what they did. The way they've allowed themselves to think and allowed their thinking to become an ideology, is simply patterned on what we know and love, God help us. It's sort of lowering.'[8]

Her later dislike of a declared ideology is inevitably reflected in the form and content of her fiction, where she continually abuses ideologues and organises the ideas content of her novels into a decentred, multi-viewpoint structure. It is difficult to believe she considers her writing (unlike that of declared feminists) to be non-ideological. Her comments on Sufism (a philosophical outlook with which she replaced Marxism) approve intuitive insights. The reading process of a novel structured like *Shikasta* encourages an intuitive grasp of the shapes inherent in the whole. But the reader brings her own ideology to bear on the reading. Lessing's own problems with an ideological position (even if she regards it as common sense) are indicated by the discrepancies in the narrative voice in all her novels.[9]

The authorial presence in her earlier work is manifest most clearly as that of a 'detached observer'.[10] This presence and her powerful talent for observation established the form of her novels. Nicole Jouve indicates very effectively how Lessing begins the sequence *The Children of Violence* very much in the mode of the classic realist novels of the nineteenth century. The author is definitely a voice, almost but not quite moving the protagonist (and the reader) towards greater wisdom through a series of carefully selected experiences. The novels' metalanguage posits a scheme of values assumed to be shared by writer and reader and to which the protagonist eventually coheres or learns from but, as Jouve points out, it doesn't quite work here. It isn't just the language. The promise which seems implicit in the first two novels of the sequence indicates that Martha Quest will eventually find wisdom and or fulfilment. She works through situations and relationships which should bring her satisfaction – sexual relationships, marriage, motherhood, but none of them fulfil her. Lessing views these situations and relationships with a clear detachment and from a woman's point of view and so cannot, despite the energy of the form in which she's writing, allow them to become the end of the quest. Martha (following Lessing's own experience) then tries party politics. There is no ironic edge leading the reader to perceive Martha as a Candide figure who moves naively from sex to marriage to motherhood to politics expecting fulfilment from each. Rather, the form becomes impossible to maintain.

Lessing's writing appears to follow a roughly chronological line, echoing her own experience and following the drive of her intellectual interests. The exception is her early childhood, which does not surface until *Memoirs of a Survivor*. Her early novels still rely on the 'privatised world of personal relations'[11] where women appear marginal to the world of work and politics because of the concentration on their private, sexual lives. However Lessing's realistic presentation brings into focus particular areas of women's experience such as the discomfort of menstruation, childbirth and childcare, and the marginalisation of women in most political movements into coffee makers, canvassers and group protesters. The effect of her penetrating observation is to subvert the possibility of a fulfilled female protagonist – the heroine just moves on.

This outstanding ability to report what she perceives gives a great sense of authenticity to the early novels. So much so that Lessing has often been used as a documentary source. Two examples will suffice. Judith Arcana in her book *Our Mothers' Daughters*[12] includes personal accounts by many mothers and daughters of their experiences in these roles, of their problems and difficulties in a male-dominated society. Quotations from Lessing's fiction are inserted several times among other women's autobiographical comment.

> Earlier, her mother had agonizedly told her that 'it was a woman's role to sacrifice herself, as she had done, for the sake of the children . . . And what will people say?' In these last two phrases she strikes at the heart of the matter – the strength of our mothers' socialisation as women, and our own.

Arcana comments on the fiction in the same way that she comments on the personal records, and includes Martha Quest's fictional mother among 'our mothers'. Marga Kreckel, an experienced psycholinguist, quotes Lessing's fictionalised presentation of group behaviour as:

> An excellent description of a homodynamic sub-code is given by Doris Lessing in 'Martha Quest'. She highlights the conventionalised interaction pattern and its group-cohesive effects on the 'kids' of the 'Sports Club Gang': 'The girls were, it was assumed, responsible for the men. Even the child of seventeen who had left school the week before . . . would instantly assume an air of madonna-like all-experienced compassion; she did not giggle when this wolf or that moaned and rolled his eyes and . . . his face would assume the agonized, frustrated look which was obligatory, while he said, "You're killing me baby . . . " '[13]

In these quotations used as documentary evidence Lessing has noted the pressures of women's lives, the way they are controlled by tradition (often passed on by other women), and by the necessity of organising their own lives always in relation to those of men.

This sense of authenticity coupled with an author in the position of detached observer leads to an extreme kind of authority in the text: a female version of Hemingway's 'This is how it was.' Eventually one viewpoint, however skilfully observed, could not be enough. Also, this authorial stance positions the reader very tightly even though, as Jouve shows, the authorial consciousness which claims to be complete has many gaps. There are narrow limits as to what can be signified, whereas in her later novels readings can be much more various.

Lessing interrupted the writing process of *The Children of Violence* series with *The Golden Notebook*.[14] Here, the protagonist is decentred, concentration on the heroine's psychological life is deliberately fragmented and the novel functions differently for different readers. The text is like a drawing that contains more than one subject, for example a rabbit or a vase of flowers depending on how you look at the outline. You can't see both together but once you know there is more than one image you can move from one to the other quite rapidly.[15] Some readers saw the book as helping to raise women's consciousness of their situation and actual experience within society, others saw it as an experimental *nouveau roman*. Still others read it as an account of what happened to thinking members of the British Communist Party, the dissolution of the communist dream. Jean McCrindle writes:

> *The Golden Notebook*, unlike anything or anyone else at the time, was saying maybe this optimism doesn't actually help us, maybe we ought to look at the dark sides of our movement and admit the possibility of failure. . . . I think Doris Lessing somehow allowed me the possibility of pessimism – allowed the possibility of failure and still surviving, because you could emerge somehow with a kind of bedrock of truth. So, for me, her pessimism was a kind of renewal of politics, that they could be more open and honest. . . . I certainly didn't read *The Golden Notebook* as a rarified literary text.[16]

Subsequently, and according to Lessing more and more often, readers read the book as an account of a mental breakdown. A similar fragmentation of text is used in *Shikasta*, so that a number of structures can be seen simultaneously within the novel, although they are not compartmentalised so sharply as the four notebooks.

In the last novel of the *Children of Violence* sequence Martha eventually disappears from the text. At the beginning of this long novel, *The Four Gated City*, the same detached observer is present, this time free from community ties or guilt, in London. But just as there are surprisingly few black characters in the first novels of the sequence which take place in Rhodesia so there are large lacunae in the representation of the working class. I found the opening sections of this novel particularly unpleasant, where English working-class specimens are observed and reported on. No doubt the prejudices of my own working-class background precluded my sympathy for such grimly documented detail. Later 'salt of the earth' characters seem equally false. It was hardly better if more 'truthful' in *The Golden Notebook* where 'An old woman came in once a week to clean the place' (p. 52). She is an amenity like the gas cooker and is not considered as having any part in Anna's experience, though employment practice might be considered relevant to a Marxist viewpoint. Detached observation has its limitations. As a Marxist it wasn't just that Lessing couldn't write the socialist-realist novel but she would never be able to write effectively about working-class characters. This problematic position possibly accounts to some extent for the change of direction, perhaps instinctive, in Lessing's writing. 'We live in a series of prisons called race, class, male and female.'[17] She has spent a considerable time as a writer attempting to move out of what she sees as imprisoning viewpoints.

Science fiction gave her that opportunity to leave her 'prisons' by the structural possibility of an entirely objective (because alien) narrator. As Lorna Sage states: 'Canopus is a "new" space, a no man's land where gender and genre are provisional.'[18] The Canopean, Johor, who 'compiles' most of *Shikasta* is androgynous and both he and Ambien II, the narrator of *The Sirian Experiments*, are virtually immortal. Her desire to speak out against oppression could be realised only on a limited scale in her previous novels and had to be confined to the experience of her characters. Now she was no longer tied to the authenticity of her text. For the first time she could deal with issues globally, rather than in particular, and became one of the few women writers to fictionalise war.

Ursula Le Guin understands this desire to preach. '[The lure of the pulpit] is a very strong lure to a Science Fiction Writer, who deals more directly than most novelists with ideas, whose metaphors are shaped by or embody ideas, and who therefore is always in danger of inextricably confusing ideas with opinions.'[19] She is explaining, even apologising for, the strength of message in *The Word for World is Forest*, another book dedicated to uncovering the unpleasant nature of colonial exploitation. Lessing uses the genre to deal in hypothetical ways with the vast amount of informed knowledge she has acquired. The violence which has been endemic in *The Children of Violence* but never really confronted until the last novel of the sequence, which is part of the inner and outer life of the narrator in *Memoirs*, becomes the most important and ubiquitous theme in *Shikasta* and *The Sirian Experiments*. In neither text is there a protagonist who experiences or uses violence. The author's (and our) vast knowledge of violence, brought to us through newspapers and televison, becomes the basis of the novels.

> The educated middle class . . . all know that war rages most terribly in various parts of Africa and Latin America; that wars of a particularly ghastly kind have recently concluded in Southeast Asia, one of which at least was distinguished by the mass use of napalm and chemicals; that wars everyone agrees may become total are endemic in the Middle East between contestants not renowned for moderation. They would probably agree that from a removed viewpoint, let us say that man from Mars, it must look as if the planet has been boiling with war through this century. Each war shifts the emphasis towards the mass killing of civilians. No part of the planet has escaped.[20]

Lessing wrote this as part of a newspaper article, yet it could easily be fitted into the text of either novel. Newspaper knowledge and its effects have appeared in her fiction before. A wall covered with pieces cut out of newspapers is one outward sign of Anna's mental turmoil in *Notebook*, and Martha's gloom in *FGCity* after her daily ritual of reading the papers indicates western enervation from the mass media's bombardment of catastrophic news. In the same novel information gained from papers and other sources is used to plot the growing signs of nuclear holocaust. This miasma of information which surrounds most of us all the time could not be effectively used from the position of a detached observer, authenticating experience. In SF, however, it becomes the starting point for all hypotheses about the planet.

Violence can be attractive. It is possible that many if not 'every woman adores a fascist'[21] or a Heathcliff. Even Buchi Emecheta in *Destination Biafra*[22] has trouble deglamorising the myths surrounding the motivation for aggression, although she tries very hard to write from the woman's point of view and asks several times what would have happened if women had been in charge during the Biafran war. SF surprisingly allows for such a deglamorisation. Lessing can reduce the impact violent and aggressive acts would have if connected with an individual character, victim or hero, particularly if that character were given a fine detailed context. In effect she reiterates her experience of colonialism so that it becomes a metaphor for the situation of our planet. We are seen to be very much impoverished by the colonial experience and our wars are the frenetic posturings of beings with little or no self-determination. The Marxist delineation of history has become that of dis-aster, the misaligning of the stars, and via this metaphor she can explore the parameters of violence, looking closely at racism, young terrorists, and the rise in refugees as well as concurrently presenting violence as a historical factor through centuries of the planet's experience. The longevity of the main narrators allows for a vast time dimension.

Empires abound in SF, both as a device for ensuring a series of novels and also to signify a power struggle. Quite often empires are evil. The signification is usually simple: the empire represents a massive concentration of power which is being used against a small planet or rebel starship. Therefore the concept of imperialism and its traditional role in SF becomes an appropriate and subtle structural device for Lessing since it is fundamentally concerned with the moral problems arising from an extension of power.

She considers several salient features of colonialism. First, the powerlessness of the colonised. Two empires 'share' the planet, another exploits it piratically. Both *Shikasta* and *The Sirian Experiments* reveal the estrangement of the colonised from their own history, from decision-making, from areas of their own land as well as from power. The point of view is almost entirely that of the enlightened coloniser or bureaucrat not those whose history and experience are being marshalled according to imperial directives. It could be argued that Lessing takes the events out of time, and certainly out of the twentieth century, by encoding them within myth.[23] Although she no longer holds a Marxist view of history (if indeed she ever held one completely) she retains the determinist approach. Our planet's fate is determined by stellar alignments, and the particular variety of degradation our species has undergone is incidental to that fate.

Lessing calls SF writers 'these dazzlers' who

> have also explored the sacred literatures of the world in the same bold way. They take scientific and social possibilities to their logical conclusions so that we may examine them. . . . Shikasta has as its starting point, like many others of the genre, the Old Testament. (*Shikasta*: x)

There were giants; there was a Garden of Eden; celestial visitors did descend; Sodom and Gomorrah were punished. And how do we get back to the beatific vision of that Garden? One of the differences between her first novel series and the second is that in the first the opportunity for development is in exile and then madness, whereas in the second the establishment of harmony and peaceful relationships comes about by extraterritorial imperial influence. No human beings by themselves can progress to salvation. Shikasta or Earth, as a colony, is not allowed self-determination.

The history of the planet Shikasta is fitted into the myth of the Fall. Lessing gives a clear indication of life in a Garden of Eden where the people mystically submit to a sense of order:

> there had even evolved a science of being able to distinguish, in very early childhood, where an individual needed to live. . . . It was no means always so that every member of a family would be suitable for the same city. And even lovers – if I may use a word for a relationship which is not one present Shikastans would recognise – might find that they should part, and did so, for everybody accepted that their very existence depended on voluntary submission to the Great Whole. (*Shikasta*: 26)

Carnivores and herbivores co-exist happily, lions lying down with lambs, and society is centred on the city. The cities, which are very unlike twentieth-century urban centres, are all based on mathematical shapes and at the end of the novel people are again building such cities but not in any planned way. Their knowledge comes instinctively. The first era of Edenic happiness and order – generally referred to, says Ambien II, as 'The Golden Age' – is followed by a period of decline roughly equivalent to our known history, our consciousness of time, our apple of the knowledge of good and evil. 'This garden could not be maintained as it had been' (*Shikasta*: 44). Yet the break in the intergalactic 'lock' which regulated the system was caused by a new stellar alignment: 'we are all creatures of the stars and their forces' (p. 40). That, plus a comet, allows the forces of disorder from the Puttioran Empire to succeed in the form of an invasion from its outpost, Shammat.

The effects of the Fall are revealed through a range of symptoms: a move away from egalitarianism, the introduction of slavery, the incidence of murder, the unnecessary slaughter of animals and 'premature' ageing. The First Law of Canopus had been 'we may not make slaves and servants of others' but this was ignored. Women's position of inferiority on Shikasta is presented as a symptom of degradation, one that occurred after the failure of the Canopean Lock. Ambien II believes that such discrimination is the product of a warped psychology which in turn distorts the victims' (or women's) psychology. She would like to come back and research this matter thoroughly so that she 'could return home with a contribution to our Studies in Perverted Psychology. But first things first.' In later history the North West Fringers – that is, Europeans – are seen as particularly callous and perverse:

> Retreating from these colonies they left behind technology, an idea of society based entirely on physical well-being, physical satisfaction, material accumulation – to cultures who, before encounter with these all-ravaging Northwest fringers had been infinitely more closely attuned with Canopus than the fringers had ever been. (*Shikasta*: 87)

The 'last days' are roughly equivalent to our last three decades and the next and are, according to Canopean records, the most degenerate and brutal. Lessing uses as pathological symptoms of social disease guerrilla violence, particularly that of young terrorist groups, race violence and the mindless brutality of the young, this last being a recurrent theme in her writing. We are given lists of different kinds of terrorist, thumbnail sketches of specific characters. The voice is very much that of an aid to study, direct and straightforwardly explanatory.

> INDIVIDUAL SEVEN (Terrorist type 5) This was a child of rich parents, manufacturers of an internationally known household commodity of no use whatsoever, contributing nothing except to the economic imperative: thou shalt consume. (*Shikasta*: 137)

If this information is linked with that in an essay 'Additional

explanatory information 1', a despairing piece about the generation gap, plus comment from Chinese overlords about the
Armies of the Young, a particular hypothesis becomes apparent.
The tendency for differences between old and young to increase,
if extrapolated from the present situation, must lead to the death
squads and the widespread refugee camps. Her name 'Armies of
the Young', while sounding sinister, is in fact an accurate description of most armies.

The SF genre particularly favours hypotheses as structural
devices. Lessing formulates a trial where black people try white.
This is reported by a Chinese delegate, soon to be one of the
overlords of the planet. The Canopean official Johor, in human
form, organises the prosecution:

> I open this Trial with an indictment. That it is the white races
> of this world that have destroyed it, corrupted it, made possible
> the wars that have ruined it, have laid the basis for the war
> that we all fear, have poisoned the seas, and the waters, and
> the air, have stolen everything for themselves, have laid waste
> the goodness of the earth from the North to the South and
> from East to West, have behaved always with arrogance, and
> contempt, and barbarity towards others, and have been above
> all guilty of the supreme crime of stupidity – and must now
> accept the burden of culpability, as murderers, thieves and
> destroyers, for the dreadful situation we now all find ourselves
> in. (*Shikasta*: 315)

In the trial Lessing is indicting the white races in a court largely
composed of representatives from ex-colonies. Yet the trial simultaneously occurs in a higher court since a Canopean, Johor, is
involved and all the material is kept in Canopean archives to
be read by Canopean students. Europeans are overwhelmingly
condemned not only for being inhumane to fellow humans but
also for neglecting the 'true way'. Their real crime is, after all,
'stupidity'. Lessing's own sense of anxiety, perhaps of complicity,
is indicated in the disproportionate amount of space given to the
past and present history of Rhodesia in a trial concerned with
worldwide exploitation. Racism is demonstrated theatrically and
formally but the speeches are almost a litany, the rhetoric is used
as an absolution, perhaps for the writer and the reader. Within
the novel's action the trial prevents widespread genocide of the
white.

Lessing decentres *Shikasta* by constructing it as a series of documents, allegedly a textbook for Canopean students studying the history of their own empire. It is intentionally fragmentary, apparently allowing for a number of viewpoints, though the authorial empathy for the victims of oppression is abundantly clear as is the desire to catalogue acts of violence. It is also, like the Old Testament, a book implying redemption. Shikasta is redeemed by the intervention of Canopean officials, often on an individualised basis, causing people to meet, be married or regenerated in their next time round. Earth seems to be a place of Purgatory where people have to live out their sins until they expiate them through a series of lives. As George Sherban, Canopean made flesh, says to his human sister: 'if you can't face all this, then you'll have to come back and do it all over again'.

This imperial intervention, helping here and there on a piecemeal process which is nevertheless systematic (Johor, like all other Canopean officials, receives orders) is apparently the form of imperial rule approved by Lessing. In *The Sirian Experiments*, the third novel in the *Canopus in Argos* series, the book is narrated through one voice. Ambien II is rewriting the official text of Sirian history and indicates her growing awareness (it takes millennia) of Canopean methods and finally not only agrees with them but works alongside Canopean officials. Much of the book is given over to the Sirian experiments in colonisation, and their attempts to breed races particularly suited to specific environments. The Sirians keep both 'natives' and imported extra-terrestrial animals in controlled areas and look after them in much the way we might look after baboons which we were going to use in our experiments with car crashes. Ambien II comes to see that the subsequent brutal behaviour of certain Shikastan inhabitants is often a development or distorted version of Sirian conduct. The 'wisdom' of the author encouraging a protagonist in an acceptable direction has been replaced by a lengthy discussion of the process of moving in an acceptable direction. And instead of one protagonist gaining knowledge, Ambien II is part of a group, and what we are shown is the gradual change of her mind set and the probable chain reaction she will begin among other members of that group. Individual knowledge is of no particular benefit.

Lessing explores the relationship of oppressor to oppressed. Miscegenation, the fate of all colonised peoples, occurs,

sometimes as a result of lust (oxygen appears to act as an aphro-
disiac), sometimes to add a few high-quality genes to the general
population, sometimes for breeding purposes only. Even our genetic history has been tampered with. Ambien II's account also
deals with the gratuitous violence which appears part of colonial
rule. Her bureaucratic experiments are linked with subsequent
brutalities encouraged by aliens from Shammat. As colonisers
Sirians have at hand a fund of 'inferiors' upon whom they can
experiment or inflict pain without fear of reprisal. Yet their experiments always fail, their natives degenerate and revert back to pre-
human intelligence. Ambien II learns from Canopus that the only
good form of colonial rule is nudging things along in the right
direction. If a tribe of Indians appears to be doing well, support
it. If a race is definitely on the way out, help it expire with dignity.
Lessing presents this kind of imperial rule as the most efficacious.
It is of course secret and unknown to those who are colonised.

In conclusion, the realist form Lessing began with proved too
insecure for her extraordinary cognitive scope. She chose to move
away from presenting women's marginality in the world of
power and politics, from images of enclosure and a concentration
on domesticity and sexual relationships. SF offered a viable way
of dealing with wide-ranging issues such as violence, group minds
and mass communication not possible in her previous approach
and allowed her the perspective of people moving across time.
She presents an alternative view (perhaps a woman's view?) of
violence to that gratuitously shown in daily newsreels, TV drama
and cartoons. It is no accident that the Shammat warlord, Tafta,
is revealed as an expert in communications.

It is now commonplace for Lessing to be described as a pro-
phet[24] and her works as prophetic. I expect she has as much (or
as little) likelihood of being prophetic as intelligent SF writers of
the 1930s, 1940s, 1950s. In many ways her SF writing seems like
expiation[25] rather than an expression of 'other people' or proph-
ecy. She states that the exploited peoples of Shikasta were always
closer than the white races to the Canopean way of life yet she
details their oppression rather than valorises their lifestyle. Her
readers are the exploiters, the 'North West Fringers' whose inhumane behaviour is indicted. It is almost as if the writing and
reading of the text might expiate a sense of guilt, of inadvertent
collusion in colonial violence and the rape of the resources of the
planet.

NOTES

1 Julia Kristeva, 'L'ethique de la linguistique', *Critique* 30 (March 1974), 322. 'La question ne manque pas de se poser: où est-on, si l'on n'est pas du côté de ceux que la société gaspille pour se reproduire?'
2 Doris Lessing, *Shikasta*, London, Cape, 1979; *The Sirian Experiments*, London, Cape, 1981, *passim*.
3 Possibly a more precise term would be ontogenetic but that seems unnecessarily pedantic.
4 Interview in Heide Ziegler and Christopher Bigsby (eds), *The Radical Imagination and the Liberal Tradition*, London, Junction Books, 1982, 198.
5 *Shikasta, passim*.
6 Scott Fitzgerald, *The Great Gatsby*, New York, Scribner, 1953 edn, 182.
7 Doris Lessing, *Briefing for a Descent into Hell*, London, Cape, 1971.
8 Doris Lessing, 'A very practical sort of mystic', *Guardian*, 15 May 1981, 11.
9 These discrepancies are commented on more fully by Nicole Jouve, 'Of mud and other matter', in Jenny Taylor (ed.), *Notebooks, Memoirs, Archives*, London, Routledge, 1982, 75–134; and Lorna Sage, 'The available space', *Women's Writing: A Challenge to Theory*, ed. M. Monteith, Brighton, Harvester, 1986, 24–32.
10 Jouve, op. cit., 110.
11 Patricia Stubbs fits Lessing (and others) in at the end of her admirable account, *Women and Fiction 1880–1920*, London, Methuen, 1979, 233. Lessing's early writing does concern itself with women's internal experience and domestic life. Presumably she found herself as confined as a novelist writing about the actual experience as she had been as a human being. She then began to deal with planetary concerns and altered the form of her novels to do so, simultaneously changing the generic expectations of her readers. So although Stubbs is right to include the early work here, the later novels are a different matter altogether.
12 Judith Arcana, *Our Mothers' Daughters*, London, Women's Press, 1981, 163.
13 Marga Kreckel, *Communicative Acts and Shared Knowledge in Natural Discourse*, London, Academic, 1981, 38–9.
14 It is interesting to note that this 'interruption' occurred at the age of crisis for many creative artists, late 30s–early 40s. See Gail Sheehy, *Passages*, New York, Bantam, 1977, 365–74.
15 Anne Cluysenaar uses this analogy when discussing poetry, in *Introduction to Literary Stylistics*, London, Batsford, 1976, 17–18.
16 Jean McCrindle, 'Reading *The Golden Notebook* in 1962', in Taylor, op. cit., 48.
17 Ziegler and Bigsby, op. cit., 199.
18 Sage, op. cit., 24.
19 Ursula Le Guin, *The Word for World is Forest*, London, Gollancz, 1977, 7.

20 Doris Lessing, 'These shores of sweet unreason', *Guardian*, 25 September 1982, 11.
21 Sylvia Plath, 'Daddy', *Ariel*, London, Faber, 1965, 54.
22 Buchi Emecheta, *Destination Biafra*, London, Fontana, 1983.
23 See Darko Suvin's comments on myth, *Metamorphoses of Science Fiction*, New Haven, Yale University Press, 1979, 16–27.
24 For example, Jouve, op. cit., 123, and Ziegler and Bigsby, op. cit., 190.
25 Ziegler and Bigsby, op. cit., 204. It is interesting to note here that *The Marriages of Zones Three, Four and Five* began with a therapeutic exercise.

Part II

Aliens and Others:
A Contemporary
Perspective

Chapter 5

Mary and the monster:
Mary Shelley's *Frankenstein* and
Maureeen Duffy's *Gor Saga*

Jenny Newman

During the wet summer of 1816 the talk between the men at the Villa Diodati often turned to science. Byron, Percy Bysshe Shelley and Polidori (possibly the most knowledgeable) were discussing the latest experiments enthusiastically, including Galvani's development of electricity by chemical action, and Erasmus Darwin's observation of the activity of bacteria in dead organic matter.

According to the 1817 preface to *Frankenstein*,[1] Mary Shelley almost always confined herself to the role of passive listener. But when Byron suggested that each of the four summer visitors to Switzerland write a ghost story, it soon became obvious that it was in her that the new scientific inquiry had taken deepest root. *Frankenstein*, completed in England the following May, was her own troubled response to the masculine spirit of competition promoted by Byron. The composition of this 'scientific romance'[2] was to span some of the most disturbing events of her young life, out of which she created the first work of science fiction, one of the most powerful myths of Romanticism, and a text which embodies a profound division in her own experience. I am not claiming that this particular 'disentangling' of the text is more valid than any other. With every page of *Frankenstein* reminding us that reading is an act of interpretation, the narrative structure does everything to discourage monolithic theories.

Shelley continued to work on *Frankenstein* back in England. By December 1816 she had reached the crucial chapter 4 (5 in the 1831 edition), which begins with the words she cited later, in her 1831 introduction to the novel, as the very first words she wrote. The pressures to write a masculine epic must have been strong. Her husband-to-be was reading her *Paradise Lost* out loud. 'He was forever inciting me to obtain literary reputation' she wrote in that same Introduction. Her stepsister, Claire Clairmont, gave the same impression of the Shelley family, later and less reverentially: 'In our family, if you cannot write an epic poem or novel that by its originality knocks all other novels on the head, you are a despicable creature, not worth acknowledging.'[3]

Critics and biographers have often dwelt on the difficulties of Shelley's life during the composition of *Frankenstein* – poverty, and separation from Percy Bysshe Shelley when he was either hiding from creditors or else away from their lodgings trying to raise money. She had been ostracised by her father, William Godwin, and many former friends after her elopement, and betrayed by her own biology into a disastrous series of pregnancies and miscarriages. Understandably, perhaps, her biographers dwell less on the fate of Percy Bysshe Shelley's wife. But contemporary society was well aware of the scandal. For the first time the world was seeing Mary very differently from the way she saw herself. *Frankenstein*, like 'The Rime of the Ancient Mariner,' which the girl Mary Godwin heard read aloud by the poet, deals with an inescapable guilt too deep for orthodox shriving. Its exploration of a fanatical spirit of inquiry leading both to irresponsibility and an inalienable sense of connection between two people who loathe each other, turns Percy Bysshe Shelley's Promethean optimism upside down.

Contemporary Marxist and feminist critics have given Mary Shelley a hard time. Franco Moretti, for instance, claims that the monster represents a newly emergent proletariat, with his desire to breed a pointer to the feared proliferation of the working class; and then accuses the author of being reactionary for having Victor Frankenstein refer to the monster's desired progeny as a 'race of devils'.[4] The feminist interpretation in Sandra M. Gilbert and Susan Gubar's *The Madwoman in the Attic* is more sympathetic, but rather matronising. Here Shelley, a 'puzzled but studious Miltonist', produces a Gothic psychodrama which is also 'a version of the misogynistic story implicit in *Paradise Lost*'.[5]

It seems likely that the character of Victor Frankenstein was based on Percy Bysshe Shelley, as many critics assert.[6] Victor was the pen name he often used in his juvenilia; and the notion of victory recurs frequently throughout his poetry, usually as a point of aspiration. The word itself recurs frequently, too, and is the final one in *Prometheus Unbound*. Victor Frankenstein, the idealistic young seeker after truth with a burning desire to 'penetrate the secrets of nature', resembles a nightmare version of the boy Shelley growing old enough to do damage.

So if Frankenstein in this particular configuration resembles Percy, who is Frankenstein's monster? Again, interpretations vary – the monster as proletariat,[7] as the unacceptable side of the hero,[8] as Mary Shelley's 'overstrained, intellectual conscience',[9] as reason in isolation,[10] as the embodiment of Frankenstein's ambition,[11] and as the author's first, nameless baby who died shortly after birth,[12] to name only a few, and without wishing to dispute these readings.

In my suggested interpretation, as in Gilbert and Gubar's, the monster's unique experience of knowing what it is to be born free of history, his social illegitimacy, his namelessness, 'nameless as a woman in a patriarchal society'[13] make him figuratively feminine. Mary Shelley had long been familiar with the idea of women as monsters, having read the reviews of her dead mother's works, where men like William Duff, writing in the Aristotelian vein where women are 'monsters, not quite human, not quite animal', describes Mary Wollstonecraft, the 'hyena in petticoats', as freakish because she overstepped the 'natural and proper bounds for a woman'.

So what relationship in the novel does Mary's monster bear to Victor, his/her manufacturer? At points s/he appears to be auditioning for the role of wife, hoping to share an identity with Frankenstein's family, struggling to acquire its culture and showing an almost obsessive interest in its domestic minutiae. The yearning to be with his/her master on his wedding night is born out of an understandable desire for revenge after Frankenstein's failure to construct a mate. Weddings in nineteenth-century fiction are notorious for being interrupted. But what distinguishes *Frankenstein* from *The Bride of Lammermoor*, for instance, or *Jane Eyre*, is the monster's desire to interrupt not the wedding ceremony or the wedding breakfast, but the bedroom scene. Suffusing the menace is a sexual overtone which threatens consummation as well as disruption.

The distance from which the monster pursues the maker betokens a respect which intensifies into conjugal concern when the flight is reversed. As the man pursues the monster he acts on his/her sustaining words of advice, such as 'You will find near this place, if you follow not too tardily, a dead hare; eat, and be refreshed',[14] or 'Wrap yourself in furs and provide food'[15]

– examples of their mutual dependence preventing them from killing each other; when the maker dies, the monster can only disappear from view to commit suttee on the polar snows.

Many men besides William Duff have described the second sex as monsters, including Percy Bysshe Shelley himself, who in a letter referred to his union with one he knew well as 'a dead & living body . . . linked together in loathsome & horrible communion'.[16] His is the living body in the metaphor. The dead one belongs to his wife – not Mary but Harriet Shelley, a woman three years his junior whom he had recently abandoned to live with Mary. At the time he wrote these words she was pregnant by him, and still very much alive.

Harriet too had once, as Lorna Sage puts it, been galvanised 'into a dazzle with idealist electricity'.[17] Presumably the young Mary Godwin believed that the marriage had fizzled out by the time she eloped with Percy Bysshe, and that Mrs Shelley was reconciled to her husband's departure. Having scrutinised all the evidence about the life of her dead mother, Mary Wollstonecraft, Mary Godwin must have known how serious the results of behaviour like hers might be. Wollstonecraft, on returning from Scandinavia to find out that Gilbert Imlay had left her yet again, soaked her clothes to make sure she would sink, and tried to drown herself in the Thames. By living with the husband of another young woman just as much a mother as she, and with – legally at any rate – a greater claim on her husband, Mary Godwin, daughter of a feminist mother and a father who advocated free love, placed herself at a painful point of intersection between these two idealisms.

Mary's journal entry for 6 December 1814 shows that the birth of Harriet's child became a source of resentment:

> a letter from Hookham to say that Harriet has been brought to bed of a son and heir – S. writes a number of circular letters on this event which ought to be ushered in with ringing of bells &c. for it is the son of his *wife*. . . . a letter from Harriet confirming the news, in a letter from a *deserted wife*, telling us that he has been born a week.[18]

This is not an attack on Harriet herself, but on her husband's behaviour, and on the irrefutable link forged anew between the married couple by the arrival of a 'son and heir'. It makes the birth of Mary's own illegitimate baby a few weeks later look particularly poignant. She was two months premature, and died before she could be given a name. (The son and heir did not himself live long enough to inherit the Shelley estate.)

Mary usually worked on her novel when Percy Bysshe was away from home. Early in December 1816 she wrote to him saying she had just completed chapter 4. A few days later she received the news that Harriet Shelley had drowned herself in the Serpentine – a tragic action replay of Wollstonecraft's attempted suicide, but this time successful. Harriet, like Mary herself, was pregnant again, but probably not by Percy Bysshe Shelley. Claire Clairmont, who was living with Percy and Mary at the time, described the event in a letter to E. J. Trelawney in 1878:

> One morning Miss W— — visited H— — and the latter was very low at receiving no letters from her lover – and expressed a fear that he did not really love her and meant to abandon her – for she remarked I don't think I am made to inspire love, and you know my husband abandoned me – the Eg [*sic*] of that day, a dark November Eg – with rain – at eight o'clock she went into the park and threw herself into the Serpentine.[19]

Mary Shelley's diaries, impersonal to the point of being little more than reading lists, contain only passing references to her writing – she keeps her 'workshop of filthy creation' as private as Frankenstein does.[20] But the parallel is clear between the 'dreary night of November' which sees the birth of the monster in the crucial chapter 5, and the one described to Trelawney. Mary cites that famous opening sentence of chapter 5 as the first fruits of her imagination all those years later, and Claire Clairmont, so close to her at the time of Harriet's suicide, echoes them, unconsciously perhaps, in her letter to Trelawney.

The dreadful *dénouement* of Harriet's life intensified Mary's own anxieties about the fate of her hideous progeny. And the first Mrs Shelley's death highlighted the callousness of her husband's behaviour. His subsequent escape in the preface to *Prometheus Unbound* to what he calls 'beautiful idealisms of moral excellence' looks evasive by comparison with Mary Shelley's engagement with the notions of moral responsibility he seemed reluctant to contemplate.

Soon after Harriet's suicide Mary become Mrs Shelley II, marrying, like her mother before her, without any great belief in the institution. Her express purpose was to help her husband gain custody of his two children by his first wife. The episode concluded with his new wife's induction into the Fall – not the Biblical or Miltonic version but a feminist kind, where free love and a consideration for other women become incompatible. Here possession of a kindred spirit – masculine – means expulsion of another woman from the Garden. Mary Shelley becomes a latter-day Eve, who in an apocryphal version of the Bible dispossesses Adam's first wife, Lilith – ironical in view of Gilbert and Gubar's argument that Mary Shelley reworked *Paradise Lost* all too dutifully.

The mortuary monster coming to life may be not so much to do with Shelley's own experiences as a mother, as critics have often suggested, as with a distaste for this mess of Victor's own making. By killing herself, Harriet Shelley ensured that her dead body remained linked with her husband's in a 'loathsome & horrible communion' that even he could not have anticipated when he wrote those words. In the second wife's account of the making of a monster its manufacturer denies all responsibility for it – as does the second scientific inquirer, Captain Walton. Their two epics frame the monster's own account of its doings. The author's official sympathies are with Frankenstein. But the monster's predicament remains the most moving part of the book – even though Shelley has locked it inside the innermost Chinese box of the narrative, and filtered it through not one male consciousness but two.

Second wives were commonplace in the nineteenth century, largely because so many first wives died in childbirth. Shelley was unusual in having to cope with an earlier incumbent who was, for a short time, still alive. In the Victorian age Jane Eyre nearly becomes a fictional counterpart. In Charlotte Brontë's novel the figure of the first wife, completely cut off from authorial sympathy before her rescue by Jean Rhys in *Wide Sargasso Sea*, and furnished, like Shelley's monster, with shaggy locks and a bestial mien, forces us to notice her unusual plight even if we are not officially asked to sympathise with this later version of a woman seeing her rival as a Gothic monster.

In the 1980s, with one couple in three divorcing, living first wives are no longer so rare. But the topic still provokes feminist writers – witness the recent spate of novels like Carol Clewlow's *A Woman's Guide to Adultery*. The blurb for the paperback edition of Fay Weldon's *Remember Me*, where a dead first wife comes back to haunt the second, might have appealed to Harriet Shelley herself: 'Second wives beware. First wives take heart. Your power is more than you know.'

That single laboratory experiment in *Frankenstein*, born out of the new science, brought forth a novel set of dilemmas which women writers are still exploring today. 'The Modern Prometheus', as Mary Shelley subtitled her novel, remains more modern than its author could have guessed. Fay Weldon's latest novel, *The Cloning of Joanna May* (1989), is the most recent book to reinforce the link between the modern variant of Frankenstein's experiments – genetic engineering – and a masculine inability to feel. But Maureeen Duffy's *Gor Saga* (1981) is more original, because for the first time the problems of *Frankenstein* are resolved in a collective rather than an individual fashion.

Like *Frankenstein*, *Gor Saga* is written under the influence of a Darwin; but this time it is Charles, not Erasmus, and what Milton called original sin is suggested here by our proximity to the apes. The fascist state in this futuristic world attempts to establish middle-class supremacy by reinforcing a rigid division between it and the working class, which is held by the bourgeoisie to resemble anthropoids.

In Duffy's novel we watch an attempt to forge the missing link in an artificial insemination scene which reads like a parody of *The Origin of Species*. This time the scientist, Forester, attempts to create new life by impregnating a gorilla, significantly called Mary. Although he uses a syringe, the sperm is his own. His act of making fits comfortably – or uncomfortably – into a tradition of Gothic eroticism. Like the shuddering of Frankenstein's monster at the moment of making, or Lucy's blood transfusion in *Dracula*, Forester's tremor of excitement while pressing the plunger between Mary's bright pink buttocks is a possible representation of a man-made orgasm.[21]

Clearly Forester is a latter-day Frankenstein, with his dactyllic surname beginning with 'F', and his mental lust to beget life with power rather than tenderness as he 'apes' female creativity. Eventually a baby is born, half man, half gorilla, after a hard and bloody birth while Mary screams with pain and rage.

The name chosen by Forester for this new species is hominid, and the young specimen is fostered among the working class or 'nons', in the belief that it will pass more easily as human. Forester's sympathetic, middle-class wife, Ann, refuses to use this derogatory term, preferring 'ordinary people' instead. But 'non' is more precise, suggesting as it does not proximity to the apes, but a class impoverished not only financially but culturally, easily manipulated by advertisements into buying surplus products. One such is the unnutritious breakfast cereal advertised during one long, hot summer in the over-populated city. The reward for buying far more than needed is a free disc of the pop song, 'Girl in a Red Car.' With its tale of the working-class boy longing for the uptown girl it becomes a class-based parallel to the exploitative miscegenation which produced the little hominid.

Maureen Duffy, like Mary Shelley, wrote a late preface to a first novel. Duffy's first novel is the autobiographical *That's How it Was* (1962), which describes going to grammar school from a working-class point of view. In her 1982 preface, Duffy explains how she came to write the science fiction *Gor Saga* nearly twenty years after the more directly autobiographical work, using what she calls 'species-ism' as a metaphor for the way she'd felt divided by the experience.

Although the hominid has a first name – Gor, short for Gordon, but also suggesting gorilla – he has no family name, and no rightful place in society. Like Shelley's monster, he is denied knowledge of his origins, which Forester hides in his laboratory for fear of rivals imitating his experiments. He too can be said to occupy a feminine position in society, close to nature, alien to culture, with a particularly painful point of entry into the symbolic order. Shelley's monster had found, among other books, a copy of *Paradise Lost* 'lying' on the ground – what Lorna Sage calls a promiscuous text,[22] ready to be possessed by anybody – although its authority is clearly enough inscribed on the cover in the name of John Milton. In Gor's world books are not so freely available. Ann Forester hoards what battered old copies she can find to distribute among the nons, while her brother-in-law continues to develop the microfiches which have almost totally replaced them. But if the written word is obsolescent, science has advanced, and Gor has an operation on his vocal cords which enables him to speak. Afterwards he is fostered in Forester's own family, and comes to identify himself as middle-class.

As in *Frankenstein*, it is the monster's nascent sexuality that provokes the major crisis. In the earlier novel, the monster wants a mate, and rebels when Victor fails to equip him with one. In *Gor Saga*, Ann Forester gives a party for her teenage daughter, and someone spikes the punch. Adolescent passions run high, and, in complete ignorance of any kinship, Gor kisses his half-sister. When Forester finds out, he banishes Gor, and it is now that the hominid's lack of social identity counts against him. As Forester never registered his birth, he is ineligible for any human right – food, work or shelter.

Which century makes life easier for a monster on the run, the early nineteenth, or an apocalyptic version of the late twentieth? Switzerland may once have been associated with the Reformation and Republican enlightenment, but by the eighteenth century it had become a closed society, with the government in the hands of an oligarchy.[23] The English Walton forms a contrast to the Swiss Victor in his egalitarian approach to discovery, turning back from the ice floes in response to his crew's terror – but even in the floating democracy of his ship there is no place for the monster.

Maureen Duffy depicts a world where, as Marx had predicted, an economic crisis has deepened the fissure between the classes. The landscape of Shelley's England was beginning to be changed by the rise of industrialism. Duffy's descriptions chart a post-capitalist decay. Gor manages to establish squatter's rights for himself in a derelict house – but soon desperate loneliness drives him out again into a world of inner-city riots, gangs of homeless youths, a metered water supply and privatised bus companies that looks disconcertingly more like ours than when the book was written. Yet the rigid division between nons and the middle class engenders a society more susceptible than Frankenstein's to social change, and accessible to outsiders like Gor. At his wits' end, he stumbles on the urban guerrillas (a pun here?), who make him a member of their socialist collective. If it wasn't beleaguered by the state it would be utopian, with its presiding matriarch in the shape of Mrs Bardfield, who had been a much-loved 'non' foster-mother of the infant Gor.

From here Gor sets out under cover of darkness to decode the mystery of his origins, raiding Forester's laboratory on the downs above Salisbury. In the Preface cited before, Maureen Duffy says that the relationship between the mother and child is the basis of all her fiction, and that every nativity is *the* Nativity. In this case, Gor's unravelling of his own genesis – the account begins with a series of notes in diary form, a typically feminine form of creativity – looks like a particularly cruel travesty of the maternal instinct. It was a Nativity all right, complete with Mary in the shape of an ape mother, dangling her babe by the ankle, its head only an inch away from the cage floor, while Jo-Jo, the gorilla mate she had rejected, stands by disregarded, a St Joseph figure to one side of the manger.

In a scene reminiscent of *Oedipus Rex*, that tale of a classical seeker of his own origins, Gor seizes a poker from the long-dead fire of an old rectory, and goes to confront his maker – the only one he'll ever know, given that the priest in the rectory had told him that as far as hominids are concerned God does not exist. Only the arrival of Ann Forester and William Bardfield, the matriarch's son, prevents Gor from striking his 'father' dead, so the castration rests at a symbolic level. But it is further than Frankenstein ever got, and it is enough to liberate Ann, who finds the courage to leave her sexually unresponsive husband. Gor's ambiguous sexual identity – feminine in relation to society, yet unable to engender children of his own – plays its part in this feminist version of Sophocles' story. We see the mother, unlike Jocasta, surviving guilt to assume a fuller sexual identity as she falls in love with William. Together they will live – with Gor and anyone else who wants to – in the urban guerrilla camp where William is already a leader. The final scene is one of rejoicing. Although Gor has not found a biological identity, he has acquired the social one denied to him by science (malevolently) and religion (intending to be benevolent), science and religion being presented as unsatisfactory forces here, both in their different ways symptoms of the 'species-ism' that Duffy is castigating.

Mothers are scarce in *Frankenstein*: Victor, Elizabeth, Justine, Safie, Agatha and Felix are all motherless. And the opening sentence of *Gor Saga* reads: 'He never really knew his mother.' At the end of the book Gor finds out from Forester that Mary died miserably – or was terminated – as an expendable part of what Gor himself has already come to see should be an animal commonwealth, not an animal kingdom. But all Gor's other mothers – the human foster mothers – reappear in the urban guerrilla camp, where a collective celebration after a victory over the state soldiery makes Gor's private misery manageable at the end of the book.

Both Frankenstein and Forester 'ape' women's creativity by engendering new life; and their fiercely masculine lust for power results, in these two female texts, in 'feminine' progeny – as though their perverted procreative drive is bound to result in rebellious daughters.

The narrative structure of *Frankenstein* sustains Shelley's ambivalence about her monster, exploring his grief after severance from his maker, but finally abandoning him on the ice with no critique of Frankenstein's behaviour anywhere in the narrative. Maureen Duffy, writing after Marx and the upsurge of the women's movement, reworks Shelleyan ambiguities by placing Gor firmly at the centre of his own saga, and excluding Forester from the scene of rejoicing at the end. It is a futuristic vision in a genre still considered marginal – but both the future and marginalia have, in their different ways, always been important places for women writers to work out alternative theories of human relations, and their implication for the present. 'The Crowning of Gor', as the last section is called, challenges the notion of the individualistic epic hero by praising the collective rather than the individual victory, reminding us 200 years after the French Revolution which inspired the writers of the Romantic movement that liberation is best achieved communally.

NOTES

1 Shelley wrote in her introduction to the 1831 edition of *Frankestein*: 'I certainly did not owe the suggestion of one incident, nor scarcely one train of feeling, to my husband, and yet but for his incitement, it would never have taken the form in which it was presented to the world. From this declaration I except the preface. As far as I can recollect, it was written by him.'

2 Patrick Parrinder, *Science Fiction: Its Criticism and Teaching*, London, Methuen, 1980, 8.

3 Mrs Julian Marshall (ed.), *The Life and Letters of Mary Wollstonecraft Shelley*, 2 vols, London, Richard Bentley, 1889, 2, 248.

4 Franco Moretti, *Signs Taken for Wonders*, London, Verso and New Left Books, 1983, 86.

5 Sandra M. Gilbert and Susan Gubar, *The Madwoman in the Attic*, New Haven, Yale University Press, 1979, 224–5.

6 E.g., Rosie Jackson, '*Frankenstein*: a myth for women', *Women's Review* 12 (October 1986), 16; Christopher Small, *Ariel Like a Harpy: Shelley, Mary and Frankenstein*, London, Gollancz, 1972, 101, and Mary K. Patterson Thornburg, *The Monster in the Mirror: Gender and the Sentimental/Gothic Myth in Frankenstein*, Ann Arbor, UMI, 1987, 8.

7 Moretti, op. cit., 86.

8 Thornburg, op. cit., 79.
9 This is Richard Church's view, cited in Muriel Spark, *Child of Light: A Reassessment of Mary Wollstonecraft Shelley*, London, Tower Bridge Publications, 1951, 137.
10 Spark, op. cit., 137.
11 William A. Walling, *Mary Shelley*, Boston, Twayne, 1972, 38.
12 Ellen Moers, *Literary Women*, London, Women's Press, 1978, 96.
13 Gilbert and Gubar, op. cit., 241.
14 M. K. Joseph (ed.), *Mary Shelley: Frankenstein*, Oxford, Oxford University Press, 1980, 204–5.
15 ibid., 205.
16 Frederick L. Jones (ed.), *The Letters of Percy Bysshe Shelley*, Oxford, Oxford University Press, 1963, I, 402.
17 'The available space', in Moira Monteith (ed.), *Women's Writing: A Challenge to Theory*, Brighton, Harvester, 1986, 21.
18 Paula R. Feldman and Diana Scott-Kilvert (eds), *The Journals of Mary Shelley 1814–1844*, 2 vols, Oxford, Clarendon, 1987, II, 50.
19 Quoted ibid., 151.
20 *Frankenstein*, 55.
21 Maureen Duffy, *Gor Saga*, London, Methuen, 1981, 1983 edn, 10.
22 Monteith, op. cit., 16.
23 Thornburg, op. cit., 72.

Chapter 6

Pets and monsters: metamorphoses in recent science fiction

Lisa Tuttle

What does it mean for a woman to turn into an animal? What does it mean for a woman to dream, to fantasise, to write about women turning into animals? It can represent escape into wildness and the delights of strength and sensuality, or it can express the limitations of a purely physical existence, the frustrations of being denied a share in human culture.

In folktales, not only do animals talk, but there is often no perceptible difference between them and humans. Indeed, a reading of Claude Lévi-Strauss implies that, in symbolic terms, the difference between men and women is far more profound than that between men and animals.[1]

Today, in urban western society, wild animals have largely vanished, those which once worked for and with humankind have been reduced still further to the status of raw material to satisfy our needs, and the only direct relationship most of us have with animals is with pets: animals made over in our own image. Yet still the memory of animals haunts us, symbols of another kind of life, of other ways of being.

The connection between Man's use, abuse and objectification of animals with men's treatment of women has been made before. Elizabeth Fisher[2] suggests that it was the domestication of animals which provided the model for human slavery and led to male control of female reproductive capacity, while Susan Griffin[3] explores in depth the patriarchal concept which identifies women with nature as matter to be shaped by the needs of men. Men have so often identified Woman as Other, out there, the opposite of cool male intellect and civilisation, a part of the warm, squishy, undifferentiated natural world from which men are born but quickly escape, that it is not surprising if women sometimes choose to speak from that position, to look back at Man, who is the self-proclaimed outsider, and give the animal inside a voice.

I don't think any useful or interesting generalisations can be made about the state of SF in the 1980s without examining far more books, and at greater length, than is feasible in this one, brief chapter. But certain themes and issues do become popular at different times, reflecting shared preoccupations, contemporary problems, and the spirit of the age. What looks like great diversity from the middle (where I am) will look a lot more homogenous in ten or twenty years' time, when 'Eighties SF' will have as specific a meaning as to subject and style as 'Fifties SF' does now. I don't know what that will be and I am not trying to provide any sort of definition of modern feminist SF here. Instead, I offer a personal response to one particular, repeated theme.

It struck me in 1988 that, in my random reading over the course of a few months, I had come across the same idea in the works of several different, personally admired, women writers: the idea of women who were transformed into animals, or animals who changed into women. Carol Emshwiller's first novel, *Carmen Dog*[4] which begins '"The beast changes to a woman or the woman changes to a beast," the doctor said' (p.1) was only the most obvious example. There was also *The Book of the Night* by Rhoda Lerman,[5] in which the heroine spends her earliest years disguised as a boy and later turns into a cow, and *The Daughter of the Bear King* by Eleanor Arnason[6] about the adventures of a Minneapolis housewife who discovers she can turn into a bear, and travel to another world, not always at her own will.

At this same time Ursula Le Guin's stories and poems about animals were collected and published together as *Buffalo Gals and Other Animal Presences* and also in shorter fiction, Pat Murphy, Sara Maitland, Tanith Lee, Suzy McKee Charnas and others were writing about metamorphoses from human to animal.[7] I don't know how, or if, this is significant, but I do know that the subject appeals to me both intellectually and emotionally, both as a reader and as a writer (my own foray into this territory, 'A Mother's Heart: A True Bear Story' was written in 1973, published in 1978)[8] so I thought I would take this opportunity to ask myself why, and what it might mean.

In the *Metamorphoses* of Ovid,[9] when the gods turned individuals into animals it was usually as punishment, such transformations being considered intermediate between the usual sentences of either exile or death, although occasionally it might be a (rather drastic!) form of rescue from the old 'fate worse than death', as when Daphne preferred to become a tree rather than lose her maidenhood to Phoebus.

For Ovid, the transformations had a reason and tended to be the conclusion of the story he had to tell. By contrast, the metamorphoses depicted in recent fantasy and science fiction by women are the beginning rather than the end; the reason for their happening of far less importance than how the metamorphosed women respond to their changed circumstances.

'Rachel in Love' by Pat Murphy must be one of the most popular works of science fiction published in the late 1980s. It first appeared in the pages of *Isaac Asimov's Science Fiction Magazine* (April 1987), where it subsequently came top in that year's readers' poll, went on to win the Nebula Award for short fiction, and was reprinted in several 'best of the year' anthologies.[10]

Rachel is a chimpanzee; she is also a teenage American girl whose electrical brain patterns – equated in the story with the personality – had been recorded by her father, a maverick scientist. When the girl died tragically young, her father imposed her 'electric mind' upon the brain of a young chimp, 'saving his daughter in his own way' (p. 161). The story opens with the father dead, Rachel suddenly alone in a potentially hostile world. She has been treated as a beloved daughter; now she is locked in a cage at the nearby Primate Research Center, treated with benign neglect by researchers who see her as 'good breeding stock'. She makes friends with the janitor, a middle-aged, rather slow-witted deaf man named Jake, with whom she can communicate in American Sign Language (ASL). She begs him to let her out, promising to help him do the cleaning, and when the cleaning is done they share Jake's dinner and whisky, then, as he settles back with a pornographic magazine, Rachel reads a *Modern Romance* she has found in the trash. As the nights pass, and under the influence of these magazines, Rachel comes to believe that she is in love with Jake. But although he is fond of her, he cannot respond to her sexually, and will not help her escape. To him, she is only 'a very strange monkey'. In frustration (and in heat) she approaches a male chimp called Johnson and, after mating with him, makes her escape, taking him with her. Hiding out in the desert, Rachel has a dream in which her father tells her it doesn't matter what anyone thinks of her, for she is his daughter.

I want to be a real girl, she signs.

'You *are* real,' her father says. 'And you don't need some two-bit drunken janitor to prove it to you.' (p. 185)

She wakes, feeling happy and knowing her dream is true. She and Johnson set off for the ranch house that was her home, unaware as yet that they have become folk heroes in their absence, and that the house and surrounding land has been left in a will to 'Rachel, the chimp I acknowledge as my daughter' (p. 187).

It's a happy ending worthy of the fairytales Rachel loves, and it is not surprising that 'Rachel in Love' is such a popular story, with men as well as women. It is, like a lot of popular SF, a coming-of-age story. Sexuality, *the* major issue for teenage girls, is foregrounded. Although Rachel's problems appear to be caused by her unusual situation – being a girl trapped inside a chimp, or a chimp with a girl in her brain – that is really circumstantial. What really matters to her, what she worries about, is what all adolescents worry about. Who am I? Will I always feel at odds with myself? Am I attractive? Will I ever meet anyone who will love me? During the course of the story, Rachel comes to terms with her physical self in a most laudable way. She realises she will never look like the pale, hairless sex-objects in Jake's magazines, rejects the conventions of pulp romance as unreal, and finds satisfaction with Johnson. Sex becomes simple, a natural part of life, not the obsession humans have made of it. Neither pornography nor romance apply to chimpanzees. She is fond of Johnson, and feels both protective of and protected by him. He will never be her intellectual equal, but he will learn from her, and she finds his silent presence a comfort. Also during her sojourn in the desert Rachel's human and animal selves accept each other, and she becomes fully integrated. This is expressed through a dream in which the blonde, pale-skinned Rachel, lonely and crying inside the house, looks out into the darkness and sees a face with 'jug-handle ears and shaggy hair. When she sees the face, she cries out in recognition and opens the window to let herself in' (p. 188).

Rachel has come to terms with who she is. She has accepted herself, and she is happy, and due to a series of fortuitous chances the outside world knows she's not 'just' a chimp, so her happiness will be allowed to continue. The implication of the story, that self-acceptance is the most important thing, will not be put to the cruellest test. Whatever happens next, Rachel is not going to be shoved back in a cage and treated as experimental animals generally are. Her physical safety and comfort have been provided for thanks to her father's money, and the curiosity and good-will of the public should secure her a certain amount of freedom. Neither entirely human nor entirely chimpanzee she is a unique individual; a new kind of person. But there are no others like her. She is the exception.

Imagine this story without the science fictional element. Imagine Rachel not a girl in a chimp's body, but a person in a girl's body. She is both person and girl, but in a male-dominated society where 'man' is considered a synonym for 'person' Rachel finds she is forever defined by her blonde hair and pale skin as 'girl'. And 'girl' precludes 'person'. No one will listen to her or take her seriously. If she does manage to make some intellectual or social impact, will that be because she has 'the mind of a man' in the way that Queen Elizabeth I, despite having 'the frail body of a woman' had 'the heart and stomach of a king'? Just how meaningful is Rachel's self-integration if all she can ever be is an honourary man, a token woman; if she is unique, if she is a freak, if only inherited money permits her to remain free, if the rest of an unjust society remains untroubled and unchanged?

It might seem unfair, or eccentric, to demand politically correct feminist insight from what is after all an enjoyable and light-hearted story, but something about its popularity makes me uneasy. Of course it is popular; it tells us, men and women both, what we want to hear, that we don't have to struggle to change the world, it's enough to accept our selves – and our places – in it. This is a dangerously inward-looking view, and reflects one of the ways in which the spirit of the 1980s is in full flight from the political engagement of the 1960s and 1970s. So often these days, as in this story, the personal is not the political – the personal is simply the personal, and matters so intensely that it wipes out the political. But to some readers it might come as a revelation that Rachel is not saved by the love of a good man (or even a good chimp) but by herself, that she can reject the commercialised romance of magazines and makeup without dooming herself to a sexless existence, and that she can value herself for what she is, even when that is judged 'abnormal' by others. At the end of the story, Rachel is what she is, and content with it, and this positive reading cannot be dismissed in a world where romantic fiction of the *Love Confessions* sort that Rachel reads is still too much with us.

Very different from the easily attractive morality of 'Rachel in Love' is Suzy McKee Charnas' 'Boobs', narrated in the authentic voice of the modern American teenager: 'The thing is, it's like your brain wants to go on thinking about the miserable history mid-term you have to take tomorrow, but your body takes over' (p. 18). Yes, it's another coming-of-age story, quite specifically about puberty this time. Kelsey thinks that 'becoming a woman' – her body becoming unreliable, developing breasts and having periods – is simply *gross*. Until one night her body *really* changes, into that of a sleek, powerful, absolutely gorgeous wolf. She's a werewolf, and from now on, once a month, she'll go out at night and prowl, and hunt, and kill – taking a bloody revenge on those who give her girl-self a hard time during the day – starting with the horrible boy who used to grab her breasts and called her 'Boobs'.

When this story was first published in an American science fiction magazine, the (male) editor found the heroine of the story too unsympathetic, and requested a minor change to the ending to make her sound a little less cold-blooded; the original ending was restored for its inclusion in *Skin of the Soul* (1990), the horror anthology I edited for the Women's Press. In an afterword written especially for that anthology, Suzy McKee Charnas commented that although some might find it disturbing, the wolfish violence of the narrator does reflect 'the tendency of the young toward a very very narrow morality ("What hurts me is unforgiveably awful and what I do is okay")' and 'the surprising failures of empathy in children' (p. 38).

Without going so far as to approve Kelsey's behaviour, I think it would be hard for anyone who has suffered through female adolescence not to feel cheered by and get a vicarious thrill from her ability to strike back at those who hurt her. It is pure fantasy, of course, and the pleasure the reader gets comes from that very fact. Kelsey's transformation into an animal is empowering; it's a physical expression of the anger which is allowed no outlet from her human, daytime self. The first time Billy grabs her breasts at school she hits out at him, and he socks her in the face, breaking her nose, teaching her that he is capable not only of humiliating her, but of hurting her badly. Her stepmother tells her: 'If you fight with boys, you're bound to get hurt. You have to find other ways to handle them' (p. 19). And so she does – by becoming a wolf. As a girl, she doesn't stand a chance against the boys, but as a wolf she's stronger and faster and nastier than any of them, and that secret knowledge makes the daytime humiliations bearable.

The Jungian interpretation of identifying oneself with an animal is that it represents integration of the unconscious, and rejuvenation through a return to the source of life.[11] While 'Rachel in Love' is very consciously about the task of integration, in 'Boobs' such a happy outcome is clearly impossible. Although Kelsey's animal and human selves share a common consciousness, girl and wolf lead separate lives; the wolf must be kept secret and only allowed out at night. Society will not tolerate the animal self, which poses a clear threat to it, and in order to survive Kelsey must be careful to cover her tracks and pretend she is nothing more than a normal girl. Normal girls certainly don't kill the boys who harrass them; normal girls aren't even supposed to express their anger.

Both of these short stories concern private, individual experiences, if not exactly outside society, then effectively on its edges. The novels I now consider explore the effects of female transformation on society – even, ultimately, on the whole universe.

In *Carmen Dog*, all of society is breaking down as women start turing into animals and animals into women. No one knows why this is happening, although there are suggestions throughout the book linking women with nature, and female fecundity with a sheer delight in change and growth, implying that this is how things are meant to be and that the apparent fixity of material form until now has been a male invention. The universe is ready for a change, and what could be more natural than for that change to begin with women? The males don't change, and men, as you might expect, attempt to take control by all their usual means.

Within this grand chaos is set the story of Pooch, originally a pedigree setter bitch, who is becoming a young woman even as her mistress is changing into a snapping turtle. This is not exactly a coming-of-age story, but perhaps a coming-of-humanity story as Pooch rescues the baby from the unloving jaws of its mutating mother, flees from police, is captured by a mad (?) scientist, escapes, is seduced by a sybarite, joins a revolutionary feminist movement (the SPCAC: Society for Prevention of Cruelty to All Creatures), finds true love with the gentle Bert, becomes an opera singer, and eventually knows the sweet fulfilment of all her dreams as wife, mother ('a litter of three: setters and all male, so there will be no hope that they might ever become human and artists in their own right'), singer, composer, and fully human being. And as for the universe, the author says on the last page:

> It is, in short, harmonious with itself. (Which is how Pooch is, as well as Bert, and how the baby grows up to be also.) And whatever it may be (which can be argued by the experts for a long time) or may come to be, it is recreating itself every fraction of a second, even as you or I. (p. 148)

Although there is a sense in which *Carmen Dog* can be read as a sort of housewife's liberation story – Pooch escaping the thankless life of doormat and dishwasher and winning self-respect through her adventures in the wider world – the novel has more to do with the importance of change in general (identified with the female principle) than with specific, and merely local, manifestations of sexual politics. Although the novel is much lighter and funnier than Susan Griffin's very serious *Woman and Nature*, the two books are actually concerned with the same subject: the destructive division between man and woman, civilisation and nature, Man and Matter.

There are thematic parallels between *Carmen Dog* and Rhoda Lerman's *The Book of the Night* which also, in the best science fictional tradition, tackles such great questions as the nature of the universe and the meaning of reality.

Near the beginning of *The Book of the Night* the narrator speaks of the brief moment between ending and beginning, 'the moment of chaos, of a higher order, the disorder of the Gods, but order nevertheless' (p. 9) when change is possible. If the change is willed, 'then change becomes not evolution but exaltation' (p. 9). In that moment, without will, she tells us: 'I became, somehow, a cow' (p. 9).

The change to animal, like Kelsey's becoming a wolf, is connected to puberty and sexuality. Celeste – forbidden to tell anyone her name – has been living disguised as a boy with her father on the island of Iona where the monks call her CuRoi. It is when she falls in love with the new Abbot, when he recognises that she is a woman, when she is about to be exiled, that she is transformed (or, more likely, despite her belief that she was without will, transforms herself) into a cow – a particularly beautiful small white cow – and so is allowed to stay, part of the monastery's herd.

It is difficult to do justice to *The Book of the Night* in a brief description. It is set in that moment mentioned above, the moment of change, chaos and the coming of a new order. Iona is somehow, mysteriously, outside of time. Although Celeste and her father appear to have arrived from the twentieth (or at least the nineteenth) century, and her father continues to send and receive mail from the Edinburgh Natural History Society, on the island the monks are caught up in the tenth-century struggle of whether or not to concede to the leadership of the Roman church – not to mention the conflict between the dark god Seth and the Christian God. Everything is breaking down and reforming, including the language in which the story is told. Lerman was inspired in part by the work of Nobel prizewinner Ilya Prigogine, *Order Out of Chaos*, which suggests that self-organisation might be an inherent property of matter, almost as if matter has mind and evolution is willed. Where most feminist science fiction can, almost by definition, be said to question the nature and natural-ness of male-dominated society, *The Book of the Night* goes still further, as Sarah Lefanu has suggested, breaking down not only the female role in society but the very idea of femaleness; interro-gating not only culture, but nature.[12]

Why does Celeste/CuRoi become a cow? It is the most practical choice for satisfying her immediate needs. Her female nature having been discovered, she can no longer stay on the island as one of the monks. But as a cow she can become part of the monastery's herd, much loved and well-treated by the monks. Nor does she give up her newly-discovered sexuality. As a cow she is unquestionably female, and so lovely that the Abbot Thomas – to his dismay and her delight – is consumed with lust for her.

On a deeper level, in world mythology the cow – white, horned, milk-giving – is one of the most common manifestations of the Great Mother and the creator of the world. Before the change Celeste has been told by the monks to surrender herself to God, for 'He is the Creator. You are only the creature' (p. 153). Yet her father, although he appears to accept the rule of the patriarchal church, contradicts what the monks have taught his daughter, and sows a fruitful confusion in her mind by telling her: 'There is no ultimate but yourself. You are your own poem' (p. 153).

The dog is also a traditionally female symbol as an emblem of faithfulness (appearing for this reason on funerary monuments to women in the middle ages) and 'man's best friend'. It is loyalty which leads Pooch to take over more and more of the household tasks, and it is her new role as housekeeper/babysitter, as much as anything, it seems, which causes her to be perceived as a woman instead of a dog.

Neither the wolf nor the chimpanzee is tied symbolically to the female. Much of Kelsey's delight in her wolf form comes from her perception of it as being essentially sexless – like her own slim, sleek self before the changes of puberty – although she *is* a she-wolf, as an inspection of her underparts reveals: instead of 'boobs bouncing and yanking in front' she has 'two rows of neat little bumps down the curve of my belly'. As for Rachel, of the four characters, she is the only one who cannot possibly have chosen her animal self in any sense; the only one who was made an animal by a man, her father.

Just as, presumably, none of us (even if we might, on some kind of Prigoginic interpretation, choose to be born female) would ask to be born into a world where that meant being treated as something less than fully human, Rachel does not ask to be reborn as a chimpanzee. Once she has been, her first difficulty is to accept herself for what she is, both girl and chimpanzee.

Is this, perhaps, what every woman in our sexist society has to confront? The task of integrating the fact of being female with the fact of being human despite the messages all around declaring that the two are not compatable, that the male is the norm and the female something other? Is writing about women who are animals a way of expressing how cut off and alienated women often feel from male-defined, male-dominated, male-*limited* 'human' culture?

That might seem rather obvious. What I find so interesting in the books and the stories I have read is that, even if the origin of this woman-into-animal theme springs from feelings of frustration and alienation, through the act of creation, the writing of fiction, it becomes something positive, rich and joyful. This is particularly noticeable in the two novels I have discussed, for they are, above all, celebrations of diversity, growth and change. Life in them is identified with the female principle, while the male principle – fixed, controlling, terrified of chaos – is obviously doomed.

This may be the beginning of a new kind of celebration of the female: not what men have defined in the past as feminine, but an investigation into what it means to be human, when human is female. The first step towards creating something is to imagine it. In the past, men created Woman; now women are throwing out the old rules and beginning to create themselves. Or, to quote from *The Book of the Night*: 'The creature becomes Creator.'

NOTES

1 'We know what animals do and what beaver and bears and salmon and other creatures need, because once our men were married to them and they acquired this knowledge from their animal wives': Hawaiian Indians quoted by Claude Lévi-Strauss in *The Savage Mind*, as quoted in 'Why look at animals?' in John Berger, *About Looking*, London, Writers and Readers, 1980, 2.

2 Elizabeth Fisher, *Woman's Creation: Sexual Evolution and the Shaping of Society*, New York, McGraw-Hill, 1980.

3 Susan Griffin, *Woman and Nature: The Roaring Inside Her*, New York, Harper & Row, 1978.

4 Carol Emshwiller, *Carmen Dog*, London, Women's Press, 1988.

5 Rhoda Lerman, *The Book of the Night*, London, Women's Press, 1986.

6 Eleanor Arnason, *The Daughter of the Bear King*, London, Headline, 1987.

7 Ursula Le Guin, *Buffalo Gals and Other Animal Presences*, Santa Barbara, Capra, 1987; Pat Murphy, 'Rachel in Love', first published in *Isaac Asimov's Science Fiction Magazine*, April 1987; 'Seal-Self' and 'Lullaby for My Dyke and Her Cat', in *A Book of Spells* by Sarah Maitland, London, Methuen, 1987; 'Sirriamnis' and 'Because Our Skins Are Finer' from *Dreams of Dark and Light* by Tanith Lee, Sauk City, Arkham House, 1986; 'Boobs' by Suzy McKee Charnas from *Skin of the Soul*, edited by Lisa Tuttle, London, Women's Press, 1990.

8 Lisa Tuttle, 'A Mother's Heart: A True Bear Story', *Isaac Asimov's Science Fiction Magazine*, January 1978.

9 *The Metamorphoses of Ovid*, translated by Mary M. Innes, Harmondsworth, Penguin, 1955, 231.

10 Including the only 'Best SF' collection of British origin, *The Orbit Science Fiction Yearbook*, edited by David S. Garnett, London, Futura, 1988; all quotations and page numbers refer to this edition.

11 See J. E. Cirlot, *A Dictionary of Symbols*, London, Routledge & Kegan Paul, 1971, 13.
12 Sarah Lefanu, *In the Chinks of the World Machine: Feminism and Science Fiction*, London, Women's Press, 1988, 99.

Chapter 7

Between the boys and their toys: the science fiction film

Susan Thomas

Fritz Lang's *Metropolis*, premiered in Berlin in 1927, ends with these words: 'There can be no understanding between the hands and the brain unless the heart acts as mediator.'[1] The film was an attempt to examine some of the industrial and scientific themes troubling Europe in the 1920s, and was based on a novel by Thea von Harbou, Lang's wife and close collaborator, in which the central female character, Maria, symbolises the heart as mediator between the labouring classes and the ruling elite.

Deep in the bowels of the ultra-modern city of Metropolis, the workers labour in soulless conditions. Maria counsels them to endure in the knowledge that a saviour and intercessor will deliver them. However the boss, Joh Fredersen, aware that discontent is brewing, commissions an inventor to make a mechanical replica of Maria which is then programmed to incite revolt. This gives Fredersen an excuse both to suppress his workforce violently and to turn the people against 'Maria', because 'her' actions have put the lives of their children in danger. However, Fredersen's son, Freder, has fallen in love with the real Maria and discovers his father's plot. While the workers pursue the robot Maria and try to burn her as a witch – thus discovering her mechanical identity – Freder saves the children and reinstates the real Maria. At the end of the film Freder, his father, and Maria are reconciled, and a symbolic handshake reunites the boss and his workforce.

The whole plot rests on the potentially disruptive presence of Maria. Her good, pure femininity – she is both Virgin and mother – is an essential part of the organicist vision, for it enables her to be the 'heart' of the city. . . . Gender comes to play a complex role in the film. The real business of life, whether it is labour or running Metropolis, is done by men, yet they lack some essential element to make them whole, and it is this ingredient which good femininity can contribute.[2]

Things haven't changed very much. Contemporary society has dealt with or learned to live with some of the socio-economic issues raised by *Metropolis*, but it still retains the concept of the feminine principle as the moral fulcrum of society. This device has been much used in contemporary science fiction films made for children, where the idea of the intelligent machine[3] provides a vehicle through which issues of power and sexuality may be examined and resolved for the young male audience.

This chapter examines some of the ways in which women are shown to intervene between boys and their intelligent machines in children's science fiction films. Techno-fiction films for children seem to be mainly directed at a male audience, with the intelligent machine central to the action providing a safe vehicle through which the young boy can explore his rite of passage into the adult world. Perhaps the major problematical areas for the pubescent boy are his relationships with power and with sexuality – both of which strongly reference his relationships with women and girls. The films under discussion here demonstrate some of the ways in which women are active as the 'heart' at the interface between the boy and his machine.

I have chosen to discuss two films which explore some of the ways in which the young boy perceives and deals with his transition into the adult world. In each of the narratives the point where woman and machine meet provides the catalyst for change, and the woman becomes an icon for emotional and sexual maturity. In *Short Circuit*[4] the outcome of this meeting is the boy's reconciliation and growth, whereas in *Tron*[5] the result is an endorsement of his desire for stasis – to put it simply, it approves the choice 'not to grow up'.

The first thing to be aware of upon encountering a fictional intelligent machine is that it has the property of taking *any* form. It is a constructed imaginary being, and as such may be female, male, animal, bird, fish, alien – benevolent, hostile, stupid . . . there are endless possibilities. Because it has such flexibility, the author's conceptualisation of it is an invaluable marker by which we can decode the narrative. But when the young female filmgoer sets out to find her own alter ego amongst these fictional machines she is likely to be disappointed. Why? Because most science fiction films are made by men for a largely male audience, and there is no need to construct a synthetic woman deliberately – that is what actresses are used for.[6] The function of the androids, robots and computers is to act as a channel, or alter ego, through which the (male) audience can solve its emotional dilemmas.

In such films, the myth of the subversive female character makes her a willing accomplice to a male victim of corporate or technological strength. Operating outside the rules of masculine elitism, she provides the shelter of emotional sustenance. But the price she demands for that support is high. She requires him to confront issues of morality, sex and love – roughly in that order. Sometimes the male character finds that if he succumbs to the feminine principle he is thus empowered to defeat his enemies. On other occasions, as in *Tron*, he is able to take the help offered but to avoid giving the implicit return for it. In essence, control of an intelligent machine can allow its user to bypass his sexuality: if he has the ability to create his own electronic children then he has no need for the biological act of procreation. And however useful a woman may be in helping the male to achieve power for himself, once the balance of power is restored she is rediscovered as a threat. Conversely, the male who has an instinctive disregard for power, or who comes to recognise its fragility, is shown as willing to be taught and rehabilitated by the woman.

In the standard representation of the intelligent machine in children's science fiction films the primary relationship is between a machine and a single male or group of males. Their physical age can be variable, but their emotional age is generally about 13. Sometimes the machine has a childlike nature, taking the place of a real child in the action (*Short Circuit*) and sometimes it simulates an opponent locked in combat with the central character (*Tron*). Whereas in several films this combat is logistical rather than physical, *Tron* contains elements of both.

Character development common to both narratives strongly references Freud's theory of the Oedipal stage between primary narcissism (love for self) and attachment to loved objects (love for another). This becomes the central theme, activated by the presence of a single female character. Jordonova asserts that in *Metropolis* it is 'femininity, triggering sexual attraction, which is the dynamic for introducing change into the system'.[7] In the films under discussion, the central characters are similarly offered an opportunity for change. But they must choose whether or not to accept it.

As the 'heart', the woman is seen in one of two roles. Either she is a touchstone for normality and security, or she acts as interpreter between a man and a machine which has gone out of control. It is important to recall that, unlike *Metropolis*, these films were not made to be watched by politically aware adults, but for a generally male audience aged between about 10 and 15. It is no accident that these films deal covertly with issues of sex, power, and identity, since these are precisely the issues with which their young audience is grappling.

Short Circuit demonstrates some of the ways in which power and sexuality may be perceived by the pubescent male. A malfunctioning weapons robot is nourished into synthetic human intelligence by a woman who also defends it against capitalist aggression and teaches it about sex, love and morality. Since the machine is invariably the child of the man in these films, the robot's designer learns the same lessons and the film ends with the three of them driving off into the sunset to a new life together. The robot is reconciled with its 'father' and becomes both son and lover of its 'mother'. The attitudes of the other male characters in the film reflect simplistic male codes relating to aggression and sexuality.

Here we have an example of an Oedipal structure in which the self undergoing change is split between the robot and its maker. This dualism allows the man to learn by proxy through his robot, who is a mirror into his other self, that it is safe to proceed to the third Freudian stage of development, namely a surrender to the laws of necessity, or reality.

The film opens with a battlefield scene – poppies are mown down by weapons robots as they trundle around a field blowing things up. This is a commercial armaments demonstration. Newton Crosby, the robots' designer (young and handsome but socially inept) privately expresses his reservations about the applications of his research. Meanwhile the visitors are served drinks and canapés by robo-servitors with female voices and little metallic breasts. Just then an electrical storm breaks and Robot No. 5 is hit by lightning, suffering a short circuit. It wanders aimlessly until it finds itself outside the perimeter fence, where it takes delight in the countryside, and trundles around requesting input

– in other words, the short circuit has created within it the capacity to learn. It now has artificial intelligence.

After a series of mishaps Stephanie finds the machine in her mobile snack truck – she is a professional caterer. She also collects animal waifs and strays, and easily appoints herself a surrogate mother to the robot. When she encounters No. 5 she assumes that it is an alien visitor, and she welcomes it into her home with excitement ('I just knew they'd choose me!') She complies with its requests for information by teaching it as much as she can until she goes to bed exhausted, leaving it to draw more input from all-night TV.

In the morning Stephanie is at first enchanted by No. 5's aesthetic appreciation of nature, but soon she discovers that it is in fact no alien, but a robot. She immediately turns against it and phones the company to collect it. She is negative and hostile to both the company director and to No. 5, but while she waits for it to be collected she observes that the machine has developed an understanding of the meaning of mortality. Delighted at copying its jumps, it accidentally steps on a grasshopper and calls to Stephanie to 'reassemble' it. She angrily explains that it cannot be reassembled – it is dead. The robot has behaved in the way she expects from a weapons machine, but she is concerned to find that No. 5 has been emotionally affected by its discovery of organic death. She begins to rethink her attitude towards it, so that when Newton Crosby arrives to take it away, explaining to her that it is a lethal weapon, she passionately defends it: 'But it's not that kind of robot.'

Later that night it returns to find her in the bath; this scene merits some examination because it is here that 'the look' as politicised gesture comes into play. Laura Mulvey has examined the importance of scopophilia in some detail,[8] and I refer the reader to her definitions of the two contradictory aspects of the pleasurable structures of looking in the conventional cinematic situation. They are as follows:

1 The pleasure in using another person as an object of sexual stimulation through sight. This implies a separation of the erotic identity of the subject from the object on the screen (active scopophilia).
2 The pleasure issuing from an identification with the image seen.

This is a function of the ego libido, involving the spectator's fascination with and recognition of his like.

The two aspects described above are both present in the bath scene in *Short Circuit*. First, in the simplest of devices, it allows the young male viewer to gaze at a woman in her bath. Second, it elicits a tension between the sexual inexperience of No. 5 and the spectator's libido. Both the machine and the boy-viewer stand on the threshold of discovery, and Stephanie's response confirms the erotic potential of the meeting.

The scene begins with Stephanie soaping herself in a luxurious bath when she hears noises outside. She becomes afraid. Here, the viewer is the subject, actively looking at the object (Stephanie) with erotic enjoyment heightened by suspense.

Then No. 5 enters the bathroom, and Stephanie expresses delight that it has escaped. No. 5, however, is surprised by the change in her physical appearance – we know that she is naked, although we can only see her head and shoulders above the bubbles.

No. 5: Stephanie! Change colour!
   (Stephanie looks shocked and sinks lower into the bath, grabbing a towel to cover herself with.)
No. 5: Attractive! Nice software! Mmm!
   (Its large mechanical eyes look her up and down.)
Stephanie: (shyly) Boy, you sure don't talk like a machine.

Once No. 5 has entered the room the ego libido of the subject comes into play. The viewer identifies with the erotic pleasure articulated by the machine, and thus in Freudian terms the self is able to direct the libidinal drive towards an object external to it. No. 5 is a surrogate for the viewer's desires, and Stephanie takes this desire seriously, despite the fact that it comes from a machine (or, in the viewer's terms, despite the fact that it comes from a 12-year-old boy).

Any uncertainty about the nascent eroticism of their relationship is dispelled later that evening when the woman and the machine dance together. (It is worth noting here that No. 5 has the physical proportions of a large man, and that he frequently mimics the voice of John Wayne!) Stephanie is now in her nightdress. She is clearly bemused by the effect that No. 5 has on her – in many ways it's the man she's always dreamed of – but it's a machine. No. 5 cannot accept this barrier however, and as she lies back in his 'arms' for the big finish to their dance it expresses a desire to stay with her permanently.

Stephanie: Oh No. 5 you don't know what you're saying.
   (Cut to shot from No. 5's viewpoint of Stephanie stretched out before it)
No. 5: (gravely) No. 5 know.
(They continue to swing around the room together)
No. 5 (singing) More than a woman, More than a woman to me.
Stephanie: Oh No. 5.
(They pull closer together in the dance)

In the morning No. 5 cooks breakfast in a comical scene which nevertheless has overtones of a post-coital meal. What has happened during the night?

As the narrative progresses, the audience shifts its immature sexual curiosity to an identification with No. 5's practical experience. During the film various views of masculinity are demonstrated:

1 Rather than No. 5, it is the military and the corporation who behave like cold and calculating robots.
2 Stephanie thinks that men are all alike – callous and cruel. No. 5, although connoting masculinity in voice and attitude, is acceptable to her and can therefore elicit her tolerance.
3 Newton Crosby is gentle and likeable but lacking in self-confidence: 'Well, girls are not my best suit'.

Crosby and Stephanie have produced and nurtured the robot between them, and it therefore takes on their characteristics, as though they were 'real' parents. The machine is the child of the man, but No. 5 has grown up in Stephanie's company, so that even when the 'father' and 'son' are reconciled, No. 5 won't let Crosby examine his circuits: 'My switches are my own'. In this articulation of the Oedipal fear of castration it demands the right to a separate identity, thus moving towards an identification with the power of the father.

After the final battle in which No. 5 defeats the military by sacrificing a lookalike machine (an act of throwing away an incomplete consciousness which demonstrates No. 5's alignment with humanity against its own kind), Stephanie hugs it and

Newton Crosby shakes its 'hand'. As the three set off for a new life together in the wilderness No. 5 declares that he would prefer to be called Johnny. The all-American family is restored, and presumably at this point 'Johnny' sublimates his Oedipal claim on his 'mother' and returns her to his 'father'. Or does he?

Computers provide the individual with a respectable excuse for social isolation. The arcane art of hacking is one of the few hobbies which may begin in early adolescence and eventually lead to respected and often highly profitable employment. There is no requirement of emotional maturity in computer science, and, indeed, the more singleminded the programmer the more he can achieve. Hacking is concerned with winning and with testing oneself against the odds. Safe parameters are set, however, because one's opponent is only a machine, and hence totally predictable, but at the same time (and this is the great lure of the computer) it is reactive to its user and therefore provides a simulation of a real relationship with a real person. Its user-friendliness offers a seemingly legitimate escape from the complexities of interpersonal relationships. Many programmers speak of the 'Vulcan mind-meld' which can be experienced: a sense of telepathy with the computer which can be achieved by 'personalizing the interface'.[9]

Consequently the two major attractions of computers could be described as, first, the escape from the world of 'real' emotions and, second, the opportunity to win in a safe environment – whether it be through playing games or through programming. But where does this touch upon the issue of gender?

We have already seen that in some children's films the female principle is juxtaposed with an encounter with a cybernetic personality in order to ease the boy's rite of passage into maturity. Other films, however, propose a different scenario in which rejection of a woman in favour of a machine is used to endorse a stance of continued isolation and emotional arrest – in other words, a definite choice towards withdrawal from adulthood. This choice is made very clearly in the Walt Disney film *Tron*. The film is aimed at a specialist audience, and it has since become a cult film for hackers of all ages. However, despite the masculine nature of hacker culture, the character of the male lead role is defined by his relationship with the only female character in the story. This apparent anomaly has a purpose, however, because it allows for a reconciliation with the male reading of power, whilst at the same time avoiding an entrance into the world of sexuality and ending with an endorsement of the impulse to remain the outsider.

It begins with a liturgical version of hacker mythology:

> This is the story of two worlds and the beings who inhabit them. One of these is our world, the one we can see and feel. The world of the 'users'. It lies on our side of the video screen.
>
> The other, an electronic micro civilization lives and breathes just beyond our grasp. This is the world of the 'programs'. Because we, the users, have created this new world, part of us lives there too. On the other side of the screen.

The film uses the computer screen as a mirror through which the self moves in order to operate in the rule-governed world of programming. It enters the version of reality inhabited by computer games-players in which battles are constantly won and lost, but at the same time control is maintained because the programmer is, after all, the original progenitor of this world. Jacques Lacan has suggested that this mirror stage, *le stade du miroir*, occurs before the establishment of a vision of the self as whole, followed by a move towards sexual identity. Significantly in *Tron*, the result is stasis and a refusal to proceed beyond the 'mirror world'. The story is as follows.

Millionaire Dillinger has become rich on the proceeds of video games, the programs for which he has stolen from a hacker named Flynn. Flynn is dedicated to retrieving the evidence of his authorship from the mainframe which runs the games. Meanwhile Alan, Flynn's rival in love and an employee of Dillinger, is engaged in devising a tron program which will trace misuse of the mainframe. (The word 'tron' is a Basic word meaning 'trace on', and functions as a search mechanism within a program, looking for errors and illegal entries.)

Unfortunately Dillinger has programmed the master control program (MCP) of his mainframe so effectively that it now controls him and is engaged in taking over all the other functions of the computer for its own dark purpose. The inside of the computer is shown to be functioning as a separate world in which each program has an identity similar to that of its user on the other side of the screen. The MCP has declared that belief in the user is an outmoded and illegal religion and is engaged in appropriating programs for its own use. In this world, the enforcers are the space invader programs who police the other programs, and dissenters are disposed of in the arcade games, rather like the way that the Romans threw the Christians to the lions. Indeed, dissenting programs are given the chance to renounce their belief in the user before being condemned to death. The substitute for death is 'de-resolution', in which the programs disappear from the screen and cease to exist.

Imprisoned in the catacombs of the video-games sector we meet Ram. (This is another Basic word meaning 'random access memory' whose role is to enable users to load and retrieve data. Obviously this is another threat to master control.) In a high tower lives 'Input-Output' (IO), an elderly sage and the counterpart of Walter, the system's original programmer in the human world. IO is aware that his role as contact for the users is under threat of elimination as the MCP proceeds with its plan to debar the users from the computer.

Returning to the user side of the screen, Flynn is engaged in the input of yet another search to find the file which will prove his authorship of the games programs. We then watch his program as it attempts to fulfil its mission and is de-ressed by the MCP's fighting force. Flynn sees his program 'crash' on his side of the screen but has no real conception of what it all means. He joins forces with Alan, the author of the tron program, who has also lost his program somewhere inside the system, thus demonstrating that their rivalry over the woman is not allowed to affect the male bond. Seeing Flynn as a major threat, the MCP absorbs the man and turns him into a program in order to eliminate him in a game. Once inside the machine Flynn encounters Tron, Alan's missing program, who of course looks just like his author, and together they defeat the MCP, enabling Flynn to return to his human state, obtain the copyright, and take Dillinger's place as millionaire proprietor. At the end of the film, when the MCP is defeated and communication with the users restored, the scene features the spreading light and awe-inspiring music which generally accompanies depictions of Christian resurrection. Referring back to the earlier pseudo-gladiator episodes, this scene addresses the mythology of church-based capitalism wherein property rights are restored to the virtuous, because although hackers are anarchists on a personal level, their isolated personalities generally deter them from organising against the *status quo*.[10]

But where are the women in this film? Laura is the token

female, a programmer working on the project which enabled the MCP to absorb Flynn into the machine. Her connection with the aggressive machine implies some degree of collusion with its attack on Flynn, but this is not explored in the film. However, her status as expert programmer is secondary to the fact that she was once Flynn's girlfriend, but now lives with Alan. Encountered within the machine her role is somewhat vague, but she acts as a guide to the adventurers and facilitates their victory. It would seem that as a woman she can work both with and against the organisation. Her creative involvement with the system becomes secondary to her emotional involvement with the men. But perhaps this analysis works better the other way. It is more likely that the plot demands a character who is willing to subvert the system, and that this flexibility of commitment can only be provided by a woman, who provides the traditional bridge between the hero and the world of power. The part Laura plays, although minimal, merits some close examination because it is through her that we understand the relationship of the hacker, Flynn, to the 'real world'.

Although Flynn, Alan and Laura are all computer experts, only the latter two are trusted employees. Flynn is the enemy of the company. He is an individualist who has been dismissed by Dillinger and now owns a video games palace, of which he is undisputed king. In the games world he is a hero because of his talent at the keyboard. His mastery can be explained by the fact that his relationship with the machine is extremely intimate. The games are his children, his family, the blood of his blood. He is that arch-American stereotype – the lone cowboy riding along on the edge of society, but Flynn has replaced the horse with his keyboard.

When the three meet each other inside the machine, their stereotyped natures are heightened by the danger they encounter. Flynn is the hero who apparently dies but then returns, whilst Tron (Alan) honourably perishes in the execution of his duty, leaving Flynn with Laura. But this fantasy world is becoming too accurate a mirror of real life for Flynn. 'Many fantasies of dualism are dramatisations of the conflict of the self torn between an original primary narcissism and an ideal ego. They depict a desire to return to a condition *preceding* the mirror stage.'[11] In the real world Flynn must be on his own: it is necessary for him to give up the comforts of home and hearth in order to devote himself to his computers, and so at the end of the film Flynn is once more alone as he descends in his helicopter to take control of Dillinger's empire. Laura has served to illustrate an option which the hero *could* take, but will not, because he is essentially independent and unneedful of the trappings of socialised society. She represents the commitment to emotion and sexuality which is so feared by hackers.

The twin mythology described above – the escape from the world of emotions and the opportunity to win in a safe environment – has been realised in a way which is most satisfying to the computer freak. His fear of emotional rejection has been neatly allayed: inside the machine Laura has demonstrated that Flynn *is* physically desirable, but in real life he chooses to reject her, thereby releasing himself from any real and possibly painful commitment. At the same time the game-players' fantasy of the screen as a truly dangerous world has been realised and their private mythology of games-playing as the exercise of power has been endorsed.

An essential feature of the plot dictates that any program contains so much of its author's character that it becomes an extension of him or her. Thus the 'baddies' are Dillinger and his alterego the MCP. Tron has a high level of integrity equal to that of its author. Flynn is brave and dynamic. Laura is – well, on either side of the screen, she's just the woman. As a character she has little depth, because her significance lies in her role of the mother/sister/lover who works with Walter (father/teacher/establishment morality) to devise the transference machine which allows the MCP to attack Flynn. Once again, the Oedipal structure is in operation. But whereas in *Short Circuit* dualism occurs in the Oedipal self, here it can be found in the father figure. Both Dillinger and Walter symbolise the father at different stages of the development of the ego. Dillinger threatens Flynn with symbolic castration by the theft of the programs through which Flynn constructs his identity, and Walter holds the power to design Dillinger's weapon, the transference process. Indeed, both conspire to produce the means by which Flynn is thrust unwillingly into the mirror world and the Oedipal dilemma, but here he is able to reconcile his libidinal drive and emerges unscathed, and unchanged.

The essential components of the narrative are that the immature male (early in the story Laura, exasperated by Flynn's attitude, complains: 'You can see why all of his friends are 14 years old') is given a clear choice between the socialised world of sex (Laura) and responsibility (corporate employment), and the world of machines. The machines offer him power and control – albeit within a very restricted field. He takes the latter, and is vindicated in his choice.

The hacker mentality is a common strand in both films. Sherry Turkle has extensively studied the hacker, and it is useful to refer to her evidence.[12] One of the hackers she interviewed, Burt, had this to say:

> I think of the world as divided between flesh things and machine things. The flesh things have feelings, need you to know how to love them, to take risks, to let yourself go. You never know what to expect of them. . . . I stay away from the flesh things. I think this makes me sort of a non-person. I often don't feel like a flesh thing myself. I hang around machines, but I hate myself a lot of the time. In a way it's like masturbating. You can always satisfy yourself to perfection. With another person, who knows what might happen? You might get rejected. You might do it wrong. Too much risk.[13]

Turkle found many computer enthusiasts who would agree with Burt's lonely testimony. They were all male. But the hero of *Short Circuit* is willing to engage with the subversive other, as the workers of Metropolis followed Maria over sixty years before. The reward for their passage through the sexual barrier, however, is contact with the usual chivalric feminine ideal, and as such does not serve to further the liberation of women from the entrapments of male ideology.

And lest we forget, the ruling capitalists in *Metropolis* created an almost fatal combination in order to control the working classes – a cybernetic woman.

NOTES

1 *Metropolis*, dir. Fritz Lang, 1927.
2 L. J. Jordonova, 'Fritz Lang's *Metropolis*: science, machines and gender', *Issues in Radical Science* 17.
3 There is much dispute about the nature of intelligence as applied to either humans or machines, but the central feature seems to be an ability to learn from experience. In other words, we know that computers are able to absorb enormous quantities of data, but in

order for them to be deemed 'intelligent' they must be able to formulate their own questions and revise their existing store of information accordingly.

4 *Short Circuit*, dir. John Badham, 1986.

5 *Tron*, dir. Steven Lisberger, 1983.

6 However, life is sometimes stranger than science fiction. The philosopher Descartes was reputed to own an automaton named Francine who bore a strong resemblance to his well-documented estranged daughter, also called Francine (N. Frude, *The Intimate Machine*, London, Century, 1983).

7 Jordonova, op. cit., 18.

8 Laura Mulvey, 'Visual Pleasure and Narrative Cinema', *Screen* 16, 3 (Autumn 1975).

9 Jargon for specifying the way in which a system operates to suit one's particular preferences.

10 Groups like CHAOS, the notorious West German hackers club, hack into world-wide weaponry systems for the excitement of the challenge rather than for political ends.

11 R. Jackson, *Fantasy: The Literature of Subversion*, London, Methuen, 1981.

12 Sherry Turkle, *The Second Self: Computers and the Human Spirit*, London, Granada, 1984.

13 ibid., 203.

Chapter 8

Your word is my command: the structures of language and power in women's science fiction

Lucie Armitt

One of the frustrations felt by some readers and critics of science fiction stems from the fact that, despite the potential for innovation inherent in the apparently limitless narrative possibilities of the genre, in actuality such innovation is rarely fully realised within either content or form.

My first serious encounter with science fiction was through an interest in the political implications of language and its structures for women. Language is of paramount importance with regard to how we structure reality (providing a cognitive framework for compartmentalising objects and sensations into linguistic units of meaning). Indeed it has been argued that: 'reality construction is probably to be regarded as the primary function of human language',[1] a claim which emphasises the need for women to challenge the patriarchal bases of language if we are also to challenge the patriarchal bases of society. However, trapped as we are within a patriarchal linguistic and social framework, it is very difficult for any writer to distance herself from that framework and write through and about alternative structures whilst still aiming to depict reality as it is lived and experienced. As this essay sets out to demonstrate, it is not enough merely to challenge surface manifestations (with revisions of words such as 'chairman', 'mastery', 'authoress' and so on, important though such revisions are), but we must also analyse and subvert the deep structural principles of language. Because of its ability to provide the writer with this much-needed distancing from lived reality, science fiction is an obvious choice for the writer intent on such exploration. The two novels upon which this essay focuses (Doris Lessing's *The Marriages Between Zones Three, Four and Five*, and Suzette Elgin's *Native Tongue*) succeed in illustrating two important issues: first, that the power structures upon which societies depend are structured by and through the structures of language; and, second, that by providing a fictional context for what has otherwise been largely theoretical abstraction, contemporary science fiction by women has made a by no means insignificant contribution to the current theoretical debate on women's relationship to language – and thus power.

An essential starting point for any critique of language as a power base *of* or *for* society is to demystify this ability to shape and control our thoughts, perceptions and behaviour. In *The Marriages Between Zones Three, Four and Five*[2] Doris Lessing begins with a vision of language as pre-eminently deterministic of behaviour patterns in both the individual characters and the societies depicted. To language is attributed an autonomy outside of human communication and almost pre-existing of any social referent whatsoever. She personifies language as a pseudo-deity whose origins are unquestioned, and whose demands remain unchallenged: 'there was an Order, and it said, simply, that she must go', (p. 13). Throughout the novel the main protagonists' behaviour is directed and determined by this 'Order', a term for which we are given no further definition, and which incorporates for the reader the dual implications not only of the linguistic imperative but also of a hierarchical power structure (both implications being significant to its understanding). So the main characters of the novel are impelled to act by unspecified drives and urges which have no contextual reference and which are never fully explained, but which exist and are articulated and understood solely at the level of language. The narrative opens:

> Rumours are the begetters of gossip. Even more are they the begetters of song. We, the Chroniclers and song-makers of our Zone, aver that before the partners in this exemplary marriage were awake to what the new directives meant for both of them, the songs were with us, and were being amplified and developed from one end of Zone Three to the other. (p. 11)

It is perhaps fitting that rumour should be the catalyst which initiates the narrative, it being the one form of utterance which typically lacks a definite source or origin for its existence. In addition, it is all the more fitting that the event concerned is a marriage, because mainstream linguistic theory has frequently used the social contract of the marriage vow as the primary illustration of the 'illocutionary speech act', a term which is of value to this argument because it hints at the power which even conventional linguistic theory attributes to language as the initiator, as well as the descriptor, of social codes. The term 'speech act' refers to an utterance which not only articulates, but actually brings into being a particular state of affairs.[3] Thus, for example, in speaking the words which form the marriage vows, the marriage itself is brought into existence. It is created *by* and *through* language. As is clear from the quotation cited above, once the rumour is initiated in *The Marriages*, the marriage is seen to exist, and neither Al·Ith nor Ben Ata has the power to change events, which are from then on pre-ordained.

I would not wish to suggest, however, that Lessing's vision of language is that of an entirely self-referential or self-perpetuating system (an approach which would toe the line of traditional linguistic theory). Many of the theories put forward both by psychoanalytic and later structuralist theoreticians could be usefully applied to this text, particularly where they have relevance to women's marginal position to the Symbolic Order or to the dominant discourse. At one point in the narrative Lessing refers to the orders by which Zone Four functions as 'ukases' (p. 251), a term deriving from Tsarist Russia, and which has come to take on the meaning of 'any arbitrary order.'[4] The implications of this word are doubled by the pun inherent in this definition which refers to the arbitrary nature of the power base upon which Zone Four (and by extension the patriarchal establishment) is based, and which makes fully apparent (i) the intrinsic nature of the relationship between language and the structures of power; and (ii) the fact that such structures are not pre-ordained at all, but entirely arbitrary.

Hélène Cixous distinguishes between the Realm of the Gift and the Realm of the Proper (*Propre*),[5] a distinction worth applying here as Zone Three could be considered representative of the former, and Zone Four the latter. From a linguistic perspective this is manifested through Zone Four's barked commands and imperatives (one might well say that 'sentences are passed' on the ordinary people of the zone by those positioned higher up the military hierarchy), while Zone Three's communication works via finely tuned spatial techniques which take us beyond the limits of word and sentence. The confusion and dislocation felt by Jarnti and Ben Ata at encountering Zone Three (either directly or via Al·Ith) is due to the fact that – their commands being misplaced and indeed irrelevant in that region – they lack any ability to shape or construct reality through language. The linguistic units which frame the commands simultaneously pre-package their perceptions of reality. Under the rules of the Realm of the Proper, language ap-*propr*-iates, leaving no room for the creation or generation of the alternative visions associated with the Realm of the Gift.

Science fiction often draws very closely on narrative devices and structures common to other forms of popular fiction, and in some ways the narrative concerns of *The Marriages* works through similar methods to the folktale or quest allegory. The story of a queen of one land who marries the king of another in order to restore harmony to her realm is a conventional one within such literature, and in line with the allegorical form both Al·Ith and Ben Ata are personifications of the abiding characteristics of their own respective zones. In this context Waelti-Walters' comments on the fairytale form are significant:

> Woman is gift and possession . . . the touchstone of the whole system of values men in our civilisation have built up between themselves and which has taken symbolic form in language.[6]

Initially, as implied above, Al·Ith embodies the Realm of the Gift and Ben Ata the Realm of the Proper, the two forming an irreconcilable dichotomy. Through their enforced marriage, however, these contrasting features gradually become blurred, and Al·Ith in particular forms the site of the conflagration of the two, rendered visible through her pregnancy with Arusi. Thus she takes on board this role of the touchstone of the value system, her victimisation at the hands of a hostile system becoming more and more apparent as the narrative progresses. Waelti-Walters' comment refers to the linguistic implications of this (the use of the term 'symbolic' here relating to the importance of language in the forging of social codes, rather than the more specific psychoanalytic definition of the term). The basic structuralist argument, deriving from the work of Ferdinand de Saussure,[7] argues that language operates via a system of signs (the sign being the twofold combination of the sound/word and the mental concept) which take on meaning in relationship to each other and the system as a whole. Later advocates of structuralism came to believe that this linguistic model could usefully be applied to other social codes and to the workings of literary narratives, one of the most important of these being Propp's *Morphology of the Folk Tale*.[8] Lessing's narrative works quite closely along folk-legend parallels, about which Propp notes: 'Functions constitute the basic elements of the tale, those elements upon which the course of the narrative is built'[9] – the 'function' in this sense being the way in which any particular action or event takes on significance (or indeed signification) within the narrative as a whole. In the traditional folktale, 'functions' take on significance primarily as they relate to, or derive from, the underlying moral code (which structuralist critics would also interpret as a linguistic code), this being the *real* (if frequently disguised) power behind its telling. As various critics, including Waelti-Walters, have shown, this moral code is not an apolitical guideline for children, but a product of the prevailing ideology out of which the tale arises, and which seeks primarily to protect the *status quo*. This is where *The Marriages* departs from the afore-mentioned model. Lessing not only foregrounds ideology within her narrative framework, but demonstrates the significance of language to it. The Chronicler is the persona whose main function is to stress the folk-legend quality of the tale. He it is who interrupts the narrative, just as the reader forgets that this is a story told by a storyteller, to remind us that chroniclers in the two zones frequently take one scene and depict it in very different ways, turning it in the process into history or myth (fact or fiction) as best suits their purposes. So Lessing's Chronicler reminds us that language plays a central role in the *construction* of so-called 'truth' (to 'chronicle' an event being to present it as 'fact'); thus truth is never absolute, but at all times remains a subjective – and in this context an ideological – construct, something that can work for good or ill. As the Chronicler states: 'Describing we become. We even – and I've seen it and have shuddered – summon' (p. 243).

But language is not just depicted as a key to power in this novel, it also becomes one of the fundamental keys to knowledge. It is through writing his version of the story of Al·Ith that the Chronicler learns: 'I write in these bald words the deepest lessons of my life' (p. 242), lessons which Al·Ith will come to share. Referring to the intrinsic relationship between language and our perceptions of reality, Grace comments that, through language, 'we do not just see shifting patterns of light, we see people and objects and actions'.[10] When Al·Ith attempts to initiate herself into

Zone Two without being granted access to it by 'the Order', she stands just over the threshold of the zone and considers:

> that all around her, above her, were people – no, beings, were something, then, or somebody, invisible but there. . . . Almost she could see them . . . as if flames trembled into being. . . . One moment she could see them – almost. Then could not, and there was nothing there. (p. 238)

Lacking 'the Order' (which Lacanian theorists could here interpret as the Symbolic Order) which, through language, would initiate Al·Ith into the ways of Zone Two, reality is not merely fragmentary, but lacking in all forms of structure. Outside language, as theorists from both Lacanian and structuralist schools agree, we lack the code via which sensory impressions can be deciphered and understood.

But Al·Ith's ex-centric position *vis-à-vis* the Symbolic Order is not unambiguously depicted as a disadvantage. Despite the fact that she becomes the inevitable and pre-ordained victim of 'the word', it also becomes apparent during the course of the narrative that only the women of Zone Four (who are very much located on the margins of that zone and its *raison d'être*, and precisely *because of* this position) can recognise and acknowledge the friction between the seemingly inconsequential surface structures of linguistic utterances and the highly subversive deep structures which give rise to them. These women are associated with the traditional oral/spatial forms of communication: song and story, an association which counteracts the traditional patrilinear linguistic/philosophical position which privileges writing over speech as the proper medium of the rational (considered more 'logical' because less immediate and emotive), and hence the 'natural' vehicle for knowledge and learning.

Through their songs these women glimpse a potential for change, the source of which they perceive to lie within the higher realms of Zone Three, and which they explore through disrupting the usual connection between the words of the song and the gestures of their bodies. We best understand Lessing's depiction of this dichotomy through applying Kristeva's concept of the signifying process 'semanalysis'.[11] Just as the workings of the poetic text emerge as a result of the juxtaposition of the pheno- and genotext inherent within poetic language, so the women's songs function in like manner. They are structured via the conventional rules associated with the nursery-rhyme form: there is no unusually subversive use of syntax, and the *meaning* (in terms of communicative competence) follows a kind of *kindergarten logic* which, while perhaps dissatisfying to the adult listener/reader, is seemingly in keeping with the accepted rules of the genre; rhyme, rhythm and intonation being the more significant elements. Kristeva notes: 'The phenotext is a structure (which can be generated, in generative grammar's sense); it obeys rules of communication and presupposes . . . an addressee.'[12]

All these criteria are fulfilled within the surface structure of the songs, but on another level Al·Ith recognises that: 'there was the oddest contrast between their demeanour and what surely had been, at least to start with, some playground counting game?' (p. 166). Underlying the structure of these songs as phenotext is a subversive process, which neither the women nor Al·Ith can articulate or fully understand but which is clearly of great significance as a means of challenging the insular militarist preoccupations of the zone as a whole. The Chronicler informs us that 'it is through the unexpected, or the sidelong, or the indirect that truths come our way' (p. 175) and it is within the 'absences' or disjunctions which disrupt and disturb the relationship between song and gesture that the importance of the rituals become apparent. Kristevan analysis locates the phenotext within the Symbolic Order, and the genotext within the semiotic. From this perspective the genotext bursts through the conscious structure as a product of the split subject's unconscious psychic processes; a theoretical position which clearly parallels both the women's sense of being torn between loyalty to their menfolk and a passion for the 'heights' of Zone Three; and their lack of ability to articulate or define what it is that they nevertheless experience as a drive or an urge which must be fulfilled. In this sense the meetings can also operate for the *reader* as a 'working through' of the frustration felt by those who, despite the recognition that language marginalises women, are either silenced by the inability to voice alternatives or – faced with the claim that 'every language has a sufficiently rich vocabulary for the expression of all the distinctions that are important in the society using it'[13] – consider their recognition of this marginality proof of neurosis or inadequacy. Chomsky's work, to which the above refers, is particularly interesting in this context because it is so symptomatic of patrilinear approaches to language study. Not only is this apparent in the underlying ideology of his theory (which, not uncommonly, poses as apolitical and thus 'scientific'), but also in his methodology. His transformational-generative approach to linguistics sought to analyse the surface grammatical structure of the sentence by demonstrating that it derives from a deep structure based on the principles of 'logic' (an analysis which he demonstrated by means of tree diagrams and mathematical symbols). In this sense Lessing's use of the secret women's meetings also operates as a means of challenging such highly patriarchal theories, implying as she does that the deep structures of language are not so much 'logical' as 'ideo/logical' and must be acknowledged as such.

Al·Ith, at least in part, functions as a representative of the woman who, in coming to recognise her relationship towards language (and thus society) as marginal, is forced to confront this new awareness from a position of complete isolation. *The Marriages* is both a fable of knowledge and a fable of power,[14] but the knowledge which Al·Ith gains through the course of her task diminishes her power both by alienating her from home, husband and people and by stripping her of her title and role of Queen. In Suzette Elgin's *Native Tongue*[15] we return to this position of alienation, but in doing so consider how women are devising positive alternative strategies for language, and thus for power.

Whereas *The Marriages* is at the fantasy end of the science fiction spectrum *Native Tongue* is, in some respects, far more akin to the 'harder' techno-fiction novel. Elgin uses a specific futurist setting (the narrative takes place in the United States between the years 2179 and 2212) and takes as a central feature of this setting the technological gadget referred to as the 'Interface'. The science upon which the narrative focuses is, however, that of linguistics, which functions as the basis of the social hierarchy. This hierarchy, as in *The Marriages*, is depicted as absolute and unbending, and in Elgin's novel operates along the following principles. Babies of the 'Lines' (the name given to linguist households) are *Interfaced* with aliens from birth, in an attempt to teach the infants to speak alien languages, so that communication and negotiations can be facilitated throughout the galaxy. Ironically, of particular significance to the maintenance of the power structure are the female linguist infants, who are each trained to communicate in several terran and alien languages in order to be able to conduct the required role of interpreter to the greatest possible level of efficiency. Not surprisingly, this ability to pick up multiple languages and translate information between cultures (a process which necessitates a significant understanding of one culture's set of structural principles in order to reconstruct another's through language) is not considered to be a powerful or creative ability by the male linguists:

> The interpreter was paid no more attention than a business machine, especially if she was a woman; after all . . . a circuit will carry any message you want to send over it, but you do not assume from that fact that it understands what you have said. (p. 193)

For our purposes, the most interesting part of Elgin's description of the Interface is that it can be effectively compared with psychoanalytic theories of how we enter into the order of language. During the Interfacing process infant and alien face each other through a transparent barrier, a process which seems to concretise Lacan's theory of the child's entry into the Symbolic Order at the mirror stage of development.[16] To explore this comparison in greater depth, it is important to recognise that the linguists are capable of carrying out this assimilation process perfectly. Yet when the non-linguist households attempt the same process in a bid to wrench power from the linguists, horrifying things occur to their infants. They either implode physically or, as in the case of the 'tubies', become completely incapable of communication at all. The parallel widens in the case of the 'tubies', as their resulting symptoms parallel the manifestations of psychosis, in which the infant remains within the Imaginary Realm, driven solely by inarticulate and unarticulated drives and desires, and is unable to interact on any level with society.

At first sight Elgin's position here provokes a very similar suspicion to that held by critics of the Lacanian theorists, concerned by the extent to which biological determinism is seemingly prioritised over and above sociologically defined criteria, as the root cause of this phenomenon. A Kristevan reading of the process, however, might help to dispel such reservations. The linguist infants, being members of the dominant *social* group, are entering a Symbolic Order controlled by that group. The non-linguist infants, however, are being forced to enter a Symbolic Order to which neither they nor their parents have full access. Kristeva's approach is important because she argues that Lacan's

Symbolic Order is also a 'social' order created and structured by and for patriarchy. As Moi explains: 'It is difficult, then, to maintain that Kristeva holds an essentialist or even biologistic notion of femininity . . . [her] emphasis on marginality allows us to view this repression of the feminine in terms of *positionality* rather than of essences.'[17]

Elgin's stance also foregrounds the importance of the link between the social hierarchy and the speaking subject's position within language. Women have no choice but to enter the Symbolic Order (notwithstanding the trauma and repression inherent in the assimilation process) if they are to interact with other human beings on any communicative level whatsoever. Similarly, the infants have no choice over their involvement in the Interfacing process, the result of this process, as already mentioned, being determined by their position within the *social* hierarchy.

Elgin's treatment of the power of names and the naming process returns us to a consideration of the *masculine* Realm of the Proper as Cixous defines it. In *Native Tongue* names are used to label and define women in terms of the patrilinear genealogy of households in much the same way as they are in our own culture (thus upon marriage the central character becomes Nazareth Joanna Chornyak (her father's name) Adiness (her husband's name),[18] a naming which assigns her to, and categorises her as a member of, the household of a particular (male) linguist, to be disowned only as and when he considers her to be past her sexual and/or reproductive usefulness). Dis-owned women live in the women's community: Barren House, a name which clearly reflects the phallocratic bias of the society. Defending the name, Thomas Chornyak, head of 'the Lines', notes:

> if it was to do all over again we wouldn't call the place Barren House. That seems cruel, and in the worst of taste, looking at it now . . . it was taken for granted that that was just a kind of working title, and that a new name would be chosen quickly – it just never happened . . . it's a tradition now. . . . It's just a name. (p. 121)

Nevertheless, in this otherwise rather dismal view of the future, Barren House is the place where the spark of subversion is kindled, and where the seclusion of this community transforms isolation into refuge, women coming to value and care for each other as individuals. The importance of language as a power base is no secret to these linguists, and the primary task becomes to craft carefully and lovingly a women's language that *will* aim to place their concerns at its centre.

It is worth comparing some of the features of this women's language, which Elgin calls Láadan, with Irigaray's concept of *le parler femme*.[19] The most striking characteristic of Irigaray's concept is her claim that it *already* exists at all-women gatherings as a spontaneous presence. Those who have attended women-only conferences or workshops may know the truth of this within a limited social context, but the difficulty with Irigaray's position on this is that she seems to neglect any sociological referent, talking instead in terms of an unconscious discourse which 'resists and explodes every firmly established form, figure, idea, or concept'.[20] At first glance, therefore, there is seemingly little similarity between Irigaray's concept and Elgin's depiction of Láadan. In contrast to a *resistance* to form and figure, Elgin emphasises precisely how much care these women place upon the tight structuring of Láadan.

However, there is a more applicable feature of Irigaray's work on women's language, which resides in her approach to structures. She claims that the linear form of our own language is patriarchal in conception, seeing this as an extension of the patterns of binary logic so prevalent in the intellectual foundations of our society and our language. Undergraduates are still taught the basic linguistic theory of relative meaning by using the following primary example:

$$\text{'man'} = +\text{male}$$
$$\text{'woman'} = -\text{male}$$

In taking this as a starting point for theorising our understanding of the world around us, the relationship between women, language and power as the establishment intends us to perceive it is all too clear.[21] On a less extreme level, the linguistic choices we make in articulating a spoken or written utterance follow a series of basic either/or choices which are conveyed along a chain (the sentence). Traditional linguistics expands upon this binary practice when theorising grammatical meaning by employing a two-dimensional structure composed of the paradigmatic and the syntagmatic axes, the first being the 'vertical' axis which relates to possible either/or choices within the same grammatical class (the choice between the terms 'this' or 'that' and so forth) while the syntagmatic axis represents either/or choices along a 'horizontal' axis, involving the ordering of words and phrases within a sentence. In this context, Elgin's labelling of the linguist dynasty as the 'Lines' is surely significant. She appears to sympathise with this critique of linearity, making clear the fact that in a women's language there would be 'no particular reason to expect that . . . languages would have verbs, subjects, or objects' (p. 210), the different grammatical classes of terms being the necessary foundation for a linear structure. Altering the structures necessarily alters our perceptions of the environment, but a problem remains. However convincing the argument, in claiming that women's discourse instinctively rejects linearity as a structure Elgin fails to provide any feasible alternative. This is an important flaw.

The ideological basis of Láadan's construction as Elgin depicts it is extremely appealing, and acts as a highly effective contrast to that of the male linguists. The male linguists employ a discourse whose inherent philosophy is elitist and exclusory and which privileges power, deceit and manipulation. In contrast, Elgin's language aims to include as many women as possible, and the phonetic choices involved in its construction reflect this: 'they hadn't wanted other women to have to struggle to pronounce it just because those whose lot it was to construct it happened to have English as their first Terran language' (p. 160). Throughout our history those discourses traditionally associated with the establishments of power and authority – the political, the medical, the legal or the religious – have all been of an exclusory nature, favouring certain 'privileged' educational and social backgrounds. As such it is surely no surprise that, until recently, few women have managed to gain access to these fields at all.

The situation for the women of Barren House, however, is not straightforward. Despite their awareness that Láadan has the power to subvert and disrupt the social structure through which they are victimised, the way forward is filled with trepidation. From the psychoanalytic perspective on gender orientation and binary opposition referred to earlier, if women are equated linguistically with 'minus maleness' rather than 'plus femaleness', then the creation of a woman-centred language merely serves to place us in the middle of an absence:

'Is it a time for celebration, do you think?' hazarded Grace.

'. . . It's a time for terror. That much is certain.'

'It's stepping out into the void,' said Susannah solemnly. (p. 254)

This piece of dialogue between three of the women of Barren House underlines the real power of the *status quo*. While existence at the bottom of the social ladder is never pleasant, there is at least some security in knowing one has a place within it.

But what of innovation? Concluding – as we began – with frustration, irrespective of the importance of Elgin's approach to the subject of women and language,[22] *Native Tongue* remains a particularly frustrating novel. This is primarily because the political implications of syntactic structures, which Elgin raises on a discursive level, are not concretised within the narrative form. This polarising of language as dialogue and language as literary medium oversimplifies, and thus reduces, the impact of feminist theories of the importance of language as a means to change. The appendix of terms Elgin provides at the end of the book merely emphasises this shortcoming. In listing these she takes the first steps towards presenting Láadan as a feasible language, but fails to consolidate her position. Taking just one example, the term 'ramime' is given the definition of 'to refrain from asking out of courtesy or kindness' (p. 303) which seems to imply a verb-like function. The existence of a term which at least *approximates* to a verb without any syntactical context denoting otherwise cuts across her own position as noted above, and suggests a reassertion of the patrilinear form rather than a movement away from it. Furthermore, as stated at the beginning of this chapter, alternative structures cannot be conveyed by re/formations at the level of the word.[23]

But these reservations are by no means entirely restricted to *Native Tongue*. This need to confront conventional narrative structures as they have relevance to the relationship between women and language is an area which few writers of science fiction have dealt with adequately. The deconstruction of language as content is important, as both *The Marriages* and *Native Tongue* demonstrate, but perhaps the deconstruction of language as form and structure is more significant. Literature, before it is anything else, is a linguistic construct. To dissociate form from content, by opening up a dichotomy between the use of language within the text and the use of language *as* text, is an evasion of the real task in hand. Huntingdon notes that the science fiction genre, 'which one might expect to explore the possibilities of fictional styles and forms, has traditionally conformed closely to a clear and powerful set of stylistic narrative conventions'.[24] In a different context, John Fiske claims that: 'Like language, narrative is a basic way of making sense of our experience of the real.'[25] If the aim really is to challenge the linguistic structures upon which patriarchal society is based, this aim must be demonstrated through the structures of narrative. Not only does narrative 'make sense of' the real, it also *constructs* that writer's perceptions of the real (thus emphasising its subjective nature).

This is not to overlook the problem of reception, which is a very real one for science fiction writers in particular. Conventionally, readers of science fiction have been attracted to the genre precisely *because* content is prioritised over form, and experimental syntax and avant-garde forms will undoubtedly alienate some of those readers. Two of the most unconventional science fiction novels ever published in terms of experimental syntax and disrupted and unreliable narrative structures are June Arnold's *Applesauce* (1966) and Mary Staton's *From The Legend of Biel* (1975).[26] Neither, however, are currently in print in either Britain or the United States. Writing about avant-garde forms in general, Susan Suleiman notes that because:

> They resist the reader's attempt to structure or order them in terms of previously learned codes of reading . . . it is hardly any wonder if the first reaction of a reader is one of defensive counterattack: she/he calls the text unreadable, which is to say both unintelligible and not worth reading.[27]

Difficult such forms undoubtedly are, but does this justify our reluctance to write or to read them? One novel which has admirably demonstrated that experimental narrative can and does have a place within science fiction is Joanna Russ' widely read and highly acclaimed novel *The Female Man*,[28] which 'in its very form disrupts the limits of the present ideological system'.[29] More novels of this kind are needed. Without such writing we can only ever go halfway towards a new language, a new reality, and indeed a new future. At its best science fiction must shake us from our complacences. For women this is no luxury.

NOTES

1 George W. Grace, *The Linguistic Construction of Reality*, London, Croom Helm, 1987, 139.

2 Doris Lessing, *The Marriages Between Zones Three, Four and Five*, London, Panther, 1985. (All quotations cited are from this edition.) From here on I refer to this novel as *The Marriages* for the sake of brevity.

3 J. L. Austin, *How To Do Things With Words*, Oxford, Oxford University Press, 1962. This example taken from the 1980 edition, ed. J. O. Urmson and Marina Sbisa, 130.

4 This definition is taken from *The Concise Oxford Dictionary*, 6th edition, 1976.

5 Hélène Cixous and Catherine Clement, *The Newly Born Woman*, Manchester, Manchester University Press, 1986, 80–1. Originally published as *La Jeune Née*, Paris, Union Generale d'Editions, 1975.

6 Jennifer, Waelti-Walters, *Fairy Tales and the Female Imagination*, Montreal, Eden, 1982, 78.

7 Ferdinand de Saussure, *Cours de linguistique generale*, Paris, Payot, 3rd edn. Trans. *Course in General Linguistics*, London, Fontana, 1974.

8 V. Propp, *The Morphology of the Folk Tale*, Austin, University of Texas Press, 1975.

9 ibid., 71.

10 Grace, op. cit., 119.

11 See, for example 'The system and the speaking subject' (1973) and 'Revolution in poetic language' (1974) both in Toril, Moi (ed.), *The Kristeva Reader*, Oxford, Blackwell, 1986.

12 ibid., 121.

13 John Lyons, *Chomsky*, Brighton, Harvester, 1977, 21.

14 In Patrick Parrinder, *Science Fiction: Its Criticism and Teaching*, London, Methuen, 1980, 81, the author differentiates between these two categories, which he considers to be the two major classes of science fiction used as fable.

15 Suzette Haden Elgin, *Native Tongue*, London, Women's Press, 1985. (All quotations cited are from this edition.) Originally published 1984.

16 See, for example, 'The mirror stage as formative of the function of the I' (1949) and 'The function and field of speech and language in psychoanalysis' (1953) both reprinted in Jacques Lacan, *Ecrits: A Selection*, London, Tavistock, 1977.

17 Toril Moi, *Sexual/Textual Politics*, London, Methuen, 1985.

18 In addition to the comments I make here, I am indebted to Mair Evans for drawing my attention to the fact that the name 'Adiness' is a pun on the phrase 'add an s', the letter s at the end of a name referring originally to 'son of'.

19 Luce Irigaray, *This Sex Which Is Not One*, Ithaca, NY, Cornell University Press, 1985, 135. Originally published as *Ce Sexe qui n'en est pas un*, Paris, Editions de Minuit, 1977.

20 ibid., 79.

21 As an undergraduate during the early 1980s I was given precisely this

example as illustration of this theory, something which unintention-
ally provided me with one of my first exercises in consciousness
raising. I was therefore particularly interested to discover quite
recently that in *What Is Linguistics?* Elgin herself uses this same example, but reverses the gender orientation: 'A feature matrix is prepared
by choosing a set of particular characteristics that can be used to
define the set of objects or entities to be classified, and then specifying
each   such   object   or   entity   as   plus   or   minus   that
characteristic . . . [Therefore] if you have the feature [female] you do
not need the feature [male], since [-female] will automatically provide
you with it' (p. 9).

22 This is in no way an attempt to criticise Elgin's work on women
and language as a whole, and for any readers interested in the subject
of women and language I would strongly recommend her pioneering
publication *A First Dictionary and Grammar of Láadan*, from which the
appendix to this edition of *Native Tongue* is taken.

23 Marge Piercy's *Woman On The Edge of Time* (1976) does tackle the
relationship between language and power structures by focusing on
language at the level of word and morpheme, and does so very
successfully. However, her success is at least in part due to the fact
that her aims are less ambitious than Elgin's, and thus arguably less
capable of challenging the *status quo* on anything but a surface level.

24 John Huntingdon, 'Science fiction and the future' in Mark Rose (ed.),
1976, *Science Fiction: A Collection of Critical Essays*, Englewood Cliffs,
Prentice Hall, 1976, 161.

25 John Fiske, *Television Culture*, London, Methuen, 1987, 128.

26 I refer anybody interested in researching this area further, to Natalie
Rosinsky, *Feminist Futures: Contemporary Women's Speculative Fiction*,
Ann Arbor, UMI, 1984. In this excellent publication she discusses
both of these texts and their experimental narrative structures in some
depth.

27 Susan Rubin Suleiman, 'The question of readability in avant-garde
fiction', *Studies in Twentieth Century Literature*, 6, 1–2 (Fall/Spring
1981/2, 17–35.

28 Joanna Russ, *The Female Man*, New York, Bantam, 1975. First British
publication London, Women's Press, 1985.

29 Tom Moylan, *Demand The Impossible: Science Fiction and the Utopian
Imagination*, London, Methuen, 1986, 65.

Chapter 9

'I'm not *in* the business; I *am* the business': women at work in Hollywood science fiction

Erica Sheen

I

This chapter is concerned not so much with SF literature itself as with the use made of it by the Hollywood film industry. My main aim is to give detailed readings of two SF films of the 1980s, but before that I want in this first section to give some general sense of the terms on which those readings will be made. I take as a simplified starting point the fact that SF has its roots in utopian fiction, a literary genre that looks beneath the surface of the determining conventions of society, and tests historical contingencies by subjecting its behavioural principles to an experimental relativism. Such a project clearly renders possible a reconsideration of the nature of sexuality and gender: other chapters in this study suggest the extent to which this has been the case, and how successful it has been. For my purposes it is important to note that a significant development relevant to the possibility of such a reconsideration was the growing interest in alien or artificial life forms; that this interest was itself focusing on SF literature in the 1940s and 1950s, when Hollywood was struggling to establish socioeconomic structures for its survival as an industry; and that it quickly became one of the first points of contact between that industry and the SF genre. I shall not however be discussing SF films of this period: my initial purpose will be to establish the preoccupations that underlie the development of this interest in the 1980s. My concern will be to try to show that narratives about the sexual identity of artificial life forms use cinema's increasing self-consciousness about the process of image-making not to test conventional definitions of gender but to consolidate them.

But why should the film industry need to function in this

particular way? Broadly speaking, because such a consolidation was the kind of work it needed to perform for itself, as well as the product its culture required of it. Brian Stableford points out that in the 1950s, in particular, optimism about the place of automation in modern society began to give way under the pressure of anxieties about the implications of 'progress':

> In the post-war period the encroachment of the machine upon the most essential and sacred areas of human activity and endeavour became a plausible theme in sf. There are a number of stories in which artists see themselves replaced by machines . . . and the replacement of humans by androids or robots even in the most intimate of relationships became a popular theme.[1]

In fact many of these stories are only metaphorically concerned with machines; their interest is often more deeply in issues of gender that can be addressed in this indirect way. What is being displayed is anxiety about what is in cultural terms a paradigmatic instance of the encroachment of the non-human upon the human: the replacement of the masculine by the feminine.

Social conditions in the early postwar period gave such a process of replacement a significant literal and metaphorical reality. In the USA and in Great Britain reconstruction of the economy required the stimulus of new technology, particularly domestic technology with its broad market and self-creating demand, encouraging a certain appetite for social and economic competitiveness within the workforce. But this structure of material desire was built on unsteady foundations. The emphasis offered by the new boom industries of advertising and publicity on images of the housewife and children was to some extent a containment of an uneasy awareness that – as a gender – women had asserted a very different potential during the war years. Of course women at work was by no means a new or even a twentieth-century phenomenon, although it was one that had become increasingly significant in the interwar period up to 1939. But the particular circumstances in which women worked in 1939–45 had offered something normally associated with men: an identity *as a workforce*. As a result, in the postwar years there was a confidence, even a glamour, available for women within a reconstituted workforce in which most men felt themselves newly insecure. Film and television became the media for the containment of these anxieties. Cosily domesticating TV series burgeoned in the 1950s – an interesting example of a prime new product attempting to consolidate its own market, and of the 'universal' cultural stakes involved in such a consolidation. Almost invariably, these series encouraged a balance in women between a bright new 1950s independence and an appropriate domestic submission. But, coming from a hi-tech industry, it was a form of encouragement that created its own problems. The rise to the challenge of post-war prosperity, the technological sophistication of the domestic market in an attempt to stimulate the economy at all levels – all these established a mode of work that added further difficulties to the way men in particular understood their role within it. A market dominated by technology creates a characteristic form of supply, structured by repetition at the levels both of production and consumption. At both, the point is to give impetus to the process of repetition; to perpetuate the employment it can create. As a predominating rationale of employment, repetition reinforces the loss of a goal-oriented concept of production which had paralleled the characteristic 'male' emphasis on material productivity and achievement. Arguably it relates – both structurally and evaluatively – to modes of productivity, including domestic and biological ones, that have typically been associated with women. But postwar society has been remarkably creative, and successful, in its realignment of these values with the masculine. At its very centre is a series of industries which enshrine the whole concept of replication within cultural aesthetics. These 'arts' industries – the film and music businesses – came to prominence as employers and producers in this postwar phase. Dominated as they are by the concept of recording as employment, their products refer directly to the processes that produced them, and their function as products is to repeat themselves: to get 'replayed', and to get the process of production replayed so that new products to play and replay can be made. Within such conditions of employment the idea of 'the performance' has a central importance, focusing the aestheticising function of notions of the one-off, the unrepeatable, within a system of production in which products are not an end in themselves but a way of reproducing work; a system which must be regulated in a way that ensures that that work continues. As we shall see in the films I shall discuss, the result of this happy and timely ideological conjunction of concepts of work, productivity and performance has been the reformulation of the potentially disabling processes of repetition and replication as a specific masculine teleology – at the expense, specifically and necessarily, of the feminine. One of the most important channels for this reformulation has been film, adapting technology that is a product of the cultural milieu which is the source of the anxieties it needs to contain towards the very process of containment. The refinement of that technology towards the virtuoso techniques for image-making of the 1970s and 1980s represents a climax in that process of containment which expresses itself in the appropriate rhetoric of the SF blockbuster.

It will be apparent that the terms of the last part of this discussion are part of the intellectual property of postmodernist theory, currently enjoying an enormous vogue amongst young – particularly male – academics.[2] But I do not want to cast what I want to say within that particular discourse precisely because it seems to me that postmodernist theory is itself a token 'radical' version of that masculine teleology. For instance, in a recent study Steven Connor gestures towards the recognition that postmodernism performs this particular function for masculinity at the expense of feminism, but himself reproduces the authoritarian marginalisation he attempts to expose in his own tendency to allow his analyses to establish aestheticised frames of reference of which the social values remain unchallenged. He refers to *Blade Runner*, from which the quotation of my title is taken and which I shall be discussing later, as 'impeccably postmodernist', but is not concerned to consider the patriarchal analysis of agency beneath the surface of a prestigious cultural style.

Just how hard-line that patriarchalism is becomes apparent if we retrace the trajectory of the film industry's other great resource in the development of this masculine teleology: the star system. Across the watershed of the Second World War, this had already become a focus for the problems that the presence of women in the workforce had begun to create; its history clearly reveals both the anxieties I have been attempting to identify and typical ways of resolving them. Cathy Klaprat[3] has analysed Bette Davis' career at Warner Brothers from 1932 to 1949 in terms of 'the Star as Market Strategy', outlining the phases in the development of her narrative role in terms of an exercise in product differentiation; becoming a star meant she could keep generating work. Interestingly, the emergence of Davis' assertive persona is linked with increasing marketability as a star. The studio made calculated use of public perception of her as an aggressive female: emphasis on Davis as a 'sexually menacing destroyer of men' is fed back into her working relations with her co-stars: 'Who will be the real star of the film . . . who will give the best performance, Muni or Davis?' A threatening ambiguity between the possibility of a man being unable to work and active female sexual agency displays itself in advertisement captions like 'Bette Davis smacks 'em where it hurts' and 'I'll destroy your ambitions, your hopes'. However this is not related to the acquisition of any real power within the industry; as Klaprat observes:

> She never did earn the right to choose her roles or to have a say in her publicity. On the contrary, as Davis' name grew larger on theater marquees, the studio consolidated more control over her career.

The assertive female roles of the industry's late studio phase were an effect, not a threat: a kind of 'permission' granted within the system for assertion against the system. At the time, it was more in its interests than against them.

But in the 1950s the studio system began to break up, and with it both its defining conditions of employment for its stars and the tailored fit between their images and the interests of the industry. One of the decade's most important commodities, Marilyn Monroe's sexy image evidently did an important piece of work both for postwar consumer culture and for the film industry. But in the last phase of her career she tried to give economic reality to the resistance that existed in Davis at the level of image. This can be seen as an attempt to establish a different kind of agency within the process of image-making: Monroe walked out on Fox while in the process of making a film, and joined the Actor's Studio in New York: she also formed her own production company.

But the extent to which it is undesirable for women to succeed in constructing a position that serves their own needs, and the lengths to which an industry will go to suggest that its conditions of employment are exactly what a woman needs anyway, can be seen from a film which deals with the sort of questions that gather around a self-destructive career like Monroe's. I'm going to look briefly at George Cukor's musical *A Star is Born*, because its narrative has what might appear to be surprising points of contact with the two SF films I shall be considering. My discussion of it here can be seen as an attempt to establish the 1950s subtext to which these films apply the rhetoric of SF in their attempt to 'naturalise' the priority of masculinity over the process of image-making.

Made in 1955 and starring Judy Garland and James Mason, this is the story of a rising female star and a falling male one. From this point of view it initially seems a remarkably frank record of the growing opportunities for women within a system which men are no longer able to dominate, but in the last analysis this film by a director who has something of a feminist reputation reasserts very traditional values indeed. Norman Maine (James Mason) discovers a young singer, Esther Blodgett, a.k.a. Vicky Lester (Judy Garland). His own career sinking into an alcoholic haze, he nevertheless unselfishly helps her to the success which he sees is so 'naturally' hers. We see Esther being 'made up' for her screen test, and Norman taking it all off again so that the real star can shine through. Marriage follows – but soon founders because the man is by now far less successful than the woman. He commits suicide to prevent her from giving up her career for his sake; but she abandons it out of grief anyway, until a (male) friend talks her into a triumphant comeback on the grounds that her husband died for her career so she should fulfil it for his sake. Her return to the public gaze is accompanied by the proud announcement of herself as 'Mrs Norman Maine'.

Notice the definitions that are being established here. Both Garland's stardom *and* her naturalness are man-made: indeed, any contradiction between the two is resolved in that fact. In professional terms her authority is dependent on him: its competitive force is registered, but in terms of identity it is more a feature of his than of hers. The curious process of cultural parthenogenesis by which this star is 'born' is registered in the title – an appropriation of the vocabulary of female creativity by a male system. A powerful female voice is given full presence but it is a voice that is quite literally switched on by the men: this film's reflexive interest in the technology of film production relates its concerns to those of SF, as we shall see. Like Rachael in *Blade Runner*, Garland is not in the business; she *is* the business. The worker has been converted into the product, her personal power as the former into marketability as the latter. When considering what exactly is at stake here, it's worth remembering that Garland's own story was more like Maine's than Lester's.

At this point it might be useful to bear in mind the suggestions of feminist psychoanalysts who have reacted against the anti-feminism of Freudian and Lacanian analysis, particularly since the SF films I shall be discussing reproduce psychoanalytical narratives in a curiously accurate way. Luce Irigaray[4] has described Kate Horney's exposure of the concept of penis envy 'as a defensive symptom protecting the woman from the political, economic, social and cultural condition that is hers at the same time that it prevents her from contributing effectively to the transformation of her allotted fate'. More latterly, Hélène Cixous[5] has asked '[What] If it were to come out . . . that the logocentric project had always been undeniably to found (fund) phallocentrism, to insure for masculine order a rationale equal to history itself?' Both of these point to ways in which a particular historical paranoia about women taking an active generative part in a socioeconomic system could be contained by narratives in which men take over the role of production, and do so by eliminating from it any serious social power in the female role. In my discussion of John Carpenter's *Starman* (1984) and Ridley Scott's *Blade Runner* (1982) I shall intermittently be using Lacanian techniques of analysis, but only in the spirit of this perception. The relevance of this theoretical discourse, and the way it fits the narratives of these films, derives from its parallel investment in the naturalisation of male frames of reference. It should be seen as a descriptive tool, not an analytical one. I hope this first part of my discussion has helped to identify the material terms upon which we should read Hollywood's often uncanny re-production of 'a rationale equal to history itself'.

II

Feminist critics have long recognised that male creativity needs redefinition as a certain privileged access to structures of production. In terms of access to funding and technical resources you cannot get much more privileged than the Hollywood producer of an SF 'blockbuster' of the 1970s and 1980s. The virtuoso techniques of image-making to which I have already referred enabled the filmmaker to reassert his presence in a market for visual stimulation increasingly dominated by television and the pop culture. But such acts of assertion remain concerned with the kind of hidden ideological agenda I have been outlining. In this respect, discussions of postmodernism have been of some use in helping to characterise a particular link between the late 1970s/1980s and the 1950s. Steven Connor, discussing 'the collapse of the modernist ideology of style', identifies

> the nostalgia or retro film . . . [which] set[s] out to recreate not a particular historical setting but the cultural experience of a particular period, so that, in the cases of *Star Wars* and *Raiders of the Lost Ark*, what is being evoked is not an actual past but rather the kinds of narrative experience – the adventure story, the science fiction movie – that seem to typify the experience of the 1950s.[6]

But again he does not concern himself with what ideological interests this retrospection serves. A generation on, these 'narrative experiences' are stories told by the film industry to control the threatening anxieties embedded within the discourse of which it is both recording and repetition. Their narratives dominated by the cyclical structures of the patriarchal family, these films reveal both their obsession with and need to control the history of their own production. Like rehabilitated offenders on show, they have become part of the particular extension of those structures known as education. *Star Wars* and its subsequent sequels must have been very comforting films for postwar fathers, offering the children a vindication of the concept of heroic male agency in recognisably postwar terms: the contrasting but complementary poles of the adolescent idealist Luke Skywalker, striving to retrieve the legacy of his father's identity, and the freebooting, opportunistic 'mercenary' Han Solo come together to form a masculine analysis of significant social action which also has as its mission the containment – via hidden family ties with the one and romantic love for the other – of the initially politically and emotionally independent Leia. The mission involved in a narrative like this makes itself clear in the kind of audience construction which this film helped to pioneer. With films like *Star Wars* SF made a decided move away from the characteristic clientele for utopian fiction – relatively intellectual, adult and socially critical. This was an increasingly adolescent market: interest in this kind of filmmaking can be seen as an attempt to assert the Hollywood point of view over a voracious as yet relatively unformed consumer. The films I shall be looking at pick up the *Star Wars* audience a few years later: as such they can be seen to consolidate and extend its terms of social and political conditioning.

One of the most authoritative aspects of these rehabilitated SF narratives is their insistence on a positive, productive relationship with 'the world we live in': film actor Ronald Reagan was clearly aware of the force of this when he used the title *Star Wars* to project his fantasies about defence onto the realities of the US budget. Ostensibly, advanced techniques for image-making do enhance the utopian pretensions of these narratives, enabling the SF filmmaker to extend a capacity for realism. E. Ann Kaplan[7] has identified realism as 'the dominant Hollywood style . . . an apparent imitation of the social world we live in'. She has suggested that it 'hides the fact that a film is constructed and perpetuates the illusion that spectators are being shown what is "natural"'. As far as SF films are concerned it is equally important to stress what she calls 'the constructed nature of the image', because it is through this awareness that these films assert a selective control:

> Embedded in a particular social and institutional context, the cinema works to suppress discourse, to permit only certain 'speakers', only a certain speech. What critics call the enonciation of the cinema (its processes of saying) cannot be distinguished from the enonce (what is said).

In the films I am going to discuss, realism and constructedness work together in the interests of such a suppression. I now want to look in some detail at the narrative and technical means by which this is effected. As we shall see, the question of permission to speak becomes at times a critical issue in the resulting representation of the feminine.

III

Starman (1984) and *Blade Runner* (1982) differ significantly in that in the first the artificial life form is a man, in the second it is a woman. However, while they promote very different aspects of a definition of male stardom, there is absolutely no essential difference in the way this bears on the representation of women. In both, masculinity is presented as 'real' – natural and naturally productive, femininity as constructed – the product. In fact the ability of these two films to reach the same position along such different routes is part of how inescapable that position appears to be.

Starman is an interesting parallel to *A Star is Born* in its use of a distinctly cinematic form of parthenogenesis. Here too the title has a peculiarly symbiotic relationship with the ideological subtext of the film industry's working structures, but in this case its two terms are statically oppositional, setting up a mythical antithesis between the transcendental and the material. This stasis is itself a form of privilege, freeing the concept of male stardom from the containing determinisms of social processes. Such a freedom is given full expression within the text.

A mythical quality was certainly something that the star of this film, Jeff Bridges, could bring to the project. Already a star in his own right, stardom was also a legacy to which he had been born. He is a 'second generation' actor with a father well-known in television work in the 1950s and 1960s, who continues to make films intermittently with his sons – sometimes *as* their father. In fact Bridges is a star in whose characteristic narrative role the economic potential of patriarchal structures receives full development. His films are frequently concerned with the theme of filial relations, and with the special forms of empowering that the role of son can offer. Often this has specifically material concerns: *Stay Hungry* (1976); *Success* (1979); *Winter Kills* (1979) and *Jagged Edge* (1985) are all concerned with the nature of heirdom as a form of agency. *Starman* elides the distinction between stardom and heirdom in a peculiar compression of patrilinearity: Bridges has a role which is effectively as the son of himself becoming his own father. The 'Starman transformation' scene, in which he creates himself as Starman out of cinematic images of himself, offers a striking visual realisation of this intensely self-investing mode of production and reproduction.

Starman manifests himself on earth in the form of Scott, the dead husband of Jenny Hayden (Karen Allen). Before this happens Scott's 'star'-like qualities have already been made clear as she yearningly watches a home movie of him. The film thus begins with a film: the Starman is a star in the *role* of a man before he becomes a man pretending not to be a star. The excitement of this tension – and its underlying erotic capital – is brought out in comments that emphasise the unlikely symbiosis between the two:

'Do you seriously expect me to tell the President that an alien has landed, assumed the identity of a dead house painter from Madison Wisconsin and is presently out tooling around the countryside in a hocked-up orange and black 1977 Mustang?'

says George Fox, the security chief who is trying to track him down. Starman learns to handle sex by watching Burt Lancaster on a hotel TV. 'I never knew it could be like this', the woman says. Good sex, of course is never anything to do with a woman. The insistence on this exclusively masculine aspect of the star's powers is already obvious in the 'transformation': Starman produces himself as a baby that immediately becomes an adult, thus bypassing any active female generative or nurturing agency just as later in the film he makes Jenny Hayden pregnant despite the fact that she's incapable of conception.

The same bypass is evident in his language-learning activities. Of course it's Jenny's language that he imitates, but he doesn't really *learn* it from her. There is a comic gap between the comprehensibility of her explanations and his capacity to reproduce her phrases in an appropriate way at telling moments. One such moment comes at the end when Starman is about to rejoin his countrymen and needs to establish the linguistic basis for a final separation:

'Tell me again how to say goodbye.'
'Kiss me and tell me you love me.'
'I love you.' (He kisses her.)

He directs the scene; he simply allows her to script it. Despite the flimsy plot device of a recording sent into space on Voyager II, from which he has assimilated a working acquaintance with the surface structures of English, Starman's language is essentially self-generating. We shouldn't give any thought to how many times he's had to play and replay the record to get the hang of it: here repetition is unproblematically elevated to the level of performance. Starman's skills are mimetic – and to recast mimesis as a process that gives masculinity priority not only over the capacity for meaning within discourse but also over an essential linguistic productivity takes us back to sixteenth-century humanist thinking – which suggests something of the political and economic scope of stardom as a social role. (It's perhaps worth bearing in mind that Bridges got an Oscar nomination for this part.) Feminist critics of Renaissance intellectual history have made clear just exactly how economically motivated humanist thinking was. Jenny Hayden's response to Starman is kept within boundaries that even those early humanists would have found distinctly limited as a basis for female agency. It is insistently intimate: no social morality or intellectual curiosity for her. The journey she takes with him across the United States – an atmospheric recording of this Hollywood topos of personal self-discovery – is for Jenny simply a journey into her body: towards the baby that will give her a future. Significantly there is no engagement with the social implications for her of all this: unlike *Blade Runner*, this film evades the representation of work completely. We don't know whether Jenny works or how she could support a baby or relate to society as a single parent. A reference to a piece of early-seventeenth-century popular culture shows how regressive this narrative is. The relationship between Caliban and Miranda in Shakespeare's *The Tempest* – identified now as science fiction not only by Renaissance scholars[8] but also (perhaps more authoritatively) in its transformation into what has been heralded as the 'cult' musical *Return to the Forbidden Planet* – clearly specifies the active teaching role taken by Miranda, the significance of Caliban's sexual response to it, and of both these for the roles they both play in the higher socioeconomic stakes with which Prospero is playing. Caliban mistakes his position in this relationship as a generative one: he has tried to 'rape' Miranda and is enslaved for it. His colonised status, and the role of language within it, thus becomes explicit. Interestingly, the treatment of these themes in *Starman* fudges colonialist issues in particular, and in doing so it reveals the way – in a culture in which 'postwar' is synonymous with 'Cold War' – the Hollywood SF film used gender as a second front to deal with broader tensions about transgressive outsiders.

In this respect, Starman's role performs an interesting piece of work, one which shows just how privileged masculinity can be, even when it takes the form of an 'invader'. The film's colonialist 'sympathies' are developed through the young ET investigator, Mark Shermin, whose presence in the film gives expression to a deceptively elevated post-imperialist discursive idiom. When he finally comes face to face with Starman, his colonialist's curiosity gives way to a specious altruism: 'there are so many things I'd like to ask you . . . is there anything I can do for *you*?' There is a curious effect at work here. The parallelism between Shermin and Jenny's attendance on Starman sets up a strategic confusion within the analysis of desire in this film, one which elevates the masculine to the level of disinterested social exploration and at the same time relegates Jenny to the inarticulate and sub-political. In its elision of the difference between stardom and alienation, the terms of the cultural consumption of the 'other' in this film camouflage its positioning of the female – abjection to a transcendent masculinity located mythically *within* that culture. In a sense, it's more important to be male than it is to be American, although in fact this film illustrates the way the concept of representation at the service of stardom offers a release from the embarassment of that particular logic, making it possible for masculinity to be seen as essentially American, a function of Americanness. The circularity of this shows how deeply and essentially femininity is itself the very type of the 'other'.

There is not much about the way 'the gaze' is treated in this film that might encourage us to think otherwise. Karen Allen should have the defining gaze: as the film begins, she is, like us, watching a film. The cognitive role this establishes should give her a lot of power over the inexperienced being that takes the form of the man whose image she now possesses. But in fact this image possesses her. Her gaze at the beginning is balanced by the one that ends the film, as she watches Starman disappear: it is a gaze kept in place by his. In that first scene her gaze into the film is simply a rather furtive reconstruction of the gaze that she is more legitimately performing within the film: at him, as they sing together. Allen seems in fact to have been cast as much as anything for her amazingly large and liquid eyes. In fact she never actually seems to see anything. Her look is always somehow a seeing of what's not there: her husband. At its most intense it passively imitates a sustained *active* feature of Starman's gaze: he doesn't blink. As with language, so it is with gaze; only *his* is generative. And this too is seen as deriving from his powers of mimesis. Having realised human form, the alien switches on the home movie that Jenny has been watching, watches Jeff Bridges fool expertly around with a gun, imitates equally expertly – and shatters the mirror into which he had previously directed a first self-realising gaze. So much for the mirror phase. Feminist critics should be so lucky.

I have suggested how frequently heirdom features in the narratives of Jeff Bridges' films. The alien's legacy to Jenny isn't just the baby that will be born: there is also the glowing ball which will enable the boy (of course) to make contact with his own 'star' destiny. All this echoes the way economic advantage re-emerges in a symbolic form in Bridges' films. Star status works as both investment and dividend: father and son of itself. As I've suggested, such a narrative shows how the film industry's particular resource – the production of images – can help contain any potential leakage within its system, even as it reinforces that containment with a 'universality' that enables it to provide the same service for its audience.

IV

Blade Runner offers an emphasis less on the star itself than on the star system as a whole. This is partly the result of the placing of the star within the narrative – as a narrator, precisely, which makes him at once both central and transparent: an observer that is pretending *not* to be a point of view. It is from this careful positioning that Harrison Ford derives most of his power in this film.

It is not in fact an unusual form of positioning for this particular star. Ford's narrative role tends to work in an almost opposite way to that of Bridges. As an actor entering Hollywood, he came from 'nowhere', and in the formative stages of his career his 'image' was characterised by a marked *absence* of social and familial pre-positioning. Early roles exploit a certain charismatic isolation, although this, like the very different situation in Bridges' films, is seen to have characteristic economic implications: it has its own form of capital. As Han Solo in the *Star Wars* trilogy he is, as we have seen, a mercenary who is at first detached from the 'positive' familial values represented (unknowingly) by Luke and Leia; love for Leia brings him back within the fold. Ford continued to play roles in which isolation plays against the impetus towards deeper socialisation. Sometimes his films end with a 'tragic' exclusion from such participation; sometimes – as in *Witness* (1985) and *Mosquito Coast* (1986) – they play with his 'principled' involvement in values which fail to realise themselves in a difficult or corrupt society. In the light of my observations in section II it's interesting that as his career progresses his roles have begun to display more social and personal attachments, particularly of the fatherly kind. The latest *Indiana Jones*, offering the two-star partnership of Ford and Sean Connery, proclaimed: 'This time he's bringing his Dad.' It's worth noting the complementary function of the father/son relationship within this marketing strategy: the earlier film *Blade Runner* also offers a two-star structure (Ford and Rutger Hauer) but it is a competitive one, one that results in the survival of Ford at Hauer's expense, thus providing a narrative that reinforces the marketing focus on the single star.

This balance between inclusion and exclusion has produced some interesting narratives: screenplays which play with ideas about inner and outer communities, membership and alienation. One might say that Ford's narrative role is compatible with a high degree of 'textuality', or internal textual coherence. One result of this is that he has been associated with 'clever' films with high production values. But high production values – Barry King[9] has noted their function as a distribution strategy – are not necessarily the same as high moral values, although again they may be packaged as such, and that is indeed the case with *Blade Runner*. In fact, when stardom is the item on offer, it's depressing to note just how similar the hidden agenda of the 'good' film will be to that of a 'bad' one, which is one of the points of my comparison between these two particular films.

Blade Runner is based on Philip K. Dick's novel *Do Androids Dream of Electric Sheep?*[10] which explicitly takes on some of the issues which glimmer fitfully across the surface of *Starman*: the question of empathy between human and non-human life forms; its implications for ethical and moral decisions about social living. But it differs enormously from the novel, and the ways in which it does so change its direction seriously from a text that deals with gender in a relatively demystifying way to a text that ultimately endorses a highly conventional positioning of femininity.

Like *Starman*, *Blade Runner* is a story of a woman 'made' by a man; of how the woman gains entry to the Symbolic Order through the rejection of a supposed unity with an illusory mother and an acceptance of the defining status of 'the law of the father' via a submission to the demands of male sexuality. *Blade Runner* aligns itself with the anti-feminist values of this analytical approach by suggesting that such a submission is the only way for a woman to 'make it'. Rachael (Sean Young) is a 'replicant' (Dick calls them androids) who doesn't actually know that she is a replicant until she becomes involved with Deckard, the Blade Runner (Harrison Ford), whose job it is to 'retire' these life forms when they get out of line. Significantly, this knowledge is negotiated through the introduction to sexuality, and a relationship with Deckard replaces the unreal past she has lost: implanted memories of a mother, and early 'experiences' of her female body (which include realising she doesn't have a penis). There is thus a link between Rachael finding out that she is artificial and becoming real through it: a situation which reflects quite accurately the Lacanian approach to the problematics of the female Imaginary. Deckard's power over this balance is expressed in the equation between the development of their relationship and his revelation that Rachael doesn't have a 'termination date'. Clearly the particular kind of entry into the Symbolic that one achieves through a star is of a transcendent kind, as we have already seen in *Starman*.

But it should be observed that beneath this intensely 'psychoanalytical' narrative there is an implicit concern with the working structures of the film industry itself. *Blade Runner* makes general use of the representation of work, but doesn't come clean about its interest in this. For a start it uses its star in a fairly evasive way. I observed earlier that Harrison Ford's role is a transparent one: much of the charisma of this film is displaced from star to location. But that inevitably feeds back into the concept of stardom – the setting, Los Angeles, is the point of entry for this transcendental dimension, and an association between the male object of desire and LA itself is an essential aspect of the economic operation of stardom. The star focuses the meaning of a privileged workplace, and vice versa. It could be suggested that stardom essentially has such connotations: 'stardom' is to 'star' as 'kingdom' is to 'king' – a metonymic extension of a certain form of power from person to place. And in both cases uncertainty about which way the metonymy goes is part of its effect.

Self-consciousness about LA as a workplace dominates *Blade Runner*, and although it is represented in 'realistically' futurist terms the sense of place dominating this film is clearly the classic sense of place of Hollywood cinema. This is still the Dream Machine. The film is structured around ideas of image-making: LA is where the genetic designer Tyrell and his assistant the toymaking J. F. Sebastian are located. It's where the replicants come to seek the secret of immortality. The value of these creative activities becomes specifically masculine in their alignment with

Deckard's male violence as the Blade Runner, which has the function of preserving the absolute distinction between 'reality' and the copy. The connection between these two areas of the film echoes the work done on behalf of the film industry in general by the idea of masculinity (and conversely on behalf of masculinity in general by the film industry). It enables the star to be seen as the 'maker', rather than the structures of production that surround the making of the film. This provides a self-protecting, self-perpetuating mystification of the analysis of agency within the system. At the end Deckard is told: 'You've done a man's job, sir', which resonates across the making of Rachael as a 'woman' as well as the unmaking of Roy Baty as a replicant. In fact Baty predetermines his elimination by trying to compete as a potential maker. He begins the final showdown with the challenge: 'Show me what you're made of ' – a competitive star structure that hints that the basis of this contention is that fundamental investment, the star's performance. (The concept of performance as an aestheticised transformation of masculine interests is a central issue in this film, as in *Starman*, and one to which I shall return shortly.) Here, as in *Starman*, female sexuality is used to displace the anxieties of that competition. Like Baty, Rachael is an outsider, but she's let in to show there *isn't* a principle at stake. The selection of the term 'retirement' to describe the destruction of a replicant is intended to point out the ironies of fine metaphysical distinctions concerning the definition of 'life', but its connotations about employment are perhaps more significant. It offers replicants a symbolic participation within the working structures of human life, to which they have never been admitted, *after* it's too late for them to do so.

Blade Runner neatly sidesteps these issues by turning LA into the place 'real' people don't want to be. It implies a split between LA and the world of film through its own particular version of the colonial theme, the process of demonisation as disavowal procedure: 'it's not that we won't let you in, it's just that we think you'd be happier somewhere else'. When Deckard hears that the replicants have returned to LA, he expresses surprise that they want to come back knowing they will be killed, a logic that coexists uneasily with the fact that he's apparently very good at his job. In LA 2019, the Dream Machine itself is somewhere else: 'A new life awaits *you* in the Off World Colonies: a chance to begin again in a golden land of opportunity and adventure.' The rhetoric is unmistakably Westward Ho.

But while in realist terms this broadcast from a huge hovering video machine opens up a gap between LA 2019 and the Eldorado of the twentieth century, its implications as both message and image close it. When a realist sense of place is applied to Hollywood itself what it has to be realist about is its constructedness – and this is a constructedness which works as much in the interests of masculine power as that of *Starman*. Indeed, if the coolness of Ford's human role in a film filled with more extrovert artificial life forms could be said to lose some of the performance advantages available to Jeff Bridges, he clearly recoups all that and more in a special relationship with this setting. Here, the techniques and technologies of film making are 'naturalised' as features of the physical environment of LA: place becomes location. Lighting is significant; the first images of the film flash out of the blackness of an empty screen as a spout of flame shoots upwards into the twilight of the twenty-first century. High-contrast, deeply angled lighting plays constantly across the city: it has become a massive film lot illuminated by 'low-key' lighting, that basic ingredient of *film noir*, a genre to which this film is closely related.

Film noir has always had its own special relationship with the Los Angeles area; its balance of moral compromise and filmic style is the tradition within which the narrative idiom of *Blade Runner* is placed. But its main contribution is the way it recasts the uncharismatic character of Dick's Rick Deckard by placing him within a prestigious form of cinematic narrative – providing him with the linguistic and behavioural style which establishes his position within the narrative as that of a controlling authenticity. It also establishes the frames of reference for a conception of performance which is essentially anti-feminist. A consideration of the film's representation of the gaze will help us see how this is worked out within the film.

As I have said, Deckard's position as narrator to some extent masks the omniscience of his point of view. Visually, the emphasis throughout is on the replicants' gaze, but it is an emphasis that confirms Deckard's defining status in the narrative. For since replicants are constructed, their gaze is constructed too; fragmented, broken up, never whole – the film is full of isolated images of eyes, and of eyes as objects. Consequently their gaze is seen as essentially 'belonging' to someone else. In a sense Baty's primary mission is to gain control of his visual experience: he says to the Japanese eye designer: 'If only you could see what I have seen with your eyes'; and to Deckard he laments the visions that will evaporate in his death: 'I've seen things you people wouldn't believe . . . I've watched sea beams glitter in the dark . . . all these moments will be lost in time'.

But whilst we share his heroic contempt for Leon's dependence on false visual memories – photos – we are directed towards a different response to Rachael's photo of her mother – and this is a significant split in our response. This question of fragmentariness reflects the theory of the Imaginary, in which the child constructs itself as a 'whole' from its own mirror image and as a result begins the process of identifying itself as an 'other', which leads to the entry into the Symbolic Order and the completed identification with the masculine identity which can provide the effect of that self-unification. We saw Starman getting over this difficult phase with remarkable ease. The point about the replicants is that, unlike humans for whom the 'law of the father' is the basic condition of entry into society, they are actually forbidden entry even though they must operate within its terms. From this point of view their psychic conditions of existence are fundamentally *feminine*. It is significant that the narrative, whilst prepared to allow them an elegaically heroic status, refuses assertive 'male' attempts to take control of their desire and gives permission only to the 'female' that seeks such control in the only way that society permits it: through passive identification with a man. But what are the implications of this when what is under consideration is the particular form of entry that is represented by work?

One of the things dropped from Dick's novel is *his* policeman's overwhelming and rather petty concern with pay. Ford's Deckard has all the conscious economic marginality of a *noir* gumshoe, but he also has his more elevated sense of being part of a story. *Blade Runner* offers the characteristic *noir* analogy between the detective's business – detection – and the plot of the film. That analogy transforms routine and repetition (Deckard has five 'retirements' to do, and he doesn't want to do any of them) into teleology. Indeed, the impetus towards this transformation is seen in the very creation of the replicants to relieve 'real' humanity of precisely those degrading forms of labour, even whilst the mode of production that brings them into being has the essential form of such work. In the replicant, the process of replication achieves a complex transference: it is present in Rachael's recognition that she is not a member of a firm that makes replicants but rather one of the products, and consequently the potential victim of a quality-control process that insists on one hand that the latter be indistinguishable from the former, and on the other that it be kept distinct: 'I'm not *in* the business, I *am* the business.' But she is not aware of the further significance of the gender to which she has been constructed: that process of transference reduplicates itself within the replicant species in its internal subdivision into male and female. We have something like this in *Starman* in the way masculinity is seen to have priority over femininity even when that masculinity is embodied in an outsider. Like Deckard, replicant 'men' have a teleological momentum – even Leon, who initially has a menial job at Tyrell's. We're told that he and Baty are trying to infiltrate in order to get information, so he's actually *performing* being a menial. But the position of Zhora – the first female replicant to get 'retired' – is very different. She has a job which the plot fails to link up with the infiltration scheme. It thus has no apparent connection with her long-term interests. And she is a striptease artist – a performer whose mode of performance is calculated to ensure an unfavourable comparison with the values set up by the masculine version of the activity. Moral values are used to reinforce such a comparison: in order to gain entry to her dressing room, Ford poses as a representative of a 'committee on moral abuses' – trying to make sure there are no peepholes into the artists' changing rooms. But this parodic moral stance has a genuine status within the film. It conforms to a consistent aspect of Harrison Ford's narrative role, his reticent, rather shamefast male gaze. He turns away from the spectacle of Zhora's act with her snake in disgust, and a metaphor in the background commentary gives traditional status to his rejection: 'Watch her take the pleasure from the serpent that once corrupted men'.

In fact this moral point of view is the source of Ford's control of both gaze and narrative; as the film insists on the fragmentariness of what is essentially a female position, and forces quite literally into unemployment those that refuse that definition, it sets him up as unified, coherent, structured by principles. From this point of view he doesn't actually need to be seen to be working, because he embodies the containing structure of law that gives meaning to that work. He also embodies the principle of mercy which allows Rachael to live, and it is not surprising to find this socialised version of masculine sexual desire directing its redeeming powers at a female figure whose 'employment' is carefully 'domesticated' within the pseudo-familial structure of the Tyrell Corporation.

A feature of those redeeming powers is a relation of linguistic coercion which, like that between Starman and Jenny, conceals its meaning as desire beneath the 'meaningfulness' of romance. Deckard makes Rachael 'own up' to her desire for him. First he forces a sexual response from her, taking her through a catechism that is similar to Starman's ritual of parting:

'Say "kiss me".'
'Kiss me.'
'Say "I want you".'
'I want you.'

Rachael continues unprompted: 'Put your hands on me.' Like Starman's, Deckard's linguistic education of Rachael has given her a body. After 'retiring' Baty, Deckard comes back to claim her, taking control of a continued existence which now depends entirely on him:

'Do you love me?'
'I love you.'
'Do you trust me?'
'I trust you.'

What is entailed in such a trust is made more explicit in Baty's story. He tries to take control of the 'desire' represented by language, to take possession of language's constant deferral of meaning by trying to become real – to stay alive. He lets Deckard live because he wants to talk to someone as he dies. Deckard's comments on this systematically unfocus the self-constructing force of this quest, and its validity: 'All they wanted was the same answers the rest of us want. Where do I come from? Where am I going? How long have I got?' The voiceover doesn't comment on the fact that its own presence at the end of the narrative has a necessary excluding relation to theirs. As we saw in *Starman*, successful programmes of demonisation often allow themselves the luxury of retrospective acts of empathy.

The American star system does a particular kind of symbolic

work for a culture founded on a concept of an egalitarian 'enterprise' economy but which also seeks in its own interests to limit opportunities to work within that economy. A film is safe in offering limited rights of entry on the basis of sexuality to a selected woman when what it really seeks to do is exclude the challenge of which the woman is a symbol – of what is feared, as well as of the qualities and experiences that need to be accepted by women if they are to provide the behaviour which makes such fears unnecessary. The characteristic SF concern with constructedness is used in these two films to provide narratives which reinforce exactly what SF has in its power to challenge: cultural myths about the naturalisation of masculinity. Clearly, the SF narrative topos of artificial or synthetic life forms is not in itself sufficient to challenge the terms of the issues it raises. What I have been discussing is in one sense a rejection of the kind of project that underlies the 'genuine' utopian narrative: the humanist insistence on fiction's ability to suspend the 'absolute' conditions created by social history. But in another, it is an endorsement of the hidden agenda of that tradition; that the exploration of the extents of human possibility must have rigorously predetermined conditions ensuring the perpetuation of the interests of that part of the population to whom it is speaking. It is not a question that women are simply or naively excluded from such stories; more that their inclusion is an essential element of the way the process of exclusion is operated. They are not of course the only victims of this process; as I have suggested, there were other outsiders to whom it was also applied in the post-war period. But they remain the most deeply articulated symbol for it and consequently continue to be placed by a vocabulary of containment whose conditions of employment are still a basic feature of our social contract.

NOTES

1 Brian Stableford, 'Robots', in Peter Nichols (ed.), *The Encyclopaedia of Science Fiction*, London, Granada, 1981, 503–5.
2 For an influential account of processes of replication and repetition, see Walter Benjamin, 'The work of art in the age of mechanical reproduction', *Illuminations*, trans. Harry Zohn, London, Fontana, 1970. A general discussion of these ideas is provided in Steven Connor, *Postmodernist Culture: An Introduction to Theories of the Contemporary*, Oxford, Blackwell, 1989; references later in the paragraph are

to his sections on 'Postmodern TV, video and film' and 'Feminism and postmodernism'.

3 Cathy Klaprat, 'The star as market strategy: Bette Davis in another light', in Tino Balio (ed.), *The American Film Industry*, Madison, University of Wisconsin Press, 1985, 351–76; quotations from Warner publicity are taken from this article.

4 Luce Irigaray, *This Sex Which Is Not One*, trans. Catherine Porter, Ithaca, NY, Cornell University Press, 1985.

5 From Elaine Marks and Isabelle de Courtrivon, *New French Feminisms*, Brighton, Harvester, 1981, 92–3.

6 Connor, op. cit., 176–7.

7 E. Ann Kaplan, *Women and Film*, London, Methuen, 1983, 12–13.

8 David Norbrook refers to 'Shakespeare's pioneering science fiction' in his article 'What cares these roarers for the name of king?', forthcoming in a collection of conference papers from the Politics of Romance conference, Oxford, 1988.

9 Barry King, 'Stardom as an occupation', in Paul Kerr (ed.), *The Hollywood Film Industry*, London, Routledge & Kegan Paul, 1986.

10 Philip K. Dick, *Do Androids Dream of Electric Sheep?*, London, Rapp & Whiting, 1969, republished as *Blade Runner*, London, Panther, 1982.

Part III

Readers and Writers: SF as Genre Fiction

Chapter 10

Writing science fiction for the teenage reader

Gwyneth Jones

From the writer's point of view serious teenage fiction presents an interesting problem. Notoriously, one of the worst mistakes you can make as a children's writer is to 'talk down' to the reader: the best and most successful writer addresses an 8 year old as one human being to another. To re-enter the subjective world of the adolescent is much more difficult (to be compared perhaps with trying to project yourself into a constant state of having just walked into a chair in the dark; a world of convinced and continually outraged solipsism; of persecution, helplessnes and smouldering despair). Although the average 15 year old will not spend all of her or his time being an adolescent – like the rest of us she may experience a whole range of ages in a day: feeling quite childish at breakfast, at lunch rather world-weary and middle-aged – at the same time she or he is undergoing an uniquely painful and absorbing experience which has its own language, its own preoccupations, its own heightened range of emotions.

The bulk of juvenile SF, however, has traditionally been indistinguishable from the adult product except in the notional ages of the characters. Simple boys' own adventure between the stars, like girls' own romance, caters for the teenager by sidestepping the inner turmoil and offering a welcome relief. But since the rite of passage experience – a human protagonist's difficult entry into a larger world – is one of SF's most thoughtfully developed themes, there is a sense (apart from the usual derogatory one) in which the genre may be regarded as the quintessential fiction of adolescence. The conventions of SF allow, even require, that its thrills should always be laced with metaphysics – no starship epic without its burden of cosmic truth. SF is therefore ideally equipped to present in fiction an adventure with *meaning*: the kind of exteriorised and concrete rite of passage no longer provided in most societies of the developed world. Alongside the escape route, the young reader may also receive a much needed explication of the emotional maze that he is treading – a heightened self-image to hang onto until he emerges, bloodied and scarified, on the other side.

I use the male pronoun advisedly, because in the classic model of (juvenile) SF, the candidates for adulthood are invariably male. However this does not mean that girl readers have been excluded. A young woman with a healthy appetite for adventure and for self-determined achievement may find a great deal to enjoy in these stories. The icons of physical and technical competence are helpfully stripped of their usual gender-specific labels (football, motorbikes); and due to the prudery of patriarchy whereby a girl is a junior *female* but a boy is a junior person, the plot rarely hinges on a logically reversed version of the girl-gets-boy teen romance. Accepting a male protagonist on the printed page does not mean accepting one's own absence. Indeed the almost total absence of female characters makes simpler the imaginative sleight of hand whereby the teenage girl substitutes *herself* for the male initiate in these stories.

The *feminisation* of juvenile SF – a movement towards more thoughtful characterisation, higher literary standards and more female characters – may have done girl readers a positive disservice. This movement, which may be considered as roughly contemporaneous with the same developments in the adult genre, is generally associated with the emergence of certain highly effective women writers. But women writing teenage SF does not necessarily mean a better deal for girls. I shall now examine two popular and admired SF novels of this 'feminised' model, one explicitly written for younger readers and one with a teenage protagonist, and see how the young woman as central character fares in each case.

Madeleine l'Engle's *A Wrinkle In Time*[1] won the coveted Newbery Medal when it first appeared in 1962 and has remained a favourite, constantly reprinted. Its heroine, Meg Murry, is the 13-year-old daughter of a famous physicist who has disappeared on a mysterious mission. Between the braces on her teeth, her failures in the classroom and her schoolmates' snide gossip about her missing father, Meg is having a miserable time. In the humiliating situation of the (supposedly) abandoned wife, her mother, who is also a scientist but 'a beauty as well' (p. 16), maintains a serene and composed reserve. Meg's most comfortable relationship is with her baby brother, a 6 year old of prodigious intellect and semi-telepathic powers. The baby brother, Charles Wallace, has discovered three 'witches' living in a haunted house in the woods. It transpires that these witches, super-powered beings who eventually identify themselves as messengers of God (angels, in other words), have come to help Meg and her brother to rescue their father. An experiment in faster-than-light travel has led him to fall into the power of the 'Dark Thing', a force of ultimate evil which is keeping him prisoner on a distant planet. The children must 'tesser' – take a short cut through the fifth dimension across space and time – to reach him. Before the quest begins another character appears: Calvin O'Keefe, a 14-year-old basketball star who is, like Charles Wallace, a genius and emergent telepath. Calvin comes from a poor family – emotionally as well as materially impoverished – and is overjoyed at his escape into the Murrys' richer world. A romance immediately develops between Calvin and Meg.

'Do you know, this is the first time I've seen you without your glasses?'

'I'm blind as a bat without them. I'm near-sighted, like father.'

'Well, you know what, you've got dreamboat eyes,' Calvin said. 'Listen, you go right on wearing your glasses. I don't think I want anybody else to see what gorgeous eyes you have.' (p. 52)

Then, guided by the angels, the three children tesser to the planet of evil in search of the lost scientist. The rest of this transparent fable of the Cold War unfolds predictably. The mindless, regimented collectivism of the world of the Dark Thing almost triumphs; the child prodigy Charles falls into temptation through pride and all is almost lost; but through love and stubborn individuality, and with God (represented by the three angels) firmly on her side, Meg wins through to the happy ending.

The characterisation of Meg Murry, the sulky and passionate ugly duckling, is vivid and engaging. The science content of the book may be slight, and always subordinate to l'Engle's particular brand of ideological metaphysics, but it does feature a girl who is at home – notionally at least – with maths and physics. And though it is actually quite hard to recall this after the end of the story,[2] it *is* Meg alone who achieves the rescue. The quest and the victory are hers. As the viewpoint character she suffers in comparison with the two boys in that their fears and doubts are not shown. They remain the traditional boy-heroes, smooth and blank as pebbles, so that Meg's *human* weaknesses must appear to be attached to her gender. But at least she is allowed to struggle against the role of eternal weakling.

> She wanted to reach out and grab Calvin's hand, but it seemed that ever since they had begun their journeyings she had been looking for a hand to hold, so she stuffed her fists into her pockets and walked along behind the two boys – I've got to be brave, she said to herself. I will be. (p. 119)

The betrayal of the fictional Meg Murry and her readers is not in the depiction of the character herself, but in her automatic, tacit subordination. We are told that Meg is a genuine ugly duckling. Her awkwardness masks a considerable intellect, her spectacles conceal gorgeous eyes: she will blossom. The two boys, however, are more than considerable. They are *geniuses*: orders of magnitude above poor Meg, as far above her as she is above the miserable O'Keefes. The crude meritocracy of l'Engle's world view masks here a true fable. Every adolescent feels struggling inside herself or himself secret, unrecognised powers – the mysterious promise of adulthood. But Meg is cheated. She has the right stuff, but not enough of it and it is not of the right kind. It is notable that the 'secret power', by means of which she successfully survives her ritual trial, is a conventionally womanly power: her love for the wilful baby boy. Indeed her feeling towards her brother seems deliberately calculated to inculcate the bright girl reader's proper nutritive and reverent attitude towards Man: 'the baby who was so much more than she was, and who was yet so utterly vulnerable' (p. 181).

Like her mother, the beautiful scientist whose lab ajoins the kitchen and whose role is to wait for her husband, she is destined to find fulfilment not in travel through the fifth dimension, but in a serene acceptance of second place.

Alexei Panshin's *Rite of Passage* (1968)[3] is a novel of a very different kind. Here the semi-mystical voyaging of l'Engle's fable is subsumed into a fictional journey into adulthood as concrete and 'realistic' as possible. A hundred and fifty years after the self-destruction of an overpopulated earth, the human race is divided into a minority of technocrats who live in the giant 'ships' – starships in the form of hollowed asteroids – and the less privileged but far more numerous inhabitants of a hundred colony worlds. Mia Havero is a ship dweller. Like every child of the ships, where overpopulation is a continual fear, she must earn the right to adult life through a literal trial. She will be dropped into the wilderness on the surface of one of the colony worlds and left to survive there as best she can for thirty days: and it is understood that a reasonable percentage of candidates will not come home.

Rite of Passage is a classic of the genre, winner of the Science Fiction Writers of America award for the best SF novel of its year (the Nebula award).[4] Due to the nature of their subject matter many science fiction novels suffer from built-in obsolescence: the future as imagined from 1968 may in many ways seem out of date twenty years later. But the quality of Panshin's writing does much to mitigate this effect, and the depiction of believable human life in the closed ship-world remains absorbing reading. Moreover, it transpires that the ritual 'trial' has wider implications that are made fully available to the adolescent reader. At first it is presented, as it seems to Mia, as a simple adventure: the reader begins to wonder why so many well-equipped and survival-trained teenagers fail to live through a month's camping holiday. But the difficult relationship between the ships and the colony worlds has been signalled. The technocrats keep the scientific heritage of old earth to themselves, doling out trade goods so carefully that the colonists, though they have the only access to natural raw materials, cannot escape from a life of laborious subsistence. This uneven balance is maintained, when necessary, by massive and brutal intervention. Mia the child has never questioned the wisdom of this arrangement, but when her time of trial finally arrives it soon becomes clear that the only serious danger the young initiates have to face comes from disaffected colonials. Mia's boyfriend is captured. Mia tries to rescue him and in the subsequent embroglio they kill a man and uncover a budding anti-ship rebellion. Through this experience Mia comes to understand that the despised 'mudeaters' are human, that they hate her, and that (though she is forced to fight them for her life) their bitterness is justified. At the close of Panshin's story there are no solutions in sight, but a dynamic of continuing development has been established. The adolescent's successful journey has not been to the false close of a happy ending, but a genuine entry into a larger sphere of action.

In some ways, *Rite of Passage* is a model example of science fiction writing for adolescents. The tone is never didactic. There is a direct assurance in the presence of the first-person narrator which is instantly convincing: Mia may be technically a junior citizen but she never considers herself an incomplete person. As is frequently the case, the science in this fiction is not where the reader might expect to find it. Not much understanding of physics or cosmology will be gained from consideration of the hollowed asteroid or its means of travel through 'discontinuity'. And yet the book teaches, for the problems it discusses are those of our world, as well as Mia's. The difficulties of life in a closed environment (such as the surface of one small planet) are tackled: and the simple diagram of a colonial system in action is thought-provoking, stimulating and contentious.

Furthermore, Mia Havero appears completely unburdened by the ideological baggage of 'femininity' which Madeleine l'Engle imposes on her heroine right from the start. She has no dependents and few superiors, she even enjoys the highly ungirlish privilege of being disliked and not worrying too much about it. She is physically daring and temperamentally quarrelsome, her intellectual ability is unhampered by mysterious mental blocks or abject self-doubt. At the same time she is not a heroic pebble but a creature of thought and feeling, openly emotional and (sometimes) responsive to the needs of others. In short, Mia is neither a girl nor a boy: she seems to represent an ideal of unconditioned young personhood. Even the inevitable boyfriend does not seriously dent her autonomy.

But there are problems. In *A Wrinkle in Time* Meg Murry is surrounded by females in positions of power, albeit always secondary power – the angels, her mother. Mia is completely alone. Her father is chairman of the Ship's Council while her mother is absent, reportedly 'difficult', and has no job but just a scorned artistic hobby. Her tutor is a man; his wife only appears when she brings in the food. Among her peers she is a tomboy among the cissy girls; and the only other adult woman with a role in the story is an irresponsibly fecund criminal, justly (and Mia concurs with this view) sentenced to banishment.

Given this background, it comes as no surprise when Mia's
lonely idyll of equality begins to break down, and the underlying
assumptions of the writer and his world show through. The actual
menarche passes with a formal nod: 'I had my first menstrual
period . . . a sign that I was growing up but that's about all you
can say for it' (p. 118). But thereafter Mia becomes, as if Panshin
considers this inevitable, deeply interested in clothes, and
intensely concerned that she should be recognised as a girl. Her
relationship with her boyfriend Jimmy Dentremont changes. By
the time they set out on the trial she has become the dependent
partner. Her role in the violent climax, though courageous and
active, is clearly that of a *woman*. It transpires that, contrary to
previous evidence, Mia is squeamish about violence while Jimmy,
though by nature 'a more humane, open person' (p. 223), is
immediately successful as a killer. Somehow he has the right to
take human life, while Mia does not, and by exercising that right
before her solemn and wondering eyes he seems to set the seal
on his superiority.

> 'I did not blame Jimmy at all. If I had been able to act, I
> would have done as he had, simply in order to stay alive.
> And . . . it cost him greatly to shoot that man. If I had the
> opportunity I would make the proposal that no man should be
> killed except by somebody who knows him well enough for the
> act to have impact. . . . Death is important enough that it should
> affect the person who causes it.' (p. 223)

On Mia and Jimmy's return, the council votes that this dangerously rebellious colony should be annihilated. The young people
are appalled, but only by the inhuman scale of the punishment.
The rule here is survival of the fittest, and the ability to kill, not
in anger but as of right, is the ultimate survival skill. For Mia
there is no retraction of that fatal moment of respect for the
dealer of death, for the longer reach and the stronger arm. And,
although the book insists on her equal adulthood, unquestionably,
inevitably, the larger world she has entered is a man's world.

It is evident that there is a great difference between feminised
and feminist SF in the juvenile as in the adult genre.[5] In the
former, girls are allowed to enjoy the adventure and the intellectual stimulus of SF through imaginary characters of their own
gender, but only under certain conditions. The teenage heroine
of the future is either a privileged anomaly, whose privileges are

automatically rescinded when she reaches sexual maturity, or else she accepts from the start a subordinate, nutritive role.

Though both the books discussed have been around for a long time it would be a mistake to consider their assumptions as outmoded. Lists and bookshop shelves still abound with juvenile SF of the same kind – the story 'about' the superpowered girl warrior who backs Prince Wonderful in his battle against Ultimate Evil, then throws away her sword and falls contentedly into his arms; or 'about' the girl of our world who makes the sandwiches, screams, asks stupid questions and falls madly in love, while her brothers and the dishy alien tackle the machinations of the intergalactic mind-police. The best of these books are not only popular but extremely well written, and though the generic 'romance' formula on which they are built does not challenge the sex roles, it is not crudely derogatory towards girls and women. Perhaps the worst thing that can be said about *feminised* teenage SF is that it reflects all too accurately the state of affairs in the present day.

What would be so different about a specifically feminist teenage SF? Of course it must entertain, or nothing else follows; ideally it should be well written. But along with entertainment and a good prose style it should offer an alternative (whether in a notional future, a formal Utopia, or a new perception of the present) to the misogyny, both covert and open, of everyday reality. It should also provide at least the hope of access to science and technology. It may be taken as self-evident that girls are disadvantaged by their fear of science, and that in our technological age this phobia represents a serious life-long handicap. SF's famous capacity for 'making the strange familiar' has a potentially useful role here. The readers may learn nothing practical (most of the science in any SF is junk, anyway) but they will still have gained if they lose some nervous distaste and acquire perhaps a little disrespectful affection for the mysteries of science and the gadgetry of technology. In the adult genre women writers and critics have been instrumental in liberating SF from the misconception that only engineering, physics and maybe chemistry 'count' as the science in science fiction. But for teenagers science that's instantly recognisable as the school-lab stuff should be preferred. The majority of schoolgirls already know too well that history is their sort of subject, while computers belong to the boys.

I also suggest that it is not appropriate, bearing in mind that all fiction is available to teenage readers if they so choose, to tackle certain standard themes from adult feminist SF. The dystopia in which girls are treated like scum may seem like just more of the same, to those 13 and 14 year olds who habitually, resignedly, surrender the lion's share of teacher's (or visiting writer's) attention to the lords of creation. On the other hand, a girls-only utopia may equally fall flat. Most girls find boys extremely interesting. Pretending that they have vanished is unlikely to appear a desirable alternative to reality, nor does it offer any new ways of dealing with the problems they cause. Moreover, the aim should not be to exclude boy readers: their attitudes too may be shifted by the right kind of fiction.

There remains the question of whether the teenagers themselves will be interested. Is it possible to attract the average 15-year-old girl to a book that's both feminist and scientific – supposing she isn't already deep into Joanna Russ? The young woman who enjoys 'feminised' SF as an exotic extension of the teen-romance genre is not interested in either hard science or uncomfortable politics. The confirmed SF reader and techno-freak who happens to be a girl is placed in a difficult position by SF that insists on raising questions of gender consciousness. It challenges the bad faith between her and the stories that engage her, and effectively stops up one of her escape routes from the problems of being a girl with inappropriate interests. The advantages of an exciting scientific read that doesn't devalue girls may be obvious – to the writer and the publisher concerned. But is there any way to present feminist SF for teenagers – or indeed any kind of feminist fiction – *without* slipping into the preaching mode?

I conclude my investigation of the case for feminist teenage SF through a description of the evolution of my own novel *The Hidden Ones* (1988),[6] to show how the ideas outlined in this essay were, in one particular case, converted into fiction.

The story that became *The Hidden Ones* first emerged as a direct reaction to, or rather revulsion from, the typical 'feminised' rite of passage story in fantasy and SF. I had grown to hate this transparent fable of the second-class citizen learning to know her place: and it seemed to be turning up everywhere, not least in my own work. I also resented the widespread assumption that girls' books should only deal with the 'soft' SF of psychic powers and hazy metaphysics. I determined to write an unreflecting SF adventure story for teenage girls: a highly coloured all-action tale starring a girl with superpowers and a charismatic woman scientist (a kind of female Dr Who). The plot would be built around a small core of unequivocally 'hard' science, and the only significant male character would be the hapless villain.

This version was a complete failure.

I decided that the spies-and-secrets plot was a mistake. I realised that it represented an attempt to escape from the 'homely' scale of events considered suitable for girls, but it wasn't working. Moreover, I'd been so afraid of girlish introspection that my superpowered teenager had become a kind of blank lay figure, surrounded by garish cardboard cutouts. After some heavy revision I then produced my teenage SF *Mark II*: which, since the basic story remained unchanged from this point, I will describe in detail.

Adele Wilmot has always known that she is different from other people. As a young child she was the focus of a poltergeist phenomenon: the resulting notoriety, in a small rural community, may have led to the breakdown of her parents' marriage. Actually brighter than average, she has given up on the education system because she is constantly in trouble. At 15 she returns to the village to live with her father and stepmother. A mysterious older woman befriends her, using the lure of science education. Adele also meets a middle-class girl of her own age who offers entry into another kind of richer world. Soon she falls under the spell of Lily's glamorous post-hippie father. Adele's secret place, the holy well that she had always felt to be connected with her own strange powers, is on his land and Mr Villiers seems to take seriously the mystical legends surrounding it. The argument of the book turns into a tug of war between Mr Villiers and his 'magical' world view, and the older woman with her promise of access to technology and science. Adele discovers that the scientist, Dr Allardyce, has ulterior motives. The laboratory proof of telekinesis is important to her work, and she wants Adele as an experimental subject. Dr Allardyce is no villain: her deception was an innocent subterfuge to get past Adele's hostility. But Adele now rejects her in disgust. What Adele does not know is that the hypocritical post-hippie has secretly sold off the holy well site to the Ministry of Defence. It will be mined for a deposit of the so-called rare-earth minerals, to be used in modern weapons development. All the charm that has been turned on

Adele has been designed to prevent her from disclosing certain information which would ruin this deal. When Adele discovers this, which way will she turn? Will her secret power be unleashed in violent revenge? Or will she be persuaded to trust Dr Allardyce once more, and enlist science on her side to save the holy well? Now read on. . . .

When asked if I'd like to offer something for a new teenage list (Livewires) being launched by the Women's Press, I did not, at first, consider this story. Several publishers had turned it down, and I felt myself that it was still a failure. But I decided in the end that they might as well see it, and so the third and most intensive stage of the book's evolution began.

It was obvious that Mr Villiers had to go. My editors rejected him as an implausible character. As a writer, I was amazed when I realised how sneakily the fascinating male had crept in, with his villain's cloak of evil powers billowing behind: and this after I had rejected the idea of a boyfriend because I didn't want Adele elbowed out of centre stage. Larger-than-life male power figures should not take up valuable space in a feminist story: to invoke the gods, even in condemnation, is to do homage. We were also dissatisfied with the guru-scientist. For the sake of simplicity I had presented science/technology as an uncomplicated good. But this is not the case. A world gets the science it deserves. And in our world a successful woman physicist is not particularly likely to have any time for idiocies like feminism or conservation. Doctor Allardyce became a much more convincing person as a hard-hearted careerist, whose interest in Adele's education really is a bit of a con. Mr Villiers turned into an overstretched cereal farmer who panics when Adele finds him out in his crooked property deal – finally a rather pitiable figure. With both significant adults demoted, Adele's choices are brought into sharp relief. When she finally chooses 'science' – and the real world – and sees the magical view of her powers as an attractive dead end, it is in full understanding of the compromised nature of its promises.

Other features of the story were subjected to the same kind of examination: for instance, the good relationship that develops between Adele and her highly conventional stepmother was one way of fending off the isolated-tomboy syndrome. The 'holy well' focus of Adele's power became a far more intensely realised and far lovelier place (in a genre bursting with phallic icons, a few images of wells and springs in secret valleys can never go amiss). The fantasy special effects of telekinesis provided most of the excitement on the SF side in my draft. In the revision demonstration of the genuinely astonishing properties of the lanthanide or 'rare-earth' minerals (the 'hidden ones' of the title) came to the fore – as did Dr Allardyce's evident and redeeming love for the real mysteries of the physical world.

But the most important revision of all was the character of Adele, and it was here that my editors gave me most inspiration. It was they who insisted that I immerse myself in the adolescent experience ('More self-obsession, Gwyneth! Put in more self-obsession!') and it was in the expression of this experience (fantastically heightened as it is for Adele) that I finally found the validation of my story. Rereading Adele now I shudder: but it was in this *person*, too ferocious, too vital ever to be contained by gender, in her unconditioned adolescent agony, that I discovered I really did have something more to offer than a sermon.

On close examination, *The Hidden Ones* shows remarkable parallels with the models of teenage SF discussed earlier. Adele's unmanageable psychic gifts echo the blocked intellectual ability of Meg in *A Wrinkle In Time* (as I have noted, the possession of secret powers is an obvious metaphor for the subjective experience of adolescence). The actual plot, Adele's thrilling fight to save the holy well, preserves traces of the knockabout adventure of my first attempt. It also represents, like Mia Havero's 'trial', the concrete form of the rite of passage, with its real dangers and difficult victory. Like Meg, Adele is faced with a task which amounts (from her point of view at least) to saving something beautiful from the forces of evil. Like Mia, she comes up against interests and preoccupations of the Big People's world which have meant nothing to her before.

I believed by the end that I had managed to express my original vision: an exciting rite of passage story that would involve hard science and would *belong* to the girl-protagonist, instead of being hijacked by cosmic truth on the one hand, or on the other by the first male character to appear on the scene. Whether or not I succeeded is for the reader to judge.

I was asked, by someone who read and enjoyed the book, how far I felt I was justified in mixing politics with fantasy; in offering unreal solutions to the real and desperate problems of someone like Adele? My reply was that the 'solution' I offer does not consist in awarding my troubled heroine psychic powers. It consists in offering a way of looking at the world whereby women and girls are coherently significant, and can interact positively with the mysteries of science and technology. This may indeed be fantasy, but it is hardly a frivolous daydream.

NOTES

1 Madeleine L'Engle, *A Wrinkle In Time*, Harmondsworth, Penguin, 1987. First published 1962.
2 The back cover 'blurb' of the 1987 Puffin edition explicitly dismisses Meg to a secondary role: 'When Charles Wallace Murry goes searching through a "wrinkle in time". . . . How Charles, his sister Meg and his friend Calvin find and free his father'. And yet the story is told from Meg's viewpoint throughout and she is clearly intended to be the principal character.
3 Alexei Panshin, *Rite of Passage*, London, Methuen, 1987. First published 1968.
4 *Rite of Passage* is 'a remarkable debut: outstanding (albeit by the standards of the genre) for its literary merit and original ideas' (David Wingrove (ed.), *The Science Fiction Source Book*, Harlow, Longman, 1984).
5 For a full discussion of these two useful terms, see Sarah Lefanu's intelligent and rigorous argument in *In The Chinks Of The World Machine*, London, Women's Press, 1988.
6 Gwyneth Jones, *The Hidden Ones*, London, Women's Press, 1988.

Chapter 11

Sex, sub-atomic particles and sociology

Sarah Lefanu

Until quite recently the mention of a category of fiction called 'feminist science fiction' would be greeted with puzzlement, incomprehension or resentment; the latter being the reaction of long-established readers of science fiction to what they see as a takeover by women of 'real' science fiction, and the two former the responses of non-readers whose preconceptions of science fiction are based on memories of *King Kong* from their early childhood (fairhaired princess-type is saved from fate worse than death) or memories of *Star Wars* from later childhood (fairhaired princess-type saves universe from fate worse than death).

But, as this collection demonstrates, there are now so many feminist science fiction writers that it is hardly possible to maintain that feminism and science fiction are mutually contradictory categories, nor indeed that these women represent some kind of raiding party on the real thing. Besides the growing numbers of feminists writing science fiction, a further indication that the genre as a whole has been changed can be found in recent male-authored science fiction. While the cannier writers of the late 1970s and early 1980s were hastily inventing some more active role for their female characters than simply a sexual one, that tokenism has been superseded by a serious attempt, amongst some writers, such as Robert Holdstock and Colin Greenland, to deal with issues of sexuality and sexual politics. Resentment against 'women's issues' still exists, but it seems to be giving way to a grudging acceptance that women really can write science fiction. A not infrequent opening to a review by a male fan of a new SF title from The Women's Press goes something like 'Although this comes from The Women's Press . . . ' and goes on to praise whatever is under review for not being (dirty word) polemical.

But while feminist science fiction no longer has to justify its very existence, there are none the less certain limiting misconceptions bruited around about it, not unrelated to that sense of resentment felt by readers who want to keep their science fiction untainted by the wild women. These appear in two major guises. The first is that SF written by women is worthy, but dull. Gwyneth Jones has wryly illustrated this: SF doesn't have to be about rockets and intergalactic wars and defending the earth and all those boyish pursuits, oh no, 'SF can be about things that are true and beautiful and womanly like sociology and town planning.'[1]

Such a view of feminist SF represents a continuation of a debate that started in the mid 1970s about 'soft' and 'hard' science fiction: 'hard' (and in the view of many, 'real') science fiction meaning concerned with traditional science, with technology, and with the hardware of the future; 'soft' meaning concerned with the new sciences such as psychology, linguistics, ecology (and sociology and town planning), with a critique of the uses of technology, and with the social structures of the future. Hard SF was associated with the traditional male writer: soft, of course, was what the women were. But it was generally admitted that these womanly concerns had a formal corollary. Women writers, and in particular Ursula Le Guin, but also others such as Vonda McIntyre and Kate Wilhelm, were instrumental in encouraging an interest amongst the readership in the quality of what was written. They were perceived as having a civilising influence (one of women's traditional virtues) on the genre.

The second major misconception is that feminist SF isn't real SF but is political polemic disguised as SF, that it consists entirely of, to quote Gwyneth Jones again, 'loving descriptions of how to run the creche on the subsistence farming cooperative'.[2] Or the reverse, horrifying descriptions of dominant men using women as breeding animals and nothing else.

Feminist science fiction does indeed include portrayals of women-only utopias, such as Sally Miller Gearhart's *The Wanderground*, which is rooted in ideas developed in the nascent second wave of feminism, or Monique Wittig's more philosophical exploration of sexual difference, *Les Guérillères*. And it includes dystopian writing in which the position of women in sexist, authoritarian and fundamentalist societies is pushed to an extreme, as in Suzy McKee Charnas' *Walk to the End of the World*, Anna

Livia's *Bulldozer Rising* (in which social attitudes to old women and the tyranny of physical attractiveness are also explored), and Margaret Atwood's *The Handmaid's Tale*. But why shouldn't it? Because these novels deal with political concerns does not mean that they are political tracts. But where the myth of the non-ideological novel is elsewhere generally accepted as dead, it seems to be alive and well in science fiction. Some readers seem to imagine that science fiction is somehow separate from, if not superior to, politics. Or that if it isn't, it should be. But it is only the beliefs and aspirations of feminist writers that are labelled as ideological; the 'normal' androcentric attitude of traditional SF is effectively invisible.

So there is some truth in what the critics say: women have brought politics into the genre. They have brought women into the genre. They have broadened its scope and have taken its possibilities seriously. But to pretend that the considerable body of feminist science fiction is either worthy or preachy or both is, to put it politely, ill-judged. To put it less politely, it is simply wrong. It suggests a defensive attitude towards an unspoken ideological position.

The hostility that is still often expressed towards feminist SF comes from a critical tradition that overvalues the content of the fiction. But in feminist SF, as in any other form of fiction, it is not so much *what* is written about that is important, but how it is written.

Now, as we move into the 1990s, feminist writers are building on the body of work produced in the 1970s and 1980s and pushing it further, challenging the distinction between hard and soft SF and showing that it is possible to be feminist without being 'feminine'. The work of two contemporary writers, Gwyneth Jones and Lisa Tuttle, exemplifies this development. Neither of them are utopian writers, although this is as much to do with political developments over the last decade and the failure of the left in Britain to grasp certain economic and cultural changes as it is to do with feminist reassessment. Nor do either of them show the slightest interest – in their fiction, that is – in town planning.

Gwyneth Jones' three novels for adults (she has also written a number of children's novels), *Divine Endurance*, *Escape Plans* and *Kairos*, are all concerned with science and technology and the relations of humans to them. *Divine Endurance* was partially conceived as a protest against Tolkien, an exploration of the thesis that 'the machines are innocent'. The narrative is structured around the journey of Cho and her cat Divine Endurance through a south-east Asian peninsula, to her capture and the revelation that she is not human but is instead a metagynoid doll, constructed to respond to the deepest desires of the human heart.

With *Divine Endurance* Gwyneth Jones found herself up against the fantasy/science fiction distinction, in which fantasy is used to describe something that isn't real. Girly stuff, in fact. While the real world is reserved for the men. *Escape Plans* is set on a world which is one vast computer, in which numberless masses have become interfaces with the machine. *Kairos* concerns a drug that affects the arrangement of sub-atomic particles, thus changing the nature of quantum reality.

All three novels show an obsession with time and reality and a preoccupation with the search for knowledge. And knowledge is less to do with state-of-the-art rockets than with state-of-the-art human consciousness. Gwyneth Jones says of her upbringing on the English metaphysical writers such as Tolkien, C. S. Lewis, Charles Williams and George MacDonald, with their themes of love and loss, sacrifice and redemption, renunciation and promise, that she found she was beginning to ask: 'where's the politics?' and further: 'where are all the women?'.[3]

Her work begins to answer that by having 'all the women' there, centrally. Relationships between women, Derveet and Cho in *Divine Endurance* and ALIC and Pia in *Escape Plans*, provide the emotional and moral centre of the novels. In *Kairos*, while men are present, the relationship between the two women of the foursome, Otto and Sandy, remains central, and the themes of love, desire, need, loyalty and betrayal are further explored in the mother/child relationships between the child Candide and Otto (his real mother) and between Candide and Sandy (the mother he runs to).

The delicate complexity of human relationships: well, what's new? Everyone knows this is an area in which women writers excel. But it's not just that Gwyneth Jones politicises this area by redefining human as female; it is that she is writing in a field that is stuck, even now, in a dualistic notion of character versus technology. And where once, in science fiction stories, the rockets were the protagonists, now it is the computer networks. Gwyneth Jones' work refuses this split between human and machine; it is not even as if it is the interface that fascinates her (although it is on that interface that the story of *Escape Plans* is set). Technology and humanity, or human consciousness, are, rather, treated as different aspects of one whole. As she has described it, science fiction is an attempt to make sense of something alien, the science trying to make sense of the outside, the fiction trying to make sense of the inside.

Her fiction is serious, committed, political. It is also clever, playful, celebratory (of language as well as of women, and not, indeed not, of technology). Her commitment to the possibilities of SF, her belief that it is the major mode for contemporary fiction, that it is privileged by its place at the cutting edge of human knowledge and endeavour, goes hand in hand with her view that that is where feminism is too. And this is where she beats the boys at their own game, being as hard and fast as they are, but never for a moment striving to be one of them.

Where Gwyneth Jones fell foul of the fantasy/SF distinction with *Divine Endurance*, other writers have found themselves excluded from a wider audience by the current mania for labelling fiction in categories of sub-genres. For women writers these labels – of SF, fantasy, magical realism, dark fantasy or horror – can be used as a stick to enforce what it is that women can or cannot do, what indeed it is permissible for them to write.

This is odd, as the boundaries between the categories are not clearly delineated and never have been. Take Mary Shelley's *Frankenstein or, the Modern Prometheus* as a case in point. It has been claimed as one of the earliest of science fiction novels, with its themes of humanity's aspirations to divine omnipotence, the search for knowledge through scientific endeavour, and the dire consequences of both. It can also be read, as Ellen Moers suggests in *Literary Women*, as a creation myth that explores the drama of guilt, fear and flight surrounding childbirth. And it can be read as a horror story. The horror in *Frankenstein* lies not just in the trappings of the monster 'out there' gibbering at the window and threatening the security of hearth and home; but in the relationship between monster and creator, in the heart of darkness around which are built all the stories within stories that form the structure of the novel, in the void where monster and creator merge into one. Loss of individual identity, being swallowed up by or absorbed into the monstrous or malign 'other', has become a central theme of horror fiction.

While the crossover between science fiction, fantasy and horror can be found in a number of contemporary writers, the distinction that is perceived between men's writing and women's writing, between 'hard' and 'soft', seems to exclude women from writing 'real' horror. This is even though in the work of such established and highly regarded SF writers as Octavia Butler and James Tiptree Jr (Alice Sheldon), the traditional horror themes of violence and vulnerability constantly occur.

Lisa Tuttle's work affords another example of the blurring of genre boundaries. And she, too, has come up against notions of what is and is not permissible for women to write. She has commented on how as a female writer of science fiction she was seen as an outsider, but while women are now accepted, however grudgingly, as being capable of writing real science fiction, she is cast once again as an outsider as a writer of horror fiction. Women can, and do, write about the supernatural, but blood'n'guts horror? No. There is a split in the perception of horror writing that is analogous to the soft/hard dichotomy of science fiction, and in those terms Lisa Tuttle, like Gwyneth Jones, writes the hard stuff. Her novels, such as *Familiar Spirit* and *Gabriel*, and her short stories, are full of violent epiphanies. Characteristically, her protagonists are women with ordinary concerns: personal relationships, work, children, with a familiar (to women, at least) sense of anxiety about their place in the world. Independent women who at some level recognise that it's a man's world and that the rules of the game are subtly different when you're a woman. Into the apparently calm surface world of these women there breaks a violent force, often sexual in nature, bringing with it the threat of loss of identity and of place, and even of life.

In America there is a small but growing body of women who write horror as well as science fiction and fantasy, such as Chelsea Quinn Yarbro, Anne Rice, Suzy McKee Charnas and Barbara Hambly. Even so, in Douglas Winter's collection of interviews with contemporary horror writers[4] only one woman, V. C. Andrews, is included amongst the seventeen authors. In Britain fewer contemporary women write in the genre, although ghost stories still flourish, and attract a variety of writers such as Pamela Hansford Johnson, Rosemary Timperley, Fay Weldon, Joan Aiken, Muriel Spark, Susan Hill, Jane Gardam and others.

There has been, and remains, a certain amount of squabbling

over the respective merits of horror and terror (as there always is when certain groups are lumped together, such as fantasy and science fiction, or thrillers and crime novels). Jennifer Uglow quotes, in her excellent though brief introduction to the *Virago Book of Ghost Stories*, Mrs Radcliffe writing in 1826: 'Terror and horror are so far opposite, that the first expands the soul, and wakens the faculties to a higher degree of life; the other contracts, freezes and nearly annihilates them.'[5]

But they are not so dissimilar. Both horror stories and ghost stories deal with fear; with loss, separation and loneliness; with the past breaking into the present; with the unconscious breaking into the conscious; with that shadowland in which women writers seem, for a variety of reasons, to move so freely. And they share with science fiction that sense of 'otherness': a concern with the effects of the strange, or the alien, or the unconscious, on the familiar and the commonplace, and an abiding interest in how the strange and the familiar can inhabit the same terrain.

There are certain fears that spring directly from women's experience, which include the fear of the violence – physical or mental – of male power and its capacity to reduce or even annihilate its female victim (as in Charlotte Perkins Gilman's classic tale, 'The Yellow Wallpaper'); the fear of the powerful nature of women's desire which, unlike men's, is allowed no public validation; the complex knot of fears that surround childbirth and maternal love.

As Lisa Tuttle says: 'We all understand the language of fear, but men and women are raised speaking different dialects of that language.'[6]

What distinguishes Lisa Tuttle from her male counterparts is the dialect of feminism that she speaks; and what distinguishes her from many of her female contemporaries is her emphasis on the physical manifestations of the shadowland. Bodies wildly out of control, colonised by other creatures, exploding, being turned inside out have become hallmarks of contemporary male-authored horror books and films, by writers like Clive Barker and Stephen King. Lisa Tuttle's visual horrors are as physically specific: a statue, in *Familiar Spirit*, that becomes a penis in Sarah's hands, arousing a lust that nearly destroys her; the transformation of Isobel into a devouring dragon in 'The Dragon's Bride'; the living breathing deadly nightmare of 'Riding the Nightmare'. These are stories about desire and its repression, about incest, guilt and revenge, about sexual jealousy, maternal love and its absence.

They are, in other words, stories about that womanly concern, human relationships. They are also stories in which the body speaks. They are full of remarkable transformations: women become men and men become women; humans become animals; dreams become reality.

The boldness of physical and sexual detail with which Lisa Tuttle describes the eruption of repressed or partially repressed material into the ordered everyday world, where everything has its place and male and female created He them, can be seen in relation to her works of science fiction. For science fiction has always offered to its practitioners the central image of a changed world. Anything can be pushed to breaking point, from the integrity of the human body to the forward flow of time to the nature of sub-atomic particles. Men no longer monopolise this kind of subject matter and gambol in it as they fancy, while women are left slogging away at the sociology and the political pamphlets. Writers like Gwyneth Jones and Lisa Tuttle are there too, playing with science and sex, with machines and bodies, with time and memory and language, and claiming both the conventions and the concerns of science fiction and horror for women. It is an encouraging sight.

NOTES

This article was developed from an introductory talk to a panel discussion with Gwyneth Jones and Lisa Tuttle at the Lancaster Literature Festival, May 1989. My thanks to Gwyneth Jones and Lisa Tuttle, to all the participants in the discussion, and to Monica McLean.

1 Gwyneth Jones, speech given at Follycon, Easter 1988, reprinted under the title 'Riddles in the Dark', *Foundation* 43 (Summer 1988).
2 ibid.
3 ibid.
4 Douglas E. Winter, *Faces of Fear: Encounters with the Creators of Modern Horror*, New York, Berkley, 1985.
5 Richard Dalby (ed.), *The Virago Book of Ghost Stories*, introduction by Jennifer Uglow, London, Virago, 1987.
6 Lisa Tuttle (ed.), *Skin of the Soul: An Anthology of New Horror Stories by Women*, introduction by Lisa Tuttle, London, Women's Press, 1990.

Chapter 12

Maeve and Guinevere: women's fantasy writing in the science fiction market place

Nickianne Moody

Science fiction studies are in the anomalous position of having to maintain an amplitude which accommodates an academic approach towards popular reading material. Where the genre is more generally considered legitimate for study, an assumption has been made that science fiction is composed of classics plus a wide-ranging morass of lesser quality work. The texts for inclusion in scholarly commentary or the school curriculum have been thrown up in spite of the genre's commercial nature. The larger latter group is more representative and has a poor standard of literature at its best and ideas at its worst. This group follows themes which are directly subject to market forces, space being another exotic backdrop to more regular formula fiction, as it is theoretically understood.

Certain recognised subgenres or marketing categories are found in this despised second group. One of the more notorious is 'sword and sorcery' although, as Marion Zimmer Bradley has pointed out in *Sword and Sorceress*,[1] this subgenre has been used by women writers to promote the 'strong' female character. Included most definitely in this area is the rising number of historically oriented novels found on science fiction shelves, despite the subgenre's equation with poor literary quality. Alternate history is an accepted subgenre but fantasy/romance is not so highly regarded by purists. David Pringle suggests: 'The popularity of historical fiction is waning while that of fantasy is waxing, so nowadays historical novels tend to come packaged as fantasy.'[2]

In several cases, for example Persia Woolley's *Child of the Northern Spring*, this redefinition has occurred. Whether this has been implemented by publishers/marketers, booksellers or readers is difficult to judge. Grafton's 1988 paperback edition of Woolley's series is clearly categorised fiction/romance but commonly stocked by booksellers in the science fiction/fantasy section.

The 1980s have demonstrated a resurgence of popular interest in the medieval period, which has certainly made itself felt in fiction. A growing number of books are using medieval backgrounds, and conform to two images of the period, either an image of reality contrary to the Victorian ideal or an image which is part of the accumulating fantasy of a quasi-medieval period. It is possible that this dichotomy has developed through the detail required for fantasy-role-playing games and the licence given by the American Society for Creative Anachronism.[3] This group gathers members together to recreate the period not as it was but as it should have been. The fan organisation and purchasing power of both these groups have encouraged the appearance of similarly oriented science fiction/fantasy novels.

Alternate history is more traditionally concerned with rematches of actual battles and has long been a legitimate science fiction speculation. *If It Had Happened Otherwise*,[4] published in 1931, contained the alternative histories and universes of scholars and historians, and included 'If Lee had not won the Battle of Gettysburg' by Winston Churchill. The historical novel in mainstream literature has been a rhetoric by which writers have been able to examine sensitive subjects of their own time, thus evading criticism without resorting to satirical fantasy. Gothic writers felt they could not be held liable for the sensory excesses of their plots because, although the sentimentality was Victorian, the setting was medieval. Historically oriented fantasy on science fiction shelves may well be a repackaging of material which does not conform to the stringent formula of romance. This type of fantasy offers the woman writer the opportunity to re-evaluate women's history from her own perspective in regard to the interpretation of evidence. Furthermore, it substantiates the 'strong' female heroine as something more than science fiction – a heritage.

Through Tolkien and earlier Victorian fantasists such as William Morris the medieval period has been presented to the reader as a golden age. In science fiction texts it has quite often been infused to provide an alien culture with recognisable similies. That the dragon was as big as an elephant may be implausible as a comparison on a planet that does not have elephants, but still acceptable to the reader. However, references to guilds, attitudes, weapons or lifestyles may take on a historical/medieval appearance because they are at once distanced and familiar. The associated magic of the period is as stimulating to writers as transgressions of its social order. From amongst this growing subgenre women writers have predominantly chosen two now familiar historical settings for fantasy, rather than romance, novels – Arthurian and Celtic. This builds on a much older tradition and with the recent proliferation it would be a formidable task to encompass the whole. It would also be impractical for the purposes of this discussion to attempt an in-depth account or analysis of the number of writers, of either sex, who have experimented with or retold the Arthurian/Celtic cycles. The consideration offered is therefore limited to central themes in the two areas and their more general relation to feminist appraisal and science fiction consumption.

Reinterpretations of the legends of Arthur

The warrior leader Arthur figures both in folktales and classical literature. Both of these forms have been open to regular reinterpretation or appropriation since the sixth century.[5] Arthurian romance has been a legitimate fantasy setting for many writers including Tennyson and Cocteau.[6] Since Tolkien, fantasy has become recognised as an independent genre and many contemporary writings on the older theme have been placed in this category and sold on science fiction/fantasy shelves.

The recent upsurge in new writing about Arthur, or the reprinting of such fiction, is the work of male as well as female writers. This discussion however is more concerned with why women continue the tradition and explore this heroic/masculine set of story lines. More generally, Arthurian themes used by women and found on science fiction shelves point to the areas in which women's writing is normally ascribed, and changes occurring at the present time in regard to the composition of works, writers and audience.

The overall legend comprises a series of stories, which may exist independently or combine to provide a fantasy narrative. The stories include those of Arthur's birth, Avalon, Tristan and Isolde, Lancelot and Guinevere, the quest for the Holy Grail, the various associated histories of the Knights of the Round Table and the political implications of the text. Thematically they are extremely complex, as well as very adult in their subject matter. However, as with most fantasy, Arthur is a character who has been drawn upon to provide reading material for children.

This highlights a major problem that women experience in writing for the science fiction and fantasy markets. Books by women originally conceived for an adult audience will be perceived by the publisher as suitable for a juvenile one. This has happened a great deal with 'shape-changing' stories, one of the attractive elements of the Arthur tales. Shape-changing is an ability which has traditionally been attributed to witches. It belongs marginally to the Arthurian tradition but is primarily a thematic concern of women writers in its own right. An example of a novel categorised as juvenile but intended for an adult audience is Meredith Ann Pierce's *The Woman Who Loved Reindeer*.[7] It is interesting to note the number of women who have written on the Arthurian theme for children: Susan Cooper, Andre Norton, Penelope Lively, Nancy Bond, Gwendolyn Bowers, Helen Clare, Jane Curry and Rosemary Sutcliffe, to provide some examples. These pieces of juvenile fiction explore themes and problems rather than simply tell expurgated versions of the legends. For example, Pat O'Shea's *The Hounds of the Morrigan*, which is more Celtic than Arthurian, was published in hardback as a children's book but categorised as fantasy for the 1988 paperback version and subsequently sold on adult shelves.

It has been difficult for authors to site the Arthurian situation in space, but not impossible. C. J. Cherryh takes the personalities of the legendary characters, and imposes them on clones which crew the spacecraft in *Port Eternity* (1982). Andre Norton's *Merlin's Mirror* (1975) accounts for Merlin's magical abilities as extraterrestial technology. John Brunner has also recreated the environment of the legends, but a direct treatment in a science fiction context has never been given. Therefore this discussion examines fiction that is heroic, mythopoeic, satirical and humorous[8] but maintains a connection with the science fiction genre and publishing category because they are sold together. Phyllis Ann Karr, for example, who wrote *The Idylls of the Queen* (1982) which can be categorised as a murder/mystery, found that her early work was classed as sword and sorcery when she had no idea what the term meant.[9]

One of the benefits of being placed on science fiction/fantasy shelves is that the writer can be freed from having to work within the constraints of women's romance. The romantic intrigue, the love affairs that play a part in Arthurian legend, are mostly morally illicit. This is taboo in standard romance novels.[10]

The main love triangle of Arthur, Lancelot and Guinevere is adulterous. For the others, Elaine of Astolat, Igraine and Isolde, it is unrequited and tragic. It is interesting to note that although Guinevere is often used as an allusion, as in Evelyn Waugh's *A Handful of Dust*, the character has not become a popular synonym for an adulteress.[11]

Against the background of the prominent male characters are female ones whose choices and actions do affect the world around them. The original tales and subsequent writings have dwelt significantly on the major love triangle within a romance framework. Mary Ellen Chase's *Dawn in Lyonesse* (1938) has her narrator read the story of Tristan and Isolde. In doing so she comes to terms with a comparable bond between her husband and a friend. The third part of Gillian Bradshaw's Arthurian trilogy, again republished in one volume, as *Down the Long Wind* (1988), and commonly stocked on science fiction/fantasy shelves, tells Guinevere's story from her own perspective. The story is told in retrospect by the queen from a convent where she has become the abbess. Sharan Newman's trilogy also tells the legend sympathetically from Guinevere's point of view. The character of the queen is portrayed in a great variety of ways which range between Tennyson's fallen woman and a powerful matriarch. The musical film version of the love triangle, *Camelot* (1967), was lightly comical but very ironic as it examined emotions within a stale marriage.

The tale is very difficult to construct as a romance because the ending is unresolvable. Therefore there is much more scope for exploration. In fact the themes of illicit sexuality and paternity are very similar to a more recent development in women's commercial writing – the saga. Here a story may feature strong, uncompromising female characters whose power lies either in their parental origins or their ability to choose the father of their child. These deceptions and allegations continue to fuel the plots of television series such as *Dynasty* and the 'bestseller' novels of writers such as Judith Krantz.[12]

Such deceptions occur frequently in Arthurian legend. The major three instances are perpetrated by Merlin in order to provide a king who will unite the Britons. Igraine, the mother of

Arthur, was already married to the Christian Gorlois when Merlin chose her and Uther Pendragon as parents for the future king. Thus Gorlois' features were superimposed on Uther's to allow the conception. Arthur was similarly deceived by Morgaine, Gorlois and Igraine's daughter (and thus his half-sister), which resulted in the birth of Modred. Quite often Modred is presented as his nemesis. In the third instance Lancelot is also enchanted into believing Elaine of Corbonnic is Guinevere so that Galahad can be born.

Merlin and Morgaine are also major protagonists in the legends, which introduces a further element of the appeal of the stories. The legend of Arthur, like many other epics, probably draws its durability from the fact that it was first told at a period of transition. As well as using the framework of stories to re-examine women's position during the period and justifying or questioning interpretation of characters' motivations and actions, women writers can also explore another prevalent theme. Up until the ninth century, Arthur is not a paragon of chivalry but a semi-divine hero who quarrelled with the early church.

Women writers quite often restore the pagan background as an integral part of the legend. Marion Zimmer Bradley's *The Mists of Avalon* (1982) revolves around this conflict. Catherine Christian reworks Malory in a more pagan than Christian, post-Roman Britain. By doing this, writers can remove the romantic chivalric element and explore aspects of women's lives and situations. It is not only women writers who do this: N. Tolstoy's 1989 novel *Merlin* takes a more realistic view of the extent of Christianity and paganism in the Britain of the period. Vera Chapman's extension of the basic legend rejects the associated courtly love of the legends. She has several extra female characters, including a daughter to Arthur and Guinevere, who suffer slavery, unhappy marriages, rape and violence. Concentration on the magical elements and the Celtic background gives the opportunity for the female writer to create strong and mature female characters and observation.

Bradley in particular excels in this. *The Mists of Avalon* is a significant break from her more usual science fiction. She produces a distinct fantasy novel with a keen feminist insight. Morgaine is the central character but most of the females associated with the legends are called to give their viewpoints. Apart from Guinevere, who is a Christian, the others have close familial ties and are of a pagan religion, worshipful of the mother goddess, which is in conflict with the rise of Christianity. Through this her narrative leaves Arthur's heroic chronicle in preference of the affairs and activities of the women.

The paternity of children, the power of women, adultery and rejection of pagan superstition (women's lore) are Roman and Christian concerns. They are of little consequence to the pagan matriarchal societies depicted by the fantasies although there are expectations governing them. Through her Christian marriage Igraine no longer has the option of choosing the father of her child, although her older pagan religion requires a child born of her lineage and Uther Pendragon. This child, conceived adulterously, results in the death of the Christian husband, setting the half-sister Morgaine against the half-brother Arthur, with catastrophic results to Merlin's or the mother goddess's plan. Morgaine's weapon against Arthur is his son/nephew who was conceived incestuously.

Arthur has traditionally been seen as a Christian king with his order of virtuous knights and his association with the Grail legend although its nature and theirs is open to interpretation. Amongst the recent Arthurian publications is a trilogy written by Stephen Lawhead which is published by Lion. Lawhead examines three main male protagonists in his books, *Taliesin*, *Merlin* and *Arthur*, and although he does not ignore the pagan associations the trilogy is published by and adheres to the publisher's specialisation in work reflecting Christian interest. In addition both C. S. Lewis and Charles Williams have worked with Arthurian themes in their Christian-oriented writings.

Removed from the constraints of the early Christian church's expectations of women, the Arthurian legends provide many interesting female characters. Bradley competently demonstrates this and includes women who are in dilemmas of their own making. Thus Igraine is a pagan married to a Christian, Guinevere is married to a man she 'betrays' and Elaine is the mother of Galahad. Elaine is especially interesting because as a Christian woman she is portrayed as either naive in the seduction of Lancelot or sanctimonious in her conflict with Guinevere.

Thus women can be seen in positions of power and active in society only when the early Christian notions of their place are removed through either matriarchal respect, a religious sorority, or by being in possession of knowledge. Merlin's sister Ganieda and his last love Nimue act as teacher and pupil, and are able to comprehend the basis of their power intellectually as well as execute emotionally. Merlin's wife Guedoloen is more of an archetype compared with the complex Celtic women that are examined in the following section, yet she is still an aspect of the earth goddess. Morgaine is descended from the triple Irish goddess the Morrigan, and in many of the stories, not just children's fantasy, she is the epitome of evil and Arthur's arch-enemy. In truncated versions of the tale she is the dark power. Many other retellings refer to her as the (or a) wise woman. In this context she is similar in stature to the Circe legend and a patriarchal conception of the learned woman.

When we examine the Celtic elements in women's fantasy writing, which is more versatile, we find the same licence and situation. To examine alternatives to women's contemporary situation writers do not have to leave the planet merely to go back in time. The market for such speculation is still science fiction, for within such environs the writer does not have to be artificial, clinical or dogmatic in her construction, as criticisms of recent 'feminist' science fiction suggest.[13] Using this tradition may not necessarily be a conscious effort to write feminist literature or experiment with feminist theory. The attraction is a framework for women-centred fiction without a denial of action.

With the growth of feminist thought, particularly in the United States, has come the rejection of patriarchal iconography and this has included aspects of Christianity. This in turn has led to the rediscovery of earlier pagan systems of worship or awareness, characterised as New Age.[14] The Irish concept of the other world was a land of women. The mythology surrounding Arthurian legend is that of finding routes into other worlds that coexist. The principle deity that concerned itself with society was the mother goddess in her three aspects. There is historical evidence to suggest that in the brief period between the Roman and Christian rule in Britain a matrilineal society existed, if not a matriarchal one. This is at the time in which Arthur appears and proves to be of great interest in women's speculation. So women's writing quite often moves from the Christian middle ages to the pagan dark ages.

It must be stressed that these stories could not be published or marketed as romances, although they may be read by such audiences. They may be considered so erroneously by a non-romance-reading audience and they may be read by people who do not generally choose to read science fiction. However they are considered more suitable for the broader marketing category of science fiction/fantasy. They have been published in great profusion since the 1970s because of developments inside and outside feminism and science fiction. The gradual acceptance inside the genre of female authors and criticism has helped, as well as the critical and commercial success of *The Mists of Avalon*. This is not to say that women's considerations of Arthurian themes are any better than men's, but to attempt to explain why the legends are so popular as speculation under the banner of science/fiction fantasy.

The warrior queen

Arthurian legend provides a structured fantasy setting, which allows women writers to explore the position of women outside contemporary values and stereotypes. It does however remain limited, because of its early Christian overtones and the presence of the warrior king. Celtic myth, while still maintaining familiarity for both reader and writer, offers another legitimate role for female characters, that of the warrior woman or warrior queen. Guinevere is definitely representative of feminine qualities and, before her 'lapse', many feminine virtues. However she is in many accounts the traditional idea of a queen, an adornment to a king with no state powers beyond the political alliance of her family and the status of queen mother. There are a great many novels which have strong central female characters within the home and spheres of domesticity, but the Celtic environment offers equal status to women in all areas as would be expected for men of the same social level. Quite often these narratives fall into a similar formulaic heroic vein as would be anticipated for a male hero but others are intricate and well researched.

In Irish mythology Maeve is one of the most prominent of all the heroines and deities. One of her battles is the subject of the twelfth-century manuscript the *Tain Bo Cuailnge*.[15] Its subject matter, Maeve and her male adversaries, predates the Christian era. She is the embodiment of male and female principles and has many positive qualities. She is assertive, intelligent and wise, strong, beautiful, proud, a good horsewoman and a noted warrior. She is the daughter of a high king married to a minor king of her own choice with whom she can organise her own lifestyle.

As a queen, in many of the legends her privileges exemplify the attractive status of women in Celtic society. Moyra Caldecott,[16] who has written extensively on the subject, notes that women could own property, give judgement and speak in counsel, and were not restricted in their movements or actions by legal or social expectations of decorum. In addition, women's sexual needs were legitimated and respected, as is graphically part of many of the stories. This egalitarian attitude towards women was reflected by Welsh law up until the time of the union with England. Contrary to English law a Welsh woman had a right to own property, not to marry against her will and to seek divorce on the grounds of adultery.

A frequent response in discussions with female fans as to why they read or had started to read science fiction was that it allowed women to participate. Women at science fiction conventions could point to a great many examples of outright sexism and inherent chauvinism found in early and mature science fiction. However, they enjoyed reading writers such as Heinlein because, although he uses superwoman stereotypes, his female characters are active. These women and girls are fully able in physical and mental terms and *expected* to contribute on all levels to the new societies in space. Women have a very high profile, sometimes independently of being the romantic interest. Of more significance than the precocious and curvaceous younger characters, Heinlein provides the 'honorary male' pioneers, women who recall a long and full life in space.

Thus science fiction is attractive to these readers because of these outward female protagonists with whom the readers feel they can identify. Even books with male lead characters encourage more identification than real-world adventure novels because of the proviso of the future that is open to change. The Celtic period as a fantasy setting offers the same mobility for female characters without the author having first to construct a world that enables him/her to do this.

Moyra Caldecott has written a great deal of fiction and analysis based on Britain's early history or ancient British mythology, and her work focuses on female personalities or characters from the period. Her novels contain extensive commentary on the fictional text including chronology and notes for further reading. A number of the novels were published originally by Arkana, a former imprint of Routledge which specialises in more esoteric work or fiction. More recently Caldecott has been published by Arrow and Corgi and joined mainstream science fiction shelves. Her trilogy *Guardians of the Tall Stones* has been collected into one volume for publication. These stories link together the majority of ancient civilisations of the Iron Age. In her anthology *Women in Celtic Myth* Caldecott tells eleven stories which focus on Celtic women and in a second section provides commentaries which are related to contemporary understanding and insight. Elsewhere she has examined early British tribal queens and abbesses.

The stories collected in *Women in Celtic Myth* illustrate several themes connected with an overall reading of the opportunities offered by the Celtic framework. It is the themes from these myths and their images that women are reworking in their contemporary narratives. Celtic tales offer the female character much more scope than the legitimation of playing sword and sorcery. There are several demonstrations in the stories chosen that Celtic women were valued as much for their minds as for their bodies and the pursuit of one usually ended in disaster.

Celtic love stories reflect contemporary problems where partners have equal rights and expectations. The stories may explore external or internal jealousy and rivalry but sexual fidelity is not an expected virtue. The relationships are based on understanding the need for personal development, and meeting this with support from both parties. The story of Deirdre is a romance which is both haunting and picturesque. More thought-provoking is the story of Emer and Cuchulain which is poignant as the female character matures and learns both compromise and adherence to self.

Grania is another story in Caldecott's collection which has a vindicating interpretation. The Celtic cycles offered Caldecott the choice of a great many stories which feature women. The story of Grania has a noted similarity to that of Eve, with a woman tempting a virtuous man with forbidden fruit for which he is punished, although in this instance the woman is prepared to take the consequences and the actual punishment is more a visitation of the sins of the father. After the event the woman is restored to her original husband and the experience forms part of her personal quest for knowledge and enlightenment. A final theme is Caldecott's choice of story concerning Maeve and Findabair, that of mother/daughter relationships. Other mythologies find that of mother/son to be more important. Allusion to the former relationship comes in the truncated form of the wicked step-mother, or the daughter who must grow up without her mother in order to be free to act.

As well as providing a period background of magic and tra-dition the Celtic framework is readily transported to science fic-tion settings. Patricia Kennealy's *The Copper Crown* (1984) does have 'Kelts in space'. These are the descendants of the historical Earth race who left the planet via the lost technology of Atlantis, because of the encroachment of Christianity. The text acknowl-edges Arthurian legends, and the culture of Celtic society exists against a backdrop of interstellar activity and technology. The culture is attractive because it balances male and female qualities: Kennealy creates a technological society that can spare time for aesthetics. Thus the position of women in the society is justified without their having to forfeit their femininity. Many visions of future and space from writers of either sex have called upon female characters to do this.

Rather than using the setting simply as a framework for fantasy fiction many novels take a more historical approach to the material used. Attitudes towards the inclusion of magic are quite ambivalent. The historical novels may again use the familiar heroic fantasy format of the unification of Britain but may well include women warriors and diplomats. In Kathleen Herbert's *Queen of the Lightning* (1983), for example, the main character is legitimised by her descent from Arthur. Herbert has familiarised herself with the dark age period, by studying Welsh, and has also conducted first-hand historical research and physically examined the region in question. She is a novelist in other historical areas and her sleeve notes state that she has been awarded the Georgette Heyer Historical Prize and studied at Oxford under Tolkien. Her knowledge about her subject is indicative of a substantial trend. Repeatedly the decision to write in this period is backed by a great deal of scholarly endeavour not normally associated with the exoticism of providing a cursory background for a romantic novel. This is also reflected by women writing on Arthurian themes, many of whom have read or studied Malory and Vulgate, two major historical sources, in the original. Gillian Bradshaw studied classics at the universities of Michigan and Cambridge and her novels have been reviewed in various popular magazines as well as the more scholarly *History Today*. The latter reports a criticism made of one of her other novels in which Bradshaw depicts a woman doctor in a fourth-century setting. Despite her knowledge of the period, the afore-mentioned critic challenges the historical accuracy of such a depiction, claiming that women doctors did not exist at the time.[17]

Novels such as Cecelia Holland's *Pillar of the Sky* are remarkable in their scope and very far removed from the usual battles of dark and light opposing forces. Holland writes of a similar period to the one under discussion. Here a matriarchy comes into conflict and declines in the microcosm of one tribe through the egotism of two male leaders and the responses of their female counterparts. It is a successful fulcrum from which to examine how the evolution of women's current position has resulted and it is full of insight and rationalisation. It is an excellent example of the place this setting has for experimentation with feminist thought or perspective in a time-honoured science fiction tradition.

Apart from offering this in the abstract, the reiteration of the tales of Celtic women also provides a more direct and humanistic approach to questions of contemporary relationships. Caldecott has noted different attitudes to sexuality and honesty in relationships in accordance with which many partnerships are enacted in fiction. Joy Chant has written *The High Kings* (1984) as a mixture of fact and fiction. The structure of the text is a series of tales about the ancient Celts which are being told to King Arthur and his Court by his bard. These stories contain points that are illustrative to the king and to the reader regarding Celtic culture and society. In the latter respect points are emphasised by non-fictional commentaries included by Chant in subsections to the chapters.

In her commentary on Celtic marriage and Celtic women, Chant notes that women had equal status with men in regard to government and war, and that descent was matrilineal. There were three types of marriage generally adhered to although the law listed ten kinds of living arrangement. Therefore a choice could be made between temporary and permanent relationships, fiscal status and kinship, but all were honourable within the society. Several of the stories Chant retells are associated with reactions to divorce and with ignominious divorce.

This century's changing attitudes to women's position, the status of marriage and its expectations has significantly affected women's social situation. Legal and social attitudes hold a great deal of ambiguity and affect most women in more than theoretical terms. Reading popular fiction is put forward as escapism. Radway's examination of romance readers shows that within marriage women read to make time for themselves and in the hope of learning and experiencing.[18] The change in stability in the married state may explain the growing popularity of the saga and its ideology as well as the appeal of science fiction. Both differ from the romance, as the heroine or the author may have different goals than simply the resolution of the romantic situation.

The images found in Celtic myth therefore prove extremely attractive. They provide a women's fantasy of freedom and equality which has historical support. The licence to experience opposite qualities to the feminine can also be reversed. The culture allows for the 'feminine man', which in Arthurian legend has sometimes been interpreted as Christian man. Feminine principles in men are encapsulated in the prestige of the Bard: the man open to emotion and expression. All careers are necessarily open to all, with the exception of maternity. Scholarship, statecraft, art, manufacture or war are open to both sexes and equally evaluated by society. There is also the possibility of a female sisterhood as well as easier social intercourse with men. Along with these observations Chant offers positive action for women's problems. When Vannolandua is supplanted by a younger woman she raises an army to restore her position, killing her rival and her husband in the process.

So the Celtic background provides a very fluid landscape within which the woman writer can work. The association it encourages means that she can communicate with men and other women, through a story that is able to satisfy any desire to explore female character and position and is commercially viable. It lifts a lot of constraints to writing without imposing new ones. (The technicalities of science or a new planet/society may of course also do this.) By its very nature Celtic society encourages women to question their heritage and, as has been demonstrated, the leaders in this area of writing are learned in lore and historical accuracy. Rather than a historical or sanctimonious lecture the stories retain a vital nature and appropriate exciting and absorbing heroic fantasy. Apart from the work of Leigh Brackett this has been a very strong male preserve. The stories are an exploration and dissemination of a history that has been denied women through more general forms of discourse.[19]

Feminist critics have noted that science fiction holds a special potential for women writers. Freed from contemporary realism it offers unconstrained narrative settings, such as those utilised by writers such as Marge Piercy and Doris Lessing. This is especially the case for women who want to visualise or explore the cultural and societal possibilities for women outside current patterns. It is accessible to those who wish to project feminist thought into a market situation where it can communicate beyond theory. It is also available for women who want to write about women with no thought towards feminism *per se*, but who have found that realism or conceptions of realism have made their work difficult.

Science fiction has always been a medium for the transferral of ideas as well as entertainment. One in which writers and readers have been invited to criticise what they are reading and how it relates to reality, as much as they are willing to suspend disbelief. Fiction provides a wider forum for feminist theory and popular fiction the widest. However, writing about what has not yet come to pass is difficult because nothing can be established without a contemporary point of reference for the reader. Constructing future societies where women are equal in heritage, dominant politically or have different social arrangements requires a lot of invention. This may have subsequent complications which affect the story line. Science fiction, despite its pretensions, remains a commercial genre.

Dark age Britain, because of its equality in gender rights and social organisation, provides an attractive setting that is just as nebulous in prospect but a little more concrete in the reader's mind. It also maintains magic as a 'feminine' alternative to technology and offers a firm basis for the concepts of magic. It is also far from being a pretty fairyland with regard to conventional quasi-medieval fantasy settings. The dark ages have an extremely uncivilised aspect involving tribalism, continual war and barbaric customs and ritual.

As well as this brutal aspect, the legends and folklore from which knowledge of the period derives encourage a franker examination not only of the nature of women but their relations with men. Marriage returns to the idea of a partnership which was lost entirely in the nineteenth century in which science fiction developed. The narratives pursued can also open up adventure plots previously closed to the female protagonist. It is in our own history and not an imaginary or alien culture that women can travel where they will, defend themselves and choose their own sexual partners as well as professions and lifestyle. It is not that human nature is any different but that the legal and social mechanisms, such as hypocrisy and double standards, which permit segregation of rights have been radically altered.

In challenging patriarchal notions of traditional folklore such as the legend of King Arthur, and general historical misconceptions of this period, women have either felt that they must justify themselves or, perhaps, that they must encourage further study and so have included fact with their fiction. This does not detract from the excitement of the adventure stories which, although allowed far more leeway when marketed for a science fiction audience, must meet the demands of a commercial genre, which in this instance is successful 'sword and sorcery'. This historically aware variant of sword and sorcery provides much more than passive escapism. It provides a workspace for women to experiment and create as well as seeding tenets of feminist consciousness in a fictional form which has the accessibility of romance.

NOTES

1 See, for example, Marian Zimmer Bradley (ed.), *Sword and Sorceress*, vols II and III, New York, Daw, 1986; and vol. V, New York, Daw, 1988. 'Heroic fantasy' is a synonym for this type of fiction.
2 David Pringle, editor of *Interzone*, made this introductory comment to a brief review of Mary Mackey's *The Last Warrior Queen* which he considered to be 'a case in point': *Interzone* 14 (Winter 1985/6).
3 The Society for Creative Anarchronism is a statewide American association founded by Diane Paxton and others in the early 1970s. It promotes medieval craft, lore and re-enactment similar to British societies like the Sealed Knot (Civil War battles) but with more interest in wider medieval society in an ideal sense.
4 Edited by J. C. Squire.
5 Y. Gododdin by Aneirin, *c.* the sixth century, noted part of the tradition well before the main associated period of writing. Also Culhweh and Olwen, *c.* 1100, the first full-scale romance about Arthur: R. F. Hobson in 'The King who will return', The Guild of Pastoral Psychology Lecture 130, July 1965.
6 Tennyson is at the forefront of the Arthurian renaissance in Victorian England writing many poems recreating aspects of the legends. His first was 'The Lady of Shalott' in 1832 and many of his poems were used as themes by Pre-Raphelite painters. Cocteau wrote the play *Les Chevaliers de la Table Ronde* in 1937 and also used Arthurian material in the screenplay for *L'Eternel Retour* in 1943.

7 Jan Bogstad, University Wisconsin–River Falls, in several conference papers, has noted other occurrences both in regard to women's choice of shape-changing fiction and women writers experiencing difficulty in writing for a non-juvenile audience.

8 Arthurian tales have been written in many different styles. These categories, which Waggoner expounds in *The Hills of Faraway*, (New York: Macmillan, 1978) are taken up and employed by R. H. Thompson in his article 'Arthurian Legend and Modern Fantasy' in Frank N. Magill (ed.) *The Survey of Modern Fantasy Literature*, vol. V, Englewood Cliffs, Salem, 1983, p. 2299.

9 Personal letter discussing Karr's contribution to a fantasy-role-playing game based on Arthurian legend, 1987.

10 To see the stereotype and further comments on the nature of romance writing and readership see Janice Radway's *Reading the Romance*, London, Verso, 1986.

11 One of the houses in the novel has its bedrooms named after Arthurian characters; the bedroom of the adulterous wife is called Guinevere.

12 Judith Krantz is foremost in a group of commercially successful women writers who have concentrated on women's entry and progress in glamorous worlds and occupations, subverting the more usual romantic archetypes and moral boundaries. *I'll Take Manhattan* (New York: Bantam, 1987), which was subsequently made into a mini-television series, sold 477,212 copies in the 1987 US and UK markets. Jackie Collins sold over one million copies of *Hollywood Husbands* (London: Pan, 1987) in the same period (figures taken from Alex Hamilton's compilation for the *Guardian* reproduced in *The Writers and Artists Yearbook*).

13 For example Lee Montgomeries's reviews of *In the Chinks of the World Machine*, ed. S. Lefanu (London: Women's Press, 1988), *The Judas Rose*, Suzette Haden Elgin (London: Women's Press, 1988), Anne Livia's *Bulldozer Rising* (London: Onlywomen, 1988) and Esme Dodderidge's *The New Gulliver* (London: Women's Press, 1988) in *Interzone* 25 (Sept./Oct. 1988). The tone and major criticism of the reviewer is summarised effectively by this quotation: 'Long essays on Tiptree, Le Guin, Charnas and Russ show Lefanu's sympathies at full stretch and illustrate the Women's Press thesis that the SF medium offers women new metaphors, new imagery, new ways of writing and new freedom to subvert and challenge social determinism. Subversion is a tactic of the underbitch, whole new prejudices have to be invented to keep the resentment simmering. Like the unfathomable discrimination against linguists in Suzette Haden Elgin's *Native Tongue* and its equally implausible premise that women could have calmly and universally relinquished all their hard-won rights at the first accusation of genetic inferiority.'

14 This is a difficult term to define outright but it refers to the 'Age of Aquarius' which is a more peaceful stage of human activity after the more violent Piscean one and covers a plethora of beliefs and practices surrounding alternative science, medicine, philosophy and tech-

nology. For a broader acknowledgement of the activities and beliefs connected with the term see Marilyn Ferguson's *The Aquarian Conspiracy*, London, Paladin, 1982.

15 The *Tain Bo Cuailgne* is the chief epic of the Ulster cycle of legends which comprise Irish mythology. The stories predate the Christian era and contain those of Deirdre as well as Maeve. The principle story concerns Queen Maeve of Connaught's raid to steal the Brown Bull of Cuailnge.

16 The main concentration of Caldecott's work is in her retelling and critical notes on many of the Irish and Welsh myths and legends which refer to women and are collected in *Women in Celtic Myth*, (London: Arrow, 1988). However she has also written novels based on the lives of early Christian or pagan women.

17 This information and not the aforementioned criticism came from a review of her latest work, *The Colour of Power* (London: Weidenfeld & Nicolson, 1989), in *History Today* 39 (July 1989).

18 Radway, op. cit.

19 This refers to women's virtual omission from history except as wives and mothers up until the recent period. Much of the general understanding of women's role at various stages of society has accepted this ideology even when evidence has shown them to be in possession of a great deal of power and responsibility, as well as living very active lives. Much women's history has been belittled or disguised by the reiteration of legends, for example Matilda, wife of William the Conqueror, doing little more than embroidering the Bayeaux tapestry and Eleanor of Aquitaine poisoning her husband Henry II's mistress.

REFERENCES

This is a brief list of texts which reflect the points discussed and sources used; it is by no means exhaustive.

Marion Zimmer Bradley, *The Mists of Avalon*, London: Sphere, 1984.

Gillian Bradshaw, *Down the Long Wind*, London: Methuen, 1988.

Moyra Caldecott, *Guardians of the Tall Stones*, London: Arrow, 1986.

Moyra Caldecott, *Women in Celtic Myth*, London: Arrow, 1988.

Joy Chant, *The High Kings*, London: Unwin, 1987.

C. J. Cherryh, *The Chronicles of Morgaine*, London: Methuen, 1985.

C. J. Cherryh, *Port Eternity*, London: Gollancz, 1989.

Kathleen Herbert, *Queen of the Lightning*, London: Corgi, 1984.

Gerhard Herm, *The Celts*, London: Methuen.

Cecelia Holland, *Pillar of the Sky*, London: Gollancz, 1985.

R. F. Hobson, 'The King who will return', The Guild of Pastoral Psychology Lecture (130), London; East Dulwich, July 1968.

Patricia Kennealy, *The Copper Crown*, London: Panther, 1986.

Norris J. Lacy, *The Arthurian Encyclopedia*, Woodbridge: The Boydell Press, 1986.

Caitlin Matthews, *The Celtic Tradition*, Shaftesbury: Element Books, 1989.

Pat O'Shea, *The Hounds of the Morrigan*, Harmondsworth: Penguin, 1988.

Fay Sampson, *Wise Woman's Telling*, London: Headline, 1989.

Susan Shwartz, *The Woman of Flowers*, London: Pan, 1987.

Charles Squire, *Celtic Myth and Legend*, North Hollywood: Newcastle Publishing Co., 1977.

R. J. Stewart, *Merlin and Woman*, London: Blandford Press, 1988.

Raymond H. Thompson, 'Arthurian Legend and Modern Fantasy' in *Survey of Modern Fantasy Literature*, ed. F. N. Magill, vol. 5, Englewood Cliffs: Salen Press, 1983.

R. H. Thompson, *Return from Avalon: A Study of the Arthurian Legend in Modern Fiction*, Westport: Greenwood, 1985.

Joan Wolf, *The Road to Avalon*, London: Panther, 1989.

Persia Woolley, *Child of the Northern Spring*, London: Panther, 1988.

Chapter 13

'Goodbye to all that . . . '

Josephine Saxton

The whole question of science fiction, even without the added problem of gender, is vexed. Science fiction is not only all things to all women (and men), but is now merely a label stuck upon a jar filled to breaking with all kinds of things. The kind of jar I mean is the one on the mantelpiece into which are put pins, hairgrips, rubber bands, receipts, old lipsticks, plastic gewgaws out of the cornflakes and anything else which does not properly quite belong elsewhere. It may also harbour valuable jewellery and large notes, but it is not the jar containing the pot pourri, because some of it stinks. There was a time when a sound definition of the term was 'stories in which some scientific idea was extrapolated, and was integral to the action and plot'. This has not been the case for a long time. It would seem that anything with a streak of 'otherliness' fits the bill, alongside the usual hard core of spaceships and robots.

I can only at first have been drawn into the SF net by some loose connection with psychology – a very soft science in the way I presented it; many novelists by that definition would be writers of SF. One of my influences at the time of first publication was Kafka. I thought to take his little doors and walk through them into vast worlds. I ended up being branded a writer of weird tales.

Over the years during which I have been a writer, in spite of all my efforts to dispense with the SF label, I have fluctuated violently between being proud to be one of an elite of highly informed, intelligent and brilliant writers, and appalled and frustrated at being thought merely a genre writer, one of a company who produce lurid junk about green jelly, improbable spaceships, monsters and morbidities. The real problem lies largely within the minds of other people, who often fail not only to discriminate between good and bad fiction, but also to understand or believe that within a genre there could actually lurk some works of excellence.

I did not set out to be a writer of science fiction, because at the age of 7 I was not aware of its existence. I wanted to be a writer, which to me meant poems, stories, plays and journalism. I also wanted to be an artist, and paint as good a picture as Holman Hunt's *Light of the World* in the front of my prayerbook (we were not a religious family, I was a rebel), and the illustrations in comics. A few years later I planned to be a great scientist, when I began to realise how science connected to everything, and lay underneath all other realities as invisible reactions, worlds within worlds. I had a homemade chemistry set in the attic, producing beautiful blue powders and green crystals. When I learned something of vitamins in domestic science, a lifelong passion for human body chemistry began. I was surely the only child ever to secretly drink codliver oil because it contained vitamins A and D, and to scrump Bramleys rather than Pippins because of the higher vitamin C content, and the pectin. I was within an ace of producing a magic potion, it now seems, which might have turned me into a scientist, an artist or a corpse.

Above all I wanted to write, but for a long time did not know quite what, except it would be different to anything else ever done. I did not know, of course, that this is the worst possible thing to do if you wish to sell to a publisher, and be widely read. I was also still ignorant of much that had gone before, a common trap, and SF was still a tiny specialist affair, on a secondhand bookstall which I had not yet visited. But it was too late, I was on the road to being original (not necessarily excellent, but original). And I was heading unwittingly right away from the lofty immortality which I craved.

My reading then included, as well as the usual English children's comics, *Pilgrim's Progress* by John Bunyan, which was the only book in the bedroom of the small rented house where I then lived, apart from an illustrated *Lamb's Tales from Shakespeare*. Shortly after that I acquired *Alice in Wonderland*. I had been reading for three years without help, was particularly in love with Rupert Bear, and had earlier read some of the horrors of the Brothers Grimm, and a collection of adventures of the denizens of a farmyard who spoke like human beings (I recall Septimus

Slug, Henrietta Hen, Cedric Centipede and the like, which I dramatised for the class at school who gave it rave reviews), and a story called *The Friendly Man* which was a kind of children's version of *The Legend of the Wandering Jew*. Later that year I acquired a secondhand copy of *A Christmas Carol*, complete with ghost, and discovered the *Just William* books in the library. Those familiar with my work will readily recognise the strange mixture of metaphysics, metamorphosis, other worlds, spiritual angst and dark humour which in my case has been sheltered inadequately under the enormous umbrella of SF. That the gaudy and glorious illustrations in Arthur Mee's *Children's Encyclopaedia*, particularly of the enormous flames on the surface of the sun, added to the SF orientation of my later creations does not explain why every child who sees them is not affected thus, and begin to create new worlds on the page. In my case the imagery burned deeply. An inherent taste for the marvellous, mysterious and morbid was being richly fed.

By the time I was in my early teens I had avidly consumed Jules Verne, H. G. Wells, Velikovsky, Heyerdahl, ancient South American civilisations, *The Three Faces of Eve*, Freud, Victorian books of unfortunate freaks, Alaister Crowley, and every travel book I could find. We also read Wordsworth for 'O' level and, by coincidence, *Pilgrim's Progress*; and the heady mixture of Christian self-correction and the pantheistic glories and mystical *Intimations* of Wordsworth made me recognise qualities and possibilities about life on this alien planet which I have never found cause to reject. It was not until I was pushing 30 that I began reading Jung, which influenced the whole of my work and a lot of my life (doing a module in psychology some years after that, I was appalled to discover that this meant studying the behaviour of woodlice!).

At the age of 15, at the end of my formal education for some twenty or more years, apart from a spell at a strange little art school, I was *still* unaware of science fiction as such. What I was looking for in my reading, which also included the Bible and any other religious work which came my way (*Foxe's Book of Martyrs* was lent to me by my family doctor, who turned out to be a heroin addict), was some other, more exotic state of being, some loftier place where I felt my frustrated and stifled soul should surely dwell. This is of course exactly what attracts most of the readers to SF.

How was I to know that my then very strong ambition to produce works of fiction the like of which the world had never seen was headed not in the direction of 'literature', but genre fiction? That is the kind of distinction only acquired in the company of literary people, and there were none in my life at that time. By the time I was undergoing a literary module as part of a late attempt to realise another ambition (to be a biochemist), in the same confused university which apparently believed that woodlice have a psyche (but who is truly yet to say they do not, as they've been on this planet much longer than we have?), I was able to answer back rather sharply when the professor in charge of our seminar rounded on me with acerbity for stating that Orwell wrote SF. Although now I do see what gave rise to his attitude, it is still irritating that he and many in his sort of position are so insular in their reading.

By that time I had published three novels and several short stories, held the opinion that Scott Fitzgerald was no great shakes, and was not about to perjure myself in essays to get a good grade. My novels had been published under an SF label, but they were not SF *at all*. This was due partly to a series of accidents, and ironically also to my own naivety at sending my first short story to an SF magazine on the same grounds later used by publishers: namely that it was so odd it *had* to be SF.

I was to discover that there was more to writing than just getting into print. There were reviews, marketing, publicity, and that thing which I had not even for a moment considered – public taste. But by then it was too late. I had long since been through the SF addiction stage, where to be without an SF story in the hand brings on acute feelings of deprivation, and was also becoming more critical. I rediscovered English and American novels, the French *nouveau roman* which for a while seemed fascinating (Robbe-Grillet's *Jalousie* being completely hypnotic), and was actually also writing some stories which *were* SF, having scientific ideas as an integral part of their fabric. I still did not realise that to write SF *per se* was the death of a literary reputation. I was to discover painfully and slowly that most people held the views of my reactionary and elitist professor, did not know that SF could by then encompass surrealism (again, not exactly widely popular then, although most TV ads now employ its imagery and spirit), or that the general reader of paperbacks did not give a damn about modernism, or Virginia Woolf.

I had also discovered good modern writers, and enjoyed H. E. Bates, Rebecca West and Iris Murdoch, all of whose novels I have read at least three times and will read again. I was offered Doris Lessing by Langdon Jones, a radical surrealist writer of the time, but was profoundly bored with her political stuff, and later found her 'SF' a thin icing on thick westernised Sufism. I belonged to no literary gangs at all, I was at odds with most popular opinion except for my own obsessions, but I had the ghetto mark tattooed on my soul. I was deeply obsessed with Gurdjieff and Ouspensky, who at that time were very esoteric. I was an isolated housewife who lived through books and mail, and cleaned the house and cooked, intoning as a mantra 'The daily round, the common task, would furnish all we ought to ask'. I was in a ghetto of one, thinking I had got a foothold in the world I craved.

Worse was to come: there was a ghetto within a ghetto. I was a 'woman writer', or 'authoress', and later the feminists reached out to claim some of my work as if it had come from the childless radicals in boiler suits. I affected bib and brace, for a while, but it cut no ice because I also wore eyeshadow and a chic haircut, glossy with Vidal Sassoon. I intentionally wrote a couple of feminist stories (not very strong). Later my anger grew, as it does when you begin to see how you have been cheated of your life, and the writing got better, but never reached the dedicated radicalism to satisfy the far left. I was too soft, too hooked on love, too likely to crack up laughing at the wrong moment, and too individual to represent a group. I read of, wrote of, dreamed of spiritual freedom because I had never had any other kind, and had not yet realised that economic power rapidly does away with subjection. Had I been born rich, or become rich, everything would have been quite different. I would have been idle, vain, wild and then as like as not dead. . . . I would have travelled and had no time for writing. When you are in prison for a number of years, writing helps to channel your madness.

Feminist writer? If you like. I had, after all, always been my own kind of fierce feminist, as what woman is not unless she has been lobotomised? I had somehow landed between two stools, not exactly in the shit, but in an unpropitious position. As a woman, it had earlier been hinted, I should have been writing romance and children's stories, or blood-soaked detective novels with plots resembling a knitting basket after the kitten has played with it. But I had no interest in writing for love-starved women, or children, or people who confuse crossword puzzles with literature – very weird indeed.

A female SF writer? An acquaintance who read my first published story, *The Wall*, quite seriously suggested that I should see a psychiatrist. At the time I was rather hurt by this, but now think that, in essence at least, he was probably right. I was producing things straight from the unconscious mind, and not understanding them myself until years later. I still do that sometimes, which makes it impossible for me ever to produce popular fiction. In that, you need to communicate right from the surface to the surface, while giving the lie that something important is being conveyed. And I was doomed as a bestselling SF writer also, for I was very interested in exploring ideas, and in having real people in my stories, and had become interested in language and style at the expense of narrative drive, which to be truthful I had never heard of. The plot was never as important as the changes which took place inside the characters. I was an alien in an alien country, in a ghetto, and the wrong sex.

And yet we are told by Brian Aldiss[1] that the first SF writer was Mary Shelley. Aldiss generally has a poor appreciation of female SF writers, never slow to illuminate our tub-thumping motives for using the genre, as if those male SF writers who aspired to do more than tell a mere tale had not always done the same. To read his work (or that of his apprentice gynaecologist David Wingrove) in *Trillion Year Spree*[2] is to feel knuckle-rapped and dispirited to say the least. I rate most of my work not being mentioned (other than one story being blessed with the word 'sexy', which it is not). Aldiss and his ilk mistrust SF written by women, because women using SF to air their political, emotional, religious and philosophical aims show clearly that these do not often coincide with those of men. This is true especially of those men who wrote the SF of the 1940s–1970s (with notable exceptions such as Theodore Sturgeon), whose average SF *She* is an archetype become a modern cliché, epitomised in Kenny Everett's Karla of the enormous boobs – of both meanings.

My more recent central character, Jane Saint, I deliberately gave a mixed bag of SF clichés to deal with. I took glamour (she has long red hair, the archetypal anima turn-on), an irritating talent for getting lost, monsters, cliff-hangers (literal), a quest or two, arrogant bastard males, a touch of cops-and-robbers chase, and so on; rolled these in wholemeal flour and fried them in Cold-pressed Extra Virgin Olive Oil until done.

Jane Saint wakes up to where she is at and what she is supposed to be doing, she begins to speak as a real person instead of a ninny, she fights back, and she wins. But she was not born like that. She began life as a minor character in a much earlier work which sought to be a metaphysical adventure on a monumental scale. Nobody, thank heavens, liked it enough to publish it at the time. Joanna Russ very kindly read it some years later (I was still sneakily fond of it and could not see where it had gone wrong), and she came straight back with a marvellous hatchet job, pointing out that all the best action had been given to the male characters, and that the whole book seemed to endorse the *status quo*, rather than point to any changed future: my first-ever brush with feminist politics in literature! After I had come out of hospital I eventually wrote a short story for Jane, using one of the sequences formerly given over to male heroism, except that by the end of the story it had all quite changed. Later, I wrote a whole book of her adventures, taking episodes in the same way, and it worked fine; my heart was in it at last.

Alas, work cushioned by inflatables, or objects to absorb male disdain of unglamorous females (the Dogs of Star Wars), is still being written and read by the ton. Examples abound in the work of Robert Silverberg and, in a way more subtle and sinister because the hatred and fear is presented in excellent writing, the work of J. G. Ballard, who specialises in the dark side of the anima, the *femme fatale*. This for me was a dreadful discovery, for he had long been a hero of mine, before I woke up to what he was really saying, albeit with style.

Unfortunately some women SF writers continue the debasement. Jody Scott's work is in direct emulation of the violent, amoral, cruel and tit-stuffed work of the big-time male SF writers, the difference being that the aggressive character is female. Scott is a skilled writer, often funny, witty and perspicacious. But then so, in another mode, are Jerzy Kozinski, Saul Bellow and Norman Mailer; if they were women it would still be surprising to find their works in a feminist imprint. The subject is not only vexed, but complex in the extreme.

Very early in my career, when the SF vortex was sucking me in to what I naively considered a literary clique, I had the idea that I might do better under a male pseudonym. Michael Moorcock adamantly stated that being female was a distinct advantage, in a field where women were sparse. In myself, then, I was a curiosity, a monster. It is likely that I would soon have been rumbled, because although I had no intention of writing *as a woman*, or especially *for* women in particular, I did so simply because I am one, and also because I detest violence and pornography, making a clear distinction between these and their more creative counterparts: action and eroticism.

You do not have to toe a party line in order to make political statements, for they arise naturally out of the material in hand. This is only one reason why I prefer Murdoch to, say, Drabble or Weldon. Murdoch can say everything there is to say about the uncaring husband and the desperately wretched abandoned wife without needing to raise female consciousness to demented intensity, or setting the scene in a separatist universe, although this can be salutary at times. She can also hint at other realities in an unforgettable way, whereas so many SF 'other realities' slip off the mind like butter off hot beans. Hatred can whip up resolve, as in Weldon (and Russ), but hatred and bitterness are not thus dissolved, but strengthened.

James Tiptree Jr is a brilliant writer who hid her sex for a long time, and caused furore at the revelation. Tiptree is a writer who deserves recognition outside the SF ghetto but the label is firmly stuck, whereas Lessing and Weldon gained a following in the mainstream prior to dabbling in the 'supernatural'. Had Weldon begun with the material of *Puffball* she might have become a kind of Dennis Wheatley. If Angela Carter had begun in SF instead of being later claimed by the fans one hesitates to speculate what she might have produced, but it would surely have made our toughest proponent, Ms Russ, look like Barbara Cartland.

It is possible that having a male pseudonym creates a new persona, as I think it might have in the case of Tiptree/Sheldon, but I doubt it did in the case of the Brontës, or George Eliot. My own work is often, regrettably, too clearly derived from female wretchedness: menstrual blood, floods of tears, the sweat of fruitless toil; it is drenched in the fluids of childbirth, and is sometimes what Harry Harrison has derided as 'tears and Tampax SF'. I am thoroughly tired of that kind of thing myself, perhaps because these days I am a happier sort of person. I have dwelt too much, like Margaret Drabble, upon domestic angst and oppression. But that is not all. There have been stories where I sought to control all that angst, or to metamorphose it, and truly that is what I meant to do all the time. But misery sticks like porridge, mouldering away in unstylish and unclear splodges. I have been a victim of my own ingrowing mysticism, and had forgotten that some of my juvenilia were adventure stories, with a female character crash-landing in the Amazon jungle, finding a lost civilisation and so on, complete with Anacondas. Such adventures that I later wrote were allegorical, or sought to explore difficult ideas about the nature of time and eternity, inspired by scientific articles on atomic physics in the 1960s, with the spiritual flight taking precedence over the physical. But then, we are still awaiting *Pilgrim's Progress* the video. . . .

I have been accused of writing only cardboard male characters: all bad guys or very weak people, shifty, perverse, arrogant, selfish and idle. This puts me in quite the position of the male writer who typecasts his females and gives them no real life. Unfortunately, then and now, I am often guilty of feeling that most men *are* cardboard, or at most made of puppydog's tails. In my new series of Jane Saint[3] readers will find that I am making a sincere effort to rectify this, and even offer a (fantastic and metaphorical) solution. This is the first work of mine not set with its feet on Earth to appear without an SF label. Those SF readers who have read *Jane Saint and Other Stories*[4] will find the 'other stories' largely not science fiction at all; most notable of these is 'The Message', one of two works of mine of which I am proud, and which readers outside the genre will never see.[5] Some of those young people at conventions who dress as the characters in endless trilogies may have taken a chance when they bought copies of my book, but I know that most of them will either be bewildered or bored by Edna, who gets no nearer to SF than having a mystical experience. It is not the stuff that young testosterone-inspired dreams are made of, no worlds are conquered or threatened, there are no leather-clad torture scenes in the dungeons of Alpha Centauri, no dolphins with in-built computers sport in the purple waters of some planet with so many Xs and Ks in the name that no human tongue can pronounce it, and no great Warlord Lizard stands in a massive hall with 1930s Nazi decor to announce the end of the Earthlings.[6]

Dangerous monsters can work as metaphors for the dark and inhuman side of our nature. Paradoxically, to battle with darkness in the form of horrible aliens may represent, not a triumph over evil, but a schizophrenic state where we come to believe that we are always on the side of right, that the inflated ego has conquered the shadow. I recently tried to convey this idea to a young (male) SF fan and he quite clearly thought me deranged. But I feel that in the constant reading of these tales we also dwell upon cruelty, war, rape, genocide, awful methods of making other races die, torture and all the morbid and vile junk which is an integral part of the genre. I cannot bear to read such SF, certainly cannot and do not want to write it, and despair for the results of widespread education if it is used for this purpose.

Has there ever been such a taste for horror, the very stuff of insanity, as now? SF is internationally popular now, but the kind of SF which really drags them in is hardly wholesome, nor is it the true SF of real scientific extrapolation. Exceptions of course include the charming *ET* (which should have been written by a woman), and the sentimental *Close Encounters* which wasn't, thank goodness. SF based on real scientific ideas got left behind when science itself suddenly became so abstruse that no single writer could possibly keep up with all the available material. SF writers have had to sink to the once-despised level of inventing their own science, which is nothing more than magic. It has become an infinite remixing of the same elements. And women are imitating the leading men, and the men of the early days of SF at that, rather than coming out with original work. It would seem that anything of importance that women have to say about being women, through SF, has already been said by Joanna Russ, Ursula Le Guin, Tiptree Junior, Marge Piercy and a few others. Here I purposely have not listed Anne McCaffrey, who has been writing as long as any of the above and outsells them considerably, because she is a writer of romance – fantasy without polemic – which endorses the very situation which feminist writers abhor (although at least she does not murder innocent dragons but falls in love with them, which is an improvement on St George).

I have a novel going the rounds of the publishers at this time which has been rejected twelve times on the grounds that the editors do not know how to *handle* it. Genre labelling by publishers is restrictive, damaging and patronising to the reading public, about whom I am convinced publishers know nothing, although they do know how to manipulate them. It is applicable only for narrow parameters, for the story which is tailormade by a skilled hack to a specific demand. If I write a story in which a horse is shot in a desert, does that make it a western? Most of my work has been given an SF label for no better reason. Why did I not submit it, or get a suitable agent to submit it, to 'mainstream' publishers? I did, but the label was the kiss of death, and this was both before and after the weird had seeped over into the mainstream to the extent which it now has.

In addition to this, a work must have a 'line', be aimed at a 'market', some particular age group, sex or even race. At a creative writing bash last year, after I had spoken, read and answered the usual questions, a young black girl approached me, obviously very disappointed. I was, for one thing, a Women's Press writer, and she had expected that I would have more to say about the plight of black women. I could only say 'Well, I am not black, and it honestly never occurred to me to write a book about the subject.' I am basically on the side of all oppressed, but she was not satisfied. Some writers make it their business to write whatever is in demand, and very wise too, for this makes money; but it doesn't often make good books, it creates ephemera. I told the girl to write her own, and I hope she succeeds, for she might be able to write from her heart and experience. Her audience will be black female SF fans. Eventually, perhaps, bookshops will keep a special shelf for these, as they now keep a special shelf for SF, and a special shelf for feminist works, and for SF feminist works (thus ensuring that no chauvinist male who does not like SF, and a great many women who do not like SF, will ever read any of it voluntarily).

Brian Aldiss still peels off his label from time to time, and J. G. Ballard has now succeeded very well after many years. Iain Banks somehow managed to be published outside of SF and be taken up by SF fans as well – a *coup d'état* indeed. For myself, I withdraw completely, unless I can attract a wider reading audience. I am sick to death of having my work misrepresented, and put out in frightful covers and under other people's flags. A book of quite apolitical short stories, *Little Tours of Hell*,[7] was published under a feminist label, and that some men read and enjoyed them was an accident. I am not a 'signed-up card-carrying' member of anything. I am perpetually on the sidelines, which is where novelists belong, because from there they can see what is going on. If I see anything from out here I will possibly write it in some form or another but, with the exception of the occasional short story which *insists* upon some SF format, never science fiction, political fantasy, horror or anything morbid or with a frightful unhappy ending. Naomi Mitchison has said to me on several occasions that I really should write more happy endings; how very true, people need them.

I no longer want to delve into subterranean realities, point out how awful life is, or even begin to think of remarking in story form upon what is right or wrong. I haven't a clue, have no answers, have come up with no workable utopias, and I detest sub-topias and alternate worlds. I am bored with chimeras and chemistry, physics and psychics, visitors from elsewhere both benign and hostile; I am no longer taken with technology, and I have no impulse to show in fiction what is better done in TV documentary. I have no further wish to be in the least bit didactic, do not find the Tarot titillating, robots make me yawn. I do not care if I never see another vision and will never again invent one, and do not think that post-nuclear landscapes are the stuff of entertainment or illumination. Exotic landscapes of other worlds are vulgar, and flying beyond the speed of light, or by instant transmission, is a cheap literary trick to get characters from one stage-set to another quickly. Interior worlds of the future always resemble ubiquitous shopping malls, often in winter, and who wants to read about that? Stories about future overpopulation give me acute claustrophobia and a sense of 'told you so', and so on, *ad nauseum*.

SF has had it with me, and this gives me a true sense of spiritual freedom. I feel like Christian when he reaches the Wicket Gate and his Burden rolls off down the hill. Goodbye the weird and wonderful, goodbye the morbid and marvellous, goodbye the straining to be original and fantastic and strange beyond belief. Goodbye symbolic towers, levitation, thinking slime, ghosties, hallucinatory clarities and above all, goodbye pushbuttons and screens.

What, if anything, do I plan to write, as a writer, as a woman, or a person? This is to be my secret, and at least some of it will be under another name.

NOTES

1 See, for example, his novel *Frankenstein Unbound*, London, Cape, 1973.

2 Brian Aldiss and David Wingrove, *Trillion Year Spree*, London, Gollancz, 1986.

3 *Jane Saint and the Backlash*, London, Women's Press, 1989.

4 *The Travails of Jane Saint and Other Stories*, London, Women's Press, 1986.

5 The other is a novel now out of print: *The Weltanschauung of Mrs Amelia Mortimer and Friends* (1970), which I was browbeaten into entitling *Vector for Seven*.

6 I did once write of a Warlord Lizard (briefly, in *No Coward Soul*), but did so purely to show that there is a part of the human brain which deals with this kind of thing.

7 Josephine Saxton, *Little Tours of Hell: Tall Tales of Food and Holidays*, London, Pandora, 1986.

Bibliography

Science fiction: primary texts referred to in this collection

Arnason, Eleanor (1987) *The Daughter of the Bear King*, London: Headline.

Atwood, Margaret (1987) *The Handmaid's Tale*, London: Virago.

Burdekin, Katherine (1937) *Swastika Night*, London: Lawrence & Wishart, 1985.

Charnas, Suzy McKee (1979) *Walk To The End Of The World*, London: Gollancz.

Dick, Philip K. (1972) *Do Androids Dream Of Electric Sheep?* London: Panther.

Duffy, Maureen (1981) *Gor Saga*, London: Methuen.

Elgin, Suzette Haden (1985) *Native Tongue*, London: Women's Press.

Emshwiller, Carol (1988) *Carmen Dog*, London: Women's Press.

Gearhart, Sally Miller (1985) *The Wanderground: Stories of the Hill Women*, London: Women's Press.

Haldane, Charlotte (1927) *Man's World*, New York: Doran.

Jones, Gwyneth (1984) *Divine Endurance*, London: Allen & Unwin.

Jones, Gwyneth (1986) *Escape Plans*, London: Allen & Unwin.

Jones, Gwyneth (1988) *The Hidden Ones*, London: Women's Press.

Jones, Gwyneth (1988) *Kairos*, London: Allen & Unwin.

Lee, Tanith (1986) *Dreams of Dark and Light*, Sauk City: Arkham House.

Le Guin, Ursula K. (1971) *The Wizard of Earthsea*, Harmondsworth: Penguin.

Le Guin, Ursula K. (1977) *The Word For World Is Forest*, London: Gollancz.

Le Guin, Ursula K. (1987) *Buffalo Gals and Other Animal Presences*, Santa Barbara: Capra Press.

Le Guin, Ursula K. (1988) *Always Coming Home*, London: Grafton.

L'Engle, Madeleine (1962) *A Wrinkle in Time*, Harmondsworth: Penguin, 1987.

Lerman, Rhoda (1986) *The Book of the Night*, London: Women's Press.

Lessing, Doris (1979) *Shikasta*, London: Cape.

Lessing, Doris (1980) *The Marriages Between Zones Three, Four and Five*, London: Cape.

Lessing, Doris (1981) *The Sirian Experiments*, London: Cape.

Livia, Anna (1988) *Bulldozer Rising*, London: Onlywomen.

Maitland, Sara (1987) *A Book of Spells*, London: Michael Joseph.

Moore, C. L. (1981) *Northwest Smith*, New York: Ace.

Murphy, Pat (1987) 'Rachel In Love', first published in *Isaac Asimov's Science Fiction Magazine*, April 1987.

Panshin, Alexei (1968) *Rite of Passage*, London: Methuen, 1987.

Piercy, Marge (1976) *Woman On The Edge Of Time*, London: Women's Press.

Russ, Joanna (1985) *The Female Man*, London: Women's Press.

Sargent, Pamela (ed.) (1978) *Women of Wonder: Science Fiction Stories by Women about Women*, Harmondsworth: Penguin.

Sargent, Pamela (ed.) (1979) *More Women of Wonder: Science Fiction Novelettes by Women about Women*, Harmondsworth: Penguin.

Saxton, Josephine (1986) *Little Tours of Hell: Tall Tales of Food and Holidays*, London: Pandora.

Saxton, Josephine (1986) *Queen Of The States*, London: Women's Press.

Saxton, Josephine (1986) *The Travails of Jane Saint and Other Stories*, London: Women's Press.

Saxton, Josephine (1989) *Jane Saint and the Backlash*, with *The Consciousness Machine* reprinted, London: Women's Press.

Shelley, Mary Wollstonecraft (1818) *Frankenstein or, The Modern Prometheus*, ed. J. Kingsley and M. K. Joseph, Oxford: Oxford University Press, 1980.

Tuttle, Lisa (1973) 'A True Bear Story', first published in *Isaac Asimov's Science Fiction Magazine*, January 1978.

Tuttle, Lisa (1987) *Gabriel*, London: Sphere.

Wittig, Monique (1979) *Les Guérillères*, London: Women's Press.

Science fiction: a selection of secondary texts

Albinski, Nan Bowman (1988) *Women's Utopias in British and American Fiction*, London: Routledge.

Albury, David (1985) '"E.T.": technology and masculinity', *Issues in Radical Science* 16.

Aldiss, Brian and Wingrove, David (1986) *Trillion Year Spree*, London: Gollancz.

Amis, Kingsley (1961) *New Maps of Hell: A Survey of Science Fiction*, London: Gollancz.

Asimov, Isaac with Warrick, Patricia and Greenberg, Martin (eds) (1984) *Machines That Think: the Best Science Fiction Stories about Robots and Computers*, London: Allen Lane.

Branham, Robert J. (1983) 'Fantasy and ineffability: fiction at the limits of language', *Extrapolation* 24 (Spring): 66–79.

Buchen, Irving H. (1977) '*Frankenstein* and the alchemy of creation and evolution', *The Wordsworth Circle* 8, 2 (Spring): 103–12.

Burgin, Victor, Donald, James and Kaplan, Cora (eds) (1986) *Formations of Fantasy*, London: Methuen.

Del Rey, Lester (ed.) (1977) *The Best of C. L. Moore*, New York: Taplinger.

Garnett, David S. (ed.) (1988) *The Orbit Science Fiction Yearbook 1*, London: Futura.

Griffiths, John (1980) *Three Tomorrows: American, British, and Soviet Science Fiction*, London: Macmillan.

Gubar, Susan (1980) 'C. L. Moore and the conventions of women's science fiction', *Science Fiction Studies* 7.

Jackson, Rosemary (1981) *Fantasy: The Literature of Subversion*, London: Methuen.

Jackson, Rosie (1986) 'Frankenstein: a myth for women', *Women's Review* 12 (October).

Jones, Gwyneth (1988) 'Riddles in the dark', *Foundation* 43 (Summer).

Jordonova, L. J. (1985) 'Fritz Lang's *Metropolis*: science, machines and gender', *Issues in Radical Science* 17.

Lefanu, Sarah (1988) *In The Chinks Of The World Machine: Feminism and Science Fiction*, London: Women's Press.

Le Guin, Ursula K. (1989) *Dancing At The Edge Of The World*, London: Gollancz.

Le Guin, Ursula K. (1989) *The Language of the Night*, London: Women's Press.

Lewis, C. S. (1982) *Of This and Other Worlds*, ed. Walter Hooper, London: Collins.

Manlove, Colin (1982) *The Impulse of Fantasy Literature*, London: Macmillan.

Meyers, Walter (1980) *Aliens and Linguists: Language Study and Science Fiction*, Athens: University of Georgia Press.

Monk, Patricia (1980) 'Frankenstein's daughters: the problems of the feminine image in science fiction', *Mosaic* 13, 3–4 (Spring/Summer): 15–27.

Moylan, Tom (1986) *Demand The Impossible: Science Fiction and the Utopian Imagination*, London: Methuen.

Nicholls, Peter (ed.) (1979) *The Encyclopedia of Science Fiction: An Illustrated A to Z*, London: Granada.

Palumbo, Donald (ed.) (1986) *Erotic Universe: Sexuality and Fantastic Literature*, New York: Greenwood.

Parrinder, Patrick (1980) *Science Fiction: Its Criticism and Teaching*, London: Methuen.

Parrinder, Patrick (1980) 'Descents into Hell: the later novels of Doris Lessing', *Critical Quarterly* 22, 4, (Winter) 5–25.

Plessis, Rachel Blau Du (1979) 'The feminist apologues of Lessing, Piercy and Russ', *Frontiers* 4, 1: 1–8.

Rabkin, Eric S. (1976) *The Fantastic in Literature*, Princeton, NJ: Princeton University Press.

Rohrlich, Ruby and Baruch, Elaine Hoffman (1984) *Women In Search of Utopias: Mavericks and Mythmakers*, New York: Schocken.

Rose, Christine Brooke (1981) *A Rhetoric of the Unreal: Studies in Narrative and Structure, Especially of the Fantastic*, Cambridge: Cambridge University Press.

Rose, Mark (ed.) (1976) *Science Fiction: A Collection of Critical Essays*, Englewood Cliffs: Prentice-Hall.

Rosinsky, Natalie M. (1982) 'A female man? The *Medusan* humor of Joanna Russ', *Extrapolation* 23, 1 (Spring) 31–6.

Rosinsky, Natalie (1984) *Feminist Futures: Contemporary Women's Speculative Fiction*, Ann Arbor: UMI.

Scholes, Robert and Rabkin, Eric S. (1977) *Science Fiction: History, Science, Vision*, New York: Oxford University Press.

Shinn, Thelma J. (1986) *Worlds Within Women: Myth and Mythmaking in Fantastic Literature by Women*, New York: Greenwood.

Suvin, Darko (1977) *Metamorphoses of Science Fiction: On the Poetics and History of a Literary Genre*, New Haven: Yale University Press.

Thompson, Raymond H. (1983) 'Arthurian legend and modern fantasy', *Survey of Modern Fantasy Literature* 5.

Thompson, Raymond H. (1985) *Return From Avalon: A Study of the Arthurian Legend in Modern Fiction*, New York: Greenwood.

Veeder, William (1986) *Mary Shelley and Frankenstein: The Fate of Androgyny*, Chicago: University of Chicago Press.

Weedman, Jane B. (ed.) (1985) *Women Worldwalkers: New Dimensions of Science Fiction and Fantasy*, Lubbock: Texas Tech. University Press.

Wingrove, David (ed.) (1984) *The Science Fiction Source Book*, Harlow: Longman.

Wolmark, Jenny (1986) 'Science fiction and feminism', *Foundation* 37 (Autumn): 48–51.

Additional bibliographical material

Abel, Elizabeth (ed.) (1982) *Writing and Sexual Difference*, Brighton: Harvester.

Arcana, Judith (1981) *Our Mothers' Daughters*, London: Women's Press.

Austin, John Langshaw (1976) *How To Do Things With Words*, Oxford: Oxford University Press.

Balio, Tino (ed.) (1985) *The American Film Industry*, Madison: University of Wisconsin Press.

Bassnett, Susan (1986) *Feminist Experiences: The Women's Movement in Four Cultures*, London: Allen & Unwin.

Benjamin, Walter (1970) *Illuminations*, London: Fontana.

Berger, John (1980) *About Looking*, London: Writers and Readers.

Chodorow, Nancy (1978) *The Reproduction of Mothering: Psychoanalysis and the Sociology of Gender*, Berkeley: University of California Press.

Cixous, Hélène and Clement, Catherine (1986) *The Newly Born Woman*, Manchester: Manchester University Press.

Cirlot, J. E. (1971) *A Dictionary of Symbols*, London: Routledge & Kegan Paul.

Clewlow, Carol (1989) *A Woman's Guide to Adultery*, London: Michael Joseph.

Connor, Steven (1989) *Postmodernist Culture: An Introduction to Theories of the Contemporary*, Oxford: Blackwell.

Dalby, Richard (ed.) (1987) *The Virago Book of Ghost Stories*, introduction by Jennifer Uglow, London: Virago.

Daly, Mary (1979) *Gyn/Ecology: The Metaethics of Radical Feminism*, London: Women's Press.

Dixon, Bob (1977) *Catching Them Young II: Political Ideas in Children's Fiction*, London: Pluto.

Duffy, Maureen (1983) *That's How It Was*, London: Virago.

Elgin, Suzette Haden (1979) *What Is Linguistics?*, Englewood Cliffs: Prentice-Hall.

Elgin, Suzette Haden (1981) 'Some proposed additions to the glossary of needed lexical items for the expression of women's perceptions', *Lonesome Node*, 1: 2–3.

Elgin, Suzette Haden (1988) *A First Dictionary and Grammar of Láadan*, Ozark: SFSFSF.

Feldman, Paula R. and Scott-Kilvert, Diana (eds) (1987) *The Journals of Mary Shelley 1814–1844*, 2 vols, Oxford: Clarendon.

Fisher, Elizabeth (1980) *Woman's Creation: Sexual Evolution and the Shaping of Society*, London: Wildwood House.

Fiske, John (1987) *Television Culture*, London: Methuen.

Fordham, Frieda (1966) *An Introduction to Jung's Psychology*, Harmondsworth: Penguin.

French, Marilyn (1985) *Beyond Power: Women, Men and Morals*, London: Cape.

Gilbert, Sandra and Gubar, Susan (1979) *The Madwoman in the Attic: The Woman Writer and the Nineteenth Century Literary Imagination*, New Haven: Yale University Press.

Gilbert, Sandra and Gubar, Susan (1988) *No Man's Land: The Place of the Woman Writer in the Twentieth Century*, vol. 1: *The War of the Worlds*, New Haven: Yale University Press.

Grace, George W. (1987) *The Linguistic Construction of Reality*, London: Croom Helm.

Griffin, Susan (1978) *Woman and Nature: The Roaring Inside Her*, New York: Harper and Row.

Grimshaw, Jean (1986) *Feminist Philosophers: Women's Perspectives on Philosophical Traditions*, Brighton: Wheatsheaf.

Hill, Douglas E. (1985) *Faces of Fear: Encounters With the Creators of Modern Horror*, New York: Berkley.

Hume, Kathryn (1984) *Fantasy and Mimesis: Responses to Reality in Western Literature*, London: Methuen.

Irigaray, Luce (1985) *This Sex Which Is Not One*, Ithaca, NY: Cornell University Press.

Jones, Frederick L. (ed.) (1963) *The Letters of Percy Bysshe Shelley*, Oxford: Oxford University Press.

Kaplan, E. Ann (1983) *Women and Film, Both Sides of the Camera*, London: Methuen.

Kerr, Paul (ed.) (1986) *The Hollywood Film Industry*, London: Routledge & Kegan Paul.

Koonz, Claudia (1987) *Mothers In The Fatherland: Women, the Family, and Nazi Politics*, London: Cape.

Kreckel, Marga (1981) *Communicative Acts and Shared Knowledge in Natural Discourse*, London: Academic.

Kuhn, Annette (1982) *Women's Pictures: Feminism and Cinema*, London: Routledge & Kegan Paul.

Kuhn, Annette (1985) *The Power of the Image: Essays on Representation and Sexuality*, London: Routledge & Kegan Paul.

Lacan, Jacques (1977) *Ecrits: A Selection*, London: Tavistock.

Lacy, Norris J. (1986) *The Arthurian Encyclopedia*, Woodbridge: Boydell Press.

Lessing, Doris (1981) 'A very practical sort of mystic', *Guardian*, 15 May.

Lessing, Doris (1982) 'These shores of sweet unreason', *Guardian*, 25 September.

Lyons, John (1985) *Chomsky*, London: Fontana.

Marks, Elaine and Courtivron, Isabelle de (eds) (1981) *New French Feminisms*, Brighton: Harvester.

Matthews, Caitlin (1989) *The Celtic Tradition*, Shaftesbury: Element Books.

Mendilow, A. A. (1952) *Time and the Novel*, New York: Humanities.

Michie, Donald and Johnston, Rory (1984) *The Creative Computer*, Harmondsworth: Penguin.

Moers, Ellen (1978) *Literary Women*, London: Women's Press.

Moi, Toril (1985) *Sexual/Textual Politics*, London: Methuen.

Moi, Toril (ed.) (1986) *The Kristeva Reader*, Oxford: Blackwell.

Monteith, Moira (ed.) (1986) *Women's Writing: A Challenge to Theory*, Brighton: Harvester.

Moretti, Franco (1983) *Signs Taken for Wonders: Essays on the Sociology of Literary Forms*, London: Verso.

Nichols, Bill (1981) *Ideology and the Image: Social Representation in the Cinema and Other Media*, Bloomington: Indiana University Press.

Norris, Christopher (ed.) (1984) *Inside The Myth: Orwell, Views from the Left*, London: Lawrence & Wishart.

Pratt, Annis (1982) *Archetypal Patterns in Women's Fiction*, Brighton: Harvester.

Propp, Vladimir (1968) *The Morphology of the Folk Tale*, Austin: University of Texas Press.

Rose, Jacqueline (1984) *The Case of Peter Pan, or, the Impossibility of Children's Fiction*, London: Macmillan.

Rosen, Philip (ed.) (1986) *Narrative, Apparatus, Ideology: A Film Theory Reader*, New York: Columbia University Press.

Rossi, Alice S. (ed.) (1988) *The Feminist Papers: From Adams to De Beauvoir*, New York: Northeastern University Press.

Small, Christopher (1972) *Ariel Like a Harpy: Shelley, Mary and Frankenstein*, London: Gollancz.

Spark, Muriel (1951) *Child of Light: A Reassessment of Mary Wollstonecraft Shelley*, London: Tower Bridge Publications.

Squire, Charles (1975) *Celtic Myth and Legend*, North Hollywood: Newcastle Publishing Co.

Stewart, R. J. (1988) *Merlin and Women*, London: Blandford Press.

Stubbs, Patricia (1979) *Women and Fiction: Feminism and the Novel 1880–1920*, London: Methuen.

Suleiman, Susan Rubin (1981) 'The question of readability in avant-garde fiction', *Studies in Twentieth Century Literature* 6, 1–2 (Fall/Spring): 17–35.

Swinfen, Ann (1984) *In Defence of Fantasy: A Study of the Genre in English and American Literature since 1945*, London: Routledge & Kegan Paul.

Taylor, Jenny (ed.) (1982) *Notebooks/Memoirs/Archives*, London: Routledge & Kegan Paul.

Theweleit, Klaus (1987) *Male Fantasies*, vol. 1: *Women, Floods, Bodies, History*, Cambridge: Polity.

Thornburg, Mary K. Patterson (1987) *The Monster in the Mirror: Gender and the Sentimental/Gothic Myth in 'Frankenstein'*, Ann Arbor: UMI.

Turkle, Sherry (1984) *The Second Self: Computers and the Human Spirit*, London: Granada.

Vogel, Amos (1974) *Film as a Subversive Art*, London: Weidenfeld & Nicholson.

Waelti-Walters, Jennifer (1982) *Fairy Tales and the Female Imagination*, Montreal: Eden.

Walker, Barbara G. (ed.) (1983) *The Woman's Encyclopedia of Myths and Secrets*, New York: Harper & Row.

Wehr, Demaris S. (1988) *Jung and Feminism: Liberating the Archetypes*, London: Routledge.

Whittaker, Ruth (1988) *Doris Lessing*, London: Macmillan.

Wollen, Peter (1973) *Signs and Meaning in the Cinema*, Bloomington: Indiana University Press.

Wright, Elizabeth (1984) *Psychoanalytic Criticism: Theory in Practice*, London: Methuen.

Ziegler, Heide and Bigsby, Christopher (eds) (1982) *The Radical Imagination and the Liberal Tradition*, London: Junction.

About the contributors

Lucie Armitt is based in the Comparative Literary Theory Department of the University of Warwick, where she recently convened an international conference on the subject of Women and Science Fiction. She is also currently setting up a networking organisation for women writers and critics in the SF field. She is a part-time lecturer at the University of Warwick and Bolton Institute of Higher Education, and is also in the process of completing her PhD on women's fantasies in contemporary literature.

Susan Bassnett is Head of the Graduate School of Comparative Literary Theory at the University of Warwick. Her research interests are many and varied, and she has published work in the fields of translation studies, experimental and women's theatre, and women's writing. Her publications include *Feminist Experiences: The Women's Movement in Four Cultures* (1986), *Sylvia Plath* (1987), *Elizabeth I: A Feminist Biography* (1988) and *Magdalena: International Experimental Women's Theatre* (1989).

Sarah Gamble has recently returned to the UK from a one-year lectureship in the English Department of the University of Seville. She is currently completing her PhD on contemporary women fantasy writers at the University of Sheffield, while lecturing part-time at Sunderland Polytechnic.

Gwyneth Jones is an established writer and critic of science fiction and fantasy. She is the author of three novels for adults: *Divine Endurance* (1985), *Escape Plans* (1986) and *Kairos* (1988); and has also written several works of fiction aimed at the teenage/-child reader including: *King Death's Garden* (1987), *The Daymaker* (1987), *Transformations* (1988) and *The Hidden Ones* (1988). A short article on women and science fiction entitled 'Imagining things differently' was published in *Women's Review* in January 1986, and she has also written numerous critical articles for the following SF magazines: *Interzone*, *Foundation* and *Vector*.

Sarah Lefanu is the editor responsible for The Women's Press science fiction series. She has also co-edited two anthologies of original fiction: *Despatches From the Frontiers of the Female Mind* (1985), and *Colours of a New Day: Writing for South Africa* (1990). Her first full-length critical work, *In The Chinks of the World Machine: Feminism and Science Fiction*, was published in 1988, and she has also contributed essays on science fiction to several critical anthologies on the subject of popular fiction.

Moira Monteith is Principal Lecturer in the English Department of Sheffield City Polytechnic. She has been closely involved with the Sheffield Women and Education Group writer's collective which, among other titles, has published a series of non-sexist and non-racist science fiction books for young children. Her best known publication to date is the Harvester anthology *Women's Writing: A Challenge to Theory* (1986), although she has also published articles on Marge Piercy and Ursula Le Guin, and an essay on Maxine Hong Kingston's *Woman Warrior*, which is published in Ann Thompson and Helen Wilcox (eds), *Teaching Women* (1988).

Nickianne Moody teaches in the Media and Cultural Studies Department of Liverpool Polytechnic, and is also currently involved in postgraduate research at the University of Warwick, linking science fiction with fantasy-role-playing games. She has contributed two entries, one on Christopher Priest and the other on David Lake, to the American anthology *A Reader's Guide to Twentieth Century Science Fiction*, (ed.) Marilyn P. Fletcher (1989), and is also involved in researching and editing the collected letters of Kenneth Tynan.

Jenny Newman is based at Chester College of Higher Education. She has run several workshops on science fiction, and also teaches a twentieth-century British Women's Fiction summer school at Trinity College, Oxford. She is the author of *The Faber Book of Seductions*.

Elizabeth Russell, although British by birth, has been living in Spain since 1969, where she lectures in the English Department of the University of Barcelona. Her doctoral thesis was entitled 'Utopian Dreams and Dystopian Nightmares: A General Survey of Utopias Written by Women in English 1792–1937'. She has published several articles on women's utopian fiction.

Josephine Saxton is a well-known writer of science fiction and political fantasy stories, whose current publications include *Queen of the States* and several collections of short stories, including *Little Tours of Hell* and *The Travails of Jane Saint and Other Stories*. Her latest collection, *Jane Saint and the Backlash*, was published in 1989 alongside the reprinted novella *The Consciousness Machine*.

Erica Sheen lectures in the Department of English Literature at Sheffield University, where her specialisms include film and literary theory. She has published work on Shakespeare and is working on a volume dealing with Elizabethan and Jacobean dramatists for the Open University Press's 'Gender in Writing' series.

Susan Thomas is a freelance writer who has contributed articles and short fiction to several SF magazines. She was recently awarded two writer's bursaries, and is currently working on a radio play and her second novel. In addition she teaches Communication Skills in the Computer Studies Department of Trent Polytechnic.

Lisa Tuttle is an American by birth, but has been resident in the UK since 1981. She is a freelance writer who has had articles and reviews published in *City Limits*, *Time Out*, the *Bookseller*, the *Sunday Times* and the *Washington Post*. Since 1972 she has published more than fifty short stories in various science fiction and fantasy magazines and anthologies. She has written two collections of short stories, *A Nest of Nightmares* and *A Spaceship Built of Stone*, is the author of two novels, *Familiar Spirit* and *Gabriel*, and is co-author with George R. R. Martin of *Windhaven*. She has written two non-fiction publications: *Encyclopedia of Feminism* and *Heroines: Women Inspired by Women*.

Index